# Pillars
# of Fire

# Pillars of Fire

## AN ETHER NOVEL

### BOOK TWO

LAURICE E. MOLINARI

ZONDERkidz

## Also by Laurice Elehwany Molinari

### Books

*The Ether: Vero Rising*

*The Dragon's Descent*

### Screenplays

*My Girl* (Columbia Pictures)

*The Brady Bunch Movie* (Paramount Pictures)

*The Amazing Panda Adventure* (Warner Bros.)

*Anastasia* (Uncredited) (Fox Animation Studios)

*Bewitched* (Uncredited) (Columbia Pictures)

ZONDERKIDZ

*Pillars of Fire*
Copyright © 2014 by Laurice E. Molinari

This title is also available as a Zondervan ebook.
Visit www.zondervan.com/ebooks.

Requests for information should be addressed to:
Zonderkidz, 3900 *Sparks Drive SE, Grand Rapids, Michigan 49546*

This edition: ISBN 978-0-310-73562-5 (softcover)

Library of Congress Cataloging-in-Publication Data

Molinari, Laurice E.
    Pillars of fire / Laurice E. Molinari.
        p. cm. — (The ether ; book 2)
    ISBN 978-0-310-73556-4 (hardback)
    ISBN 978-0-310-73559-5 (epub)
    1. Guardian angels—Fiction. 2. Angels—Fiction. 3. Demonology—Fiction.
4. Schools—Fiction. 5. Animals, Mythical—Fiction. 6. Good and evil—Fiction.
7. Family life—Maryland—Fiction. 8. Maryland—Fiction. I. Title.
PZ7.M7337Pil 2015
[Fic]—dc23                                                        2014031386

*Illustrations: Randy Gallegos*
*Interior design: David Conn & Ben Fetterley*

*Printed in the United States of America*

HB 10.03.2017

To my husband, Chris, who dreamed
of the Ether as a boy.

# CONTENTS

1. Medical Wonder ............................................ 11

2. Going Green ................................................ 21

3. Trial by Fire ............................................... 35

4. Tracking Unicorns ....................................... 49

5. The Hair .................................................... 67

6. New Girl .................................................... 79

7. Angel Trials ............................................... 89

8. Ariel the Power ......................................... 107

9. Children of the Fallen ................................. 121

10. Beyond the Clouds .................................... 131

11. Zombie Ants ............................................ 145

12. Invisible Angel ......................................... 157

13. Surprise Party .......................................... 171

14. Fort-i-fires .............................................. 185

15. Soul Searching ......................................... 197

16. Riddle of the Imp ..................................... 207

17. Hyena's Den ............................................ 219

18. Michael .................................................. 231

19. Pep Rally ................................................ 243

20. Unlikely Hero ........................................... 253

21. The Dreamer................................................265

22. Jacob's Ladder..........................................275

23. Pool of Truth..............................................287

24. Marsh Creatures......................................303

25. The Black Castle........................................311

26. Lilith............................................................319

27. Wreaths of Glory......................................333

28. Vero's Task.................................................341

29. The Burning Hatred.................................351

# 1

## MEDICAL
## WONDER

The moon was nearly full, but no light pierced the canopy of cloud and tree to reach the forest floor. Below the tangled branches, the woods were dark and deadly still. Not even the melodious music of the evening crickets could be heard.

From the center of the forest, a column of heavy black smoke wafted through the trees, choking the life from the surrounding air. A moment later, the eerie silence was broken. Birds screeched, branches snapped, and animals crashed through the underbrush, all fleeing in a widening ring of panic. Something was not right in the woodland.

The smoke came from a bright fire in a small clearing. A hunched figure, cloaked in shadows, slowly stepped into the light of the flames. She was a gaunt woman, and behind her trailed a carpet of coarse black hair that gleamed dully in the light. Longer than a hundred wedding trains sewn together, the hair seemed to have a life of its own, slithering around trees and rocks with the agility of a serpent. It looked endless in the dark.

When she reached the fire, the woman swept aside her ragged robe and dropped to her knees. The flames revealed cavernous wrinkles and deep black eyes. She looked to be thousands of years old.

"I am listening, my prince," the haggard woman snarled to the blaze before her. Her voice sounded like the screech of a hundred hungry owls.

"Our time runs short," said a voice from the fire. The flames rose and fell as it spoke. "The others have disappointed me greatly. But you shall not."

Eighty yards away, next to an abandoned well, a fleeing white-tailed buck unknowingly stepped on the long black mane.

"Are we sure it is one of these fledglings?" screeched the hag.

"His true nature will manifest during the Trials. Then we will know with certainty," the inferno breathed. Despite the intense heat from the flames, its tone was menacing and cold. "The child cannot live."

Suddenly, the end of the woman's hair train rose up like a king cobra readying to strike. The buck's eyes filled with terror, and he tried to bolt, but the hair coiled itself around its body with the speed of a viper. Within seconds, the panicked buck was completely encased by the hair, strangled, devoured, and then just gone.

"Don't offer me creatures of the forest," the fire said. "Offer me the fledgling, for he will be the prize of all prizes."

"I will do as my prince commands," the hag said. A smile cracked her ancient lips. "The child will not be."

As she stood up and turned to leave, the hair gliding with her, the blaze called out. "Do you loathe me?"

The woman stopped and slowly turned to face the fire. Her eyes were hollow. "I despise all that He has created. So you are no different."

Pleased with her answer, the fire let out a wicked laugh, and the hag disappeared once more into the dark forest.

⟡

Vero Leland stood with his back against the stark white wall. His gray eyes nervously scanned the room for items that could be used to injure him. There were syringes with long needles, razor-sharp scissors, and pointy scalpels on the counter. The room was filled with the nauseating smell of rubbing alcohol. Looking around at the many dangerous objects, Vero was scared. But he was more scared that the flower-themed, flimsy paper gown he was wearing would fly open and expose his pasty backside. He clutched the opening shut in tight fists.

"Sit down. You're going to rip the gown," his mother, Nora, told him. "Really, Vero, you're too old to be afraid of the doctor."

"Easy for you to say. You're not the one who's getting a shot. Just look at the size of those needles!" Vero said, nodding to a metal tray on the counter.

"I'm sure they're not all for you," Nora winked, her faint laugh lines showing.

Vero looked at his mother skeptically, but Nora's vibrant

green eyes filled with tenderness as she gazed upon her only son. "I remember your first set of shots. You were so tiny. When the doctor pricked you, you cried and cried. Then I joined in," Nora said, tearing up. "It broke my heart. The doctor thought I took it harder than you."

"Knock it off, Mom." Vero rolled his eyes. "You're so embarrassing."

"No more embarrassing than a knobby-kneed thirteen-year-old boy in a flowered paper dress," Nora replied, looking hurt.

"Sorry, but, it's just that I'm old enough to get a physical by myself. You don't need to be here with me."

"But I've always taken you to your physical."

"I'm not a little kid anymore," Vero said. "You treat me like a baby. You won't even let me have a cellphone!"

"You'll get one when you're older, like Clover," Nora said.

"See? Like a baby." Vero pouted.

Nora's expression softened. "What if Dr. Walker has questions, and you can't answer them?"

"I'm sure he could find you in the waiting room."

Nora looked at Vero, her lips pursed. She knew he was right, but it was so hard to let go. Nora had always struggled to give Vero independence. She feared for him more than for her daughter, Clover. Thirteen years later, she still regularly woke up in a cold sweat after reliving the night she had found the abandoned baby Vero in the hospital. The night a figure cloaked in a dark robe chased her through a grocery store while she clutched Vero to her chest. The night she so desperately wanted to shake from her memory, but knew she never would.

"Hello, Vero," the doctor said as he shut the door behind

him, snapping Nora from her thoughts. "How's my medical wonder doing?"

Dr. Walker had known Vero his whole life but usually only saw him once a year for his annual physical because Vero almost never got sick. Nora had brought Vero in a few times to discuss how to put more weight on him, but other than that, Vero rarely saw the doctor.

Nora stood up and opened the door. "I'll be out in the waiting room if you need me," she said.

"You're not staying?" the white-haired doctor questioned.

"No, he can handle himself."

Vero smiled gratefully at his mom. Taking one last look at her son, Nora slipped out, leaving him alone with Dr. Walker.

"So, Vero, how is everything?"

"Pretty good."

"You feeling okay? Any complaints?" Dr. Walker listened to Vero's heart with his metal stethoscope.

"No."

"Breathe."

Vero took a few deep breaths as the doctor checked his lungs.

Dr. Walker smiled. "Very nice. So how's your back?"

The question threw Vero. "Oh, um . . . my back?"

"Your mother called a while ago, said you were complaining it hurt?"

"Oh, that thing. Yeah, they bought me a new mattress, and it stopped bugging me after that."

Vero felt guilty about twisting the truth, but there was no way he could be honest. Dr. Walker would never understand that all his back pain had completely disappeared the first time he had sprouted his wings. That the back pain had actually been nothing more than guardian angel growing pains.

"Let's check your vision. Put your hand over your left eye and read the chart."

Vero covered his eye and read the chart hanging on the other side of the room. "E, F, P, T, O, Z ..." he said.

"Just read the lowest line you can see clearly," Dr. Walker interrupted.

Vero squinted as his eye scanned down the chart. "I can make out the last line. F, E, A ..." he read aloud. "R, M, E."

"That's awful, Vero! You got every single letter wrong," Dr. Walker told him. "Try the line above it."

"But I see 'em clearly."

"Remove your hand and read it with both eyes."

Vero dropped his hand from his face. He stared intently at the last line. "F, E ... A, R, M, E," Vero repeated.

Dr. Walker scribbled something on his prescription pad and tore it off with great force.

"It took thirteen years, but we've finally found something wrong with you! You need glasses, Vero," he said as he triumphantly handed the paper to Vero. "This is a prescription to see an eye doctor."

"But I'm sure I'm reading the line right." Vero walked over to the eye chart and put his face right up to it. "See? I'm right. Look. F, E, A, R, M, E."

"Interesting ... not only near sighted, but you're far sighted as well."

Then it hit Vero. The letters, F, E, A, R, M, E — they spelled out "Fear me!" He was getting a message that the doctor could not see — a message from the Ether. *Fear me?* he thought. Was he being threatened from beyond?

It had been several months since he had heard anything from the Ether, and Vero missed it terribly. He longed for the vast fields of wildflowers, so brightly colored he had to shield his eyes. He ached for the warmth of the Ether's eternal light. Most of all, he wanted to sprout his wings and soar into the Ether's brilliant blue sky. In fact, it had been so long since he was there, he had begun to worry that maybe he wasn't actually cut out for angel training, and he had been eliminated from his group of fledglings.

*Fear me.* A chill ran through Vero, giving him goose bumps. No matter how badly he longed to return there, he knew not everything in the Ether was good.

"Any questions, Vero?" Dr. Walker asked, his kindly eyes twinkling.

"No," Vero answered, relieved that there was no mention of any shots.

"Then I'll see you and your new glasses next year," the doctor said on his way out. "You can get dressed."

After the door closed, Vero reached down to grab his jeans off the blue chair. As he ripped the thin plastic belt from his waist, someone knocked, then entered without waiting for a response. Vero quickly spun around and saw a young pretty nurse holding a small metal tray. His hand instinctively pulled the back of the gown shut to hide his underwear.

"Time for your shot," the nurse smiled, flashing a set of perfect white teeth.

"But Dr. Walker didn't say I needed one!" Vero panicked. "He said I could go."

"Doctors never like to deliver bad news," the nurse smiled. "They make us nurses be the bad guys. Sorry, sweetie."

Vero looked at the woman. Even though she smiled, no warmth reached her eyes. She didn't seem at all sorry for what she was about to do to him. Perhaps after years of dealing with screaming scared kids her sympathy had turned to indifference or worse — annoyance. Vero carefully jumped up on the examination table, one hand still clutching the gown's back flaps. As the nurse rubbed his arm with a small alcohol swab, he swallowed hard. Now that he was officially a teenager, he would put on a brave face and take his shot without complaint. But deep down, he regretted sending his mom out to the waiting room. He still wanted to hold her hand.

"It'll be over before you know it," the nurse said in a flat, monotonous voice. "Hold still."

Vero looked into her eyes for reassurance, but found none. Instead, he saw red. Glowing little flecks of red. Vero gasped. He knew what those flecks meant. He had seen them before. The nurse clenched his arm, ready to stab the long needle into his soft skin, when Vero leapt off the examination table, grabbing the first thing he could reach on the counter to defend himself. Vero looked at his hand — a stethoscope! It would be about as much help as the Q-Tips that had been lying next to it.

"Tell us who it is!" the nurse gurgled deeply as she backed him into a corner.

"Who are you?" Vero yelled.

She growled, revealing that her sparkling white teeth had turned to rotted fangs, and lunged at Vero. Vero rolled underneath her outstretched legs, narrowly escaping. The nurse spun and wildly jabbed the syringe at Vero. He jumped back against the examination table. As the needle came straight for his eye, he grabbed a pillow and blocked it. The needle punctured the fabric and cotton padding, nearly stabbing his nose.

"Tell us which one of you it is!" she commanded.

Vero bolted to the door, but the enraged nurse slammed into his back before he could open it. Feeling the tip of the needle press against his neck, Vero, turned, grabbed her wrist, and with unexpected strength, twisted it, thrusting the needle deep into her shoulder and compressing the plunger. The nurse snarled, and with a final shriek, she tumbled off his back onto the hard floor. Vero was breathing so heavily, he thought he'd pass out. But he had more pressing worries. How was he going to explain the dead nurse, or whatever creature it was, lying in the middle of the room?

As Vero stared at her, he noticed the stethoscope on the floor. He bent down and quickly picked it up. He wasn't completely sure she was dead, so he grabbed a scalpel with his other hand for protection. Vero then kneeled, put in the earpieces, and placed the listening end over her heart. There was no heartbeat. Relief swept over him, followed quickly by anger. "Fear you?" he spat. "How about 'fear me'?!"

But then he heard something, a faint sound in the stethoscope. It was the distant echo of eerie cackling, and it was growing louder. Vero yanked out the earpieces and chucked the instrument to the floor, holding the scalpel in front of him like a sword. There was a demented smile on the nurse's face that hadn't been there previously. Puffs of black smoke blossomed from her nostrils.

Vero backed away as the nurse's body began to blacken. Soon, all that remained was a scorched mark on the checkered tiled floor. Horrified, Vero dropped the scalpel, ran out the door and raced down the hallway toward the waiting room.

*Annual physicals are not supposed to be life threatening!* Vero thought. When he saw his mother in the crowded waiting room, casually leafing through some gossip magazine, Vero ran into her arms. Nora was caught off guard by his embrace, and dropped the magazine. Parents and kids looked upon Vero with interest. He was still wearing his pink flowered paper dress.

"Vero, what's wrong?"

"The shot ... She was trying to give me a shot!" he blurted, fumbling over words.

Dr. Walker stood behind the appointment desk reading a patient's file. He overheard. "No shot today, Vero. Your vaccines are all up to date."

Vero let go of his mother, his common sense returning to him.

Nora stared at Vero intently, then she said, "Come on, you need to get to school."

A chubby five-year-old boy walked over to him, laughing and pointing. "I see London. I see France ..." he giggled.

Vero turned beet red.

"I see that kid's underpants!"

Vero hid behind his mom.

# 2

### ❖

# GOING GREEN

"Vero, wait up!" Tack yelled as he maneuvered over to Vero's locker in the crowded school hallway. "Where were you this morning?"

"I had to go to the doctor's for a physical," Vero said as he rummaged through his metal locker.

"Aw, man, I hate those things. All they ever tell me is that I need to eat better ... and less," Tack grimaced, running his hand through his strawberry-blond hair. "Then my mom always goes on some health food binge for a few weeks, and she puts stuff like seaweed snacks in my lunch, and we eat tofu burgers for dinner."

Vero wrinkled his nose as he pulled a dirty white sock from his locker.

"Hey, even that smelly thing looks good compared to eating a tofu burger," Tack said, nodding to the sock. "So anyway, after this goes on for a while, my dad will say he needs to go to the hardware store, and he'll take me with him. But it's nothing but a giant lie just so we can go to a drive-thru instead and get some real food. After a few days of sneaking around, my mom'll find the wrappers in the backseat of the car, she'll yell at my dad, and he'll say he'd rather die a few years earlier but happy instead of eating that weird stuff. Eventually my mom gives up, and then the next thing I know, the Ding Dongs are back in the house."

"Yeah, but don't you always have a secret stash of them under your bed?" Vero asked.

Tack shook his head dejectedly. "Not anymore. Pork Chop found them, and ate every single Ding Dong, tinfoil and all."

"That dog eats everything."

"Yeah, for the next couple of days, the grass in the backyard looked like a Christmas tree decorated in tinsel."

Vero laughed. Pork Chop was Tack's English bulldog. Vero knew about the theory that owners and their dogs sometimes looked alike, but it wasn't true in Tack's case anymore—especially since Tack had stretched out and lost all his extra weight two summers ago. Even so, Tack and Pork Chop still shared the same eating habits. Just as Vero was about to shut his locker door, Tack stuck his hand inside and pulled something out. It was a half-eaten sandwich.

"I wouldn't eat that," Vero warned him. "I have no idea how long that's been in my locker."

"Guess we're about to find out," Tack said as he shoved it into his mouth. "Think of it as a medical experiment."

"More like a science experiment on the opposite of Newton's law of gravity," Vero smirked before he shut the locker. Tack gave Vero a blank look. "Whatever. Hey, so I got it all worked out," he continued. "Henry Matson, that basket-ball dude, is gonna trade places with you."

"What are you talking about?"

"For the class photo. He's gonna switch places with you so you can be in the back row."

"Why do I want to be in the back row?" Vero asked.

"Because the cool guys are always in the back. Girls and dorks are in the rest. And it's totally humiliating if you're a guy in the front row. That will haunt you for life."

"Thanks, I guess, but won't the photographer notice he's taller than me when he lines us up?"

"Yeah, but when he's not looking, Henry's gonna change with you then crouch down for the photo," Tack answered.

"Why would he do that for me?"

"He's a freak. He likes Mallory, so I promised to hack into her Facebook account and add him as one of her friends."

"Your sister will just unfriend him when she finds out." Vero smiled.

"Probably, but by then the picture will be shot, and it won't be my problem." Tack swallowed the last of the sand-wich. He looked at the empty wrapper in his hand. "Wow, that was awful."

Tack was a faithful friend to Vero and always tried to look out for him. Their friendship went way back to pre-school when they bonded over their mutual love of Tonka dump trucks and seesaws. Growing up, they played base-ball together, sang in the church choir, had sleepovers most weekends. They shared video games and books (in Tack's case just comic books), and they even shared a toothbrush for a week when Tack forgot to bring his to sleep-away camp. Tack knew Vero's favorite color was yellow. He knew Vero cried when the class bunny died in the second grade. He knew Vero hated snakes more than anything.

Tack was confident he knew every single thing about Vero. But he didn't. For instance, he had no idea that his best friend wasn't even human or that he traveled between earth and a spiritual realm called the Ether. He had no idea that Vero was in training to become a guardian angel. And he certainly didn't know about the wings. Sure, there had been some weird things going on. Like the time Vero strangled a corn snake with his bare hands or the day he effortlessly cleared two hurdles at once on the track. But Tack thought up rational explanations for the events and then pushed them out of his mind. He never wanted anything between Vero and him to change.

The obnoxious warning bell rang, startling Tack and Vero. Kids scurried through the hallways to their classes. Tack forced Vero into a headlock, and they disappeared into the crowd.

✦

Vero stood in the middle of the packed school gym. As he glanced at the drove of kids surrounding him, he noticed that most of their summer tans had already faded. And Missy Baker, whose hair was always green for the first few weeks of school from teaching swim lessons all summer, had returned to her natural blonde shade. Autumn had definitely replaced summer.

Several photographers stood stationed around the gym, clicking fingers, as kids waited in long lines to have their yearly school photos taken. At the same time, a few homeroom classes climbed up the bleachers for their group photos. A delicate hand tapped Vero's shoulder.

"Hi, Vero. How are you?"

Vero turned around and saw Davina Acker smiling at him. He couldn't help but smile back. She was, after all, not only the most beautiful girl in the seventh grade, but also the nicest. With long, wavy brown hair, full lips, and sparkling blue eyes, Davina had every right to be stuck up, but there was nothing remotely arrogant about her. It was as if she was completely oblivious to her own beauty. Vero often wondered if Davina even owned a mirror and had ever seen her reflection.

"Hey, Davina, um ... you look ... nice," Vero stammered.

"Thanks."

"What about me? How do I look?" Tack had appeared suddenly out of the crowd.

Davina and Vero jumped back at the sight of him. Tack was wearing an obnoxiously loud purple and yellow striped shirt with mint green pants. Just looking at him, Vero thought he'd get a severe case of vertigo.

"When did you put those on?" Vero asked with a raised eyebrow and a chuckle.

"I snuck into the bathroom and changed. My mom wouldn't let me out of the house wearing this, so I stashed them in my backpack. I just really want to stand out in the picture."

"I'm sure you will." Davina winked at Vero, giggling.

"But my hair won't stay down," Tack said as he licked the palm of his hand then tried to smooth down his hair. "Think anyone will notice?"

"Trust me, that's the last thing anyone's going to notice about you," Vero reassured him.

Tack let out a huge belch. Everyone in the immediate vicinity winced and stepped back. The look on Tack's face said he was as surprised as everyone else.

"Sorry," he said. "I don't know where that came from."

"Probably from that sandwich from my locker," Vero chided him.

"That belch tasted like mayonnaise."

"My mom puts lots on all my sandwiches."

"And you let me eat that?!" Tack sounded panicked.

"I warned you!"

"Shortest to tallest," a photographer yelled to Vero's class, putting an end to the conversation.

Vero and Tack headed toward the bleachers with the rest of the kids. Most had a pretty good idea to which row they belonged. As Vero eyed a spot in the middle row, a shoulder slammed into him from behind, knocking him to the gym floor. Vero looked up and saw the shoulder belonged to Danny Konrad.

"Vero!" Davina said, seeing him on the floor. She ran down the bleacher steps. But before she reached Vero, Danny turned around and came back, stepping between the two of them. He grabbed Vero by the arm.

"Oh, sorry, Vero. I guess I didn't see you there," Danny said. To hear Danny speak, it sounded like a sincere apology. But as he helped Vero to his feet, Danny flashed him a nasty sneer.

"Are you all right?" Davina asked Vero with concern.

"Yeah, I guess," Vero said, rubbing his elbow.

Vero's face darkened as he locked eyes with Danny.

Months ago, Vero had risked his life to save Danny from two demonic maltures. He had even gone up against Abaddon, the locust king, who guards the lake of fire—a creature so frightening, he literally took Vero's breath away. And yet, Danny was still a jerk to him! But there was nothing Vero could do about it. He could never reveal to Danny that he was his guardian angel.

"We better line up," Danny said. "Sure you're okay, Vero? Or do you want me to walk you over to the front row?" He snickered.

"I'm not in the front row," Vero said, gritting his teeth.

"Of course not," Davina soothed. "You're not that short."

Vero sighed. This conversation was not going his way.

"I don't have all day, people!" the photographer said as he waved Vero to the bleachers.

There was no doubt Danny was headed for the back row. He was a year older than the other students in the class, and he was a big kid on top on that. Danny was the undisputed class bully. Or he used to be anyway, until Davina Acker showed up last year. She was new to the school and didn't know Danny's reputation. Ever since she had arrived, the most feared kid in the school had suddenly begun to soften. Danny stopped shoving innocent kids in lockers and talking back to teachers. He carried Davina's tray at lunch. Once, he even held the door open for Principal Meyers and smiled.

There was only one problem. Davina liked Vero just as much as she liked Danny, which explained why, no matter what Vero did, Danny refused to be friends with him. Vero made Danny nervous. Vero was still rubbing his elbow as he took his place in the next to last row from the back. The photographer looked the group over. He rearranged a few kids. And when he turned his back to set up the camera, Tack nudged a tall boy standing next to him.

"Henry, quick, switch with Vero."

"You're going to friend me with your sister, right?" the tall boy asked urgently.

"Yeah, I said I would," Tack promised.

Henry tapped Vero on the shoulder, and the two traded places. Henry bent his knees, and the photographer was none the wiser. Tack turned to Vero.

Vero was sure Tack was about to congratulate himself for pulling off his ruse, but instead he looked at Vero and said, "I'm not feeling so good."

Vero noted that Tack's face was nearly the same shade of green as his pants. "You don't look great."

The photographer moved behind the camera and made a few adjustments to the lens. Vero looked over at Tack. He was not smiling. He seemed to be turning greener by the second.

"Maybe you should go to Nurse Kunkel's office," Vero suggested.

"It's okay … if this guy would just hurry up and take the stinkin' picture."

"All right, everyone, give me your best smiles," the photographer instructed the class. "On the count of three say, 'cheese.'"

As the kids straightened up, the photographer shouted, "One, two …"

One count ahead of schedule, the kids simultaneously shouted, "FEAR ME." Vero looked around, completely freaked out. The class chanted the phrase over and over, with the photographer leading them, his hand up in the air—each time getting louder and louder, smiles still plastered across their faces. They appeared to be in a trance, even the green-faced Tack. Vero's heart pounded. Was anyone else aware of what was happening? Finally, the photographer put his eye to the lens and yelled, "Three!" The kids shouted "cheese" as he snapped the shot. And at the precise moment the flash went off, Tack lost his battle for control over the contents of his stomach. Chunks blew all over his classmates in the rows below. Kids screamed. Some ducked. Some ran. The sight—and sound and smell—of Tack throwing up, caused more than a handful of other kids to become sympathetic pukers. Within moments, the entire gym was in chaos: kids hurling on each other, while others bolted for the doors, slipping and sliding in vomit on the now slick wooden bleachers. The teachers couldn't control the pandemonium. Tack gave Vero a guilty look.

"Yep. That sandwich was definitely bad. But at least I feel better now."

However, this time it was Vero's turn to have an uneasy feeling churning in the pit of his stomach. And it had nothing to do with the vomit.

$$\diamondsuit$$

A loud clang pierced the air, the unmistakable sound of metal striking metal. Several more hard blows followed, then a foil thrust straight into Vero's torso. The force of the weapon made him lose his footing. He stumbled back and fell hard to the floor. Relentless, his attacker advanced. Vero looked up at the menacing steel mesh mask standing over him.

"Lucky shot," Vero said.

"If that was luck, then what were those last three attacks that landed you right on your butt?" a teenage girl's voice answered.

"Bad luck?"

His opponent removed her heavy mask. It was Clover, Vero's fourteen-year-old sister. She offered her hand and pulled Vero to his feet. Needing a bit of fresh air on his sweaty face, Vero also pulled off his mask. He blinked in the sudden light of the small sports club. Two other fencers battled in a heated match nearby. The fencing classes were over for the day, but Vero and Clover stayed behind to practice their parrying and jabs.

"What's up with you?" Clover wondered. "You can't focus at all."

It was true. The uncanny events of the day had put Vero's mind elsewhere. First the doctor's office, then the class photo — Vero was totally distracted. But he couldn't tell his sister about what had happened. Even though Clover was the only human being who knew he was a guardian angel, Vero was unsure how many details of his life in the Ether he should share with her. As wonderful as the Ether was, maltures and demons consumed by hatred also dwelled there. They terrified Vero, and he wanted to protect his sister from them, and the knowledge of them.

But as much as both Vero and Clover wanted to deny it, Clover was already at risk. She had a gift — a gift she wanted so desperately to return, like the terrible pink polka-dot dress her grandmother gave her for her last birthday. No matter how hard she tried to deny or ignore its existence, it only seemed to grow stronger. Gradually, Clover had to make peace with the fact that she saw things that other people simply did not see—frightening things, like maltures disguised as teenage boys. And closing her eyes did not make the images go away.

"I'm just tired, I guess," Vero said, which wasn't altogether a lie.

"You wanna quit?"

"No." Vero put his mask back on and smiled weakly. "Bring it."

Clover and Vero stepped into position to square off. Each placed their feet at ninety-degree right angles, remembering their instructions about the importance of proper stance. The correct foot placement created better stability and control. Both raised the blades in their hands. Dressed from head to toe in protective white garments, Vero noticed Clover almost looked like an angel, minus the wings.

It had been Vero's idea to take up fencing. After having engaged in a vicious sword fight in the Ether a few months ago, he felt he needed to sharpen his skills. Clover wasn't as excited to take up the sport, but she agreed to accompany him at her parents' prodding. They were really keen on the sport, not because they loved fencing, but because they thought it might lead to a college scholarship for both their kids.

Vero and Clover sized up one another. Fencing not only taught agility and endurance, it required a great deal of mental energy. A fencer needed to look for the vulnerable spots in his or her opponent. Vero lunged toward Clover, but she blocked his attack with her foil. Clover counterattacked harshly with an envelopment, taking Vero's blade and moving it in a complete circle, freeing the target area. She quickly followed with a jab to his chest. The match was pretty much over before it began.

"Touché," Vero conceded. "I'm done."

Clover lowered her blade and removed her mask. Vero also yanked off his mask and slid to the floor, his back against the red padded gym wall.

"I never beat you," Clover said, concerned. "Are you going to tell me what's going on?"

Vero looked at her, his eyes full of hesitation. Clover plopped down next to him. "I can handle it, you know. Somehow I'm mixed up in all your stuff too."

Vero knew it was true. It was no coincidence that Clover was his sister or that she had visions. Whatever God's plan was for him, it definitely involved Clover. He was placed into the Leland family for a reason, that much was sure. The sound of clanging metal reverberated throughout the gym as the other fencers continued to spar.

"Something's happening," Vero said at last.

"How do you know?"

"Maybe because the nurse in the doctor's office tried to kill me today," Vero said, a hint of sarcasm in his voice.

"Seriously?" Clover asked, her eyes widening.

Vero nodded.

"Which nurse?"

"She wasn't human. She was only pretending to be a nurse."

"Mom must have freaked," Clover said.

"She had no clue. She was in the waiting room the whole time."

Worry lines spread across Clover's forehead. "What if she comes back? You shouldn't ever be alone."

Her words hit a nerve with Vero. He let his mask drop to the floor between his knees. "What do you want me to do? Take my mommy everywhere with me?"

"No, but you need to be more careful."

Vero stood up and ripped off his fencing chest vest. "I am careful," he said angrily.

At the exact moment Vero threw his chest top to the floor, one of the sparring fencers hit the other's blade with such force that the protective rubber tip flew off the foil, and the weapon itself went flying end over end. Vero's eyes went wide as the sharp projectile spiraled straight toward his heart.

# 3

⬧

# TRIAL BY FIRE

Vero found himself lying face down on rocky ground, tasting gritty dirt. He rolled over with a start, clutching his chest. He felt sure he was having a heart attack. But as the moments passed, the aching pain in his chest slowly subsided into little more than mild heartburn. He spit the dirt out of his mouth and took in his surroundings. To his left, a dazzling Greco-Roman temple with immense columns perched high above bright yellow marble steps. The columns were of such vivid pastel colors they appeared to dance in the radiant light from above. Massive stone doors proudly stood in the center of the magnificent structure. Vero knew exactly where he was — the Cathedral of Angels for Novice Development, Learning and Edification, or C.A.N.D.L.E. This was the training school for guardian angels. Vero stood up, brushed off the dirt, and smiled. It had all been real. He was back. He was finally back in the Ether.

"Vero!" a boy's voice exclaimed.

Vero spun around to see a boy grinning at him. "Hey, Pax."

It had been a few months since Vero had seen Pax, but Vero would know him anywhere. Even though he was small for his eleven years, Pax stood out in a crowd without having to wear mint green pants. He wore glasses that were too big for his face, making his eyes appear much larger than they actually were. His ears stuck out far from his head, and to top it off, his hair looked as if someone placed a soup bowl on his head as a marker and trimmed the excess with a pair of scissors.

"Have you been back since, you know ... the last time?" Vero asked.

"No. I think they wanted to give us a long break after what happened."

"Probably," Vero replied. His expression turned solemn as he recalled the battle he and his fellow angels in training had fought against two maltures the last time they were in the Ether. They nearly all perished until Vero drew his sword and slayed the demonic creatures, who were then thrown into the lake of fire by Abaddon.

"We better go in," Vero said, glancing at the scores of fledglings streaming into the school.

Vero and Pax joined the other student angels as they walked up the flight of shimmering stairs. Vero noted there seemed to be a lot more students than usual, and they were all pushing and shoving to reach the top of the steps. In the commotion, he was separated from Pax. Suddenly, the crowd came to an abrupt stop. The massive main doors were shut tight. Vero toppled into another angel.

"Hey, klutz, watch where you're going!" she angrily yelled.

Vero smiled broadly, recognizing the voice. "Nice to see you too, Greer!"

Greer turned around and smiled. "Of course it is," she said without the least bit of embarrassment for her behavior.

Greer looked a little taller than the last time Vero had seen her, but otherwise there was no mistaking her. With her tough demeanor, she didn't necessarily exude the appearance of an angel, especially in ripped jeans. Her hair was short and stylish, the brown color shot through with blonde highlights. Each of her ears was pierced three times and filled with matching sets of small silver hoops. Greer radiated strength and confidence, but Vero knew her well enough not to buy it completely.

"Glad to see you're still enjoying your favorite high-protein snack," Vero joked, as Greer bit her nubby fingernails to the quick, a nervous habit that gave away the side to her most people never saw.

Greer spit a shred of her wet nail at Vero, hitting him in the chest. "Whatever, Major Loser!"

"I take it you've been away at etiquette school over the summer," Vero teased.

"Graduated top of my class," she said, unable to suppress a small smile.

A loud creaking noise filled the air. The stone doors swung open, and the lines of angels walked through, buzzing with excitement. Vero got the feeling everyone knew something he did not. He stood just inside the doors, letting kids stream past him and feeling puny as he looked from one end of the massive entrance hall to the other. The building seemed to go on forever—it looked almost as infinite as the ocean. Balconies stacked one on top of another lined the interior sides. Everything inside seemed to sparkle. The walls were a mixture of gold and diamonds. Above the balconies sat a dome ceiling almost too high to make out its intricate geometric designs.

"There you are," Pax said out of breath, as he caught back up with Vero.

"Hey, little dude," Greer smiled to Pax.

"Hi, Greer," Pax said. "Did you have a good summer?"

"Awesome summer. I'm all done with foster families. They put me in a group home."

Pax looked closer at Greer, suddenly very interested.

"And I kind of like it. Who knew?"

"But isn't that living with a bunch of strangers?" Pax said.

"Hey, when you're sharing a bathroom with six other kids, you get over that whole stranger thing real fast," Greer chuckled heartily.

As Vero laughed at Greer's comment, he noticed that Pax wasn't even smiling. What was up with him?

"Hey, what do you suppose that is?" Greer asked.

Vero and Pax followed Greer's gaze and saw what looked like a colossal cornucopia basket floating a few feet above the floor with the wide end facing down. Only it wasn't woven together with twigs or reeds, but strands of fire. They twisted in and out of one another swirling to a sharp point on top. The young angels gathered around it, but not too closely. Vero could feel the heat of the spiraling flames.

"That's some bonfire," Greer said, astonished.

Vero nodded in agreement, but then the wind chimes sounded, signaling the angels to get to their classrooms. Vero had forgotten all about the wind chimes. Back at his school on earth, a loud bell rang throughout the hallways to let kids know it was time for the next class. He so much preferred the soft, soothing rhythm of the chimes over the unnerving clang of the bell. As the gentle wind chimes played, a lovely female singing voice accompanied them, "All fledglings, please proceed to the amphitheater," she sang.

Vero looked around, wondering which door led to the amphitheater. Even though he was a student at C.A.N.D.L.E., he was not yet that familiar with the building. He had only been here a handful of times, and he never knew when he was going to return for further instruction.

"Any idea where?" Vero asked Greer.

"Nope, but just follow everybody else," she replied matter-of-factly. "And pretend like you do."

The crowd swallowed up Vero, Pax, and Greer, and when they reappeared outside through a set of wide doors, they found themselves standing on the top row of a jaw-dropping natural amphitheater. Far below them were arches of majestic stones bathed in colors of dark red, effervescent orange, and warm browns that created a half-dome backdrop over a glistening, white marble stage. Running down to the stage were row upon row of semicircular tiered seating. As angels began to fill the seats, Vero noticed that the rock benches were also made from the same unique and colorful stones. A paternal voice called from the stage.

"Everyone find a seat."

With his well-groomed silver beard and equally silvered hair, Vero immediately recognized the fatherly-looking angel to whom the warm voice belonged. It was the archangel Uriel. Of all of his instructors at C.A.N.D.L.E., Vero considered Uriel to be his mentor. It was Uriel who watched over him when he was a little kid. It was Uriel who first took him to the

Ether, and it was Uriel who saved him from the maltures on the rooftop. The tall archangel patiently waited for the young angels to settle. Two other archangels, Raziel and Raphael, stood behind him on the platform. Raphael always brought a smile to Vero's face. He was warmhearted and good-humored, so easy to like. The word "jolly" came to mind when Vero looked at Raphael's twinkling violet eyes and round, pleasant face. Plus, Vero thought Raphael's long ponytail was cool. The archangel Raziel, on the other hand, had the opposite effect on Vero. With his unkempt white hair and goatee and harsh jagged features, he made Vero tense and nervous, like he was constantly on the verge of making a mistake. Despite having the same violet-colored eyes as Raphael, Raziel's showed no warmth or charm. As Vero watched him, Raziel caught his stare. He shot Vero a look of great disdain before Vero quickly turned his head away and sat down between Greer and Pax. Uriel cleared his voice over the chattering students.

"Today is an important day," Uriel began. As Uriel spoke his voice naturally amplified out over the audience, and the angels quieted. "I'm sure you noticed the flame inside the Cathedral and are wondering what it is."

Vero noticed several fledglings around him perk up and nod their heads.

"Does anyone know why the ancient Greeks held the Olympic games?"

A fledgling stood. Vero noted that he was very tall and was built like a body builder. The group of five other angels sitting around him were equally well built. They all looked older than Vero, maybe seventeen or eighteen.

"Who's that?" Vero elbowed Pax.

"Eitan," Pax said.

"He and his buddies would make the jocks at my school look like wimps," Vero said, somewhat awestruck.

Pax nodded. "They're rumored to be future archangels."

Vero glanced back at the big angels in training. It had never occurred to him that fledglings could become archangels.

"The games were held to honor the gods," Eitan said in a booming voice that easily projected.

"Correct," Uriel said. "Go on."

"The citizens of the city-states of ancient Greece competed with one another, showing off their talents and skills in the hopes of honoring and glorifying the gods who they believed bestowed those gifts upon them," Eitan said. "It was a religious festival."

He sat back down.

"Thank you, Eitan. Exactly correct. We here at C.A.N.D.L.E. have been conducting our own games since long before the Olympic games of Ancient Greece," Uriel said. "Here we call them the Angel Trials. They occur every hundred years. In these Trials, we honor and glorify God by displaying not just our faith, but also all of the unique gifts He has bestowed. There are three challenges, each of which will test your faith and your God-given talents. One flight of fledglings, that's six of you, will be chosen to compete against the other angel schools."

A petite girl raised her hand.

"I'm confused. I thought C.A.N.D.L.E. was the only guardian angel school," she said.

"Hey, it's Ada." Pax nudged Vero.

Vero squinted. He had a hard time making out her face from such a distance, but there was no mistaking that fiery auburn hair. And when she nervously twirled her finger through her curly locks, Vero knew for certain it was Ada.

"It is, Miss Brickner," Uriel answered.

"Then who do we ...?"

"There are three spheres in the angel world," Uriel continued. "The first sphere consists of the angels of contemplation—the Seraphim, the Cherubim, and the Thrones. The Seraphim minister to God proclaiming His glory. The Cherubim guard His throne. And the Thrones dispense God's justice. All these angels dwell inside the gates, closest to God. Those positions have all been filled pretty much since the beginning of time, so there are no schools in the first sphere. However, for the purpose of the Angel Trials, the Thrones serve as judges, and their decisions are final."

Vero turned to face Greer. "Did you know about other angels?" he whispered.

Greer shook her head slowly.

"You will be competing against the angels of the second sphere. Angels who can perform limited miracles, foretell the future, and heal sickness."

Greer stood up suddenly and put her hands on her hips. "Let me get this straight; those other angels can do miracles?"

"Yes."

"And see the future?"

"Yes."

"Then we don't have a snowball's chance in you-know-where of winning this thing!" Greer said angrily.

"It is true we are the underdogs. And it's been many centuries since the guardians have won the Angel Trials," Uriel said. "But keep in mind, those angels are just like you in the sense that they, too, are in training. They have yet to completely master all those abilities. Plus, you will outnumber them. We will send one flight of fledglings from our sphere."

Raziel stepped forward. "Which is the third sphere. We are the angels of the earth — the messengers and protectors of man."

"I still say it's a lost cause," Greer said, crossing her arms.

The crowd murmured in agreement, and a look of impatience flickered across Uriel's face. He shouted out over the crowd.

"Anyone curious as to why there's a flame inside C.A.N.D.L.E.?"

The thousands of students hushed.

"Ever heard the expression 'trial by fire'?"

Vero and many of the other fledglings nodded.

"It's the revelation of a novice's true skill when under pressure. When he's put to the wall, what is he made of — what is his real character? It is usually a test of one's abilities, one's endurance, or one's belief. Corinthians states that the acts and deeds by the believer will be judged by the fire."

"If only a few angels are chosen to compete, what are the rest of us supposed to do?" Eitan asked.

"Pray for them," Uriel answered with utmost seriousness.

A complete silence came over the gathering of students as it dawned on them that these Trials might be more than just games. Perhaps there was more at stake than winning a gold medal.

"Should any angel fail during the Trials, they will find themselves singing with the choir of angels for all eternity," Uriel told them, his face grave.

Vero swallowed hard. He knew that if a fledgling washed out of training before he became a full-fledged angel, he would be sent to join the choir. Not that it was a bad thing at all to be in the choir, but glorifying God by singing was very different from glorifying Him by fulfilling your intended purpose as a warrior.

"There is to be a competition amongst all of you to determine who will have the honor of representing the guardians in the Trials," Uriel continued. "The first fledgling who completes the challenge will then select five others to make up his or her flight for the trials. They can be from your own class flight, or anyone else in training."

"What's the challenge?" Greer called out.

Uriel looked out over the crowd and waited until everyone was perfectly silent. "A long time ago before the Great Flood covered the earth, Noah was instructed to take two of every animal onboard the ark. He did as he was instructed. However, it broke Noah's heart to imprison one particular breed of animal on the ark. The unicorn. It had such a pure, free spirit that he was convinced if tied up for many hard months in the belly of the ship, the animal would surely die. So Noah asked God to spare the unicorn from the long voyage. God granted Noah's prayer, giving the unicorns wings. He opened up a piece of the sky so they could fly into the Ether, where they have remained ever since."

Uriel paused for a moment to allow the fledglings to absorb the story.

"The first one to place the palm of his or her hand on the tip of a unicorn's horn will win the competition. For the unicorn's horn holds healing powers which you'll probably need during the Trials. And, even more important, that angel shall receive a special grace from God. You will have until the light rises tomorrow morning. Good luck and happy hunting."

Vero turned to Greer. "That's it? I mean, how are we supposed to find a unicorn?"

"You're asking me?" Greer exclaimed. "I didn't even know they were real up until a minute ago!"

Uriel walked off the stage, followed by Raziel and Raphael. Vero chased after Uriel. As he headed back into the temple, Vero called out to him. "Uriel!"

Uriel stopped so Vero could catch up. "Hello, Vero."

"Hi."

"Is there something you wanted?" Uriel asked.

"I don't understand. How are we supposed to find a unicorn? I wouldn't even know where to start."

"If I told you, it wouldn't be fair to everyone else. Would it?" Uriel replied with a wink. "But here's a hint."

Vero leaned in so as not to miss a single word.

"They're white with a single horn coming out of their head." Uriel chuckled before walking away.

As Vero, watched his retreating back, he suddenly felt a wave of fear from all that he had gone through in the last twenty-four hours. "They're after me again," he shouted.

Uriel stopped and spun around. He was no longer laughing. "Who?"

"Something disguised as a nurse tried to kill me on earth."

"Did it say anything?"

"It wanted to know which one of us it was. It kept screaming, 'tell me who it is!'"

A look of deep concern crossed Uriel's face, but then he turned his back to Vero. "I'll look into it," Uriel said before walking away.

Vero stood, disappointed and surprised by Uriel's reaction.

"Where the heck are we gonna find a unicorn?" Greer asked, as she barreled over to Vero with Pax tagging along.

"I would start at the library," a girl's voice suggested.

Vero spun around. He saw Ada standing behind them and smiled at her.

"Well don't just stand there," Ada said, smiling back at Vero. "Hurry up before the others get a head start."

"But didn't you hear Uriel?" Vero asked. "He said the winner was the first one to touch the unicorn's horn."

"But he also said that person picks the others. I suggest we work together under the agreement that whoever touches the unicorn first, picks the rest of us," Ada suggested.

"Done," Pax said.

"Okay," Vero agreed.

Everyone looked to Greer, waiting for her response. She hesitated for a moment. Folding her arms across her chest, she looked carefully at the three of them. And then a smile spread across her face.

"I wanted you guys to sweat it out for a minute," she laughed. "Deal."

It was the brightest room Vero had ever seen. The walls were stark white, as was the floor, ceiling, and every bench and table. The angels' earthly clothing provided the only color in the place. The enormous rotunda was filled with scrolls from floor to ceiling. Vero got a crick in his neck as he looked up at the shelves of scrolls that stretched as far as his eye could see. It was vast, endless, and yet, surprisingly bland.

"I've heard the library is so boring looking because you're

here to learn and do research, so they don't want anything to distract you," Ada said.

"How are we supposed to get the scrolls down?" Pax asked. "I don't see any staircases anywhere."

"Fly up to the shelves?" Greer suggested.

Vero looked around. "To which one? How are we going to find a scroll on unicorns ..."

Before Vero could even finish his question, he and the others' jaws dropped as a scroll from a shelf above them, freed itself, and floated into the air. It continued its journey and landed in Vero's hand.

"I've gotta say, that was way faster than the Internet," Vero marveled.

The angels sat down at a table and rolled open the scroll. The parchment paper looked ancient. It was weathered and crinkled upon touch. But there was nothing written on the document. Disappointment swept over the angels.

"Is this some kind of joke?" Greer said angrily. "It's blank!"

"Maybe it's just written real faintly?" Pax leaned into the paper for a closer look. As he squinted his eyes, a tiny unicorn, no more than two inches from head to tail, suddenly sprang from the scroll. It was snow white with wings at its sides and a horn protruding from its head. Its long mane seemed to be blowing in a breeze. The angels watched, completely fascinated, as it flapped its tiny wings and then flew directly into Pax's left ear! Pax screamed. His squeezed his eyes closed, banging his head with his hand as if the unicorn were a nasty bug. He quickly stood and jumped on one foot as if trying to get a water bubble out of his ear. A moment later, the unicorn shot out of his right ear.

Pax slumped back down into the bench. But the miniature unicorn wasn't done. It flew into Greer's left ear next. After wreaking havoc inside her head and flying out the other ear, it did the same to Ada and finally Vero. When the unicorn flew out of Vero's ear, it landed in the middle of the unraveled scroll, and the scroll rolled itself up, swallowing the unicorn within it. It then floated off the table and flew back to its proper place on the bookshelf. The angels looked at each other, too startled to speak, and still catching their breath. Finally, Greer broke the silence.

"Wow," was all she could say.

# 4

---

# TRACKING UNICORNS

D o you know how smart I would be in school if we had libraries like that on earth?" Greer asked excitedly as she walked out of the library, flanked by Ada, Pax, and Vero.

"Even my friend Tack would get straight As," Vero commented.

The angels were amazed at how the library had worked. They didn't even have to study or read about unicorns. The information had literally flown into their heads. Instant knowledge. They now knew everything there was to know about unicorns, except where to find a real one.

"According to what we now know about unicorns, they live near rivers," Ada said, as she stopped walking and faced the others.

"And they only eat from the snowball bushes," Vero added. "Oh, and they hide in daytime."

"That doesn't really help us much," Greer said.

"Maybe it does."

Everyone turned to Pax.

"What about the big river with the three waterfalls? Once when I flew over them, I remember seeing a whole field of nothing but white bushes below."

Vero also remembered soaring over the waterfalls when he had first learned to fly in the Ether. They were a magnificent sight. One single river split off into three waterfalls placed at equilateral distance that formed a perfect triangle. They flowed into a pool, where souls bathed before they were presented to God. Uriel had rubbed water from the falls over Vero's eyelids, and when he had opened them, Vero had been able to see the souls cleansing themselves in the pool.

"Anybody got anything better?" Greer asked. "Anybody?"

Vero shook his head.

"It's as good a start as any," Ada commented.

"Hey, guys," Pax said in a low voice, nodding over his shoulder. "Look over there."

The others turned and saw Eitan and his fellow jocks entering the library.

Greer gritted her teeth. "Let's fly."

She got down on one knee, her head bowed toward the ground as she closed her eyes. After a few seconds of complete concentration, Greer's wings shot out her back, ripping her leather jacket and lifting her high into the air. Pax and Ada did the same and flew up to Greer. Only Vero hesitated. When he had first learned to fly, he had needed a running start to get airborne. Over time, he honed his flying skills, but he still lacked confidence.

"Sometime today!" Greer shouted down to Vero. "Or the super boys are going to beat us!"

Vero hunched over. He closed his eyes and pressed his fingertips to his temples and thought only of flying. He blocked everything else from his mind. He concentrated so hard, he began to shake. Suddenly, his shoulders jerked forward as his wings sprouted, tearing the flimsy fabric of his shirt. Then like a rocket, Vero shot into the air. It happened so fast, his eyes were still closed, and he wasn't looking where he was going. He didn't see the massive tree until he head-butted into a thick branch and found himself tangled like a wayward kite. Greer rolled her eyes.

"Guys, help," Vero said, turning red. "My wings are stuck."

Greer and the others flew down and landed gracefully on the tree's branches. Greer manhandled Vero's wings as she struggled to free them.

"That hurts!" Vero yelped.

"You know, it's hard to believe you're the same guy who defeated the maltures," she said. "I'm wondering if that was just a fluke!"

Greer twisted the tip of Vero's wing into an unnatural angle then yanked it free from a cluster of sharp branches.

"You don't have to be so rough!" Vero winced.

"I don't have time to be gentle," Greer answered. "In case you forgot, every other angel in the school is already out looking for unicorns!" She knit her brow. "Wow, never thought I'd say a sentence like that."

Vero stood on the edge of a branch and jumped off. His wings caught the wind, and he flapped high into the air.

"Wait up!" Greer called after him.

Greer, Ada, and Pax flew after Vero as he soared higher and higher. Vero looked below and took in the sights of the Ether. Verdant hills lush with flowers of every color imaginable. Sparkling crystal lakes. Snowcapped mountain peaks. Sailing clouds. Vero loved nothing more than the rush of the wind invigorating his face and rippling through his hair. It was a feeling of total freedom. When Vero flew, he knew he was truly a guardian angel. It was as if all his senses had come alive. As Vero and the others headed for the river, a low rumbling grew louder and louder until it filled their ears with a thunderous roar. Vero glanced down and saw the three waterfalls.

"There they are!" Pax called. "Land by the big river!"

Vero hated to leave the warm, peaceful skies of the Ether, but it was time to get serious and find the unicorn. It would be dark in a few hours. Vero dropped out of the great blue, retracting his wings a few seconds too early and hitting the ground hard. He stumbled and fell.

"Don't worry, nobody saw," Greer teased as she walked past him.

Vero looked over at her, embarrassed for the second time in just a few minutes.

Ada turned to Pax. "Okay, you brought us here, now where are those unicorns?"

"I swear this was the spot where I saw the snowball bushes," Pax said, turning around.

Vero looked out over the riverbank. Every tree, bush, and shrub was a vivid green — not a single snowball bush anywhere.

"I'm pretty sure this is where they were," Pax maintained.

"Well, they're not here, so get over it," Greer told him.

"Finding the snowball bushes is a good idea," Ada said. "Maybe we just landed in the wrong place."

"Guys," Greer said, "we've gotta figure this thing out or else it's game over for us. Now what else do we know about unicorns that could help?"

"Noah thought they had such a free spirit that it would have been a sin to lock them up," Pax said. "I suppose that's why they hide from everyone."

"That's why I think they'd be hidden deep in the forests, afraid someone will harm them," Ada reasoned.

"But there are no humans in the Ether to do that," Greer pointed out.

"Yes, but maybe there are maltures and demons that would harm any of God's creatures if they could, especially one so beautiful."

"But the Ether is way too big," Vero said. "We don't have time to search all the woods for them."

"Then let's narrow it down," Ada said. "And just because there aren't any snowball bushes here, doesn't mean Pax is wrong. They could have eaten them all and moved on, probably deeper into these woods. We can figure this out."

"What do we know about unicorns?" Pax asked again.

"They're smart," Greer said. "They can communicate with humans telepathically. They're shy."

"They have eyes that seem to be full of stars," Ada offered.

"And cloven hooves like a deer," Vero said.

"Once a year, they journey to the site of the Garden of Eden," Greer added.

"So," Pax said, "we just need to find the entrance and wait."

Greer gave Pax an incredulous look. "Are you insane? If

we can't find one stinking unicorn, how the heck would we ever find the Garden of Eden?"

"Over here!" Vero exclaimed suddenly. He was on his knees in a low muddy patch along the sloping riverbank, his sneakers sinking into the muck. "Tracks." Vero pointed. "Cloven hooves." The others crowded around to look and saw a trail of hooves in the mud. "They lead into the woods," Vero added.

"Should we follow 'em?" asked Pax.

Greer squinted at the hoofprints. "How do we know they're not from a deer? They kind of have the same hooves."

Vero leaned down to study them closer. "These look a lot bigger than a deer."

"Then let's see where they lead," Ada said.

Vero stood up. As he looked into the dark woods, a feeling of determination empowered him. "Let's do it."

The forest was dense and appeared to be very old. Its trees grew so closely together that it was difficult to tell which branches or roots belonged to which tree. A few scarce slivers of light streamed through the thick canopy of leaves. Spongy moss clung to the trunks of the trees and camouflaged entire rocks, and the underbrush was crowded with ferns and bushes, making it nearly impenetrable.

"Can anyone see tracks anymore?" Vero asked nervously as he breathed in the cool, wet air.

"Getting hard," Greer said, kicking a fern from out of her path.

"It's just too thick," Ada sighed. "The tracks are gone."

"Then forget the tracks," Pax said. "We need to look for leaves they might have eaten or small branches they could have broken. Or sometimes deer rub their antlers against trees and strip away the bark. Maybe unicorns do the same with their horns."

"Does anyone wonder why we're the only ones in this forest?" Greer stopped walking and turned to the others. "Think about it. Tons of other fledglings are out tracking the same unicorns, so why haven't we run into any of them? Maybe our idea isn't so great. Maybe they know something that we don't." She threw up her hands. "Maybe we're the idiots here."

"And we're losing our light," Pax sighed. He sat down on a fallen log.

Vero looked up at the canopy. Hardly any light was streaming through the trees. It would soon be dark, and then they would be stuck in the forest unable to find their way out. But those tracks were still their best bet at finding a unicorn. They had nothing else to go on.

"I hate to mention this now," Pax began, "but some say that Lucifer also has cloven hooves."

"What?" asked Greer, fear spiking her voice. "I never heard that. Where'd you learn that?"

"When my mom read me Shakespeare's *Othello*," Pax said.

"He's right," Ada replied.

"Of course, you would know," Greer eyed Ada. "You've probably read every Shakespeare play."

"And his sonnets," Ada added.

Greer rolled her eyes.

But then fear rose in Ada's chest. "So does that mean — could these hoofprints be a trap?" Her voice grew high and squeaky.

Suddenly, Vero heard the distant sound of crunching

leaves. His eyes darted around, looking for the source of the unsettling noise. At home, the sound of crackling autumn leaves was a sound of joy—jumping into a huge pile of newly raked leaves with friends. But here, the sound created only a feeling of dread. And the noise seemed to be growing.

"Anybody else hear that?" Vero asked nervously.

Ada, Pax, and Greer instantly hid behind him, using him as their shield.

"Get off, you guys!" Vero said angrily.

But the three would not release Vero. They pulled and tugged on him until he toppled over backward, leveling all of them like dominoes.

The last faint rays of light revealed a figure stepping out from the shadows of the trees. Vero squinted—it had two heads! Fear strangled his throat, and he couldn't even scream. As the figure stepped closer, Vero's arm instinctively rose to block his face.

"Glad to see you guys are taking this whole thing seriously," the figure said to them.

That didn't sound like the devil. Vero lowered his arm. He saw two heads, but they weren't joined. The last of the light revealed that one belonged to Kane, the other to X. X was classically handsome, with high cheekbones and a chiseled nose. His chest and shoulders were extremely well developed for someone only sixteen. Kane had a roundish face with deep-set eyes and a strong jawline.

"What are you jerks doing here?" Greer asked as she tried to push everyone off her.

X held out his hand and effortlessly pulled Greer to her feet.

"Following you," Kane answered. "We saw you coming

out of the library and figured that maybe you knew how to find a unicorn better than us. We've got nothing."

"So we've been trailing you," X added.

"We'll you'd have been smarter to follow the yellow brick road than us, 'cause we've got nothing either," Greer snapped.

"But it is good to see you guys," Vero told them.

X and Kane had been in the same class as Vero and the others. Vero had done his very first training with them, and they had taught him to fly. And when Vero needed help to battle the maltures, they were by his side.

"You too," X said.

Greer cleared her throat. "Enough with the love fest." She impatiently beckoned Kane and X closer. "The four of us have all agreed to work together, so if by some miracle one of us stumbles upon a unicorn and is the first to touch his horn, we've all agreed to pick each other for the team." Greer got up in their faces and fixed her eyes upon them. "Any problem with that?"

"No, none," X said. "If I touch the horn, you'll all be on my team."

Greer looked to Kane who hesitated for a moment and then nodded.

"Okay, good," Greer said. "Now whatever we're going to do here, it needs to happen fast because we're losing light."

"No problem," Kane said as he pulled a smart phone from his back pants pocket. He pressed a button in the middle of the screen, and the phone illuminated like a flashlight.

"You have your own cell phone?" Vero asked, his voice full of envy.

"Yeah, don't you?"

"No," Vero said. "Everyone has one but me." He turned to X. "Don't you?"

"Um, in case you forgot, I'm in a wheelchair on earth," X said. "As in ... I can't use my hands."

Pax nodded. "I'm severely autistic so I don't have one either."

"I have no parents to buy me one," Greer said.

Vero looked down. "Okay, now I feel like a big jerk."

"I have one," Ada chimed in. "Well, had. My little brother and I were fighting over it, and it fell into the toilet so my parents refused to get me another one."

Vero was about to reply when Greer interrupted, waving her arms impatiently. "I thought we were here to look for unicorns, not discuss cell phone plans!"

"Guys, look!" Pax yelled.

Vero turned around. Pax parted a clump of ferns with his hand. "Shine the light over here!"

Kane pointed the phone toward the ground where Pax stood. The white light from the flashlight app illuminated a pair of hoof tracks in the muddy ground.

"Can I have that?" X nodded to Kane's phone.

Kane handed X his phone.

"Follow me," X instructed as he shone the light in front of his shoes.

X walked ahead, spreading the fern clusters apart with his feet. As he tracked the pattern of hooves, the other angels walked closely behind him. Before long, the underbrush of ferns gradually thinned out, and the hoofprints became much easier to follow. The group soon reached a clearing in the woods. The sky above was dark and filled with stars, and Vero looked up at them as the group continued to carefully step through the big clearing. After several minutes, Greer suddenly stopped and turned around in a circle, surveying the landscape. A look of frustration came over her, and she let out an ear-shattering scream. Everyone turned around to see Greer pointing to the area around her.

"What?" Ada asked. "What is it?"

"Look at the ferns! Can't you see?" Greer kicked the fern closest to her.

The angels eyed one another. They had no clue what she was talking about.

"We've been walking in a circle!" Greer yelled.

Vero scanned the area and saw a circular path of crushed ferns. Greer was right.

"We're doomed," Pax said.

Tired, Vero laid down on a soft piece of ground.

"Not a bad idea," Ada said, and she lay down next to him.

Feeling defeated, the others joined them on the spongy, moss-covered ground. Exhaustion overtook them as they lay on their backs looking up at the sky. "The stars are so much brighter here than on earth," Pax said.

"I guess that's because the Ether is closer to them," Ada surmised. "The Big Dipper is so much easier to see."

X pointed. "And there's Gemini."

"Orion's next to it," Pax added, pushing up his glasses.

"I think I'm gonna fly out of here and go back," Greer said. "I'm tired, and I'm starving."

Suddenly, Vero bolted up. He stared at the sky for a moment, and then he turned to Greer with a huge smile. "That's too bad," he said. "Because you'll miss the unicorns."

Greer's eyes narrowed. The others quickly sat up. Vero pointed to the sky directly over them.

"That's the constellation Monoceros—as in Monoceros the unicorn," Vero said excitedly. "Remember, unicorns have deep blue eyes that seem to be full of stars. The unicorns hide up in the constellation during the day!"

"Really?" Greer said, her voice laced with sarcasm.

"No, it makes sense!" Vero insisted. "Just give it a few minutes. They'll show up."

"We don't have the time for this," Kane said, shaking his head. He looked to X for support.

X shrugged his broad shoulders, "We don't have any thing else."

Kane sighed, and then lay back on the ground. They waited and waited, watching the sky until their necks hurt. Nothing happened except that Greer fell asleep.

"Vero, you know what this is?" Ada said. "It's like in Charlie Brown when Linus and Sally spend all night in the pumpkin patch. We're gonna sit here the entire night and wait for the Great Pumpkin who's never going to show up!"

"We've given it enough time, Vero," X said, above Greer's snoring.

Vero sighed. "Good grief."

At that exact moment, the low-growing shrubs in the clearing began to change color. They turned from a healthy green to a lustrous white. Pax shook Greer awake. The angels watched in amazement as tiny white buds blossomed from the branches until they bloomed into flowers the size and shape of snowballs.

"I knew I wasn't crazy. I told you I saw those bushes!" Pax said. "They must camouflage themselves in green when they're not in bloom."

Every bush transformed into a white so bright that the

clearing seemed to glow. Vero tugged on X's sleeve as he looked at the twinkling lights above. The stars in the Monoceros constellation moved farther apart from one another, creating a large opening in the heavens. Ada and Pax gasped as one by one, unicorns dropped out of the hole in the sky, flapping their wings in the night air. After a few minutes, they landed gracefully in the clearing and shook their beautiful manes, one of them quite close to the fledglings.

"I guess they come down at night when it's safe to feed," Vero stuttered in total awe.

Greer shook her head. "Holy cow," she murmured.

"More like holy unicorn," Pax corrected.

The creature that Vero had always thought to be only mythical now stood but a few feet away. It was more magnificent than he had ever imagined. The unicorn resembled a horse, only much larger, taller than the Clydesdale horses Vero once saw in a parade. Its coat and wings were milky white, and its eyes were the color of the midnight sky. A thick silky mane ran down its neck, and it had a thin, scraggly beard, resembling a goat's. The hooves, Vero noticed, were indeed cloven. But what most mesmerized Vero was the horn that stood out straight from the middle of its forehead. The sharp, three-foot crystal horn exuded power. Awestruck and little bit frightened, the angels stared at the herd of unicorns as they grazed on the snowball bushes.

"So all we have to do is touch one of their horns?" Ada asked sheepishly as she gazed at the massive animals.

"Yeah," Pax answered.

"Okay, I'll try," Kane said, and he moved toward the herd.

As Kane approached, several of the unicorns reared and flapped their wings. The wings created such a strong wind that it reminded Kane of the gusts created by moving helicopter blades. He stopped in his tracks. The unicorns whinnied so loudly everyone covered their ears.

"Maybe finding the unicorns was the easy part," Greer said hesitantly.

"Is it enough that we found them?" Pax asked. "Or do we really need to touch the horn to get the extra grace?"

The unicorn that had landed closest to the fledglings trotted over to Vero and stood several feet away from him. It looked into Vero's eyes and held his gaze. They stared at one another with great intensity.

"Are they having some sort of staring contest?" Greer asked.

"I think he's speaking telepathically with him," Kane answered.

Vero continued to look at the unicorn for a few moments longer. Then he nodded to the animal and stepped back. Vero turned to the others.

"His name is Aurora. And he says that he decides which one of us will touch his horn to get the blessing."

"But how?" Ada wondered. "He doesn't know any of us."

"He can feel it."

"Since when did you learn to speak unicorn?" Ada asked.

"About two minutes ago," Vero said, checking his watch.

Ada stared at Vero, remembering the last time Vero had made sense of a language when no one else could. They had been trapped in the underground caverns by the golems, the brainless, giant stone creatures. Only Vero had been able to read the strange symbols on the parchment papers that destroyed the creatures. Nobody else could even see the writing. Ada had realized then that Vero had more talents than she and the others, that there was something different and special about him. And watching him stand before the unicorn now only reinforced her belief.

"Everyone line up," Vero instructed them. "We need to stand next to each other."

Pax, X, Kane, Greer, and Ada lined up on either side of Vero. They stood before the mighty unicorn. The animal towered over them. The angels nervously waited as the unicorn paced before them like an army drill sergeant inspecting his troops.

Greer swelled with hope when Aurora paused before her and looked deep into her eyes. As she stared into the eyes of the unicorn, emotions welled up within her. She felt vulnerable, like she could not hide anything. Under the intensity of Aurora's gaze, Greer began first to tremble, and then tears escaped her eyes. It was like nothing she'd ever experienced. She felt both intense shame and phenomenal joy at the same time.

"Thanks, Aurora," Greer whispered.

Then the unicorn looked away and moved down the line from Ada and then to Pax. Vero was starting to feel very anxious as the beast began to study X. He so desperately wanted Aurora's blessing, not because he thought he was special and deserved it more than anyone else, but because he felt he needed it. The archangel Michael had told Vero that so much more was expected of him, that his mission would be quite difficult, and Vero was afraid he would fail. He thought about the terrifying nurse, the strange chanting during the school picture, and he shivered. Maybe the extra strength and grace promised by the unicorn's horn could help him succeed, could protect him. When the magnificent creature moved away from X and stood before him, Vero knew that the unicorn sensed his desperation.

But after a few seconds the unicorn took his eyes off Vero and turned to Kane.

"C'mon, Aurora, old-buddy! I'm right here," Kane said out loud. He clearly wanted the blessing every bit as much as Vero. "C'mon."

Aurora tilted his head back toward Vero. Then he gazed at Kane, then at Vero again. For a moment Aurora paused, as if to apologize to him. Vero bit his bottom lip. And then, the mighty unicorn's front legs buckled underneath him, and he bowed down before Kane.

"Yes! Ka-ching!" Kane whooped.

Massive disappointment swept over Vero. His head sunk into his chest. After a moment, he looked at Kane "Congrats," he barely managed to squeeze out between his lips.

"Thanks, dude."

"Aurora wants you to place your right palm on the tip of his horn," Vero said. A large lump had formed in his throat.

The unicorn snorted as Kane approached. He lowered his head even closer to the ground so Kane could reach his horn. Kane tentatively held up his hand, wary of the sharp point. He looked back to Vero and the others.

Vero nodded toward the unicorn. "He won't hurt you."

Kane stepped forward. He stood before the amazing beast, stretched out his arm, and placed a shaky hand on its horn. Upon touch, the clear crystal horn began to shine. Every color of the rainbow radiated from it, taking form and swirling toward Kane. The colorful rays spun a web around him, wrapping him in their warm hues. After a moment, the light unraveled itself and shot off like fireworks.

❖

Deep in the surrounding forest, a pair of dark eyes, rimmed with hatred, watched as the brilliant lights ascended to the heavens.

# 5

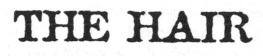

# THE HAIR

Aurora walked away from Kane and joined the other unicorns grazing on the snowball bushes. Kane felt disorientated and a bit off balance after receiving the blessing. He staggered toward the others.

"That was awesome," he blurted.

"I wonder what type of grace you'll get," Ada said.

"Guess we'll find out in the Trials," Kane answered, putting a hand on X's shoulder to regain his balance.

Suddenly, the herd stopped grazing and perked up their ears. Something had spooked them. In the distance, Vero heard the faint snapping of tree branches.

"What's happening?" Vero urgently asked Aurora through his thoughts. "What is it?"

The unicorn did not answer him, his attention too focused on the commotion in the forest. The ground began to tremble as the sounds drew closer. The brightness of the snowball bushes dimmed and camouflaged to a dark shade of green. If not for the light from the moon, the clearing would have plunged into total darkness.

Pax pointed to the dense cluster of trees behind them, while digging his nails into Vero's arm. "Look up at the trees!" he yelled.

Vero spun around and saw the distant tops of trees toppling over. Tree after tree fell in a line heading straight for them, but Vero couldn't tell what was knocking them over. The herd reared up, flapping their wings furiously as they lifted off the ground in a rush of wind. Vero shielded his eyes with his hand as he watched the unicorns fly higher and higher. After a few seconds, the stars of the Monoceros constellation broke apart and formed an opening. The unicorns flew towards it. Vero heard a whinny and realized that Aurora was still standing in the clearing. He approached Vero and stared hard into his eyes.

"You must flee the forest!" the unicorn mentally spoke to Vero. "Quickly, to the air!"

"Why? What is it?" Vero asked.

"She will devour you all!" the unicorn said. "Fly now!" Aurora was prancing nervously as the rumble of falling trees grew closer.

"He wants us to fly now!" Vero shouted to the others.

Vero watched as the other fledglings sprouted their wings and jumped skyward. It sounded as if a freight train was nearly upon them. Aurora spread his wings and leapt into the night.

"Vero, come on!" X screamed from the sky as the panicked Vero crouched down and willed his wings to open.

"I'm trying!" Vero yelled. He tried to concentrate, but it was no good. He was too nervous and distracted.

A line of trees fell on top of one another causing a chain

reaction into the clearing. The very top of one hit Vero, knocking him to the ground and pinning one of his legs. Vero froze with fear, as he watched what appeared to be a serpentine rope of hair as thick as a pillar slithering toward him. But he had no time to wonder what it was. Crawling on his elbows, Vero quickly tried to inch his way out of the tangled branches. The tip of the hair serpent had no head or eyes, yet somehow it was acutely aware of him. It advanced with amazing speed and wrapped itself around his free ankle.

"Help me!" Vero yelled as he tried to kick his foot free of the hair.

Aurora swooped down from the sky, diving close to Vero's upper body yet trying to keep his distance from the hair. The unicorn hovered over him, his wings wildly beating.

"Grab my tail!" he conveyed to Vero. "Take it now!"

Vero grabbed at the silky white tail hanging before him and caught a clump of it in his fist. The unicorn pulled Vero out from under the branches, lifting him high into the air. But the hair serpent still would not let go of Vero. As the other fledglings screamed in terror, Vero felt as if the tug-of-war would rip his foot from his leg. Aurora ferociously flicked his tail. The force was strong enough to cause the black hair to release Vero's foot, but Vero was unable to keep his grip on Aurora's tail and fell into the night air below. He landed with a dull thud on a soft bed of ferns.

"Vero! Look out!" X yelled. "It's coming back!"

The hair serpent rose up, looking very much like a provoked snake about to strike. Vero kneeled, willing his wings to open.

"Vero, you grow those wings now or I'll kill you myself!" Greer yelled.

Just as Vero sprouted his wings, Aurora circled back down and once again offered his tail. The hair stuck, but Vero flew the few yards up to Aurora's tail and grabbed hold. Faster than he could ever fly on his own, Vero and the unicorn shot straight up toward the stars, the other angels furiously batting their wings to catch them. Soon, they were far above the danger of the forest.

Aurora turned his elegant head to Vero.

"This is as far as I can take you," he said telepathically.

Vero nodded to him, releasing his tail. As the unicorn and Vero slowly flapped their wings, hovering in place, they looked each other in the eye. "Aurora, you saved me from that thing."

"I am glad to have helped, and that you are safe, fledgling. You are far too important to all of us," Aurora said.

"What was it?" Vero asked, a haunted look on his face.

"Pure evil."

Vero gasped.

"Be safe, my friend."

And with that, Aurora turned and flew up to the constellation. The unicorn's words filled Vero with confusion. What did he mean by pure evil? And did he mean to say he knew Vero was important? If that was true, why had he chosen to give the blessing to Kane?

The other angels were panting when they finally caught up to where Vero was hovering. Spellbound, they watched as the majestic unicorn slipped safely into the stars and disappeared.

"Pretty awesome," Greer said.

Pax turned to Vero. "Did Aurora tell you what that creepy hair creature was?"

"Pure evil."

❖

Light rose in the Ether. Flowers of every color turned their sleepy heads toward the golden rays as butterflies woke and opened their wings. Lush fields of grass swayed in a soft breeze. Pairs of animals grazed peacefully in the morning light. And in the middle of the marble stage of the large amphitheater, Kane stood grinning broadly while a packed audience of fledglings cheered. In a seat down in front, sat Vero next to Pax. Vero clapped his hands for Kane and did his very best to be happy for him, but the taste of disappointment was still strong in his mouth.

"We were all kind of surprised Aurora didn't pick you," Pax said to Vero.

Vero tried to look indifferent, but he couldn't help but agree with Pax. The unicorn's selection hadn't seemed fair. After all, he was the one who figured out that the unicorns were hiding in the constellation. Were it not for him, Kane and the others would have flown away and never even seen them.

"I don't know," Vero said, "Aurora took his time in choosing, and in the end he was sure it should go to Kane." Vero shrugged and hoped Pax would change the conversation.

Uriel walked onto the stage flanked by Raziel and Raphael. Vero watched as Raziel patted Kane on the back with a congratulatory smile. Then Raziel's eyes found Vero in the audience. Vero had always felt that Raziel didn't like him, and Raziel's smug expression seemed to confirm this. He had no idea what he had done to earn Raziel's animosity.

Uriel put up his hands to quiet the crowd. "Kane has won the challenge and will be the first one to represent the guardians in the Angel Trials," Uriel announced. "And as winner, he will select the five others who will make up his flight and compete alongside him."

Raphael turned to Kane. "Have you made your choice?"

Kane nodded. "X is my first pick," he stated.

X stood as the audience broke out into applause. He walked up onto the stage and took his place next to Kane.

"Greer, Pax, and Ada," Kane called.

As they stood and approached the stage, Vero's heart began to pound. He wondered why Kane hadn't called his name with the rest of them. He hoped Kane was pausing for dramatic effect. But as he watched Kane eyeing the muscular Eitan sitting in the front row, Vero realized Kane had no intention of selecting him. The thought also occurred to Greer. She crossed in front of Kane.

"We had a deal!" she said, glaring into his eyes. "You promised to pick Vero."

"You guys had a deal. I didn't really agree to it," Kane said.

"Why *wouldn't* you pick Vero?" Greer snapped. "He's the one who figured out where the unicorns were."

"But he also nearly got himself killed when he didn't get off the ground in time," Kane told her. "He put all of us in danger, and he could do it again. Danger seems to follow him wherever he goes! And Uriel agrees. I told him all about the hair monster!"

"You're a jerk!" Greer shouted.

"I'd rather have Eitan. He's on his way to becoming an archangel," Kane said.

Vero saw Raziel looking intently at Uriel. They were speaking mind-to-mind. Raziel looked agitated as he shook his head. Uriel met Raziel's gaze and then stepped between Greer and Kane. "Greer, it is Kane's choice," he said firmly.

"Well, if Vero's not on the team, then I quit."

"Me too," Pax told Kane.

Kane looked to X and Ada. Both nodded in agreement. Greer caught Kane's eyes and stared him down. As Kane deliberated, Vero felt as if he were back in gym class when he was the last one picked for a team. He wondered why teachers let the kids pick teams. Why wouldn't the teachers themselves do it and spare some poor kids from total humiliation?

"Fine! Vero!" Kane shouted unhappily.

Embarrassment more than relief seized Vero, especially when he saw Raziel storm off in a huff. And to make matters worse, as Vero took his place up on the stage, he noticed a look of disappointment come over Uriel.

❖

As Vero shuffled through the entrance of C.A.N.D.L.E., he didn't notice its flawless sparkling walls or the colorful tile designs that decorated its dome. His head was down. Why hadn't Kane chosen him willingly for his team? Did he think Vero wasn't good enough for the challenge? But most importantly, why had Uriel looked disappointed when Vero was picked to compete? Vero stopped walking and stood before the giant swirling torch. He stared hard into its flames as if the tongues of fire might offer some answers for his troubled mind.

"Hypnotic, isn't it?"

Vero turned and saw Pax standing next to him.

"Those flames swirl in and out of one another," Pax continued. "This is probably where humans got the idea for the Olympic torch."

Vero didn't answer. He stared into the fire.

"Kane was just being a jerk," Pax said. "Don't let him get to you."

Vero sighed and turned to Pax. "We all risked everythings to save him when he got stuck in that cavern. And this is how he repays me?"

Pax knew Vero was right. During one of their first training sessions, Kane got himself stranded on a rock in the middle of an acidic river. Vero and the others formed a dangerous chain with their bodies to rescue him. Any one of the angels could have wound up in that river themselves trying to help Kane. They could have "died" and been sent to the choir of angels for all eternity for Kane's sake.

"But it's not only Kane," Vero said. "Raziel stormed off angry. And did you catch the look on Uriel's face after he agreed to pick me? It's like he was totally upset."

"I saw it," Pax nodded. "And he looked really mad when Greer and the rest of us threatened to quit without you on the team. I was able to read their minds ... I don't get it, Vero, but Raziel told Uriel not to allow you on the team."

Vero's shoulders slumped. So it was true. He hadn't imagined it.

"So prove them wrong," Pax said, putting a hand on his shoulder. "Win the Angel Trials. You've gotten past golems and the Leviathan and Abaddon and found the unicorn. With you in our flight, for the first time in centuries, the fledglings might finally have a shot at winning."

Vero smiled gratefully at Pax. He was a good friend.

"Can you teach me how to read other angels' minds?" Vero asked. "You're so much better at it than any of us."

On earth, Pax was extremely autistic. He had no language and wore a protective helmet because he constantly banged his head against the wall. Vero guessed that Pax was so keen to reading thoughts because he had no other way to communicate on earth. He couldn't rely on speech so he had to live inside his own head.

"Do you ever use it on your parents?" Vero asked.

Pax's lip trembled slightly at the question.

"What?"

"I don't see so much of my parents anymore. They put me in an institution."

"Why?" Vero asked.

"I have a little sister. She's three, and they think I could accidentally hurt her." Pax fought back tears. "I wouldn't. I swear. I love her, but I can't even tell them that."

Vero's eyes filled with sympathy. "I'm sorry."

"You know, Vero, sometimes I really wish I could finish my training and be done with earth. It's too hard living this way."

Vero understood. It was difficult going back and forth between the two worlds, but he also knew he would miss his family and friends when his training was finally completed.

"I think I'm good at telepathy because on earth I want to communicate so badly. And I guess that's the key to learning it. You want to know the person without passing judgment. If they feel like they're not being judged, they'll open up to you and willingly share their thoughts. Try it. I'll think of something, and you guess what it is."

Vero stared hard at Pax. He tried to concentrate on Pax's thoughts, but out of the corner of his eye, the flames of the torch twirled in and out of one another, distracting him. Pax placed both of his hands on Vero's shoulders and turned his back to the swirling fire.

"Try again."

Vero looked at Pax with intensity. His face scrunched up so much he almost looked angry. Vero tried to clear his mind of any preconceived notions about Pax so Pax would allow him to know his thoughts. He remembered what his dad had once told him about how a coward makes snap judgments, but an honorable person searches for the truth. He wanted to be that honorable person. And then he made a connection! He heard Pax's thoughts.

"You need to go to the bathroom?" Vero said, surprised. "That's your big important thought?"

"Well, it's important to me," Pax answered. "But you just read my mind!"

"Yeah, I guess I did," Vero said, puffing out his chest.

"Uriel said we have to go back to earth before the Trials begin. It sounds like we need to rest up," Pax told Vero. "Plus, I really do need a bathroom."

"Okay," Vero said as he grabbed Pax's hand and gave it a squeeze. "And, Pax, your parents love you. I'm sure of it."

Pax looked to Vero, caught off guard before realizing that Vero had just read his mind again. Pax slowly nodded, closed his eyes, then vanished into thin air. Vero took one last look into the dancing flames before he, too, closed his eyes and recalled his last place on earth. When he opened them, he felt a small rubber tip hit his chest and bounce to the mat below. He realized he was back in the fencing gym. As Vero tried to get his bearings, a woman fencer quickly walked over and picked up the tip.

"Sorry, I guess I didn't put it on properly," she said to Vero before walking back to her mat.

"What just happened?" Clover asked Vero. "I feel like I blanked out for a second."

Vero shook his head. He didn't want to explain to her how in a matter of seconds, he had been to the Ether, escaped an evil hair serpent, befriended a mythical unicorn, and now was back. On top of that, his head was still spinning from the transition.

"Mom's out front," Vero said, looking out the window.

Vero removed the rest of his protective fencing clothing and hung them on the hooks that lined the walls. He moved very slowly as he struggled to adjust back to earth.

"I'm sorry, but I worry about you," Clover said fondly.

It took Vero a few seconds to recall their last conversation. Oh, yes. He had told Clover about the nurse who had attacked him in Dr. Walker's office. Clover had been scared for him and had scolded him to be careful. Vero had lost his temper. Now he felt like a jerk because he knew that his sister was only trying to look out for him.

"It's okay," he said.

"I know there's so much you hide from me," Clover told him. "And maybe you're right not to tell me everything, maybe I can't handle it, but at least promise me that those archangels keep you safe, that they watch out for you ..."

Uriel's disappointed face flashed in Vero's mind. He was no longer sure the archangels had his best interests at heart. But he didn't want to worry his sister.

"Yeah, they do," he said weakly.

❖

Vero sat in the backseat of his mother's minivan. He picked at a hole in the leather seat as Clover stared out the passenger window. Nora glimpsed Vero in the rearview mirror.

"Vero, stop picking at the seat. You're gonna make the tear bigger. I need to get it repaired."

"Sorry."

"And I'm sorry I was a little late. I had to stay past my shift because my replacement nurse was stuck in traffic," Nora said. She paused. "You guys are okay with me working back at the hospital, aren't you?"

"Sure," Vero answered.

"Because it's only part time. I had to jump back into nursing now or else my certification would expire, then I'd be too old to ever go back." Nora smiled. "And now that we're on the subject of age, you do know my birthday's coming up? Right?"

"Yes," Vero said.

"I don't want anything big, just a quiet meal with the whole family together."

Both Vero and Clover barely grunted. Nora turned around, glanced at Vero, then to Clover. "Did something happen at fencing? You two have a fight?"

"No, we didn't," Vero answered, a little too quickly.

"Clover?" Nora asked, raising her eyebrow.

The car pulled up in the driveway, and Nora put it into park. "No, for once Vero's telling the truth," Clover answered, then she opened the door and walked toward the house.

# 6

# NEW GIRL

Vero sat on his bed with his laptop computer as late afternoon light streamed through the window. He was working on a paper for his social studies class. Each student was given a country to research and present to their classmates, and Vero had been assigned Sri Lanka. But he was having a hard time concentrating and kept reading the same paragraph over and over, so all he knew about the country so far was that it was a small island somewhere in the Indian Ocean.

Truth was, Vero was nervous about the Angel Trials. He had no idea when he would be called back to the Ether to compete, but in the meantime, he couldn't stop thinking about it. Aurora's selection of Kane over him had rattled his confidence, and he couldn't help but worry that the Trials would be more challenging than he or the other fledglings could handle.

A pang of jealousy shot through Vero when he looked

out his window and watched his next-door neighbor, Mr. Atwood, and his teenage son, Angus, raking fallen leaves into piles. Vero envied the simplicity of their lives. He would never have that kind of ordinariness.

Vero heard a knock on the door, snapping him from his thoughts. "Come in," he called.

"Think quick," Dad said as he threw a chocolate bar at Vero.

Vero caught it, and his dad sat down next to him on the bed.

"Mom said you were studying hard, so I thought you could use a break."

"Thanks," Vero said as he ripped the wrapper off the candy bar.

As dad leaned over the computer screen, Vero noticed his father's hair was becoming much more salt-and-pepper-looking. It made him sad to think of his father getting older. Dad then asked, "What are you working on?"

"Social Studies. I have to do a class presentation on Sri Lanka."

"Sri Lanka, a small island country in the Indian Ocean," Dad read the screen, then looked up at Vero. "You've been in here for hours and that's all you've got?"

"Been going slower than I hoped" Vero shrugged.

"That's a coincidence. Sri Lanka is one of the countries I'm researching for the World Bank. They've already received aid for housing and health care, and now we're studying their water supply. Never take a glass of water for granted," Dad said, waving a finger in Vero's face.

Dennis Leland, Vero's dad, worked for the World Bank. He researched potential projects for developing countries.

The projects included things like supplying clean drinking water, building homes, repairing bridges and roads, educating children, and providing healthcare to the needy.

"Since you know all about Sri Lanka, can't you just do my report for me?" Vero asked with a pleading smile.

"Sure," Dad answered with a grin.

"Really?"

"No."

Vero frowned. If only he were back in the library at C.A.N.D.L.E., maybe a tiny island of Sri Lanka could float into his car, giving him instant knowledge.

"What's up with you?" Dad asked. "I never have to hound you to do your homework. Is there something going on?"

*You mean besides a demonic nurse that tried to kill me or the creepy hair monster that tried to strangle me or the fact that no one wants me to compete in the Angel Trials?*

"Nothing." Vero shrugged.

"Sure?" Dad eyed Vero.

"Yeah."

Clover walked past Vero's bedroom, grabbing Dennis's attention. "Clover, get in here," he called.

Clover backed up and walked into Vero's bedroom.

"Mom's birthday is coming up, and she says she doesn't want to do anything special ..."

"She says that every year," Clover interrupted.

"Yes, but she's busy with her new job, so I really think she means it this year. So that's why I thought it'd be nice to throw her a little surprise party. We can make dinner and cake. What do you think?"

Clover looked surprisingly excited about the idea. Her face lit up. "Okay! I want to decorate with streamers and balloons. And Dad, you'll have to take me to the mall 'cause there's this outfit I know she wants."

"You got it," Dad said.

"And Vero and I can make the cake."

"I don't know how to make a cake," Vero said.

"From the box," Clover said. "It's easy."

"My favorite kind." Dennis smiled to Vero. "And don't make a big one. I'll just invite the Atwoods over."

"Do you have to?" Vero and Clover asked at the exact same time.

They looked at each other.

"Jinx," Clover said.

Dennis shot them a disapproving look.

"You got a C?" Tack high-fived Vero. "Finally, you're getting the grades normal guys in the seventh grade should get."

"What about you?" Vero asked Tack as they walked across the schoolyard.

"D+," Tack answered. "Hey, it could have been worse. Could have been a D-. Although I thought the pizzas would have gotten me at least a C. That's fourteen bucks down the drain."

Tack's report was on the country of Italy. In his class presentation, he only talked about the food of the country— strombolis, spaghetti, gelato, salami, and, of course, pizza. Hoping to bribe Miss Wexler, the Social Studies teacher, he had a local pizza parlor deliver her a sausage and pepperoni pizza during the class. Tack had no idea Miss Wexler was a strict vegetarian, so the pizza had done nothing to raise his grade. However, it didn't go to waste. Nurse Kunkel had smelled it all the way down the hallway, and confiscated the pizza for herself, claiming that some kids in the class could have food allergies.

"Don't your parents get mad when you get bad grades?" Vero wanted to know.

"Yeah, but they already consider me a big disappointment so I've got nothing to lose."

Vero knew that underneath all his talk, Tack was hurt by his parents—mainly, his dad. The Kozlowski's were famous dowsers, which meant they were able to sense where water was located inside the earth. And not only water, but also oil and some minerals. Every male in the family going back generations had inherited the dowsing gift, except Tack. The line ended with him.

"Mr. Kozlowski!"

Tack and Vero turned around and saw Nurse Kunkel heading toward them. She tried to take a short cut between two outdoor circular lunch tables but, underestimating her stout size, got stuck. Tack and Vero winced as her face turned red as she tried to squeeze her way out. Finally, she shoved one of the tables up against the wall and barreled over to them. Luckily, it was past lunch so no one was sitting at the table.

"Mr. Kozlowski, I just wanted to say I thought your report was delicious. In my opinion, you deserve an A+ + on it," Nurse Kunkel told Tack.

"Thanks. I'm glad someone appreciated my efforts."

"Next time, if you get an assignment on China, I'd like some eggrolls and Chicken Lo Mein," she winked at Tack before walking away, giggling to herself.

Clover walked past and, unfortunately for Tack, caught Nurse Kunkel's wink.

"You guys make such a cute couple," she teased Tack.

"Jealous?" Tack smirked.

"Yeah, right."

"Hey, Clover," a bubbly girl's voice rang out.

Tack's eyes nearly popped out of his head at the sight of the tall blonde girl heading toward them. She had a willowy frame with high cheekbones and bright hazel eyes. Vero couldn't help but notice her, too. Just because it was forbidden for angels to fall in love with humans, didn't mean he was blind. Clover caught their stares.

"Stop drooling, you losers," she muttered to them as the girl caught up with her. "Hey, Kira."

"Hi," Kira replied.

Tack loudly cleared his throat, wanting to be noticed. Clover took the hint. "Kira, this is Tack ..."

"Thaddeus," he corrected in a somewhat British accent, once again clearing his throat and puffing out his chest.

Clover rolled her eyes at him. "Kira just moved here from Seattle. She's in my class."

Kira smiled at Vero, batting her eyelashes. "And who's this?"

"My brother, Vero."

"You guys don't look alike," Kira told Clover.

"Vero's adopted," Tack said.

"Oh, really, 'cause I am too," Kira said, her eyes wide. "Do you have any idea where you came from? Who your birth parents are?"

Vero squirmed, unsure how to answer her questions without lying. He shook his head.

"Oh, sorry, I guess that's not really any of my business," Kira smiled apologetically.

"It's okay," Vero replied.

The bell rang out over the yard, signaling that break was over. Kira turned to Clover. "What's our next class?"

"History," Clover replied. "I'll walk you there."

"It was nice meeting you," Kira told Tack and Vero before sashaying away. "Hope to see you guys around."

Tack elbowed Vero with a wink. Vero didn't share his enthusiasm. Something about seeing his sister walk away with Kira — as nice as she was — rekindled that queasy feeling in the pit of his stomach.

✦

Tack had convinced Vero to join the swim team. The swimming and diving pools were indoors, so they didn't have to deal with weather, but Tack insisted the biggest selling point was that they got to see girls in bathing suits. Both boys had given up track and field. Vero said it was because he didn't like it, but really he was just too good at the sport. As an angel, he was easily the fastest sprinter and the highest jumper, and he called way too much attention to himself. When Tack suggested they try swimming, Vero agreed because he was sure there was no chance he'd excel at it. His true nature was to soar high in the skies above, not plunge in the waters below. Everything about swimming felt wrong to him, especially the tight little swim briefs he was required to wear. Never feeling completely comfortable in the bathing suit, Vero always kept his pile of clothes nearby on a bench.

Tack and Vero sat on the edge of the swimming pool

with their legs dangling in the water as they waited for swim practice to begin.

"You know, some guys shave their whole bodies so they'll go faster in the water," Tack told Vero while splashing his feet.

"I'm not doing that," Vero said with a look of disdain.

"It could literally shave seconds off your time."

"Don't care."

"Then maybe you should try diving," Tack suggested as he cupped water in his hands and splashed it over his head.

Vero looked over at the diving pool with its one meter and three meter boards. "Nah, it's not for me," Vero replied. He was afraid if he jumped off the diving board, especially the three-meter, he'd enjoy the feeling of free-falling too much. He might wind up sprouting his wings and then really drawing some unwanted attention.

"Go ahead, try the high board," Tack urged Vero.

"No."

"Hi, guys," Davina said.

Wearing a navy blue one-piece swimsuit, Davina sat down next to the boys and also dangled her feet in the water.

"The water's warm," she said, wiggling her toes.

"Hey, Davina, tell Vero he's a wuss because he won't go off the high dive," Tack said to her.

"You don't like diving?" she turned to Vero.

"He's afraid of heights," Tack answered for him. "Isn't that it?"

"No," Vero half-chuckled. If Tack only knew how he could fly in the Ether—high above waterfalls and trees and mountains—without a care in the world.

"Then prove it. Jump off the high dive or just admit that you're a chicken."

"Okay, fine."

"Don't make him do that," Davina protested.

"I'll do it to shut him up once and for all," Vero said, pulling his feet from the water.

Tack nudged Vero. "Look who joined the swim team."

As Vero and Tack stood up, they saw Kira walking toward them. She looked even taller in a bathing suit, and with her hair hidden under a bathing cap, her face was even more captivating.

"Hey, Kira, watch this!" Tack called. "Vero is about to wuss out on the high dive!"

"Wanna watch Tack eat crow?" Vero shot back.

"Hmm. Either you chicken out, or Tack eats crow?" Kira laughed. "I'm in!"

As Vero made his way over to the diving pool, Danny walked out of the boys' locker room in his swimsuit with a towel around his neck. Kira noticed him immediately.

"Wow! Who's that?" Kira asked.

"He's taken," Tack said, nodding at Davina. "He's Davina's guy."

"He's hot," Kira said approvingly.

"Well, we don't actually date," Davina said. "My parents won't let me date until I'm sixteen."

"Oh, so you sneak behind their backs to get together with him, right?" Kira asked.

"No," Davina answered, offended.

"Well, you'd better if you want to keep a guy like that," Kira laughed.

Davina eyed Kira. "Sorry, but since when is this your business?"

Kira patted Davina on the back. "Just giving a girlfriend good advice." she smiled.

Davina shook her head, stood up, and walked over to Danny.

Tack elbowed Kira and nodded to the diving board. "Let's see if he does it!"

Vero had climbed halfway up the ladder to the three-meter springboard. To the boy who once jumped from the roof of his house, this ten-foot high dive was nothing. He reached the top and walked out onto the board as the kids watched poolside.

"Hey, Vero," Tack yelled. "You can just flap your chicken wings down the ladder, and no one will say a word! I promise!"

Kira chuckled along with Tack. Davina looked over and narrowed her eyes. Standing on the edge of the board, Vero jumped up and down on the balls of his feet. He was going to prove to Tack he wasn't afraid, and he didn't mind impressing Davina and Kira either. Vero bounced one final time and sprang high into the air. It felt so exhilarating to be airborne that he forgot he had an audience. He did a somersault, followed by a forward twist and then a reverse somersault. The kids below watched in a stunned awe. But Vero's eyes suddenly went wide with fear as he looked into the pool — it was empty, not a single drop of water!

# 7

## ANGEL TRIALS

Vero breathed in deeply. Water rushed into his lungs. He jerked his head back, coughing and sputtering, as he realized he was floating face down in a small pond. Vero swam to the shore and pulled himself onto the bank. As he took in the crystal clear water and the plush green grass, he knew he was back in the Ether. Off in the distance, above the birdsong and quiet trickle of a nearby stream, Vero could hear the faint sounds of a large crowd.

"Finally," he said as he stood. "The Angel Trials." Horror struck Vero when he looked down and noticed he was still wearing his skimpy suit. "Oh, great. Greer's gonna have a field day with this." Just then, an angel materialized beside the pond. It was Raphael, and he was holding Vero's clothes.

"Welcome back, Vero. I'm guessing you'll be wanting these?" Raphael asked as he held out the clothes to him. Vero never felt more relieved. He snatched the clothes and began to put them on over his wet suit.

"Thanks, Raphael. You're a life saver."

Raphael smiled. "Ordinarily you dress as you come in Ether. But as you will be one of our representatives for the trials, I made an exception to the rule this time. Which by the way, you need to get to ... they're gathering at C.A.N.D.L.E. I'll see you." Before Raphael vanished, his voice shouted out, "Remember, you'll need to go back the way you came!"

Vero closed his eyes and concentrated, and soon his wings burst from his shoulders, launching him into the air. Sprouting his wings was becoming more seamless. As he followed the sounds of the crowd, Vero shortly saw scores of angels below him convening outside of C.A.N.D.L.E. And not just angels in training, but angels of all ages. As he lowered for a landing, Vero spotted a group of angels who had stunningly beautiful faces. They were so striking that their beauty totally distracted Vero, causing him to body slam into a corner pillar of the temple. He dropped onto the marble steps with a thud. Unfortunately, his sloppy landing had not gone unnoticed. As the group of beautiful angels turned to look at him, Vero noticed that their features were perfectly proportioned. Their skin was flawless and milky, their bodies slender yet muscular. And on their heads, golden hair. Vero suddenly felt ugly.

"Dominions, you klutz," someone whispered in his ear.

Vero turned around and saw Greer standing beside him. She was biting her nails again.

"They're so good-looking," Vero told her.

"If we all looked like that, plastic surgeons would definitely be out of business," Greer chuckled nervously. "I mean look at 'em. They're so delicate-looking, so pretty, so sweet . . . we need to crush their golden little heads to smithereens."

Vero turned around to look at Greer. "Really?"

"Hey, they're our competition." Greer shrugged.

The Dominions carried scepters fastened to orbs of light. Vero watched as the balls of light ebbed and flowed in intensity. He wondered if the scepters had some magical powers. He walked over to a young Dominion.

"Excuse me, what do those do?" He pointed to the scepter.

The stunning Dominion stared back at Vero with a lack of expression. His look was neither mean nor kind—just impassive. Vero knit his brow, confused by the lack of response. Then the Dominion turned and walked away with the others.

"Thanks a lot, Mr. Personality!" Greer shouted after him before turning to Vero. "Who knew there was such a thing as stuck-up angels."

"Vero, Greer!"

They saw Ada and Pax headed toward them.

"Hey, guys," Vero said. "Have you seen Kane or X?"

"Not yet," Pax answered. "But we're supposed to meet up in the amphitheater."

As the fledglings made their way through the magnificent entrance into C.A.N.D.L.E., and then into the courtyard beyond, Vero noticed that the school wasn't decorated at all for the Trials. At the very least, he had expected to see a banner announcing the event. But everything looked as it had always looked. Feeling a little let down by the lack of fanfare, Vero suddenly had the sensation that he was being watched. The feeling grew stronger and stronger, almost as if someone were following him. His eyes darted around the crowded courtyard, looking for the source of his paranoia.

"Anyone else feel like they're being watched?" Ada asked the group, echoing Vero's sentiment.

Before anyone could reply, a massive round emerald object flew slowly over their heads, radiating light in all directions. It seemed to be made of two perpendicular wheels of light. A smaller wheel spun rapidly in a horizontal direction inside of a larger wheel, which rotated more slowly, vertical to the ground. Both wheels were covered with thousands of lights. The entity had enormous wings on either side, but with both wheels spinning, it was hard to tell how the wings stayed in place. To Vero, the whole thing looked like a gigantic flying version of the gyroscope he got one year for Christmas. Back on earth, the thing could easily be mistaken for a UFO.

The most unnerving thing about the object for Vero was that when he looked closely at the spinning wheels, he noticed the glowing lights were actually eyes! Thousands upon thousands of eyes covered every inch of the perimeters of the wheels—eyes that saw in every direction as the wheels spun around and around. Nothing escaped their observation. No wonder Vero had felt like he was being watched!

Vero stood with his mouth open, mesmerized. Oddly, as alien as this being was to Vero, he did not feel frightened by it. Rather, the spinning circles of eyes seemed to emanate a peaceful feeling.

"A Throne," Ada whispered as she put her hand on Vero's shoulder, also transfixed by the sight.

"Oh, yeah, Uriel talked about them," Vero recalled. "They're going to judge the Trials."

"Correct," a male voice said.

Vero turned around and saw Uriel standing behind him with Kane and X.

"The Thrones are the angels who administer God's justice and authority," Uriel nodded. "As you probably noticed, they see everything."

"I'm glad we don't have to compete against them," Kane said, staring at the huge Throne.

"It's pretty scary," Pax said.

"No," Uriel said. "The Thrones are anything but scary." He looked around at the fledglings with a serious expression. "They are the definition of humility. They lack any pride, ambition, or fear of demotion, making them perfectly objective in their dispensing of justice." Uriel gazed up at the spinning wheels. "They are completely fair."

Vero recalled Uriel's look of disappointment when Kane selected him for the team. *At least someone will be fair to me in these Trials*, he thought. The narrowing of his eyes told Vero that Uriel had read his mind. Vero blushed but didn't look away. Uriel then turned his gaze to the others.

"The Thrones will rarely show themselves to you, but know their eyes will always be watching during the competition." The fledglings watched as the Throne continued its flight, disappearing over the top of the cathedral wall. Uriel continued, "Before the opening ceremony begins, I'd like to say a few words."

They gave him their complete attention.

"Do any of you know why the ancient Greeks celebrated the Olympics? What the purpose was?"

"Eitan said the first Olympiads were held to pay tribute to the gods," X said. "The Olympians wanted to honor the gods with their God-given abilities."

"That's correct, X," Uriel said. "And as a religious ceremony, the Olympics always began with a prayer. But long before that, there was sacrifice."

"They would slaughter oxen to the gods," Pax said.

"Yes, they did do that. But that's not the kind of sacrifice I'm talking about," Uriel said. He paused to collect his thoughts. "I mean the self-sacrifice of the athletes. By denying themselves things, by giving up the comforts they cherished, and by rigorous training, the athletes prepared themselves not just for the games, but for the gods themselves." Uriel saw the confused faces of the fledglings. "The word 'sacrifice' comes from the verb 'to make sacred.' By choosing to make sacrifices, you make room for the sacred to enter your life. When you pass up material comforts in favor of a hard workout, or doing something uncomfortable, you do so with the hope and faith that God will fill the void with something better."

Uriel's words stirred Vero. He remembered one Saturday when his mom had asked him to come with her to help out in a soup kitchen. At first, he had been upset because he had planned to go to the movies with Tack—not spend the afternoon serving food to the homeless. But by the end of the day, he had been glad he'd chosen to do it, because he had felt he had made at least a small difference in some people's lives. An elderly woman had given him a grateful smile as he served her a plate of food. And although her teeth had been an absolute mess, Vero remembered it was one of the most beautiful smiles he had ever received. Uriel was right. He had given up a movie that day, but the woman's smile had filled him with a joy that had lasted till this day.

"We could sacrifice all we want, but it's not going to

change anything," Greer said, shaking her head. "Those other angels are far superior to us."

"Do you remember the story of David and Goliath?" Uriel smiled. "Of how a lowly shepherd boy took down a nine and a half foot giant with a single stone."

Greer slowly nodded.

"So nothing is impossible," Uriel told them. "To show your strength, you have to do something tough."

A blast of trumpets filled the courtyard. Their vibrant, resounding song announced the start of the Trials, and the bright melody invigorated Vero. He pulled his shoulders back and stood straight. The others, too, raised their heads high, warriors ready for battle.

Uriel smiled. "Let's go."

The natural amphitheater was brimming with angels. Not only was every seat taken — hovering angels filled the skies overhead.

"I've never seen so many angels," Ada said, squinting upward at the mass of angelic beings. "I can barely see any sky."

"And they don't all look like us," X replied.

*It's true*, Pax thought as he watched the group of the attractive Dominions walk past. Another band of angels followed, and Pax's eyes went wide. He tapped Vero on the shoulder.

Vero couldn't believe what he was seeing. These new angels had the bodies of lions with the faces of humans. They reminded Vero of the Egyptian sphinx he had studied in school. The Egyptians considered the lion to be the most powerful animal on earth, so the Pharaoh had his head carved on top of the animal to symbolize his strength.

When they passed by Vero, he instinctively took a step back. Beyond their muscular bodies and giant paws, their stern expressions told Vero these creatures were definitely not to be messed with. And when one of them flicked his tail, Vero jumped back even farther. The angel had the tail of a scorpion. At its tip were hundreds of venomous stingers. Vero had seen this type of tail before—it belonged to Abaddon!

The blare of the mighty trumpets abruptly stopped. It was only then that Vero thought to look for the source of the music.

Hovering above the dome-shaped stage, he saw four angels, two on each side, facing one another. They wore flowing white robes. In their hands were long golden trumpets. Vero smiled. He knew the image well. When he was nine years old, his family went to New York City to see the holiday decorations. These angels greatly resembled the herald angels that lined Rockefeller Center each Christmas.

Vero remembered how Clover had loved the department store window displays best, each depicting a different holiday scene—from families of yesteryear enjoying a night by the Christmas tree to elves loading the sled for Santa's big ride. His mother had loved buying the roasted chestnuts from the pushcart street vendors. His dad had most enjoyed ice-skating in Central Park. But Vero had been infatuated with the angels in Rockefeller Center. He had felt such tranquility sitting under their watch. Of course, it was years later before he finally understood why.

Despite the feverish excitement in the air, the crowd quieted when an angel took the center stage. He was a Dominion—very tall, elegant, and of course, flawless and beautiful.

Greer elbowed Pax next to her. "I can't tell if they're guys or girls," she said in a low voice.

"Me either," Pax shrugged.

"I am Charoum, an angel of silence and channeler of miracles," the angel announced. "We Dominions rarely break our silence ..."

Now it made sense to Vero why when he had asked the Dominion about his scepter, the angel hadn't replied. Vero knew about cloistered monks and nuns who had taken vows of silence, sacrificing their voices for contemplative prayer instead.

"But today I speak! On behalf of my fellow angels, we celebrate the Angel Trials along with you. We participate in the competition to honor God with the talents and gifts He's given us. We shall use those talents to win the Trials."

As Charoum said this, all the Dominions put one hand over their hearts, bowed their heads, and thumped their scepters on the floor in their version of boisterous applause.

Charoum took a step back and put his hands on a young angel's shoulders, moving him front and center. Vero instantly recognized the angel as the one who had not answered him earlier.

"This is young Dumah. As quiet as a shadow, he will represent the Dominions."

Dumah bowed his head in reverence, and, once again, the thumping of the Dominions' scepters shook the amphitheater.

Suddenly, a lioness leapt up onto the stage. Vero saw it was one of the sphinx-like angels. She moved like the great African cats he had seen in videos running across the vast desert plains—with a quick, graceful stealth. Her powerfully built body and tasseled tail of poisonous stingers spoke of danger and strength. Yet, her pretty teenage face was completely human looking. Vero was admiring her movie-star good looks when a larger sphinx-like angel with an older male face and a full mane pounced up on the stage next to her.

"I am Camael," the male angel told the crowd. "We Powers were blessed with the strength to resist evil. We were also blessed with healing abilities, and we are the keepers of history. And this is Ariel, lioness of God. With the prowess of a lion and the curative powers of a doctor, she will represent the Powers. Ariel shall bring honor to God with her talents and win the Angel Trials." With that, every Power in the place curled their tails high above their backs and shook them. Loud rattling sounds, like the shaking of a million maracas, emanated from their tails as they cheered for Ariel.

Ariel bowed her head in reverence.

Kane turned to Uriel. "Am I next? Should I get up on the stage?"

The nervous fledglings waited for a reply, but Uriel shook his head. "The Virtues are next."

"Where are they?" Vero asked, scanning the amphitheater for some type of angel he had not yet noticed.

"They're there." Uriel said. "You just have not seen them."

Vero looked back to the stage, confused. He saw only the Powers and the Dominions. But then a light began to glow next to Ariel. It started as the size of a baseball then stretched longer and longer until it reached the shape of a guardian angel. But it remained a translucent figure with no physical body. Vero had seen images of angels that people had sometimes caught on film—a silhouette of light—and these angels looked very similar. He could make out wings and a head and a body but no discernible facial features. Vero imagined that if he were to try to grab this angel, his hand would probably pass right through. Another one of these transparent angels floated forward. The voice that came forth from his luminous head was fainter than a whisper, yet Vero could clearly hear every word.

"I am the angel Vangelis. As Virtues, God has bestowed upon us great intellect along with the ability to see the future. And this is Melchor. With great stealth and foresight, Melchor shall represent us in honoring God and winning the Angel Trials!"

As he said this, a gentle ring filled the amphitheater. The high-pitched sound reminded Vero of the noise he would make every year on Thanksgiving when he ran his wet finger around the edge of his mother's good crystal glasses. As the ringing sound grew louder and louder, hundreds of baseball-sized spheres of light floating all around the amphitheater illuminated for Melchor, who bowed his head in acknowledgement.

Together with the glowing lights, the melodic ring was very comforting to Vero, and he watched them in amazement. But the sights and sounds had the opposite effect on Greer.

"Invisible, plus they can see the future? Face it, this is over before it's even begun." She sighed heavily.

Uriel tapped Kane's shoulder and motioned to climb the stairs to the stage. Kane leapt up to the first step when Uriel grabbed his arm, stopping him.

"Wait for the others," Uriel instructed him. "Go up as a team."

The other fledglings lined up behind Kane, and when

everyone was ready, they ascended to the stage as one unit. Uriel followed them and stood next to Kane.

Vero watched as Ariel turned to Camael just a few yards away.

"Why six of them? And I am only one?" Ariel complained.

"To make the competition as fair as possible," Camael hushed.

"How is that fair?"

"It's fair because your gifts far exceed those of the guardians." Camael's eyes rested on Vero.

Feeling caught, Vero quickly looked away. *Maybe Greer was right.*

"These are the guardians. Those closest to man," Uriel said to the audience. "They are blessed with a great love for humans."

Kane turned to X. "That's our big talent?" he grumbled.

Uriel placed his hand over Kane's head as if administering a blessing.

"Kane." Uriel proceeded down the line extending his hand over each fledgling. "X, Pax, Ada, Greer, ... Vero." As Uriel looked into Vero's eyes, Vero desperately searched them, looking for some sort of encouragement, a wink, anything. But Uriel only frowned and spun back around to the crowd. "With their gift of love, they vow to honor God by winning the Angel Trials."

Every archangel and angel clapped his hands and cheered. It was so loud that it sounded like one long sonic boom. Vero thought his eardrums would explode.

Once the applause had died down, Uriel raised his hands to the crowd. "May God's will be done."

The entire audience of angels of every sphere bowed

their heads in reverence upon hearing Uriel's words. After a moment of silence, several doves sprang forth from behind the half-dome backdrop of the stage. With their wings spread wide, they flew wingtip-to-wingtip, forming a perfect ring above the candidates. X squinted as he counted them.

"There're nine of them. Same number as angels competing," X told his group.

Ada looked up at the doves in reverence. "The ancient Greeks used to release doves at their Olympics as a symbol of peace," she said.

"Well, are we supposed to hold hands with these guys and sing 'Kumbaya' or whip their butts in this competition?" Greer asked. "It's getting confusing."

Ada shrugged. "Maybe it's like what Raziel told us before our first training," she said. "That a little healthy competition will push us to be the best we can be."

Greer shook her head. She looked up at the doves and watched as they rose higher and higher into the clouds before vanishing from sight—just like her chances of winning the competition, she thought—flying farther and farther away. The trumpets blared once more, and Uriel spoke.

"God appeared as a pillar of fire in Exodus to light the way for His people. You, too, are called to be pillars of fire ... to be that guiding light in the darkness," Uriel said while looking to the nine competitors. "Remember that as you begin this competition."

Uriel nodded to Charoum, who moved front and center.

"The clue for the first task is ..."

Vero leaned in. He didn't want to miss a single word.

"*They laughed at me, mocked me, and called me an ass.*

*However, today they cower should I ever pass.*
*They have felt my strength—one thousand men strong—*
*When I was called to settle a terrible wrong.*
*Yet, there is no rest beyond the clouds.*
*No rest for me, 'till I be shroud."*

Vero watched as the light that was Melchor suddenly dimmed and vanished. Ariel, the sphinx angel, sprouted wings and flew from the amphitheater. Vero thought she was so cool—a flying lion. Dumah walked away, not making a single sound. No wonder, because when Vero looked closer, he saw that Dumah's feet did not touch the ground as he walked.

With a surge of panic, Ada shook Vero. "What do they know that we don't?" She nodded at Dumah and Ariel.

"Everything, apparently ..." Pax looked frazzled.

"Everything you need to know is in the riddle," Uriel told the group. "You must solve it and do as it asks of you to complete the first challenge."

"But, Uriel," X said. "It doesn't make much sense. I wouldn't know where to begin. The first line especially—the riddle wouldn't just use that word."

"Use your strengths ... There are six of you while each other team has only one. Unlike them, you can be in more than one place at a time." Uriel looked around at the confused fledglings. "Yes, your competitors were blessed with a higher intellect. However, there is a way to become their intellectual equal."

"How?" Pax asked.

"You'll have to figure that out for yourselves," Uriel answered.

Greer stomped. "But apparently we're too stupid to do that!"

Uriel smiled at her, amused, then wrapped himself up in his wings and disappeared.

"I hate when he does that," Pax sighed.

Spinning around to face the others, Greer balled her hands into fists. "So let me get this straight. We need to be smart enough to figure out how to get smarter?" She shook her head and added sarcastically, "Makes perfect sense."

X chuckled. "I guess so."

"There has to be a way," Ada said. "Let's think it through."

Ada sat down on the stage, dangling her legs over the side. Greer slumped next to her.

"I know how," Greer said. "I say we capture that invisible light angel in a mason jar, like a firefly, and we won't take the lid off until he tells us everything he knows."

Everyone shot Greer a harsh look.

"Sure, as if you all weren't thinking the exact same thing," she huffed.

"Come on, we're losing time here," Kane said.

"Maybe it's as simple as listening to our Vox Dei," Pax said.

*Vox Dei, God's voice,* Vero thought. It had always been there for him.

"That's a part of it," Ada said, nodding. "Vox Dei will guide us, but I don't think it will solve the riddle for us."

X joined Ada and Greer on the edge of the stage. "I wish there was a scroll in the library that could tell us all these answers," he sighed.

Kane's eyes lit up. "That's it!"

"What's it?" X asked.

"All the knowledge we need is in the library! Everything we need to solve the riddle would probably be there. That's how we become their intellectual equals."

"But Uriel said we should be in more than one place at a time ..." Ada said, her brow furrowed.

"We can be, if we split up," Vero said. "Station two of us in the library and the rest out trying to complete it."

Pax looked hesitant. "But we're a team," he said.

Vero was getting more and more excited by the idea. "We'll still remain a team. We'll just be at different locations."

Greer narrowed her eyes. "Okay, let's say by some miracle, we figure it out. How will the people at the library be able to tell the rest of us what to do?" She put her hands on her hips. "I don't see any cell phone towers in the Ether." She nodded to Kane. "And apparently, you're the only one who owns one anyway."

"Pax can communicate telepathically," X said. "He should stay in the library."

"But none of us can communicate with him," Ada said. "So what good is it?"

"Vero can do it," Pax said, stepping forward.

Vero looked at Pax and felt the blood rush to his face. He never thought he'd need to use his new skill so soon. "I'm not that great at it."

"You're our best shot," Pax said.

"Then Vero stays behind, and, Pax, you come with us," Kane said.

"No," X shook his head. "Vero proved himself with the maltures, and he found the unicorns. We're going to need him."

"I think he'd be better off in the library," Kane insisted.

As Vero looked back and forth between Kane and X, he felt a knot growing in his stomach. It didn't make sense to Vero that Kane would want him in the library. Was there another reason why Kane didn't want him to go along?

"You're wrong," X said matter-of-factly.

"Then you think it should be me?" Kane asked. "Don't forget. I'm the one with the blessing, so I should be out there on the front lines."

It was a standoff. The fledglings eyed one another, waiting to see if anyone would volunteer to stay and research.

X finally stepped forward. "I'll stay behind in the library with Pax."

No one objected, but Kane shook his head at Vero. Vero stared back at him, refusing to drop his gaze.

X cleared his throat, returning the fledglings to their most immediate problem. "So does anybody have any clue what the riddle means?"

"Whoever it is, is powerful," Ada said. "And lives somewhere beyond the clouds."

Greer looked up to the sky. There were fluffy clouds as far as she could see. "That definitely narrows it down," she replied.

"They're not happy," Ada continued, ignoring her. "There is no rest for them. If I understand correctly, there won't be any peace until they're properly buried."

"Where did you come up with that?" Kane asked.

"*Yet, there is no rest beyond the clouds. No rest for me, 'till I be shroud*," Ada recited. "To shroud something is to wrap it for burial."

"So is this guy like a ghost?" Vero asked.

"Maybe," Ada answered. "But maybe not."

Pax squinted at the sky. "What's beyond the clouds? Because I think that's where you guys need to go."

"Even if we do that," Kane said, "we don't know who we're supposed to look for." He shook his head in frustration.

The group was silent for a moment, considering their options. "Standing around here is pointless," X said at last. "Pax and I will start researching in the library, and at the same time, you can let us know what you find beyond the clouds. Maybe something you see can help narrow down our research."

"What if there's nothing but clouds up there?" Greer said.

Vero sighed, afraid she could be right.

# 8

### ❖

# ARIEL
# THE POWER

There seemed to be no break in the clouds. No matter how high Vero and the others flew, they remained obscured by heavy mist. With every flap of their wings, the fledglings grew more discouraged as they could barely see each other in the fog.

"C'mon guys," Kane called. "We've got to keep going. Eventually, we'll get out of these clouds."

"Vero, are you picking anything up from Pax?" Greer asked.

Vero tightly closed his eyes and concentrated. After a few moments, he reopened them. "Nothing."

"What are they doing in that library?" Greer said angrily. Her wings were heavy with mist and were beating less and less rapidly as she grew tired.

Before the angels ever got above them, the clouds finally

broke. Kane was the first to shoot out into clear blue air. "Hey!" he shouted, pointing. "I can see land! Look down there!"

When Vero broke out of the clouds, he could see why Kane was excited. There appeared to be an island, but there wasn't any water surrounding the landmass. It was simply floating in the sky below them. As he flew closer to the island, Vero saw it was green, thick with heavy foliage.

"Should we check it out?" Vero asked the others.

"What do you think, Captain Obvious?" Greer said. "I can't fly anymore!" With the singlemindedness of a peregrine falcon after its prey, Greer nosedived for the green patch of land.

"I guess we're going down," Vero said and followed Greer.

As the angels flew closer to the island, Greer pointed out a flat mossy patch of land growing right up to the rocky edge of the floating island. Once her feet were firmly on the ground, she retracted her wings. The other fledglings also landed safely. The moment they reached the island, light rain began to fall. Kane looked up.

"Well, this can't be the right place because we're definitely not beyond the clouds anymore," Kane said discouraged.

"How do you know?" Greer asked.

"Because it's raining on us," Kane answered. "Rain comes from clouds. Didn't you ever pay attention in science class?"

"No. Why? Are you planning to be a meteorologist someday?"

"She makes a good point," Vero said. "I mean, don't you sometimes feel ripped off that we still have to do all that human stuff that we're never going to need? Study for tests, practice piano, eat brussel sprouts, shower ..."

"Gross! You don't like to shower?" Ada said with a wrinkled nose.

Vero shrugged.

"You're disgusting. Go stand over there." Greer waved one hand while holding her nose with the other. "I thought someone smelled."

Vero stepped a few feet away from Greer, but he bumped into Ada who was holding her hand over the edge of the island. Vero watched as Ada flexed her hand toward her body then moved it back over the edge. She looked like she was doing some sort of experiment.

"What are you doing?" Vero asked.

"Look." Ada wiggled her fingers. "It's not raining on my outstretched hand, but it's raining directly over us."

Vero noticed it was true. He extended his hand over the edge of the island. The rain did not touch it.

"Weird. It's only raining right over the island," Vero observed.

"That's great, but we're wasting time being here," Kane told them. "Whatever we're supposed to find is still beyond the clouds. And we're not."

"But the Ether is so completely different from the earth," Greer grumbled. "Maybe rain doesn't come from clouds here? 'Cause remember? There is no sun in the Ether, only God's light. It's not the same as the earth. Besides, the riddle said beyond the clouds ... not necessarily above the clouds."

"Guys! Quiet!" Vero said, waving his arms. "I think I'm getting something."

The group fell silent, as Vero held his hands to his

temple, eyes shut. "I definitely hear something. A voice." Vero frowned in concentration. "Pax's voice!"

"What's he saying?" Kane asked anxiously.

"He's testing to see if I can hear him."

"So they don't have any clues for us?" Kane dropped his shoulders.

"I guess not."

"Well, tell them where we are," Ada told Vero. "Describe this island to them. Maybe they can find a scroll about it."

Vero nodded and shut his eyes, conveying the message. After a few moments, he opened his eyes. "They said they're on it."

"So in the meantime, I guess we hang out here and rest up," Ada suggested.

"I'm gonna go find some shelter until this storm blows over," Greer said. "Anybody coming with me?"

Kane looked at the others in disbelief. "So we're just gonna wait here until we hear something?" he said annoyed. "Did you guys forget that this is a competition? That other angels are also out there trying to solve the riddle!"

"No, I didn't forget," Greer shot back. "But we've been flying around for hours, and this island is the first thing we've seen. I say before we abandon it, let's at least find out what it is. I don't see any point in going back up there and just flying around, hoping the answer will magically appear to us."

Kane was ticked off. On the one hand, he knew there was some sense to what Greer had said. On the other, sitting around doing nothing seemed like a colossal waste of time, and he was growing more frustrated with each passing moment. The others didn't understand how badly he wanted — he needed — to win. Kane stomped his foot. "We're gonna fail!"

Suddenly, the ground began to shake. The trees swayed. The angels looked around, panicked.

"Did you just do that with your foot?" Ada asked Kane, alarmed.

"Earthquake!" Vero shouted.

But then the trembling stopped.

"That was a short earthquake," Greer commented.

"Are you complaining?" Ada retorted. "Would you like it to last longer?"

Greer smiled. "I guess not. But we should explore this place and see if we can get out of the rain."

"Okay," Ada said. "Just give me a minute. I'm pretty exhausted." She sat on a large white stone surrounded by reddish flowers. "Wow, this is surprisingly spongy," she said, leaning her back against a large green stalk directly behind the stone.

Just then Greer screamed. Vero and Kane ran over to her and laughed as Greer peeled a small tree frog from her cheek. She dangled it by its front leg.

"He's kind of cute," she noted.

"Unless he's one of those poison dart frogs," Kane warned her.

Greer instantly flung the frog into the air. It landed on a tree branch, its suction-cup feet stuck to the bark.

"Let's get out of here," she said, wrinkling her nose.

"Where's Ada?" Vero asked.

The others spun around to the white rock where Ada had been sitting. She was no longer there.

"Where'd she go?" Greer asked.

"Ada!" Kane shouted. "Come on, we want to get out of here!"

"Ada!" Greer yelled as she looked around a clump of flowering bushes.

Vero searched in every direction but didn't see Ada anywhere. A sinking feeling formed in the pit of his stomach.

"But she was there a minute ago," Greer said, her brow furrowed in thought. "She couldn't have gone far."

"Especially with these plants growing everywhere," Vero added. "It's hard to go anywhere quickly."

"Then where the heck is she?" Kane sounded annoyed. "She's not taking the Trials seriously! She's playing games!"

"She's not the type to play games," Greer shot back at Kane.

"I know. I know," Kane sighed. "But where the heck is she?"

Frustrated, he sat down on the white rock. "Hey, this *is* soft and spongy," Kane commented, almost to himself. He looked into the sky as if hoping for divine inspiration. None came. Suddenly, the rock began to tremble.

"What the . . . !" Kane exclaimed leaping off the stone.

The other angels stood, curious and rooted to the spot, as Kane raced over to them. Greer's eyes grew hard as she spotted her frog still clinging to the bark of a tree. She yanked it off the tree, walked over, and placed the frog on the white stone. After a few moments, the large green stalk behind the stone began to move. It seemed to be unfolding from the earth up, and the white stone moved with it. The angels' heads slowly turned skyward as a beast rose menacingly over them.

Before the fledglings loomed an enormous plant, laced with white jaws and standing eight feet tall—a giant Venus flytrap of sorts, thick enough to swallow a man. It hadn't been a rock Kane was sitting on — it was the plant's tongue! And the red flowers that surrounded the rock weren't flowers after all — they were teeth! The creature closed its enormous jaws and swung its head upward as the frog slid down its throat.

"A man-eating plant ..." Greer stuttered.

Vero pointed to the plant's stalk. "Guys, look! I think that's Ada in there!"

In the stalk was the outline of Ada struggling to escape from its confines. But despite her efforts, she was slowly sinking down the stalk.

"Ada! How can she breathe?" Kane asked, his voice full of panic.

"We need to get her out before that thing digests her!" Greer shouted.

Having swallowed the frog, the plant bent back down again and placed its head, mouth open, on the ground, waiting for its next meal to sit on the white tongue.

"I say we charge the thing and rip it to pieces," Greer stated, stepping forward and motioning the others to join her.

"Greer, get back here!" Vero whispered as loudly as he dared. He wasn't sure if the plant had ears, but there was no point in risking it.

Greer returned to Kane and Vero's watch point, looking furious.

"We get it, Greer," Vero said.

"I'm not sure you do," she snapped. "Unless one of you carries weed killer on you, Ada is going to be humus if we don't do something quick."

Vero's heart was pounding. "Okay, so either we dig the

plant out of the ground from its roots, which would take a long time, and there's no guarantee it won't try to eat us while we're digging ..." He bit his lip. "Or we slice its head off when it extends itself."

"That would be doable if we could grow our swords!" Kane shouted, exasperated.

"Vero," Greer said. "You're the only one who grew a sword. Can you do it again?"

It was true. When Vero was engaged in a deadly battle with two maltures, a sword had miraculously sprung forth from his hand. At the moment he had needed it most, it had materialized.

"It appeared because someone had prayed for help," Vero explained. "I don't know how to do it myself."

"Why do they always send us out in the Ether without anything to fight with?" Kane said, pulling at his hair.

Greer spun around, scanning their surroundings for some sort of weapon.

"Here's something." Greer picked up a long heavy pointed fallen branch and handed it to Kane. "A couple good smacks might take its head off."

She bent down, grabbed two more long sticks and put one in Vero's hand. He looked down at the weapon with great reluctance.

"It's not a sword, but it's the best we've got at this point," said Greer.

"We've got to get it to extend its ugly head first," Vero said. He picked a furry caterpillar off a broad, waxy tree leaf and took a few tentative steps toward the plant's massive tongue. He stopped, summoned his courage, then ran at the plant, and chucked the caterpillar. It looked like it was headed straight for the center of the tongue at first, but the caterpillar was lighter than Vero had expected, and it landed short, on the lower part of the white tongue.

"Lousy shot," Kane said, shaking his head.

Vero dashed back to the safety of Kane and Greer and waited. Several moments passed. Nothing happened — the flower did not attack the caterpillar. The angels watched as the caterpillar began to crawl off the white tongue toward the ground.

"No, no, stay there," Greer shouted to the caterpillar, her voice tinged with urgency.

The caterpillar continued to inch its way off the giant tongue and fell to the ground.

"It's not heavy enough. It doesn't sense it," Kane said.

"I don't see anything else we can feed it," Greer said as she crept towards the flower, holding her stick out in front. "We're losing too much time. Ada could be buried in the dirt by now."

"Be careful," Vero warned her, as she inched closer to the plant.

Vero held his breath as Greer scooped up the caterpillar onto the end of her stick from the mossy ground. She held the stick over the plant's tongue and flicked the caterpillar right smack into the center. Vero breathed a sigh of relief as she turned around and headed back to them.

"Now maybe it will sense the caterpillar," she said with a smirk.

Vero's eyes went wide as he saw the flower shoot off the ground and lunge at her. "Greer!" he screamed.

The plant's jaw clamped down on Greer, catching her shoulder and pulling her toward it. She slammed on her back into the wet dirt. Vero and Kane quickly ran to aide their friend, their sticks raised. The outline of Ada's body was still apparent in the creature's stalk. Vero saw the look of terror on Greer's face as the flower's spiky red teeth pierced her flesh.

"Get off!" she cried.

Fueled by Greer's pain, Vero lost all sense of danger and charged the plant. He swung his stick like a baseball bat at the monster plant's head. The blow startled the plant, and it opened its huge mouth, releasing Greer. As it turned its attention to Vero, Kane seized Greer around the waist and pulled her safely from the flower's reach. The gigantic head repeatedly snapped forward, grabbing for Vero. It looked like he was dancing to avoid the creature's jaws, taking two steps forward and one step back. As Vero stumbled to avoid the giant mouth, he was reminded of the arcade game with the claw that dropped down, attempting to clasp a stuffed animal. Except now he was the stuffed animal! When the top row of teeth grazed his shoulder, Vero knew he needed a new strategy. He threw his wings out into the lightly falling rain and shot into air.

"Hey, I'm up here!" Vero yelled down to the plant.

As the plant's head turned upward, Vero slugged it with all his might. It was a homerun! The head swayed, stunned. Kane got airborne and glided toward the flower's head, holding up his stick.

"Why should you have all the fun?" Kane ribbed Vero.

Kane whacked the flower. The head swung from side to side, even more dazed. Then Vero hit it again.

"This is fun. Sort of an Ada piñata," Kane smiled.

Kane swung at the creature with such force that its head

slammed hard into Vero, sending him straight into the ground. As Vero tried to get up, the monster's jaw grabbed his left wing and pulled him high into the air, shaking him violently from side to side. Vero screamed when he felt his wing being ripped from his back. Greer, still writhing from her own wounds, watched helplessly from below, unable to move as one of Vero's feathers gently floated down to her.

"Kane! Help him!" she yelled desperately, clutching the feather.

Kane flew around the plant, searching for an open spot to bash its head, but every shot risked hitting Vero.

"I can't get a clear shot!" he shouted, panic-stricken.

Greer bent over and willed her wings to open, but her shoulder was too badly damaged. They would not sprout. The mouth opened, releasing Vero's wing. As Vero dropped to the ground, the mouth opened wider, aiming to gobble Vero's head. Greer tightly closed her eyes, too afraid to watch. Suddenly, out of the mist, a warlike cry penetrated the scene. Greer opened her eyes in time to see a set of claws slice deep across the flower's neck, decapitating the head from its stem in a single swipe. The flower's massive head landed on top of Vero where he lay in the dirt beneath his tangled wings. He managed to wiggle out from underneath the flower only to see the enormous stalk sway, then collapse, falling inches from his head.

Out of the green stalk crawled Ada, covered in green mucus. As she wiped her face clean, she blinked in the sudden rush of light and tried to focus her eyes. There, sitting regally before her, was Ariel, the sphinx-like Power. Ada gasped. "You," she said. "You saved me."

"Are you all right?" Ariel asked.

Ada nodded. "Just a little gross."

"More than a little," Kane furrowed his brow.

Ada held her face up to the rain, hoping to clean it.

Vero winced as he touched his back and felt the damage done to his wings. Ariel saw the pain in Vero's face and walked over to him. She placed her paw over his injured back and held it there. Vero felt warmth come over the spot, which continued to spread throughout his body. Moments later, he no longer had any pain. He reached behind him and realized his wings were completely healed.

"They're totally better," he said, astonished.

"We Powers were blessed with the gift of healing," Ariel told him.

"Well, could you bring a little of that healing over here?" Greer asked as she grabbed her bloodied shoulder.

Ariel leapt over to Greer and placed her paw on her wounded shoulder. After a few moments, Greer, too, was healed.

"You're Ariel, right?" Greer asked.

"Yes."

"Aren't we competing against you?" Greer looked puzzled.

"Yes, but a competition is no reason not to do the right thing. I'm sure if I were in trouble, you'd help me out."

"Yeah, you got it," Greer answered with genuine sincerity.

Ada smacked Kane's arm.

"What was that for?" Kane asked.

"Ada piñata? You were enjoying those shots a little too much!" Ada snarled. "I could hear you, you know."

"I was aiming for its head," Kane answered.

Ada narrowed her eyes at him, not quite buying it.

"Hey, guys, does the fact that Ariel's here mean we're on

the right track?" Vero asked. "It's probably not a coincidence that we both wound up on this island. Maybe the person we're supposed to find is here after all?"

"What makes you so sure it's a person?" Ariel said. "It could be anything."

"What do you mean?" Vero asked.

"The Powers are the keepers of history," Ariel began. "So I can tell you that in the past Trials, some of the riddles involved finding David's harp, Moses's bronze staff, Joseph's multi-colored coat ... What we seek need not be a living being."

"Then what led you to this island?" Vero persisted.

"The riddle says that whatever we're supposed to find is stronger than one thousand men. I know every word of the Bible committed to memory, and that's what led me here." She paused. "To the jungles of Geshem, home of the Children of the Fallen."

"The Children of the Fallen?" Ada said, her eyes wide.

"The Children of the Fallen," Ariel repeated with a definite warning in her voice.

The fledglings looked frightened.

"Who are they?" Vero asked.

"I can't tell you any more. This is still a competition," Ariel replied. "We are to use our given talents to figure it out on our own."

"But ..." Kane began.

Ariel turned and walked away, cutting him off. Her powerful muscular shoulders moved up and down with each step.

"Good-bye," she said. "And good luck." Ariel crouched down and, springing off her back legs, bounded into the dense jungle.

# 9

## CHILDREN OF
## THE FALLEN

Greer spun around to the other fledglings, stepping over what was left of the flower's decapitated head. "Vero, transmit to Pax and X what Ariel told us. Have them research the Children of the Fallen in the jungles of Geshem. See if they come up with anything."

Vero put his hands to his temples and tightly shut his eyes. After a few moments, he looked up. "I also told them to research the number one thousand in the Bible."

"Good. Let's go," Kane said, heading toward the jungle.

"Where are you going?" Greer said.

"Ariel obviously knows a lot more than we do," Kane replied. "She went this way so we should follow her."

"I don't know ..." Vero said.

"You got a better idea?"

Vero shook his head and followed after Kane. Ada and

Greer hurried alongside him, journeying into the heart of the dense tropical rainforest. As they walked, Vero surveyed the dense vegetation. On the ground, the shrubs had grown so tightly packed together that they swallowed his legs with every step. Trees buttressed by fifteen-foot roots towered over the crowded shrubs. Slippery mosses covered rocks and trees, bathing them in dark hues of green, while vines with woody stems climbed on anything that would support them. Colorful lichen and fungi shot out of tree trunks and up from the wet, muddy soil. The waxy, oval leaves of the trees formed a canopy over Vero's head so thick that barely any light came through. Though the thick vegetation kept most of the rain out, the air inside the forest was hot and humid.

Vero tugged at his shirt collar. "It feels like we're trapped in a giant greenhouse," he said.

"But it is pretty," Greer commented, running her hand over a smooth, broad leaf.

Suddenly, the ground beneath Vero's feet began to shake once again. It was another unnerving earthquake. As the fledglings paused, they looked up and could see the treetops dangerously swaying. Vero feared one might topple over and crush them. As Ada steadied herself by grabbing onto Vero, the trembling finally stopped. She let out an uneasy sigh of relief.

"It's the island of earthquakes," Kane said, the color slowly returning to his cheeks.

"Vero, anything from those guys?" Greer asked impatiently.

"Not yet."

"And no sign of Ariel," Greer grumbled. "Is anybody else

as nervous as I am about running into the Children of the Fallen? I mean, they don't exactly sound like sweethearts."

"No, I'm sure they're not," Ada said. "I believe Lucifer and his angels are called the fallen." She anxiously scanned the trees.

"Maybe they're not as bad as the overgrown Venus fly-trap," Kane suggested.

Greer felt a slight crunch beneath her feet. She looked down in the dim light. Littered all over the ground were corpses of dead ants—hundreds, maybe even thousands of them. She spotted a moving ant trail and stopped to watch the ants crawl over the moss-covered ground in a perfect formation to their anthill.

"What are you looking at?" Vero asked.

"Those ants." She pointed to the line of insects.

Vero raised his eyebrows. "Why?"

"I was just wondering what killed all these over here." Greer motioned to the mounds of dead ants at her feet.

"Hey, look, that guy's got a mind of his own," Vero chuckled, pointing to an ant as it broke formation from the line.

The angels watched as the lone ant moved farther away from the line of marching ants and climbed up the trunk of a leafy shrub. The ant stumbled along, walking clumsily. As it continued its climb, its tiny body started to convulse. A look of pity came over Greer. She reached out to touch the little ant. Kane slapped her hand away.

"Hey! What's your problem?"

"Don't touch it," Kane said forcefully. "It's a zombie ant."

Greer rolled her eyes at him.

"I saw it once on TV. Watch. He's going to crawl to a leaf, then bite down on the underside of it and die."

Sure enough, the worker ant climbed a bit farther up the branch. It crawled onto a leaf and flipped itself over, plunging its mandibles into the juicy main vein of the leaf. After a few moments, the angels watched as it expired, still clinging onto the leaf.

"Why did it do that?" Greer looked sadly to Kane.

"There's this parasite fungus, and it infects the ants. Then it takes over their brains and turns them into zombies."

"Oh, come on," Greer interrupted, rolling her eyes.

"It's true," Kane said. "The ant becomes a host for the parasite. It leads the ant away from the other ants and controls them to bite on the leaf. After the ant dies, a couple of days later, the stem of the fungus sprouts from the dead ant's head and shoots toxic spores to other unsuspecting ants, trying to infect them too."

"He's right. Look." Vero carefully lifted up the tip of the leaf. Several dead ants clung to the underside. Each had a long stalk that had sprouted from their heads.

"Weird," Greer said.

The drizzle continued as the fledglings trudged forward. The day was wearing on them when the canopy overhead finally began to thin out. The ground was increasingly soggy, and the mud that clung to their shoes made each step twice as heavy. Even worse, mosquitos began to taunt them, buzzing around their heads. Vero slapped the side of his face, killing one.

"These mosquitos are real annoying," Vero said, wiping blood from his cheek with his sleeve.

With both hands and arms, Kane swatted mosquitos away from him. As more mosquitos swarmed him, his movements became more frantic. It looked like he was conducting a maniacal orchestra. "These are so much bigger than our mosquitos!" he yelled.

Kane danced around like a mad man, trying to flee the swarm of mosquitos. Ada grabbed the back of Kane's shirt, and Kane stopped wildly flailing his arms.

"Look!" she yelled. "There's a hill over there, and it has an opening in it!"

A few hundred yards in front of them, the jungle widened out to a clearing. There was indeed a hill with what appeared to be an enormous cavity carved into its side.

"Maybe we can get a break from the mosquitos and go inside and rest for a while," Ada said.

Kane didn't have to be persuaded. He pressed through the overrun greenery, swatting branches and leaves from his face in an effort to reach the opening and escape the swarming insects. The others trailed right behind him. Just walking into the cave, Kane felt better. The mosquitos did not follow, and the cool temperature was a welcome relief from the muggy, sweltering air outside. Kane glanced around. It looked like a typical cave made of rock walls, yet the ceiling was fairly tall—at least thirty feet. There were several narrower tunnels that branched off from the main one.

"It feels good in here," Kane announced. "Should we check it out?"

"Why not?" Greer answered.

"Which way to go?" Kane asked as his eyes scanned the various tunnels.

Vero turned to look around and saw a splinter of light forcing its way through the dimness at the back of the main tunnel. "I see light up there," he said excitedly while scratching the mosquito bites on his arm. "Let's go that way."

"But be quiet," Ada said in a low voice, anxiously twirling her finger through her hair. "We don't know if anyone or anything is living in here."

Vero followed the stream of light with the others close behind. He had thought that caves were usually moist and damp, but the air felt dry, and he noticed that the dampness on his shirt had already disappeared. He rounded a slight bend in the cave then froze at the entrance to what was a massive chamber off the main tunnel.

"Look," Vero said, holding out his arm and stopping the rest.

The others looked past Vero and took in the sight before them. Neatly stacked on wooden shelves lay hundreds of skeletons of what looked to be gigantic humans! A huge lantern hung from the ceiling illuminating the macabre scene. From head to toe, their skeletal bodies measured about fifteen feet long. That was almost the size of a T-Rex! Their skulls were about five times the size of a normal human head, and their arms were longer than Vero's entire body. And their hands! Vero thought one could easily hold the biggest watermelon in its palm and crush it like a tiny grape. But what unhinged Vero most were the teeth—the size of a whale's.

"Giants," Greer said, her voice barely above a whisper, as if she was afraid she'd wake them.

"All I can say is that I'm glad these guys are dead," Kane said with awestruck fear.

Greer elbowed Vero. But he had both hands over his ears. His eyes looked distant, fixed on something only he could see.

"He must be picking up on something," Greer said in a low hush to the others.

Moments later, Vero put down his hands and turned to the others. "Nephilim," he said. "Pax said the Children of the Fallen are the Nephilim … giants."

"Go on …" Greer motioned.

"He said the Nephilim go back to Genesis 6. God sent several angels to earth to watch over man, but they rebelled against Him by taking human wives …"

Vero's mind strayed to thoughts of Davina. Before he had understood he was an angel, he had had the biggest crush on her. But both Uriel and Michael the Archangel had warned him that it was forbidden for angels to fall in love with humans. *"We have such great love for humans, but, Vero, we are not to fall in love with them."* Michael had assured Vero that his feelings for Davina would become less and less with the progression of his training in the Ether. It was true. He wasn't as love struck for Davina as he had once been; however, he wasn't sure if it was because he now knew he was an angel or the fact that she liked Danny over him.

"Hello!" said Greer. "Keep going."

Vero shook his head and continued. "And so the children of the women and the angels were the Nephilim … giants. They had superhuman strength, and they used it to spread violence and evil in the world."

"What happened to the angels that fathered these creatures?" Kane wanted to know.

"Abaddon has them chained in the Lake of Fire." Vero shuddered at the thought. He remembered the time when he had ventured too close to the Lake of Fire. Just being near the entrance of the pit, Vero knew it was a horrid place. He couldn't image being chained inside it for even a second, let alone thousands of years.

"That's a fate worse than death," Kane said with a solemn look.

"The fallen angels fell right in with Lucifer and his minions, and they took the human wives because they wanted to taint the human bloodline that God so cherished," Vero said.

"Why?" Greer asked.

"They were jealous and deeply offended by God's love for the humans. So they wanted to corrupt and destroy them," Ada answered.

"So that's why God sent the Great Flood, isn't it?" Vero suddenly realized. "Noah and his wife and children were the only ones not tainted by the fallen angels."

"Yes, He sent the flood to punish the wicked, to restore humanity, and to rid the earth of the Nephilim," Ada said. "In the Bible it says Noah was *perfect in his generations,* but Noah and his sons weren't the only ones on the ark. They took their wives with them. Noah and his sons were not tainted, but a wife of one of the sons was carrying the Nephilim gene, and it was passed down."

"But that doesn't make any sense," Greer said, confused. "God would have known that. Why would He let that happen?"

"Because the Nephilim still had a role in God's plan," Ada said, looking around at the giant bones. "Man needed to cast out evil for himself to make the earth his own. God just made it more of a fair fight. Because they were chained in the Lake of Fire, the fallen angels never had anymore offspring, so the Nephilim after the flood were not as powerful as the bloodlines became more and more diluted, even though they were still giants by human standards."

"How do you know?" Vero questioned.

"Because in Numbers 13, Moses sent some scouts out to explore Canaan. They came back and reported having seen giants. *'We saw the Nephilim there. We seemed like grasshoppers in our own eyes, and we looked the same to them.'* And don't forget Goliath. He was also a giant. As a matter of fact, a great number of the Philistines were believed to be giants," Ada told them.

"Wow," said Vero. "Who needs the library when you could just bring Ada with you everywhere? You know everything."

Ada blushed.

Suddenly Vero's face lit up as he put two and two together, "Whatever we're supposed to solve has to do with these giants. Uriel was trying to give us a hint. Don't you remember when he mentioned David and Goliath?"

"Yeah, he did," Greer said slowly, as the memory came flooding back to her.

"Well, I'm still glad these guys are dead," Kane said, staring at a giant's massive skull.

"Umm, I have news for you." Greer's voice was suddenly full of worry. "Someone's been visiting these graves."

The others' heads whipped around to face her.

"Look, over there . . ." Greer shakily pointed to the corner of the chamber.

Greer walked deeper into the chamber as the others followed. Ada gasped at the sight before her.

A clump of brightly colored, freshly cut flowers lay across the bare chest of one of the giant's bones.

# 10

# BEYOND THE CLOUDS

Pax's head tilted back as he looked up at the many, many scrolls shelved in the library. His mind raced a mile a minute, trying to solve the riddle. X tapped him on the shoulder, startling him.

"Sorry," X said. "Didn't mean to break your concentration. Are you talking to Vero?"

"No, and I'm feeling pretty useless to them."

"*They laughed at me, mocked me, and called me an ass. However, today they cower should I ever pass. They have felt my strength—one thousand men strong—when I was called to settle a terrible wrong. Yet, there is no rest beyond the clouds. No rest for me, 'till I be shroud,'*" X recited. "This guy may have been called a fool, but he obviously knew how to kick butt when he needed to …"

"Vero said it might not even be a person," Pax reminded

him. "Remember, Ariel said past Trials involved Biblical objects."

"Okay. I'll research Biblical objects, and you research the number one thousand in the Bible," X said. "Maybe there's a link between the two. Then again, Ariel is a competitor, so she could be trying to throw us off track."

Pax put a thought in his mind, and a scroll freed itself from a shelf and floated downward into his hand. Another landed in X's. They sat at a table and unrolled their scrolls. The number one thousand materialized and shot into Pax's ear. A teeny, tiny Bible sprung forth from X's blank scroll and sailed into his ear. X shook his head as the tiny Bible exited his other ear then jumped back into the scroll and disappeared when the scroll rolled itself up. Both scrolls flew back to their shelves.

"So what have you got?" Pax turned to him, sticking his index finger in his ear to itch it.

"Unfortunately, there's a ton of Biblical objects," X said, discouraged.

"I didn't get too many references," Pax informed him, "There's Psalm 40 that says 'a thousand years are as a passing day.' Peter said, 'a day is like a thousand years to the Lord, and a thousand years is like a day.'"

"None of those involve any artifacts," X thought out loud.

"Isaiah, 'the last of you will become a thousand.'" Pax continued reciting. "Judges, 'he struck down a thousand men ...'"

"What was that?" X's interest suddenly piqued.

"The story of Samson."

"That's it!" X yelled. "Not only did Samson kick butt ... but he used the jawbone of a donkey! It's the jawbone! Recite the rest of the passage!"

"Finding a fresh jawbone of a donkey, he grabbed it and struck down a thousand men. Then Samson said, 'with a donkey's jawbone, I have made donkeys of them. With a donkey's jawbone, I have killed a thousand men.'"

"That's it!" X shouted. "They laughed at me, mocked me, called me an ass ..."

"A donkey?" Pax wondered. "Of course! Ass is just another word for donkey."

"Yes," X answered. "They have felt my strength of one thousand men strong when I was called to settle a terrible wrong."

"After they burned his wife and her family, Samson slew a thousand Philistines."

"It makes perfect sense," X stated happily.

"And some of the Philistines were giants," Pax added. "So we're in the right place!"

"Probably." X grinned. "We still don't know where the jawbone is, but at least now we know what we're looking for."

✥

"The jawbone of a donkey?" Greer said, looking at Vero quizzically.

Vero shrugged. "That's what X and Pax say."

Greer looked around. "I don't even know what one would look like."

Without warning, the floors in the chamber began to shake. Vero's face flushed white. Ada pushed her body up against one of the chamber's ancient rock walls, bracing herself.

"I don't want any of these skeletons to fall on me!" Ada yelled to the others, looking up at the swaying shelves of bones.

Vero grabbed Ada's arm, pulling her away from the wall, "Let's get out of here!"

As they raced to get out of the burial chamber, Kane and Greer followed. The walls continued to shake, and the ground underneath them buckled. Ada stumbled, taking Vero and Greer down with her. They fell right next to the skeleton with the freshly cut flowers, and Vero noticed that the underside of one of the leaves was loaded with dead zombie ants still clinging to the vein. Seeing the ants only a few feet away, his eyes went wide, and he held his breath, afraid of catching whatever killed them.

"Get up!" Kane yelled, holding both hands out to them.

He had just pulled Ada and Greer to their feet when something massive shuffled toward them from the cave tunnel. Kane stopped short, arms out, holding Greer and Ada back as Vero stood up. Kane couldn't quite make out what was before him, but when he heard it moving closer, he quickly turned around.

"Go back!" he said in a loud whisper.

The angels retreated farther back into the chamber as the shaking became more violent. Bones rained onto the fledglings as Nephilim skeletons fell from their resting places and crashed onto the cold floor, snapping skulls from their vertebrae. The angels ducked while racing to the safety of the closest wall. Kane pushed the others behind him around a tall, wide boulder that created a gap between itself and the wall. They shrank behind the boulder and watched as a giant stepped into the lantern's light.

"I guess we know what was causing those earthquakes," Ada said faintly.

A hideous creature loomed sixteen feet tall in the middle of the chamber. Its bald head and skin were a dark grayish color, the texture of an elephant's hide—thick, with ridged creases. Its eyes were dull black. Its feet and hands were massive with yellow, cracked, and rotted nails. But what nearly caused Greer to gag were the numerous hairy warts that sprouted from its face.

"Thank God, he's wearing a loincloth," Greer whispered in disgust.

The giant's head whipped around at the sound of Greer's voice. The fledglings froze. The creature's gloomy eyes scanned the chamber, lingering over the angels' hiding place behind the massive boulder. Vero and the others held their breath and crouched down even lower. A loud, grunting sound emanated from the giant's mouth, growing louder and louder. Vero thought it was the sound of pure anguish. The giant then shuffled his enormous feet toward the front of the chamber. When he slid his feet this way, Vero noticed that the ground did not shake.

Vero wondered what the source of his pain could be. He peered around the boulder and watched as the giant bent down on one knee and picked up a severed skull. He cradled it in his massive arms as if it were a newborn then reattached it to the proper body—the one with the cut flowers lying across its chest.

As the giant wailed and kneeled over the skeleton, Vero saw a chance to escape. He motioned for the others to follow him, and they slipped out from their hiding spot, crouching down to remain hidden in the shadows. They crept along the wall, never taking their eyes off the giant who, fortunately, was too preoccupied with his own grief to notice them.

The fledglings were nearly safely out of the bone chamber when the sound of wings flapping overhead caused Vero to look up. Coming toward the angels down the main tunnel from deeper inside the cave was the lioness Ariel, and the noise of her flying was definitely loud enough to alert the giant to her presence if she flew into the chamber! Vero wanted to scream to warn her, but could not do so without putting them all in danger. But she had saved Ada and healed him and Greer after the plant attack. Next to him, Ada gasped, and Vero and Greer began waving their arms frantically, hoping to flag her off. But Ariel was flying ever closer, the noise from her wings growing with every flap. She didn't see them. Finally, Vero stepped away from the wall.

"Ariel, stop!" he yelled.

But it was too late. Ariel had flown into the chamber. The giant's head spun around toward Vero, and the massive creature quickly stood. Ariel stopped sharply, a look of horror on her face. The giant's eyes narrowed menacingly, and Vero realized they had to get out of there—fast. The giant picked up a fallen skull and whipped it at Vero. It missed, impacting the cave wall instead, chipping out a huge divot from it. The giant moved surprisingly fast to the chamber's entrance, blocking Ariel and the fledglings from escaping that way.

"Quick!" Vero yelled to the others as he retreated toward a wide tunnel that branched off from the rear of the bone chamber. As the fledglings raced after Vero, the giant ripped another skull from a skeleton and chucked it at the fleeing angels. The skull rolled like a massive bowling ball straight toward them. Just as it was about to hit Vero, he attempted something he'd never done before. Running full stride, Vero dove headfirst toward the tunnel in front of him. And the moment be became airborne, he sprouted his wings and quickly flew up and out of the skull's path. Kane, Greer, and Ada did the same. As the four of them hit the air and peeled out in formation, Vero thought of the Blue Angels jets his father had taken him to see years ago.

Ariel, flying close to the ceiling, caught up with the airborne angels. "Watch out!" she shouted. The giant picked up another skull and hurled it at the angels. When the skull failed to hit any of them, the giant let out a roar, scooped up more skulls like they were playground balls, and threw them one after another at the flying angels. The angels ducked and dodged. The skulls were thrown with such force that they exploded the cave walls wherever they impacted, making dents and creating lots of shrapnel-like debris that peppered the surroundings.

"He's got a really bad temper," Ariel said, narrowly avoiding a flying skull.

As the angels flew deeper into the cave tunnel, the sound of skulls smashing the walls became fainter. Eventually, the sounds faded completely. Feeling a little safer, the angels regrouped and found themselves in another chamber, also lit by large lanterns hung on the walls.

"He's not coming after us," Vero observed, peering back down the dark tunnel.

"That makes me nervous," Greer said. "What does he know that we don't?"

Vero shrugged. He didn't want to say it out loud for fear of scaring the others, but he also shared Greer's concerns. It was strange that the giant did not pursue them.

"This must be where he lives," Ada said, scanning the chamber as she and the others hovered above.

A crude wooden table sat in the middle of the room. It was so huge that all the angels would be able to stand underneath it without even having to stoop. An equally crude chair sat in a corner. Its frame was carved from wood, and the seat was tightly woven from thick vines. A bed, constructed from the same material, was pushed up against a wall. On the table lay a wooden bowl, roughly the size of a kitchen sink, along with a crudely made fork and knife.

"I love what he's done with the place," Greer commented, taking in the sparse furnishings.

Ariel landed gracefully on the stone floor, and the other angels followed. "His name is Ahiman," Ariel said. "He is the bone preserver, and the last of his kind."

"At least he's decorated the walls." Vero pointed to crude, yet colorful cave drawings etched all along the sides. He walked up to a drawing of three men who bore a resemblance to one another. Each had dark, curly hair, unkempt beards, and looked fairly fit. They stood before a large boat as a massive wave threatened to devour them. "I wonder who they are," Vero said.

"Shem, Ham, and Japheth—Noah's sons," Ariel stated. "These drawings recount the history of the Nephilim after the Great Flood." Ariel padded on the floor before the murals. "Even though Ham, the middle son—" she indicated "—was not righteous like his brothers, Noah allowed him and his wife, Ne'elatama'uk, aboard the ark. And Ne'elatama'uk was believed to have had Nephilim blood in her so the Nephilim genes were passed down through their children."

"That's what I told them," Ada said, nodding.

"Yes, and Ham's descendants became the Philistines and later the Canaanites," Ariel said. "The Philistines were the sworn enemies of the Israelites. Many of them were giants."

"How do you know all this?" Kane asked, his eyebrow raised in suspicion.

"She's a Power, you nimrod! Greer blurted. "As in keepers of history!"

Kane nodded, remembering.

"Funny you should mention Nimrod," Ariel said, nodding to a drawing of a tower.

"What?" Greer asked.

"The Tower of Babel. Built by King Nimrod. A giant of a man."

"Oh, well, yeah," Greer covered. "Of course I knew that. You thought that was a coincidence?"

Vero looked closely upon the tower that stretched many stories high. It reminded him of the Babylonian ziggurats he had studied in Miss Wexler's social studies class. The structure was like a mud-brick pyramid but with outside staircases, and, on the top, rose a shrine. It was so tall that it peaked up through the clouds.

"Nimrod was a descendant of Ham," Ariel told them. "And he was the founder of Babylon where they practiced many pagan rituals. He rebelled against God for killing his forefathers in the Great Flood, so he built the tower. He told those who built the tower that he was building it so high so that he could reach heaven and confront God himself. In truth, he wanted to build a structure tall enough so that if God ever sent another flood, the waters would not be able to reach him." Ariel put a paw against the wall and peered at the drawing. "God struck the tower down and scattered the people all over the face of the earth and confused their language so they no longer understood one another."

Greer chuckled as she looked at a drawing of several people a little farther down the wall. They had humongous butts and their faces looked extremely pained—as if they were severely constipated. "If I didn't know any better, I'd say these guys need a little more ruffage in their diet," she chuckled.

"They've got hemorrhoids," Ariel said.

"Seriously?" Greer crinkled her nose.

"Many generations later, when the Israelites returned to Canaan, the Philistines stole the Ark of the Covenant from them, so God punished them with several plagues until they returned it. In addition to the hemorrhoids, they suffered boils, and mice overran their lands …"

Ada stared at the drawing of hills infested with thousands and thousands of mice. The mice were devouring the wheat fields.

"Only when they gave the Ark back to the Israelites did the plagues stop," Ariel said.

"I know this one." Vero pointed to a drawing of a little kid aiming a slingshot at a huge giant. "David and Goliath."

"What happened to the Philistines?" Kane asked.

"When David came to power, he greatly weakened them, and later, Nebuchadnezzar wiped them out."

"Except he missed one," Greer reminded them.

"Ahiman was banished here to this island to safeguard the bones."

"He's not very good at his job," Greer said. "Hurling their skulls at us doesn't seem like he's exactly handling them with kid gloves!"

"Nephilim bones are unbreakable," Ariel said. "Every

time he walks into the cave, his footsteps cause the bones to crash to the ground, and he has to restack them all over again. He does it over and over, day in and day out."

"That's like Sisyphus from Greek mythology," Pax said. "He had to roll a big boulder up a hill every single day. When he reached the top, it rolled right back down. So he had to roll it up again for all eternity."

"Why?" Vero asked. "Why doesn't he just bury the bones and be done with them?"

Ariel looked at him. "Because he believes the Nephilim will come back in the end times to punish the wicked."

"The wicked punishing the wicked ..." Ada pondered.

As that sunk in, Greer's eyes fell upon the final drawing. A powerfully built man with long hair held a curved piece of bone as a weapon. He stood, angry-faced, before a mob of scornful giants. Greer closely examined the weapon in the mural.

"So that's what a jawbone looks like," she said as the others crowded around for a closer look. "Now where the heck is it?"

"I hate to bring this up, but we're still competing against you ..." Kane's eyes rested on Ariel. "We have to go our separate ways."

"So leave," Ariel answered nonchalantly, motioning toward the chamber's entrance with her paw.

Kane hesitated.

"Give my best to Ahiman on the way out," Ariel teased.

"You're really being a jerk," Greer told Kane. "Where is she supposed to go?"

"What if we find the jawbone at the same time? Then who gets it?" Kane said. "Huh?"

"Whoever grabs it first," Ariel said.

Kane considered for a moment then nodded, but he didn't look happy about it. Vero looked down, embarrassed to meet Ariel's eyes. He really did like her, but he also wanted to win. Ada saw a small passageway that shot out the back of the chamber and wandered off to explore it.

"So it's all settled," Ariel said to the group.

"Look!" Ada screamed after only a few steps.

Everyone turned around and crowded around the passageway. They were all surprised to see Dumah, arms and legs tied up not with rope, but with thick vines, lying on the ground.

"Great," Kane groaned. "Another angel."

"Did the giant do this to you?" Ada asked as she and Vero began to unravel the vines.

Dumah nodded.

"What happened?" Vero asked.

Dumah did not answer. He stared at them.

Vero then remembered. "Oh, yeah, Dominions are silent. No wonder he didn't need to gag you."

"So what if we didn't happen to see you?" Greer asked. "I mean, were you really not gonna say a word and let us know you were there? You'd rather stay tied up than speak?"

Dumah nodded.

"You take this 'vow of silence' thing way too far," Greer said, crossing her arms. "But if this whole angel thing doesn't work out, you might want to consider applying for a job as one of the queen's guards at Buckingham Palace."

"Or as a mime," Vero added.

"And I bet you're great at charades," Greer teased.

"Guys, knock it off. We need to get out of here," Kane said as the last vine fell to the ground, freeing Dumah.

"We can only go back the way we came," Ariel announced as she looked over Dumah's shoulder at the solid curved stone wall behind him.

Kane asked the question that was on everyone's mind as they walked back into the giant's living chamber. "How are we going to get past the giant?"

"Sneak past." Greer shrugged.

"You really think it's that easy?" Kane asked.

"Unless you can walk through walls?" Greer shot back.

As Greer and Kane continued bickering, Vero watched Ada. She was staring at the mural of the Tower of Babel. After a minute, a knowing smile crossed her face. Vero stepped closer, and as he watched Ada fly to the top of the mural, he too understood. "Where's she going?" Greer asked, noticing Ada.

"Beyond the clouds." Vero smiled and pointed to the drawings of the clouds just below the shrine on the peak of the tower.

# 11

---

# ZOMBIE ANTS

Ada removed a stone that was set into the wall on the peak of the tower. Down below, Kane, Vero, Greer, Ariel, and Dumah watched in anxious anticipation. Ada reached her hand inside the small cavity. She poked around for a moment, and then she felt it—something hard and curved and heavy. So heavy, she had to drop the stone and reach inside with both hands. With some effort, Ada triumphantly pulled out the jawbone and held it up for the others to see. The bone was as long as Ada's forearm and shaped like two boomerangs joined together in a "U" shape. Where the two sides of the jaw met at the donkey's front lower teeth a natural handle formed. Each side of the jaw still had a row of molar teeth intact. As Ada held it, she saw that it really was a frightening-looking weapon.

"We did it! Guardians rule!" Kane yelled, forgetting all about Ariel and Dumah.

"Congratulations," Ariel said to Kane, looking down at her paws.

Dumah gave a slight bow to Kane, and Ada flew back to the ground with the jawbone firmly in her hands. Vero and the others gathered around to inspect it.

"Hard to imagine Samson could single-handedly take out a thousand Philistines with only this," Vero pondered aloud.

"It wasn't just the jawbone," Ariel said. "He had the might of God behind him."

Kane grabbed the bone from Ada.

"Rude!" Ada yelled.

Kane laughed. "Guys, I don't think we need to be afraid of that giant anymore." He smiled brashly, holding up the jawbone. "We're going to walk right past him."

The angels walked through the tunnel back toward the bone chamber. Kane gripped the jawbone tightly in both hands. When they reached the bone chamber, Kane stopped. The angels peered around the bend, watching the giant gently restacking the skeleton bones.

"He doesn't see us," Vero whispered. "We can sneak past him when his back is turned and then make a run for the entrance."

"Everyone, quiet," Greer said in a low voice, bringing her index finger up to her mouth. "Do the 'full Dumah'!"

Dumah eyed her. A faint smile formed at the corners of his mouth. The angels watched Ahiman closely as they dodged the lantern's light and snuck along the wall through the chamber. The giant seemed none the wiser. But just as they were almost in the clear, Kane suddenly broke away from the others and walked right toward the giant.

"Hey, Ahiman, buddy," Kane yelled.

The giant dropped the bones in his hands and turned around. At the same moment, the other angels' jaws dropped. *What was Kane doing?*

"Are you insane?" Vero shouted to Kane.

"No. I'm just gonna slay him so we can get out of here," Kane proudly announced.

"But he wasn't bothering us!" Vero panicked.

Kane turned to look at Vero. "What? Did you forget that he tried to kill us first?" He looked back at the giant who was now shuffling toward them.

Vero and the others drew back against the wall as the giant's eyes narrowed. Kane stood tall, unafraid. As the giant reached down to grab him, Kane sidestepped and smacked the jawbone with all his strength into the giant's leg. The giant had no reaction to the hit. Kane pulled back his hand and slammed the jawbone once again into the giant's calf. The giant let out an angry yell. It was so loud that everyone instinctively covered their ears. Ahiman grabbed Kane and shook him in his hand. More bones fell from their shelves as the giant stomped his feet in rage.

"Kane!" Vero winced.

The giant threw Kane across the cave. He landed on top of the others, while still managing to keep hold of the jawbone.

"Ouch!" Ada yelled.

Kane quickly got off them, never letting go of the jawbone. "Sorry," he said, his eyes still wide with shock. "I thought it would work."

"Thanks, genius," Greer said, getting to her feet. "Now what?"

Suddenly, the giant seemed to lose interest in them and returned to his business of restacking the fallen bones.

"I can't believe you!" Ariel whisper-yelled to Kane. "We were almost out of here! What were you thinking?"

Kane looked to the ground.

Ariel's voice was nearly a growl. "You wanted to kill him with the jawbone? Why? The poor lonely guy stacks bones all day and cradles his dead wife's remains."

The thought of the skeleton with the fresh flowers gave Vero pause.

"Obviously the stupid jawbone must have lost its mojo," Kane said.

"As I said, it only had power because God willed it to!" she retorted, swishing her tail in frustration.

Greer inched away from Ariel's moving tail. "Can you watch that thing?" she said eyeing the stingers in the tassel.

"Well, great," Ada wailed, putting her head in her hands. "Now he's ticked off and blocking the exit. How are we going to get out?"

"I say we throw Kane to him as bait," Ariel suggested. "And then the rest of us slip out."

"I like her," Greer pointed to Ariel. "She's someone I could definitely hang with."

Ada gasped and pointed to the center of the chamber.

Without explanation, Vero had slipped away from them and crept over to the skeletons.

Ariel watched in disbelief. "Are all you guardians certifiably crazy?"

Vero snuck up on the skeleton that the giant loved most. As he reached toward the fresh flowers that still lay across its ribcage, Vero accidentally nudged a bone. The giant quickly turned toward him at the noise, but Vero dove over a mound of bones and hid himself just in time. He held his breath as Ahiman lumbered over, the giant's massive foot stomping dangerously close to his face. After a few moments, the giant appeared satisfied and went back to his job. Vero gingerly emerged from behind the pile of bones, grabbed the cut flowers off the skeleton, and raced back to the others. He handed them to Greer.

"Thanks. You shouldn't have," she said.

"Just hold 'em," Vero said sternly as he broke a long green leaf from its stalk.

He flipped over the leaf. There were dozens of dead zombie ants attached to the underside. Fungus spouts grew from their heads.

"I've got an idea," Vero said. "We need to pulverize the infected ants into powder and then blow the spores in his face so he'll inhale them."

Kane looked skeptical. "Do you think those spores will be strong enough to kill him?"

"We don't want to kill him," Vero replied. "Just knock him out."

"What if it doesn't?"

"They will make a nice addition to his bone collection," Vero answered.

Ada handed Vero a smooth rounded rock. "Here's a rock to grind 'em with."

"Glad you're the one doing that, Vero," said Kane. "I wouldn't want to touch those ants."

"I'm not going to touch them," Vero said. "But even more important, I will definitely be careful not to breathe any of the powder."

Vero set the leaf on the ground and gingerly turned both ends of the leaf upward to form a canoe. He gently pulverized the ants with the rock into the leaf, being careful not to touch them. Greer knelt down to watch and inadvertently created a minor air disturbance with her movement.

"Greer! Stop moving! Any wind and the spores could blow back in our own faces," Vero scolded. "Unless you want to become a zombie."

"You should put something over the powder so it won't blow back on you," Ariel suggested.

"Here," Ada said pulling a tissue from her pants pocket. "Place it over the leaf. Then cup your hand over it," Ada suggested. "Like walking with a lit candle."

Vero nodded and laid the tissue over the leaf. "I need to fly right up to his face so I can blow it up his nose," he explained. "Someone's gonna have to distract him."

"I'll do it." Kane stepped forward. "I'm the one who ticked him off so bad. He already hates me." He handed Greer the jawbone. "Guard it with your life 'till I get back."

"Okay, let's do this," Vero said bravely.

Kane flew over to Ahiman who was still stacking the bones, and poked the giant in the back with his finger. The giant spun around with a huge femur bone in his hand.

"Yeah, me again!" Kane taunted.

The giant's face turned purple with rage. He swung the bone at Kane who dodged it. Kane flew circles around Ahiman.

"Hey, big guy over here!" Kane taunted him. Ahiman tried to shuffle toward Kane as Kane flew around the chamber. "Now, Vero!" Kane shouted.

Vero flew up to the giant's eye level, his hand carefully cupping the leaf.

"Get close to his face!" Kane shouted "You only get one shot at this!"

The giant took another swing at Kane. Kane dove, feeling a gust of wind as the bone swished dangerously close to his head. As the giant raised his weapon for another swing, Kane decided the situation called for something crazy—he zoomed around the back of the giant and landed on his left shoulder. The giant looked left, but Kane had already flown to his right shoulder. The giant looked right, but by then, Kane had flown back to the left. A stupefied look came over the giant—and then Kane knocked as hard as he could on the top of Ahiman's head. "Knock-knock!" Kane taunted.

When the giant finally raised his eyes upwards to Kane, Vero saw his opportunity. He removed the tissue covering the leaf and blew the powder up the giant's nose, momentarily stunning him.

"Direct hit!" Kane cheered.

Vero smiled triumphantly. But then the giant did something Vero hadn't counted on. The giant opened his mouth and inhaled deeply as his eyelids closed. Vero's eyes widened in fear as he realized what was about to happen. With a sound louder than an elephant's trumpet, the giant sneezed the powder all over Vero! The zombie dust flew into his eyes, up his nose, and in his mouth. Kane shuddered. Vero instantly felt a tingling sensation that started in the back of his throat and worked its way down to his toes. He felt as if his body belonged to someone else. He stared at his hand but could not feel it. It was like someone else was controlling his mind. His wings stopped flapping, and he plummeted to the ground.

"Vero!" Kane shouted, nosediving after him.

Clasping his arm across his chest, Kane caught Vero before he hit the ground. Ariel and Dumah rose up to meet them. Together they safely guided Vero down. A loud bang reverberated throughout the cavern, and more bones fell off their shelves. The fledglings turned to see the giant clutching his head and stumbling back from a wall. He, too, was in a stupor. He walked straight into another wall, creating another mini earthquake.

"Let's get the heck out of here!" Greer yelled.

Vero could not stand. His arms and legs felt like they were a mixture of pudding and marshmallows. He grabbed Dumah's perfectly chiseled face. "Got your nose," Vero teased.

Kane slapped Vero's hand away. "Let's go!"

With Dumah and Kane holding Vero up, the angels ran out of the skeleton chamber into the main cave tunnel, the sounds of the giant's groans echoing behind them. Greer looked over her shoulder as the giant tripped over a mound of bones and face-planted onto the cold, hard floor, causing a quake so large the angels lost their footing and fell.

They quickly got back up and raced toward the cave's main entrance. They knew they had to be in the home-stretch, and yet, they still could not see the daylight. Ada wondered if perhaps night had fallen while they had been seeking the jawbone and dodging the giant.

Dumah and Kane hoisted Vero along. "You know I love you guys," Vero said slurring his words. "You guys are awesome. My best friends for life." Vero turned his head to Dumah. "Now what was your name? Oh, that's right, you can't tell me anyway."

"Shut up, Vero," Kane said. "We're almost out of here."

"Boo!" Vero shouted in Dumah's ear.

Of course, Dumah said nothing, but he looked very annoyed.

They dashed onward, but then Ada came to an abrupt halt as she tripped and nearly smacked into a wall. Her elated expression soured when she saw what was before her—an enormous boulder blocking their only way out. It completely covered the entrance, which explained why they hadn't been able to see daylight. Everyone else bunched up behind her.

"Uh-oh," Vero laughed. "Looks like we're gonna need to make a bolder plan! Ha-ha! Get it? A bolder plan!"

"No wonder Ahiman never seemed interested in chasing us," Ada moaned. "He rolled this boulder in front, knowing we couldn't get out."

Greer looked confused. "Maybe he's not such a big dumb lug after all."

"Any ideas?" Kane asked. "Because Vero's getting pretty heavy, and I can't take any more of his bad jokes."

"We could all try to push it out of the way," Greer only half-suggested.

"Way too big," Ariel said.

"We could wait for the giant to wake up. He's going to have to go to the bathroom sooner or later, and he'll have to remove the stone to go outside?" Kane tentatively offered.

Greer gave him a deadpan look. "Seriously? You sure some of that powder didn't blow up your nose too?"

"Any other ideas?" Kane asked looking Dumah squarely in the eyes.

Greer huffed. "Even if he did, he wouldn't be able to tell us!"

"I say we tickle him until he talks," Vero said, flexing his fingers.

"Will someone shut him up?" Greer said, holding the jawbone threateningly at Vero.

Dumah and Kane sat Vero on the ground. Greer watched as Dumah held out his hand and closed his eyes in concentration. After a moment, a scepter with an orb on the head of it materialized from the palm of Dumah's hand. When the orb began to send out ribbons of light, Greer banged the side of her head with her hand to make sure she was seeing straight. The lights began to swirl. The angels stepped back, as the light ribbons grew brighter and brighter. They formed into the shape of ... Greer squinted through the intense light ... into the shape of Dumah — only about five times larger. And yet, she could still see the normal-sized Dumah standing holding the scepter. The giant-sized illuminated Dumah placed both hands on the boulder and, with no effort, rolled it away from the entrance. The angels watched in amazement. Dumah then tapped the bottom of his scepter to the ground, and the 'light Dumah' was sucked back inside the orb ball. Moments later, the entire scepter disappeared back into Dumah's palm.

"Totally awesome, dude," was all a spaced-out Vero could muster.

❖

Vero lay on the moist ground in the jungle as Ariel knelt over him, her hand on his forehead, silently praying. The others crowded around. After a few moments, Vero's senses began to return to him. He sat up, looking bewildered.

"Did I just see what I thought I saw back there?" he asked.

"Yeah, Dumah was holding out on us the whole time,"

Greer said, eyeing Dumah who smiled with pride. "But why didn't you just save yourself when the giant tied you up?"

Dumah held out his wrists, the left one over the right. Greer knit her brow, unsure what he was trying to convey.

"I think he's saying because his hands were tied up, he couldn't make the scepter appear," Ada deduced, looking to Dumah to see if she was correct.

Dumah nodded enthusiastically. The ground began to shake underneath them, and the treetops swayed. The angels looked around. "I guess Ahiman is awake," Ariel announced.

"No biggie. If he comes after us now, at least we can fly off this island," Greer said.

"Let's get this jawbone back to C.A.N.D.L.E. and collect our prize," Kane said, with his hand out to Greer. "I'll carry it from here."

Greer looked to Ariel and Dumah, her eyes apologizing for Kane's insensitivity to them. After a moment, Greer held out the jawbone. A smile spread across Kane's face as he took the priceless relic from her hands. Kane looked like a proud papa laying eyes on his newborn child for the first time. He turned it over in his hands, admiring it from every angle. And then, out of nowhere, a flash of light appeared, snatched the jawbone from his hands, and vanished with it.

Kane's gloating smile disappeared.

# 12

❖

# INVISIBLE ANGEL

Vero and the other fledglings raced through C.A.N.D.L.E.'s entrance. Vero was surprised to see that no one was inside. Given all the visitors for the Trials, he expected it to be brimming with angels. The only movement was the colossal torch with its swirling flames twisting in and out of one another.

"Where is Uriel?" Kane panted.

"Everybody must be outside!" Vero shouted as he continued running toward the back doors.

The fledglings burst out the doors, headed to the natural auditorium. But when they stepped outside, the auditorium was no longer there, nor the verdant fields of the Ether. Instead, they beheld a vast expanse of rolling brown-green hills with little other vegetation. A sweltering heat hit them. It was as if they had stepped right out of the Ether and into a foreign land.

"Where's the amphitheater?" Vero asked. "Where are we?"

In the distance, a stony hill rose high above the rest, and just beneath it were throngs and crowds of angels, some standing and many hovering.

"If I had to guess, I'd say Jawbone Hill," Ada suggested, "the place where Samson defeated the Philistines."

Kane sprouted his wings and rocketed into the air. The others quickly followed. They flew over the parched grass until they reached the floating gathering of angels and pushed their way through.

"Excuse me, coming through," Kane repeated as he elbowed angels left and right.

He finally reached an opening in the crowd and glimpsed the scene below. Pax and X were standing with Uriel and Raziel near a small pile of dirt. An intense anger shot through him like a geyser when he saw the illuminated outline of Melchor, the translucent angel, triumphantly holding up the jawbone. The spectators cheered his success. Melchor knelt down before an open patch of grass that appeared to be a shallow grave, and Kane's anger reached a new height when he saw what lay inside—the skeletal remains of an animal minus a lower jaw. It had to be the donkey! The words of the riddle came back to him: *There is no rest beyond the clouds. No rest for me, 'till I be shroud.*

"No!" Kane shouted, causing every head to turn in his direction. "Stop!"

He dropped out of the sky. Vero and Ada exchanged worried looks as they followed Kane to the ground. Kane landed at the head of the grave and immediately shoved Melchor's shoulder, knocking him to the ground. Surprisingly, for looking so ghost-like, the angel appeared to have a physical form.

"You stole that from me!" Kane yelled, his eyes flashing.

Melchor met Kane's eyes but said nothing. Uriel grabbed Kane's elbow and pulled him away. Kane tried to wrestle his arm free, but Uriel's grip was too tight.

"Uriel, he snatched it right out my hands!" Kane protested. "Ask Vero or any of 'em! We found it first! The Guardians solved the riddle!"

"It's true," Vero said, stepping from the crowd.

Greer and Ada stood behind him and nodded in agreement.

"The Thrones see everything," Kane said desperately. "Ask them!"

Uriel looked to Kane and examined his pleading eyes. But after an intense moment, Uriel turned back to Melchor. "You may continue."

Outrage overtook Kane. He yanked his arm away from Uriel. "That's it?" he shouted. "So the cheaters win?"

"We were all blessed with different gifts, and Melchor was just using his," Uriel told him.

"What gift? Stealing is a gift?"

"The Virtues can see the future," Uriel explained. "Melchor saw that you and the other guardians would retrieve the jawbone—"

"So he waited and watched us risk life and limb until the moment was right?" Kane interrupted.

"He used his gifts to accomplish a task," Uriel corrected him. "The challenge was not just to find the jawbone, but to be the first to bring it back and bury it. What were you doing that enabled him to take it from you?"

"Nothing! I was just holding it and admiring it ... And then Melchor stole it right out of my hands!" Kane said.

"Holding and admiring the relic was not part of your challenge. You were to bring it back directly. There is no room for self-righteous pride when executing any of your angelic missions."

"That's not fair!" Kane shouted. "Stealing is stealing, and it's wrong! Maybe you're not familiar with the Ten Commandments? If not, I suggest you read the seventh one!" His voice was laced with sarcasm.

Vero cringed. He turned to Ada. "I can't believe he's talking to Uriel like that," he said in a low voice. Ada slowly nodded.

"First of all, Kane, the jawbone is an ancient relic and was never yours, so Melchor did not steal from you. You may have found it—actually Ada may have found it first, but you failed to protect it and bring it back here." Uriel's voice was stern and serious.

Kane's eyes locked on Uriel's.

"And as for fairness, when demons and maltures come after you with everything they've got, is your only defense going to be, 'hey, that's not fair?' Think they'll listen and back off?" Uriel asked.

Uriel's words began to register for Vero. He had fought two of Lucifer's maltures and knew how ruthless and evil they were. They would have done *anything* to defeat him.

Kane shook his head and balled his hands into fists. "This is different! We are supposed to be good! I would think at least amongst ourselves a competition ought to be fair!"

"Kane, we must never confuse the concept of 'fairness' with the much higher precept of 'justice,'" Uriel answered, his eyes softening. "It's not always easy, even for angels. Lucifer fell because he thought God's love for man was unfair to angels." Uriel paused and looked around at the fledglings.

"So you want us to fight dirty?" Kane spat out. "Undercut other angels?"

"I want you to use what God has given you ... I don't want to lose a single one of you." He put a hand on Kane's shoulder. "You might think these Trials are about winning a trophy or personal glory, but they are not. The Trials are about pushing you to become a fierce fighter, to hone your skills to better carry out God's will."

"It's totally bogus," Kane said angrily before storming away from the crowd.

As Uriel watched him sprout his wings and fly off in the direction of C.A.N.D.L.E., Vero caught a look of sadness on Uriel's face. When Kane was no longer in sight, Uriel turned back to Melchor.

"Continue."

Melchor reattached the jawbone to the donkey's skull. The small dirt piles lying next to the grave lifted off the ground as if gusts of wind had gotten underneath them. The dirt spread out over the donkey's remains, covering the skeleton. In a split second, grass grew over the hole, and the grave was completely concealed. No one could ever tell what lay underneath. Melchor turned to the spectators.

"Thank you for allowing me this honor," he said in a clear and melodious whisper.

❖

"How could you let him steal the jawbone?" X asked Kane as they and the rest of their flight stood before the giant torch back inside C.A.N.D.L.E. "Why didn't you protect it?"

"I would have," Kane answered adamantly. "The dude's invisible. How was I supposed to know he was following us?"

"Yeah, X," Greer added. "You weren't there. You weren't battling killer flytraps or a giant! You had the cushy job of hanging out in the library! At that moment, we were all just happy to be back out in the fresh air and daylight."

"This isn't doing us any good." Ada stepped in between them. "There are still two more Trials. And we'll never win if you guys keep this blame game going."

X looked to Kane as he considered it for a moment. "I'm sorry," X conceded. "I guess it is pretty hard to spot an invisible guy."

Vero heard the sound of footsteps. He turned and saw Uriel walking toward them. Uriel placed his hand on Kane's shoulder. "Kane, I know this all seems confusing to you, but you were right — the Thrones see all your actions, hear your thoughts, and listen to your words. And what they know, God knows. And that should bring you solace," Uriel looked deep into Kane's eyes.

Kane met Uriel's gaze, but he gave no indication that he understood what Uriel was trying to tell him. Kane jerked his shoulder from under Uriel's hand. Uriel turned his gaze to the others. "Go home and rest up. You'll be back here soon enough."

Uriel headed out toward the doors. Vero watched him leave, debating whether or not to chase after him. But then his legs decided for him, and he broke into a sprint.

"Uriel," Vero called.

Uriel stopped and waited until Vero caught up with him.

"Did I do something wrong?" Vero panted.

Uriel furrowed his brow. "Why do you ask?"

"Ever since the Trials began, you seem to be mad at me," Vero told him. "Like you don't want me to be here . . ."

"I'm not angry at you Vero," Uriel said. He sighed. "But yes, I wish you weren't participating in the Trials."

Vero felt as if he had just been punched in the gut. "But why? Am I not good enough?"

Uriel paused, as if deliberating a thought. "I fear you're not advanced enough."

"You think the others are better than me?" Vero asked, holding back tears.

"I pray you prove me wrong," Uriel said, and then he walked out the doors.

✤

Vero belly flopped hard, really hard, into the water. As the thud reverberated throughout the pool deck, Tack, along with just about everyone else on the swim team, winced. Vero sank into the depths of the pool, opened his eyes, and realized he was back on earth. *What was going on?* Oh yeah. The high dive. Davina. Kira. At least he had remembered to change back into his bathing suit before he left the Ether. He started swallowing water, so he quickly swam to the surface. His head broke through the water, and once again, air filled his lungs. Vero felt an arm grab him under his shoulders. Tack was swimming him Red Cross style to the side of the pool. Vero grabbed onto the ledge.

"That was intense," Tack said, his voice shaking. "You shouldn't have done that."

Vero spat out water. "You dared me!"

Vero and Tack climbed out of the pool. As Vero bent over to catch his breath, he felt someone place a warm towel around his shoulders. He turned his head and was surprised to see Kira. "Oh ... thanks."

"You okay? That didn't sound so great," she said.

"Yeah, just got the wind knocked out of me," Vero replied. He felt his face burn red with embarrassment.

A whistle blew. Vero looked over to see an angry Coach Cindy storming toward him, her long, dark ringlets bouncing with every step. Vero and Tack shrank against the wall as her fit, nearly six-foot frame towered over them.

"Leland, Kozlowski, hit the showers! You're done!"

"Why?" Tack asked.

"You know the rules. No one in the water until I arrive."

Tack opened his mouth to protest, but Kira cut him off. "Vero accidentally fell in the water and Tack bravely jumped in to save him."

Tack flashed Coach Cindy a self-satisfied look. Vero looked curiously at Kira. Why was she lying for him?

"It didn't look that way to me," Coach Cindy shot back. "I just got this job, and I'm not going to lose it because you two knuckleheads decided to break the rules! Now hit the showers!"

Vero didn't put up a fight. Truth was, he was tired from the Trials and disorientated by the transition from the Ether. All he wanted to do was go home and rest. He looked over and saw his clothes had made it back from the Ether and were piled on the bench. "Thanks, Raphael," he said in a low voice. Vero walked over and tucked them under his arm. As he and Tack walked toward the boys' locker room, Coach Cindy yelled to them. "Oh, and since both of you obviously like clowning around, I decided that you're going to be the mascots at the pep rally."

"You idiot!" Tack said as they stepped into the locker room.

"Don't blame this on me. You dared me!" Vero answered, sitting on a bench. "And I know what you're going to say … 'only the biggest dorks are the mascots!'"

"Not that. Being a mascot might be fun. Everyone will get to see my dance moves. I'm talking about when Kira asked if you were okay. You should have told her you needed mouth to mouth," Tack said. "You totally blew a perfect opportunity." He turned on a shower and jumped under, keeping his suit on.

"You talk big for someone who's never had a single date in his life," Vero said.

"Not true. Remember last year when we went to see that movie about the guy who becomes a robot?" Tack asked, squeezing a huge amount of shampoo into his hand.

"Yeah?"

"It was you, me, and Clover. And you got sick from the popcorn before the movie even began, so your mom came and picked you up, but she let Clover and me stay and watch the whole thing …"

"Is there a point to this?"

"It was me and Clover, just the two of us alone in a dark movie theater. That counts as a date."

"It was my sister!"

"You know, she's pretty good-looking," Tack said, lathering soap all over his face. "Kind of hot."

"No guy wants to hear that about his sister!" Vero said.

"I do. I hope my sisters all become the next Miss USA."

"You do?" Vero asked.

"Yeah, 'cause that'll up their chances at getting married and moving out of the house sooner," Tack said.

Suddenly the water cut off, leaving Tack with a face full of soapsuds. "Hey!" he said. "What's your problem?"

"I didn't do it!" Vero retorted as he stood and crossed over to a sink. He turned the faucet. Nothing came out. "Guess the water's shut off."

"Great," Tack said, spitting out a mouthful of soap.

❖

Yellow school busses pulled away from the curb at Attleboro Middle. They were the late busses for kids who had after-school activities. As Vero and Clover sat on a bench waiting for their dad to pick them up and take them to the mall, the school looked deserted. Vero put his head in his hands.

"What's wrong with you?" Clover asked.

"I'm tired. I really don't want to go to the mall."

"I know exactly what we're getting mom so it'll be fast.

"Better be."

Clover looked over at her brother. "Why are you so tired?"

"You wouldn't understand."

"I might. I had a stressful day too. Algebra test, world history quiz, someone slammed the door on my ponytail, and all the girls agreed to wear blue nail polish, but no one told me, so I looked like a freak with red polish ..."

Vero rolled his eyes.

Clover laughed. "Okay so maybe that isn't the biggest problem in the world."

"Yeah, well try fighting Nephilim——" Vero quickly shut his mouth. He shouldn't have said that.

"You went to angel training?" Clover asked, wide-eyed.

Vero slowly nodded.

"What was it like?"

Vero looked down, feeling uncomfortable. He wanted to share everything he learned in the Ether with his sister, but it wasn't possible. If he tried to reveal something he shouldn't, Uriel would send a siren-blaring fire truck past them or create some other loud noise so Clover would miss whatever it was he shouldn't have been telling her. There was a kid in his class last year whose father was in the CIA. Vero remembered how his friend once told him that was all he knew about his dad's job. The kid wasn't allowed to ask his own dad any questions about his work. Being a fledgling felt a lot like working for the CIA, Vero thought.

"It was kind of boring," Vero said.

"You're lying," Clover accused him.

"Of course I'm lying so don't ask me any more questions about it!" Vero looked up. "You'll force me to lie, and then I'll feel guilty about it."

"Fine," Clover said dejectedly. "I won't say another word about it." She crossed her arms and leaned back on the bench.

Vero and Clover sat in silence for a moment. Then Clover spun around to face Vero. "You know nothing about this angel thing is easy for me either! You expect me to accept it blindly like it's no big deal. No questions asked. Well, that's just unfair!"

"Oh geeze, there's that word again," Vero groaned and

sat up straighter on the bench. He could feel the frustration growing within him. "It's the same for me too, you know. Do you think they tell me everything? I only find out stuff little by little." Vero was gripping the bench armrest so hard his knuckles were turning white. "You're not the only frustrated one here!"

The anger in Clover's face began to soften. "What are Nephilim?" she asked.

Vero sighed, releasing his grip on the armrest. "Giants."

"Seriously? Like in Jack and the Beanstalk kind of giant?"

"Kind of."

"I have a hard time making sense of it. How can you be sitting here with me in a boring suburb and yet be out battling giants?"

Vero smiled grimly. "I know. Freaky, isn't it?"

Clover looked at Vero, her shamrock green eyes serious. "Just answer one question."

"What?"

"Promise me you won't lie, please ..." Clover's face was apprehensive. "I need to know."

Vero looked at her and considered carefully. "I won't lie, but I can't promise I'll answer you."

"Please," Clover said. Her eyes were big and pleading. Vero held her gaze then slowly nodded.

"What happens when you're done training? What happens to you?"

Vero looked down. He did not want to answer her question, but he knew he needed to prepare her. He turned back to her. "I won't be here anymore."

Clover's eyes instantly filled with tears. "What? You mean you'll die?"

Vero solemnly nodded. "You guys will think I've died."

"But you'll be really old when that happens. Right?"

Vero shook his head. A lone tear streaked down Clover's cheek, as the implications of his answer sunk in. Vero held her gaze, his gray eyes steady. "I'll go to my spirit form, but that doesn't mean I'll leave you. I'll always be with you."

A car horn tooted. Dad's car pulled up to the curb, and Clover quickly stood.

"Maybe I'll get hit by a bus and die before you," she said angrily as she headed for the car. "So you can see how that will feel."

The mall was nearly empty as Dad, Clover, and Vero headed for the department store to buy Mom's gift. The whole ride over, Clover had refused to talk to Vero. Now Vero thought she didn't want to look at him either, but his Dad hadn't seemed to notice. He stopped in front of a store window where all the latest sneakers were on display and tapped the glass.

"While we're here, Vero, you need new sneakers. Those things you're wearing have holes in the bottom."

Vero put his foot up on the window ledge and looked at his sneakers. Tired as he was, his dad was right.

Dad examined his shoe. "Come on, I'll get you a new pair."

"Hey, I didn't sign up for this," Clover protested. "I have a test tomorrow. Let's just get mom's gift and go home."

"Here," Dad said, as he pulled his wallet from his back

pocket and took out some cash. "Take this and go buy her gift. We'll wait here for you."

As Vero studied the shoes in the window, he saw a girl's reflection. He spun to see Kira standing behind them.

"Hi," Kira said, waving.

"Hi, Kira." Clover's face lit up.

"Is this your dad?" Kira asked.

Clover nodded and gestured to her friend. "Yes, Dad, this is Kira. She's new at school."

Dennis shook Kira's hand. "Nice to meet you."

"What are you guys shopping for?" Kira asked.

"My mom's birthday present," Clover said, "but Vero thinks we've come for new sneakers for him." She made a face.

"Vero," Kira said, half scolding.

"I'm gonna go buy a gift for my mom. I know the perfect outfit. You want to come with me?" Clover asked Kira.

"Sure."

"Don't take too long," Dad said. "We'll be waiting here."

"It was nice meeting you," Kira said. "I hope to see you again, Mr. Leland."

Vero watched as Kira and Clover walked away.

"Nice kid," Dennis said.

Vero didn't comment.

# 13

❖

# SURPRISE
# PARTY

Dad nervously tapped his fingers on the kitchen counter. Dressed in her nurse's uniform, Nora was stacking the dirty breakfast dishes into the dishwasher.

"Nora, don't worry about that," Dennis said. "We'll do them later."

"I hate to come home to a messy house."

"You'll be late for your shift," Dennis told her.

Nora looked up at the clock. "Oh, you're right," she said, shoving the dishes into the dishwasher even more quickly.

Vero walked into the kitchen, all dressed and ready for school. Dad made eye contact with him, and motioned impatiently with his hands to Nora whose back was turned to them. "I need to go to work," Dad mouthed to Vero. Vero understood.

"I can do that," Vero said to Mom. He took a juice glass

from her hand. "I have time before the bus comes. It is your birthday after all."

Nora looked to Vero. "Oh, okay. Thank you. I have to get to the hospital before the morning rush," she said glancing at her watch.

Dad breathed a sigh of relief. But then Nora opened the cabinet under the sink and pulled out the trashcan. Dad looked like he was going to lose it. As Nora pulled out the trash bag, Dad grabbed it from her.

"I'll have Clover take it out."

"Where is she?" Mom asked then shouted down the hall. "Clover! It's getting late!"

"Yes, it is. Nora, just go!" Dad raised his voice.

Nora smiled suspiciously at him, "I get the impression you want me to leave ..."

"Yes, so I can get to work!"

Nora turned to Vero and kissed his forehead, "Bye, honey."

Holding the trash bag, Dad leaned over and kissed his wife on the cheek. "Have a good day."

"Bye, Clover, honey!" Nora yelled. "Do well on your Spanish test!"

Mom picked up her purse from the back of a dining chair and walked out to the garage.

"I thought she'd never leave," Dad said after he heard the door shut. "Clover, now!"

"Where are the decorations for tonight?" Vero asked as he dropped a fork into the dishwasher bin.

Clover walked into the room. Vero and Dad gave her a look. She was wearing a full-length raincoat.

"They're not calling for rain today," Vero told her.

"Well, I heard differently," Clover said.

"But the sun's out!" Vero said.

"Who cares?" Dad said. "I'm late, but before I go, here are the instructions. All the decorations are in the dining room hutch along with everything you need to make the cake ..."

"You put eggs in the hutch?" Vero asked.

"Don't be stupid," Dad said, annoyed. "Come straight home from school, and I'm counting on you two to decorate and bake the cake."

Dad grabbed his briefcase when someone knocked on the door.

"It's Vicki," Clover said. "Gotta go!"

Dad stepped in front of her. "As soon as you get home, take the steaks out so they'll defrost in time."

"Okay, bye," Clover said as she picked up her backpack and raced to the door.

Ever since last year, Vicki's older sister, Molly, drove the girls to school each morning. Vero was rarely invited, and he missed riding the bus with Clover. Although, next year, he'd have Clover on the bus with him again when Molly graduated and went on to college.

Dad looked out the window. The school bus was pulling up in front.

"The bus is here," Dad said.

"But I'm not done with the dishes," Vero said.

"They'll be here when you get back," Dad said as he dropped the trash bag, picked up Vero's backpack and handed it to him. "Go."

❖

Tack walked down the crowded school hallway as kids

fished through their lockers while others hustled out of classrooms. As Vero got a drink from a water fountain, Tack walked up behind him and put his finger partially over the water fountain jet. A stream of water shot up Vero's nose. He turned to Tack, coughing, as water dripped out his nose.

"Got you good!" Tack laughed.

"Jerk." Vero smiled, wiping his face with his sleeve.

"Hey, stop wasting water," Tack teased. "That might just be the only water left in the whole school."

"What do you mean?"

"Remember yesterday when the shower cut off? Well, there's no water in the gym. They've got a bunch of plumbers trying to figure out where the leak is. So there's no P.E. this afternoon. Isn't that awesome?"

Vero didn't answer. He was too busy staring at Clover as she walked toward him flanked by Vicki and Kira. She was wearing skintight jeans way too snug for her body. Vero wondered if she had to butter the sides of each leg in order to squeeze into them. Her shirt was cut low, and black makeup was smudged thickly around her eyes.

"Does Mom know you're wearing that?" Vero asked with a look of disgust. "There's no way Mom and Dad would let you out of the house in that." Then Vero remembered that Clover had worn her raincoat to school. She must have worn it to hide her outfit.

"I don't mind the look," Tack said, winking at Clover.

"You need to lighten up, Vero," Clover told him.

"I think it's sweet," Kira said. "He's protective of his sister." Kira took off her white denim jacket and handed it to Clover. "Here, maybe you should put this on."

Clover pushed the jacket away. "No, I'm fine," she said, giving Vero a defiant stare. She pushed her way past Vero and Tack and headed down the hallway with Kira following.

Vero followed Clover with his eyes until she disappeared into the crowd. Vicki stood back with Vero.

"I'm not crazy about the outfit either," Vicki said to Vero. "I tried to talk her out of it, but Kira kept telling her how good she looked in it."

"Thanks," Vero said.

Vicki walked down the hall as the bell rang.

"First ball warning," Tack sighed unhappily. "Time to practice our mascot moves!"

"I gotta go return my library books on Sri Lanka," Vero said to Tack. "I'll catch up with you in a few."

The school library was quiet. Only a handful of kids sat at desks studying while a few more sat at computer workstations. Vero dropped his books into the return slot. When he turned to leave, he spotted Danny sitting at a computer. Suddenly inspired, Vero decided now was as good a time as any to try to make some inroads with Danny. If he was going to be with Danny his whole life, it might be nice to be able to stomach the guy. Vero walked over to him.

"Hey," Vero said.

Danny looked up from the computer screen. "Hey ..." he said suspiciously.

"Did you download that new zombie game where they battle alligators? It's so cool," Vero said, sitting down in the seat next to him. "You got alligators eating zombies."

Danny looked at Vero, his eyes narrowed. "What do you want?"

"Nothing," Vero said. "I was just wondering."

Danny turned back to the computer screen. "I'm busy. We lost Internet last night at my house so I need to get caught up on my emails."

"Oh, okay," Vero said.

"Hey, guys."

Vero and Danny looked up to see Kira standing over them. Vero was a little surprised. Lately, Kira seemed to show up everywhere he went.

"I overheard you tell Tack you had to return your library books, and it reminded me that I had a bunch too," Kira said to Vero as if she had read his mind.

Kira placed her hand on Danny's arm. Danny's eyes grew wide, and his arm tensed. "What are you doing?" she asked.

"Trying to answer emails," Danny said, shooting Vero an annoyed look.

Vero took the hint to leave. Yet, when he watched Danny with Kira, he suddenly felt protective of him. He walked away but then ducked down behind an aisle of books, so he could keep an eye on Danny. Kira was laughing. It seemed to Vero that she was flirting with him, but Danny didn't look particularly interested. After a few minutes, Vero became bored and turned to leave, but then he saw Davina walk into the library. Just at that moment, Kira leaned over and kissed Danny on the lips. Danny's cheeks turned bright red, and he jerked back. Davina froze. Danny looked up and saw her standing across the room. As soon as they made eye contact, Davina turned and dashed from the library, tears streaming down her cheeks. Danny jumped up and ran after her. Vero saw Kira smile and sit down in Danny's chair. She looked very satisfied with herself.

❖

"It's about time you got home!" Vero yelled to Clover as she walked into the kitchen.

Clover looked over and saw Vero standing at the kitchen counter cracking an egg into a silver mixing bowl. The kitchen looked like a disaster. The dishes were still not done from breakfast, piled high in the sink. Cake mix had spilled all over a countertop and onto the floor. The morning's bag of trash still sat by the table.

"You were supposed to help me make the cake!" Vero wiped his forehead with the back of his hand, streaking it with flour. "People are coming any minute!"

"I had an emergency," Clover said. "Kira was so upset, I couldn't leave her." She glared at Vero. "It's called being a good friend."

"What was wrong with her?" Vero asked, his eyes narrowed in suspicion.

"Danny Konrad tried to kiss her in the library today, and it totally freaked her out."

"He tried to kiss her?" Vero asked, genuinely confused.

"Yeah, Davina and a couple of kids saw it, and Kira's kind of traumatized by it."

"But that's not ..." Vero stopped himself. He realized that if he told Clover it was Kira who had kissed Danny, he would have to admit to her that he had been spying on them.

"What?" Clover asked.

"All I'm saying is that you shouldn't believe everything you hear."

"Kira isn't a liar."

"How do you know? You barely know her!"

The kitchen door flew open, and Dennis walked inside. His expectant face dropped when he saw the two of them arguing in the middle of a messy and undecorated kitchen.

"Guys, where are the decorations?" He set down his briefcase and looked around the barren living and dining rooms. "And have you even started cooking dinner for mom?"

"I'm working on the cake," Vero said.

Dad put his head in his hands and groaned. " Your mom does everything for you, and you can't do this one thing for her?" He looked up. "I'm disappointed with you two."

"I just got home," Clover said with a shrug. "We can start cooking now."

"Did you pull the steaks out of the freezer?"

Clover shook her head.

"Were you listening this morning? Now they won't be defrosted in time!"

Clover looked defiant instead of repentant.

"Take the trash out at least." Dad threw the bag to Clover, but she caught it on its side. The opening wasn't tied properly, and the garbage spilled out onto the floor.

"Seriously, Clover?" Dad yelled.

"Knock, knock," a man's voice called from the back door.

Albert Atwood walked into the kitchen followed by his wife, Wendy, and curly redheaded son, Angus, who was Clover's age.

"I don't smell the grill, yet, Leland," Mr. Atwood said, grabbing his potbelly. "I like my steak medium rare."

"Albert, be quiet," Mrs. Atwood smacked his arm. She looked around, noting the chaos. "Are we too early?"

"No, right on time," Dennis said. "We're the ones behind. Unfortunately, we're going to have to order Chinese instead." Dad fumbled in the junk drawer and pulled out a takeout menu.

"I was promised ribeyes," Mr. Atwood said, unhappily.

"Chinese is fine," Mrs. Atwood covered. "We love Chinese. Don't we, Angus?"

"I prefer Brazilian," Angus answered.

Mrs. Atwood shot him a look. "When is Nora showing up?" She asked.

"Her shift should be over ..." Dennis looked up at the kitchen clock. " ... in about a half hour. Then she's heading straight home."

"Is she working again?" Mrs. Atwood asked.

"She started working about 20 hours a week down at the hospital," Dennis said as he began to dial. "This is really bad, you two," Dennis said in a low voice to Clover and Vero.

Vero shot Clover a look as Dad ordered into the phone.

"Why didn't you go to nursing school?" Mr. Atwood turned to his wife. "You could be out there earning money too."

"Maybe I will get a job. And work the nightshift," Mrs. Atwood shot daggers at her husband.

"But I work in the day, we'd never see each other," Mr. Atwood said. Then he put it together. "Oh."

Dad covered the mouthpiece. He picked up a roll of yellow streamers from the counter and threw it at Clover. "Get going on the streamers and cake! She'll be here in half an hour!"

Just then, the kitchen door opened, and Mom stepped inside. Guilty looks came over Dad, Clover, and Vero as mom took in the sight before her. She looked confused and then crushed.

"Surprise," Vero mumbled.

"Even bigger surprise," Mr. Atwood said, "if you were expecting a steak."

❖

The dining room table was littered with Chinese takeout boxes as everyone sang "Happy Birthday" to Nora. Leaning over the dining room table, Nora admired her birthday cake despite the fact that it bore little resemblance to an actual cake. The white frosting was sloppily spread onto the top, and red and yellow sprinkles littered the icing in clumps. It looked pathetic, but Mom still smiled.

"Happy birthday to you!" everyone sang.

"Blow out the candles," Dennis said to Nora.

"You did a great job on it," she said, looking at the cake.

"Sorry, I'm not much of a cake maker," Vero said.

"You can say that again," Mr. Atwood snickered aside to Angus.

"I bet it tastes good." Mom took a deep breath and blew out the candles.

Everyone clapped except for Clover. She was too busy looking at her cellphone.

"Clover, you want to cut the cake for me?" Mom asked.

Vero elbowed Clover. She flashed him a nasty look then went back to texting.

"Clover," Dad said in a scolding voice. "Your mom's talking to you."

"Oh, what?" Clover glanced up from her phone.

"What's so important?" Mom asked.

Clover set her phone on the table. "Kira's upset. So I just sent her a photo of Two Dimension to cheer her up. It's our favorite band."

"Why is she upset?" Mom asked.

"Danny Konrad practically attacked her in the library today."

"He did not!" Vero yelled a little too quickly.

Clover looked at Vero suspiciously. "Since when do you defend Danny? The guy hates you."

"Yeah, he does," Angus smiled. "Lots of other people do too."

Mr. Atwood laughed. Mrs. Atwood slapped Angus on the back of his head.

"Unless you were there, I wouldn't comment," Vero told his sister.

"Davina saw him do it. I heard she's going to break up with him."

Vero paused for a moment. The thought of that made him feel really bad for Danny. He knew Davina was a very positive influence in Danny's life. Her kindness toward Danny had brought out the best in him. But if Davina were to shut him out, Vero feared that Danny could go back to his old mean ways. Danny was his ward, and Vero's job as a guardian angel was to keep him on the right path, even if he wasn't a full-fledged angel yet.

"Not only that, Danny sent a bunch of kids a threatening email," Clover said.

"I doubt that."

"It's true." Angus nodded his head.

"I'll cut the cake if nobody else will." Dad shot his kids a look of disapproval and picked up the serving knife. "Vero, why don't you go grab Mom's gift?"

Vero ran to the kitchen and picked up a wrapped present the size of a shirt box. He dashed back to the dining room.

"This is for you," he said handing the present to Mom. "You're gonna love it."

Nora excitedly took the present and began to unwrap it. "I wonder what it is?" she said.

Dad smiled. "Clover picked it out and said you'd love it."

Clover frowned and looked away.

Nora's excited face dropped when she saw an apron lying on top of tissue paper inside the box. It was a red and white striped apron with little rooster silhouettes on it. Vero and Dad looked equally shocked. Clover did not.

Nora slowly placed the lid back on top of the box. When she looked up again, her eyes were filled with hurt. "Sorry guys. I tried to put on a happy face with the Chinese food and the undecorated house and the awful cake, but why don't we just forget it was ever my birthday?" She shook her head and took a deep breath. "I'll see you in the morning." Nora stood and walked upstairs to her bedroom.

Dennis flashed Vero and Clover a look that let them know they were in big trouble. "Nora," he called as he climbed up the stairs after her.

"Don't look at me," Clover said to Vero. "You're just as much at fault."

"You believe this?" Mr. Atwood turned to his wife. "They give their mother something like that?"

"It's about as thoughtful as the Dustbuster you gave me on our twentieth wedding anniversary." Mrs. Atwood narrowed her eyes at her husband.

"How could you buy her that? You were supposed to get her an outfit she would love!" Vero pounded his fist on the table after the Atwoods had left. "How could anyone be excited about an apron?"

Clover shrugged. "Well, she always cooks. I thought she'd like it."

"But Dad gave you enough money to buy her an outfit, a dress or something ..." Suddenly the pieces came together in Vero's mind. "You bought yourself that outfit you were wearing at school. Didn't you? You took mom's birthday money and used it for yourself!"

Clover turned red as a pomegranate. She didn't answer.

"That's like stealing from Mom!" Vero shouted.

"I'm gonna have a lot more birthdays with Mom. You won't, so don't get all in my face about it. When you're gone, I'll be the one left all alone to take care of Mom and Dad!"

Vero's expression softened. "I can't change what's going to happen."

"Did you even try? Did you ever ask your archangels or whoever it is, if you could stay on earth?"

Vero shook his head.

"See? You don't even want to stay. I knew it." Clover stood up and turned her back to Vero.

"I'm not human," Vero began as he placed his hand on her shoulder and spun her around to face him. "I am what I am. I have to do what I was created to do." Vero saw the hurt and uncertainty in Clover's eyes. "I'll always be here. The angels are all around us. You know that. You more than anyone should know that. You see more than most people."

"Yeah, well the angels must hate me or something, because I don't see them anymore! I haven't had a dream or seen anything in almost a year now."

"Clover, that doesn't mean they hate you ..."

"Well, maybe I hate them!" Clover yelled then stormed off to her bedroom.

❖

That night, a lightning storm raged outside. Each boom of thunder seemed to shake the Leland home. Long irregular streaks of light lit up the sky. Vero tossed and turned in bed. He couldn't sleep. He kept replaying his conversation with Clover over and over in his mind. The phone on his night-stand rang. He grabbed the receiver. At the exact moment Vero put it up to his ear, a vicious lightning bolt struck and sent an electrical current through the line. His hair stood straight up on its ends and smoked as Vero fell to the floor, instantly electrocuted.

# 14

※

# FORT-I-FIRES

Vero's pajamas felt wet, and he realized he was lying on soft
grass sodden with dew. He sat up with a start and shoved
his fingers into his ears to block out the sound. The booms
of thunder he had heard on earth continued to rattle Vero's
eardrums here in the Ether. A few yards away, thousands of
angels stood around an athletic field behind C.A.N.D.L.E.
As Vero walked over to see what held the angels' attention,
he realized he was barefoot. This was the first time he'd ever
been called back to the Ether while in bed.

Boom! The sounds grew louder with every step toward
the field. He made his way through the crowd and stood on
the field's edge. Four angels stood on the far side behind a
white chalk boundary line. Vero squinted and realized three
of the angels were Uriel, Raziel, and Raphael. But he had no
clue who the fourth angel was. Out of thin air, high up in
the sky, something that resembled a Frisbee shot across the
field. Instantly, a ball of light the size of a baseball appeared

in the palm of Raziel's hand, and he flung it with tornado speed at the target. It was a direct hit. The Frisbee exploded with a thunderous bang and disintegrated into a spectacular firework display despite the daylight. *Fireworks in the day. How cool*, Vero thought.

As the fireworks faded, another Frisbee-like target materialized and streaked across the sky. This time, the light ball appeared in Uriel's hand. He hurled it at the moving Frisbee and decimated it with another ear-shattering boom.

As Vero watched, he was reminded of skeet shooting. He and Clover had always enjoyed watching it on television during the Olympics.

"It's a pick-up game of hopeball," a girl's voice said next to Vero.

Vero turned and saw Ariel. Her sleek lion's body shimmered gold under the exploding light. She gave him the look-over. Vero stood wearing his drawstring flannel pajama pants and a white T-shirt and was completely barefoot. He blushed. "What? I was sleeping," Vero said defensively, secretly relieved he had not worn his Scooby Doo pajamas to bed.

Ariel smiled.

"Now what's hopeball?" Vero asked.

"A game where the angels hone their fort-i-fire throwing skills," Ariel said.

"Fort-i ... what?"

"Fort-i-fires. They're balls of God's light that the angels throw at humans to fill them with hope."

A series of especially loud cracks split the air. Vero saw Raphael had hit three consecutive targets, each nanoseconds after the other.

"When someone has feelings of doubt or despair, the balls of light fill their souls with hope," Ariel said, "giving them both courage and encouragement."

"What makes the fort-i-fires appear in their hands?" Vero asked, his eyes wide as one materialized in Raziel's hand.

"Sheer will."

Vero continued to watch the match with amazement. "It's funny. When I was little, I was told that the thunder I was afraid of was caused by the angels bowling," Vero said, eyes fixed on the sky above him, watching the action. "I guess hopeball isn't altogether unlike bowling, only the pins are flying targets."

Then hundreds of skeet-like targets shot out from the heavens in every direction. Eardrum-thumping pops filled the air, and the ground trembled. Vero covered his ears at the sound of the rapid fire. The three archangels and the other angel threw fort-i-fire after fort-i-fire at the targets, blasting them. Vero couldn't turn his eyes away from the spectacular display of exploding fireworks. It was like the best grand finale, a hundred times over.

Suddenly, Vero had the feeling that he was being watched, and his suspicions were confirmed when a giant wheel covered in eyes appeared. Vero recognized the angel as one of the Thrones. His gyroscopic wheels continuously spun as he spoke.

"Uriel, three thousand twenty-four, Raziel, two thousand nine hundred eleven, Raphael, three thousand fifty seven, and Gabriel . . ."

*So that's who that is*, Vero thought as he looked upon the fourth angel — the archangel Gabriel. The angel turned, and Vero's eyes grew big as he realized that Gabriel was a female archangel. She didn't look to be much older than his mother. Gabriel had unusual copper-colored hair that grazed her shoulders. Her face was beautiful, as perfect and stunning as a Dominion's.

Gabriel was the one who interpreted the prophet Daniel's dream. She was the angel who delivered the news to the priest Zechariah that he and his wife would have a child despite their old age. And it was Gabriel who appeared to the young girl Mary in the town of Nazareth telling her she had found favor with the Lord.

" ... Four thousand even," the Throne angel finished before disappearing as suddenly as he had arrived.

The crowd erupted into cheers, and Gabriel bowed humbly with a broad grin on her face. Raziel, Uriel, and Raphael also cheered for her. As she stepped forward, the crowd quieted.

"Thank you, but now we must get on with the Trials," Gabriel announced. "Will the contestants please make themselves known and step to the middle of the field."

"Let's go," Ariel said to Vero.

As they made their way across the field, Vero saw X, Ada, and Kane emerging from the crowd at the other end. A light shimmered in the field's center. Vero knew the light was Melchor. And next to him stood the Dominion, Dumah.

"Vero, wait up." Vero turned to see Pax and Greer come up behind him.

Pax looked curiously down at Vero's bare feet then at his hair. It was still sticking straight up. "How did you go this time? It looks like either you saw a ghost and heart attacked, or else you stuck your finger in a light socket," Pax said.

Vero ran his hand through his hair, remembering his transition. "Definitely closer to the latter."

"As angels, we are God's messengers," Gabriel began. "It is often our job to convey God's wishes to humans, for God speaks in dreams."

Greer nudged Ada, "Finally a woman archangel."

Ada smiled and nodded.

"As Job wrote, 'For God does speak—now one way, now another—though no one perceives it. In a dream, in a vision of the night, when deep sleep falls on people as they slumber in their beds, He may speak in their ears and terrify them with warnings, to turn them from wrongdoing and keep them from pride, to preserve them from the pit, their lives from perishing by the sword ...' For your second trial ...'" Her eyes rested upon the competing angels gathered around her. "You will communicate a message to a slumbering person."

"How hard could that be?" Kane snickered to Vero in a low voice.

"It will not be as easy as you think," Gabriel said as her sparking violet eyes landed squarely on Kane.

Kane gulped.

"And what if each of us delivers our message to the human? Who will win?" X asked.

"Whoever completes the task first will be the winner because all of you will be journeying into the same person's dream."

"How?" Ariel asked.

"Ecclesiastes 12:6–7. 'Remember him—before the silver cord is severed, and the golden bowl is broken; before the pitcher is shattered at the spring, and the wheel broken at the well, and the dust returns to the ground it came from, and the spirit returns to God who gave it,'" Gabriel said.

Kane looked to Vero, his tan face scrunched up in confusion. Vero shrugged.

"Babies are born with an umbilical cord connecting them to their mother's life source. People also have a similar cord that connects their physical body to their soul. It is the silver cord spoken about in Ecclesiastes." Gabriel looked at each of the contestants. "As long as they are alive on earth, the cord remains tethered, as humans must nurture both their physical and spiritual natures. But as a person ages or suffers from a prolonged illness, the cord gradually thins. As a result, when the person nears death, the cord is so thin that when the Angel of Death severs the cord, the transition to the spiritual world is not jarring at all."

"But what if it's a sudden death, like a car crash or something?" X asked.

"Because God is merciful, the cord is cut before the body can actually feel pain. Then there are a group of angels who instantly rush in to comfort the soul to make the transition smoother. Many times, at that point, loved ones who have already passed on will also come and comfort the soul."

Vero knit his brow, trying to process the information. He had heard of the Angel of Death, and the image of an angel with black wings wearing a long dark robe and a skeleton face flashed in his mind. Gabriel turned to Vero, aware of his thoughts.

"The Angel of Death gets a bad reputation on earth," she said. "But he is a loving, kind, merciful angel. Can you think of any kinder action than to cut the silver cord thus releasing a soul so it can return to God?" Gabriel spoke softly.

Vero stared intently at Gabriel as he considered her words. So much of what he had thought before discovering his true identity turned out not to be true. Accepted notions on earth could be so completely different from God's truth. But Vero still had questions.

"Do we have silver cords?" Vero asked.

"Because angels are pure spirit, we do not."

"But we have bodies ..."

Gabriel nodded. "Yes, you fledglings do, but think of your current body as just a loaner. Because you do not have a cord, you are able to transition freely to the Ether."

Understanding flooded Vero's mind. Now it made sense how he could travel from the earth to the Ether.

"It is this silver cord that allows us to enter humans' dreams. By catching a silver wave, we can access and communicate with their spiritual nature, giving advice, wisdom, hope, comfort, or visions." Gabriel put a hand over her heart. "The purer a human is in heart and mind, the easier your job becomes. That person will be more receptive to you, and your message will be more easily understood." The archangel smiled, her teeth perfect.

Ariel swished her tail. "And what if the person isn't of a pure heart or mind?" she asked.

"Then you must work that much harder to convey your message. For that person is more vulnerable to Lucifer's tricks and shields."

Vero turned to Gabriel with a fearful look, knowing from firsthand experience just how true her words were. Gabriel held his gaze. "He and his minions can also access a human's dreams the same way. Some call these nightmares."

Vero swallowed hard.

"When a person dreams, their physical intellect becomes dormant. In accessing their dreams via the silver cord, you will see only their soul, not their physical body." Gabriel's face grew serious. "It is the soul you need to communicate with. During this particular trial, the person you are trying to reach is under spiritual attack. Their faith is in crisis, and you need to deliver them a fort-i-fire. They desperately need the light of hope, of faith."

Vero looked down at this palm, wondering how he'd conjure up a fort-i-fire. Gabriel noticed.

"The Dominion, the Virtue, and the Power have already mastered the materialization of the fort-i-fire. For the fledglings, one of you will go and take an ember from the torch burning inside C.A.N.D.L.E. Keep it on you until needed."

Gabriel extended her gaze to Dumah, Ariel, and Melchor. "You, too, will also be limited to only one fort-i-fire each."

*At least that evens it up a bit*, Vero thought.

"But how do we enter a person's dreams?" Ada asked.

"You will go to the portal of silver cords, locate your dreamer's soul, and ride the cord into their dream. Now, please follow your teachers," Gabriel instructed.

The fledglings walked over to Uriel and Raphael. They gathered around them. Raphael handed Vero a pair of white sneakers. "This is getting to be a habit."

"Thanks," Vero said, taking the sneakers. He looked curiously at Ada. She was dressed in black leggings, a button down shirt, and flats. Her hair was nicely combed, and she even wore some makeup.

"We live in the same time zones," Vero said to Ada, "You should have been sleeping like me ..."

"I sleep fully clothed," Ada said. "Always prepared."

Vero raised his eyebrows.

Uriel beckoned to the group. "Come on, but before I take you to the portal, let's collect your ember."

Uriel turned and headed into C.A.N.D.L.E. as the fledglings followed. When they reached the massive torch, they stood before it, mesmerized by its flames. Its strands of fire gave off a great amount of heat.

"Someone go on and grab an ember," Uriel instructed.

The fledglings looked to one another. No one wanted to stick his or her hand into the blazing fire.

"I think Kane should since he's our leader," Greer said.

Kane's head spun around to her. "Me? You're the tough one."

"Yeah, well, foster dad number 3 extinguished his cigarette on my arm when he couldn't find an ashtray, so I'm an ember-phobic. Sorry, " Greer said.

"I say Vero does it," Pax said, stepping forward.

"Me?" Vero panicked.

Pax spoke mentally to Vero, "Yeah, this is your chance to prove to them that you belong in these Trials."

Vero held Pax's gaze, then glanced at Uriel for guidance, but Uriel simply shrugged. Vero looked from his hand to the fire as he silently deliberated. Then a determined look came over him. "Okay."

Vero slowly held out his right arm as he stepped closer to the dancing flames, spreading his fingers wide. Sweat poured down his face, and his cheeks turned bright red from the heat. Vero inched closer as the others watched with bated breath. His eyes were fixated on the swirling torch. His index finger touched the inferno. Vero screamed and jerked his hand away. He examined the tip of his finger. A red blister had already formed.

"No way, I'm out," he said, blinking back tears. "Not doing that again."

Pax shot Vero a look of disappointment.

"Ada, what does Isaiah 2 say?" Uriel asked.

"When you pass through the waters, I will be with you; and when you pass through the rivers, they will not sweep over you. When you walk through the fire, you will not be burned; the flames will not set you ablaze. For I am the Lord your God."

Upon hearing the passage, Kane became emboldened. He stood tall and decisively walked toward the torch, keeping his eyes fixed on the swirling flames. He recited the passage in his mind as he shoved his fist into the fire. Greer flinched. Pax shut his eyes. Vero closely watched as the flames seemed to tame around Kane's hand becoming as smooth as a sheet of ice. Seconds later, Kane pulled his arm out and examined it. No blister, no burns. He walked back to the others who gathered around him, marveling at Kane's perfectly normal skin. Kane smiled at them and opened his hand. In his palm glowed a red ember—a fort-i-fire.

"Amazing," Pax said, his eyes wide.

"I doubted." Vero looked at Uriel. "Didn't I?"

"Yes." Uriel nodded. "You could have grabbed the ember just as easily."

"At least he tried," X said. "The rest of us were too chicken to even give it a shot."

"Kane, put it in your pocket and let's go," Uriel said.

This time, Kane hesitated. "It's one thing to be in my hand, but my pocket? What if my pants catch on fire?"

"You'll be fine," Uriel said reassuringly. "You won't even feel it."

Kane hesitantly placed the ember in his pants pocket. Soon, a look of relief came over him, as he felt nothing.

"Good?" Uriel asked.

Kane nodded.

Uriel's wings sprung from his back. "We've spent too much time here."

Uriel wrapped his wings around the fledglings, and the seven of them vanished from the halls of C.A.N.D.L.E.

# 15

# SOUL
# SEARCHING

Uriel unfurled his wings, and the fledglings saw nothing but bands of silver light everywhere they looked. The bands stretched so long that Vero could see no beginning or end to them. Gabriel had said they were going to the portal of the silver cords, yet this room was so vast that he could see no walls on any side. There had to be millions of cords—billions actually, whatever the world's population was—so many that they appeared to form a silver ocean. Waves and waves of silver cords flowed before Vero's eyes.

"Which one is ours?" Pax asked. "They all look the same."

Hearing Pax's voice, Vero remembered the others were standing with him. He had been so caught up in the sight, he'd forgotten he wasn't alone.

Uriel placed two fingers underneath a cord directly in

front of them. The cord, though it was made of light, had an elastic springiness to it. It bounced in Uriel's fingers.

"Here is your person. Time to catch a wave." Uriel smiled.

He took Greer's hand and placed it into the silver cord. Her body began to illuminate a silver light, and then she warped into the cord. Vero did a double take, as all that was left of her was a silver blur traveling down the cord.

"Everyone grab onto the cord," Uriel told them.

Vero clasped his hand around the cord along with the others. His body took on the same silver aura, and the next thing he knew, he felt as if he was cruising down what felt like a water slide. The ride abruptly ended when Vero was ejected from the slide and thrown onto hard land. He stood up, dazed. As he brushed himself off, he saw Greer standing next to him. He jumped back as X, Kane, Ada, and Pax tumbled off the slide and rolled close to him. Vero gave Ada a hand up as the others also stood. The silver slide was no longer in sight.

"So where are we?" Greer asked, looking around into a thick mist.

"Somebody's subconscious dream," Vero answered.

"I know that," she huffed. "But how are we going to find their soul?"

"I guess we're going to have to do a little soul searching," X joked.

Kane brushed off his pants. "Knock it off," he said. "Are you forgetting this is a race?"

Vero looked at Greer. She had her hand over her heart, fingers spread wide apart, eyes closed. Vero knew exactly what she was doing. She was listening to her Vox Dei, God's guiding voice. After a moment, Greer opened her eyes.

"I've got something," Greer said in a singsong voice.

"What?" Kane asked.

"I saw the soul of our dreamer," Greer said.

"Who is it?" Pax asked.

"I can't tell. I can only see their aura, but I'm feeling a pretty strong connection."

"How do we find him?"

"They went that way," Greer said, pointing to her left. "And we better hurry or we're gonna lose them."

The six fledglings spouted their wings and became airborne, following Greer as they flew out of the gray mist. Gradually, the haze lifted, revealing a sparkling river nestled in a lush valley.

"Look!" Ada shouted. "There's the soul!"

About 30 yards in front of the angels, a glowing, small silver-tinged cloud was flying. It appeared to have a head but no defined body. It reminded Vero of ghosts he and Clover once made for Halloween where they took Ping-Pong balls, wrapped them in a tissue and tied string under the ball. It didn't have wings but was gliding with ease, seemingly unaware of the angels behind it.

"So that's what a soul looks like?" Pax asked.

"I guess," replied Ada.

"Can you hit it from here?" X said to Kane.

Kane reached in his pocket and pulled out the ember. It instantly became a fort-i-fire in his hand. He tightly clutched it, and fixed his eyes on the soul, trying to determine if he could make his target. As if it could sense Kane's thoughts, the soul sped up and disappeared behind a mountain peak.

"Hurry, guys!" X yelled.

The angels increased their speed and followed the soul through a snowy mountain range until it disappeared from sight. Vero and the others landed on a sharp peak to catch their breath. They looked out over the mountains searching for the soul.

"I don't see it anywhere," Ada said.

Vero bent down and picked up a handful of snow. He studied it as the flakes drifted back to the ground. "Weird," he said. "This snow feels so real. But we're just in someone's dream."

X nodded. "Everything is so real. You'd never know this is only someone's imagination."

"Greer, any idea where the soul flew off to?" Kane asked.

Greer pointed to an ocean below. "There it is!"

Vero glanced downward and saw the soul swimming with a pod of dolphins. There were hundreds of them. The soul and the dolphins gracefully bounced in and out of the water.

"Think you could hit it?" Vero asked.

Kane shook his head. "Way too far away."

"Let's go then!" Vero shouted, and he dropped into the air.

The others followed. They dove down to the swimming pod. Kane eyed the soul. He held the fort-i-fire in his hand, readying to throw it. His hand went back for the launch.

"You only get one shot!" Greer yelled. "You better be sure you can hit it!"

The soul swam in and out of the water with the dolphins. Kane's eyes narrowed as he steadied his gaze upon the soul. His arm went farther back, but then a dolphin bounced the soul with the tip of his nose and flung it high up into the air as if it were a beach ball. Kane kept a firm grip on the fort-i-fire, watching as the soul continued to rise in the sky. He then lowered his hand.

"After him!" X shouted.

The angels raced after the soul. But when the fledglings looked ahead, the landscape had completely changed. Skyscrapers lined the horizon. A big city lay in front of them.

*Man*, thought Vero. *Dreams are weird.*

The soul dropped into a busy street filled with passing cars, trucks, and pedestrians, and quickly disappeared into the crowded sidewalk. The angels landed on the curb, their eyes scanning for any sign of the soul.

Pax stood on his toes to see over the crowd. "How the heck does a dolphin flick somebody into the middle of rush-hour traffic?" he asked.

"Trust me," Greer said. "I've had weirder dreams. Once I dreamt that I was half ballerina and half police dog ..." Greer stopped, realizing that everyone was looking at her. "Never mind."

"Come on, let's find him," Kane said, putting the fort-i-fire back into his pocket.

The angels looked in every direction. Vero checked the windows of a passing bus. Greer and Ada flew above the crowd to get a bird's-eye view. Then the angels heard X yell. "The subway entrance!" They followed his pointing finger just in time to see the soul disappear underground down a narrow staircase.

The angels' wings disappeared as they struggled to make their way through the throng of people all pushing toward the entrance. As Vero and the others ran down the steps, they saw bars from the floor to the ceiling blocking the entrance to the platform. The only way through was a revolving metal turnstile that was also barred from floor to ceiling. The soul pushed through the turnstile and made its way over to the platform.

"Through the turnstile!" Greer yelled.

As Greer pushed through, the turnstile came to an abrupt stop, causing Greer to bang her head on its metal spokes. Inches from her face stood a donkey.

"Hello," the donkey said.

Greer screamed. The others slammed into her from behind, causing her to hit her head on the turnstile yet again.

"Would you dopes watch out?" Greer shouted, rubbing her head.

"Well, move it or we'll lose the soul!" Vero yelled.

"I can't!" Greer said as she looked down and saw the donkey's hoof wedged between the floor and the bottom spoke of the turnstile.

"Why not?" Vero asked.

"It's just too bizarre." Greer's voice quavered.

"What is?"

"Hello, Vero," the donkey brayed.

Vero's eyes went wide.

"Yeah, now you see," Greer nodded.

Ada peered over Greer's shoulder. "Greer, you've been through the unspeakables of the Leviathan. A talking donkey should be no big deal."

The donkey snorted. "Perhaps not a big deal, but I think I'm rather unique," it replied.

"Look, we're in a hurry so we need you to move your hoof," Kane told the donkey. "And everyone behind us also needs ..." Kane looked around. The crowd of people had disappeared. The subway station was suddenly deserted except for the soul waiting on the platform.

"Everybody's in such a hurry these days," the donkey hee-hawed. "Nobody takes the time to get to know one another."

"How did you know my name?" Vero asked.

"I know all the angels. I see them all."

"Look, move now or else we'll ..." Kane began.

"Beat me?"

"Well, um," Kane stammered. "I didn't exactly say that."

"But you want to. I know," the donkey said. "It's the curse of us donkeys. Our stubbornness brings out the worst in others. I endured many beatings from my master."

"Who was your master?" Pax asked, suspiciously.

"Balaam the sorcerer."

"Yeah, that's what I thought," Pax said, studying the donkey with keen interest.

"That train is coming any minute," X said. "Everyone push!"

The angels pushed against the turnstile with all their strength, but the donkey's hoof held firmly. They were no match for it.

"Man you're stubborn," X said looking the donkey squarely in the eyes.

"Please," Ada pleaded. "You have to let us through."

"Balaam did not heed my advice," the donkey replied. "And so you are the same. Everyone thinks I'm nothing but a dumb animal."

Despite the seriousness of the situation, Vero chuckled. Kane pulled the fort-i-fire from his pocket and pushed his way to the front. "Maybe I can throw it from here," he said.

Kane shoved his hand through the turnstile spokes and pulled his arm back, aiming at the soul whose back was turned to them.

"It won't work!" Ada said, grabbing Kane's shoulder. "You're too far away!"

"Guys, maybe we should listen to the donkey," Pax said. Balaam didn't and it almost got him killed."

"Okay, fine ... who is Balaam, Pax?" Kane asked. He turned his head toward the tunnel as the fledglings heard the train approaching in the distance.

"He was a sorcerer who went to curse the Israelites, but while the donkey was carrying him, an Angel of the Lord appeared to him three times to get him to stop. The donkey could see the angel and stopped, but Balaam just thought the donkey was being stubborn so he beat it three times—"

"Savagely," the donkey interrupted.

"Savagely," Pax added, eyeing the donkey. "Finally the angel showed himself to Balaam and gave the donkey the gift of language. And then Balaam realized that the donkey had only been trying to save his life."

The donkey gave the angels an I-told-you-so look.

Vero felt desperate. "Then let us through," he said. "We are angels sent here to help that soul. It may be a matter of life and death."

The donkey still did not move. "It might be, but it would be your life, not that soul's. You are all in that soul's dream, and a dreamer can't die in their own dream. But you are just visitors ... you could die in its dream, no problem."

The whoosh of the approaching train grew louder. Its headlights lit up the platform. The train pulled into sight and came to a stop. Panic came into Kane's eyes as the train's doors opened.

"Just let me through! I only need to get close enough!" Kane shook the turnstile as the soul floated onto the train. The moment the doors began to close, the platform erupted into a ball of light so intense, the angels had to shield their eyes—the light of a fort-i-fire! After the flash of light cleared, the angels glimpsed the train pull out of the station. Vero did a double take as he looked through the windows of the last car. *Were those hyenas looking back at him?*

"You missed it!" X shouted to Kane.

"Wasn't me," Kane said, and he turned his hand to the angels, exposing the fort-i-fire still in it.

The angels looked confused. Then Dumah walked along the platform toward them, carrying his scepter.

"Look," Ada nodded toward Dumah. "It was his fort-i-fire."

Kane turned on the donkey, "So you let him on the platform and not us?" he yelled.

"And how did that work out for him?" the donkey shot back.

Greer peered at Dumah through the metal bars. "You missed, didn't you?" she said to him.

He nodded.

"So now the second trial is over for you?"

Dumah nodded again.

"Sorry," Greer said.

Dumah tapped the bottom of his scepter to the ground and vanished.

"The competition just got a little less," Kane said.

Ada noticed the worried look on Vero's face. "What's wrong with you?"

"Did anyone else see hyenas in the last car?"

The donkey loudly brayed, startling the angels.

"What? What is it?" Vero asked.

The donkey shook his big head. "Oh, the hyenas are bad. That's why I had to stop you. They're bad, very bad."

X looked frightened. "Yeah, and now the soul's alone on that subway train with them!" He glanced down the tunnel. "You should have stopped the soul instead of us!"

"Now you're calling me stupid?"

"Yeah, I am," X said.

The donkey looked hurt. "I am so underappreciated." He moved his hoof from the turnstile. "Go ahead. Go where you want."

Kane glanced at the donkey and shoved his way onto the platform. "Hey, thanks for nothing, Eeyore."

The angels watched as the donkey turned and slowly walked down the platform with his tail swinging from side to side. Vero noticed Greer looked sad as she watched the donkey leave.

"What?" Vero asked.

Greer shook her head. "He's a strange creature, but I think he was trying to help us," she said.

Vero looked back at the donkey and shrugged. "I guess, but come on, we've gotta hurry and go after that train."

"Do you think it's safe?" Greer asked.

"Probably not, but we don't exactly have a choice."

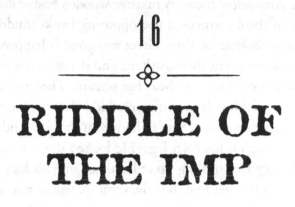

# 16

# RIDDLE OF
# THE IMP

Vero and the others flew down the long, winding subway
tunnel. Fortunately, overhead lights illuminated the train
tracks, so the angels had no problem navigating through them.

"Anybody see or hear the train up ahead?" Pax asked.

"Not me," X answered.

"Nope," Vero said.

"What if it just disappeared and we're chasing it for nothing?" Kane asked.

"We're going the right way," Greer said as she flew in
front of the others. "I still feel a connection with the soul.
And because this tunnel still exists, it means the soul is still
dreaming about it. We need to keep going."

As they continued to fly down the tunnel, the black stone
walls came to an abrupt end along with the train tracks. The
landscape changed, yet again. The fledglings saw and heard

a raging river below them. A massive wooden bridge directly in front of them connected the opposing banks. Suddenly, from the air in front of Vero, Greer was gone. It happened so fast that one moment she was there, and the next, she wasn't. There wasn't even time to hear her scream. Then to his left Vero saw something the size of a small kid clasped around X's legs. In a split second, X was pulled from the sky. And then Vero felt a tug on his own legs. He looked down to see an intensely ugly face smiling up at him, hugging his legs. Vero tried to kick himself free, but the creature would not let go. He pulled Vero to a patch of grass under the bridge and in a matter of seconds, tied his hands to a pillar. The creature instantly sprang back into the air. He could not fly, but he could jump amazing heights. Vero turned and saw Greer and X also sitting with their backs against the pillar, hands bound.

"What the heck was that?" Vero asked.

Before Greer could answer, the creature returned with Pax and tied him up with the others. Soon all the fledglings were sitting against the pillar with their hands tied behind their backs. The creature turned to his captives, and Vero finally got a good look at him. He was short—probably the height of a five-year-old—and stumpy but very thick and muscular. His nose hung like a half-filled water balloon. His ears were the size of saucers, and his lips drooped below his chin. His skin was of a greenish hue and hairy. And to make matters worse, he was humpbacked.

"That guy didn't get a break in the looks department," X said in a low voice to Greer.

"No one crosses my bridge for free!" the creature shouted over the noise of the roaring river. He turned and warmed his hands over a campfire.

"Sorry, we didn't know it was your bridge," Kane answered. "But we don't have to walk over it. We can just fly over it and not bother you."

The creature snarled at Kane. "The only way to the other side is over my bridge!"

Vero turned his head to X. "What the heck is it?" he asked in a low voice.

"Isn't it obvious?" X whispered. "A hideous creature living under a bridge? Didn't you ever read *The Three Billy Goats Gruff*?"

"A troll?"

In a flash, the troll's face was square with Vero's. Vero jerked his head back, hitting the pillar.

"A troll, you say?"

Vero winced as its horrible breath sprayed in his face. He caught the musk of fish and skunk.

"You think I'm a hideous, vile troll?"

Vero shrugged. "I don't know. But to be honest, you could really use a breath mint."

"I am no such thing. I am the most handsome of all beings," the creature snarled, revealing only four teeth — two on the bottom and two on the top. Each was sharpened to a point like an arrowhead and entirely black.

Vero raised his eyebrows to Greer. She looked equally confused.

"I am an imp."

Pax closed his eyes and concentrated. *"An imp is an evil spirit, a lesser-degree demon,"* Pax told Vero mind-to-mind. *"On earth, they are known as trolls. Obviously, he's never seen his reflection."*

"I am actually the most kindhearted, gentle creature

known, but my bridge is my only source of income. You must pay a price in order to cross it." He had to speak loudly in order to be heard above the river.

"What do you want?" Kane asked the imp.

"Our women?" Pax guessed.

Greer and Ada shot Pax the nastiest looks possible.

"Don't insult me with such an offer," the imp spat. "I have no need for such vile creatures."

Despite their grim situation, Vero chuckled.

Greer wriggled with fury in her binds. "We're vile? You need to take a look in a mirror, buddy," she said to the imp.

"Just tell us what you want," Kane said.

"Maybe I'm simply enjoying your company. Perhaps that's all I desire," the imp said. "And maybe if you got to know me, you'd see I'm actually a very good guy."

"This guy is totally whacked," Greer said under her breath.

"Perhaps if you could solve my riddle, I'd allow you to pass."

"You'll let us go?" Ada asked. "Free and clear?"

"Free and clear." The imp got in Ada's face. "But if you don't solve it, you will stay here chained to this pillar forever." He smiled maliciously.

The angels looked at one another, uncertain how to respond.

"How can we stay here forever if we're in someone's dream?" X muttered to the others.

Vero shrugged. Kane shook his head, also confused. The imp sat cross-legged on the dirt before them. He didn't wait for them to agree.

"A king had three sons. He was very old in age and

needed to choose his successor. He said to his sons, 'My children, I am old and will soon die. One of you must become the next king, only I don't know which son to choose.' So the king decided that before the sun set that day, each son would go out and prove himself deserving of the throne. Whoever proved himself most worthy would become king," the imp said.

A fly buzzed around his head. With lightning speed, the imp caught it in his hand and shoved the fly into his mouth. Ada looked like she was going to throw up. The imp belched then continued.

"The three sons set out into the kingdom that morning and returned to their father as the sun was setting. They lined up before their father's throne. 'And what have you done to prove yourself worthy of the throne?' the king asked his eldest son. The son opened a bag at his father's feet and thousands of gold coins spilled out, covering the king's shoes. 'I have spent the day collecting new taxes to honor you with,' the eldest son said.

"The king turned to the middle son. 'And what have you done to prove you deserve the crown?' The middle son laid three heads at his father's feet. 'I have spent the day finding traitors and beheading them to honor you with,' he answered."

The imp dug his hand into the dirt and pulled out a fat worm. He opened his mouth and dropped the worm into it and chewed. Ada turned her head and gagged as worm juice dripped down the imp's chin.

"'And what have you done to prove yourself worthy of the throne?' the king asked his youngest son. He approached his father, holding out his hands. They were empty. 'I am sorry, but I have nothing to honor you with. I set out this morning with my brothers, but as I walked down the lane, I came across an old woman who begged me to come to the fields, for her old husband had taken ill. When I arrived there, I found the old man lying in the field under the oppressive sun. He told me he had to reap the field and sell his crops at market before sunset or else the tax collectors would take his land. I carried the old man to his home, gave him water, then harvested his crops. I sold his crops at the market before the tax collector arrived.' The king eyed his son. 'I am sorry, Father, I am most ashamed and unworthy of the throne for I have nothing to honor you with.'"

The imp stood up.

"Now which son did the king choose?" He raised one eyebrow, chuckled, and walked a short distance away from the fledglings.

"Guys, it's definitely the last son," Vero said in a low voice to the others. "Do you agree?"

"I don't know, Vero," Pax said. "I'm not sure he sees things the way we do."

X tried unsuccessfully to scratch an itch on his head with his shoulder. "Well, the last son was motivated by goodness, and this imp claims he's actually a good guy," he said.

Greer huffed. "Yeah, most good guys tie their guests to pillars!"

"I agree with Vero," Ada said. "We're angels. I say we choose goodness. Pax?"

Pax shrugged, "I guess. We've got a one-third chance of being right."

"Greer?" Ada asked.

"Fine. But if I wind up stuck to this pillar for all eternity next to the bunch of you, I promise I will never shut up about it."

"Then we've decided," Kane said.

"We have our answer," Vero shouted to the imp.

"Yes?" the imp said, moving closer to them.

"Because he showed true kindness and compassion by putting the needs of others before his own," Vero said, "the youngest son demonstrated the true qualities of a good king. Therefore, the king chose the youngest son because, like you, he was a good guy." Vero held his breath as he waited for their captor's response.

The imp's gleeful expression dropped. Vero took this to be a sign that they had solved the riddle correctly and out-witted him. But then the imp began to smile. He fell to the ground, laughing.

"You're so stupid," he said between laughs. "You chose the goodie-two-shoes!"

Vero shrugged to the others. He could feel his heart beating faster.

The imp stopped laughing and got back on his feet. "You are wrong. The king chose his oldest son ... and his middle son. He decided they would rule together, as they had both honored their father properly."

Greer smacked her hand to her forehead, shaking her head in frustration.

"No, he didn't!" Ada said.

"Yes, he did. A good king desires only two things — wealth and the fear of his subjects. And as a matter-of-fact, the king threw the youngest son to the lions for being so worthless."

"Oh, that's ridiculous," X said.

*"I told you imps are evil spirits."* Pax spoke into Vero's mind. *"To him that conclusion would make perfect sense."*

The imp pulled a huge knife from a sheath tied around his hip. X and Ada pushed back against the pillar. Vero's eyes went wide. But then the imp stuck the blade tip under his fingernail and began to clean it. A wad of dirt came off onto the tip of the blade. He licked the tip clean. Ada's stomach heaved as he continued to clean the rest of his nails and eat the grime from underneath them.

"Relax, Ada," X said in a low voice as he watched her try to suppress her urge to vomit. "Close your eyes and think of something else."

Ada tightly shut her eyes. After a few moments, she appeared calmer.

"So we're stuck here?" Greer asked the others, the panic rising in her voice.

"Don't you live with any other imps?" Vero asked the imp as he continued to clean his nails.

"Don't be stupid. I would kill any imp that crossed my path!" he said, suddenly angry. "Death to them who would try to steal what rightly belongs to me!"

"You mean us?" Kane tentatively asked.

"Yes, you will make me six delicious meals."

Ada gasped and opened her eyes.

"Eat us!" Pax's voice cracked. "You're gonna eat us?"

Greer flashed the imp her most charming smile. "I thought you wanted us to stay with you forever?" she said, batting her eyelashes.

"After I eat all of you, then you will be a part of me forever."

Ada shrieked. "I wish whoever's dream we're in would wake up so we could get out of here!"

The imp walked over to his campfire. He picked up several branches from the ground and threw them onto the flames.

"Guys, we need to do something quick!" Pax said. "I think he's getting that fire ready for us!"

"Hey, excuse me!" Vero shouted.

The imp turned around.

"I was thinking that I'd like to be the first."

The other angels looked incredulously at Vero.

The imp walked over to Vero. "Oh, you do? Do you?"

"Yes, I'm so skinny, I'm not as good tasting as the others. So you might want to start with me first and work your way to more nicely marbled meat."

"Is that a fat joke?" Greer muttered to the others.

"You know, save the prime for last," Vero said.

The imp narrowed his eyes and stared at Vero for a moment, sizing him up, but then he chuckled. "Because I am such a nice guy, I'll grant your wish."

The imp began to cut the rope around Vero's wrists. He stopped for a moment. "If you try to escape," he whispered in Vero's ear, "I will slay all of them before your eyes."

Vero slowly nodded.

The imp sliced through the rope, and it fell to the ground. Vero stood, flexing his wrists and trying to get circulation back into them. He walked toward the swirling river.

"Hey, the fire's this way," the imp pointed.

"I know. I just thought you might want me to drink some water first. So I'll cook up plump and juicy."

"What the heck is he doing?" X whispered to Kane.

Kane shook his head. He had no idea. Vero crouched down before the river. He cupped his hands to scoop up the water. The imp kept a watchful eye on him. Vero turned his back to the imp, placed his right hand in the water, and mumbled the same passage Ada had recited moments before Kane had stuck his hand in the flames at C.A.N.D.L.E. *"When you pass through the waters, I will be with you . . ."* Just as the flames had become docile, the water around Vero's hand drew calm. A ripple expanded outward into a bigger circle, and the surface became as clear as a sheet of glass.

Suddenly Vero's body jerked. "Don't let him take me!" Vero yelled as something tugged on his arm from under the water.

"Who?" the imp shouted, alarmed.

"There's an imp in the water! He's trying to steal me!"

"Vero!" Kane yelled, thrashing against the ropes that bound him.

"Quick! He won't let go!"

The imp ran to the river's edge. Vero's body was now halfway into the river. The imp looked into the water. His eyes went wide when he saw another imp staring back at him.

"Don't you steal what is mine!" he shouted, pulling his knife from its sheath.

The imp waded into the river and stabbed blindly at the face of the other imp. Vero yanked his hand out of the water, and the currents once again grew violent. The waters swirled and knocked the imp off his feet. Yet, he was determined to kill the other imp. He stabbed wildly but, confused by the rushing waters, accidentally stabbed himself right in his thigh. He howled in pain as the water around him turned red with blood. He looked at Vero, realizing he'd been tricked. Vero waved to him as the waters swept him away.

"I'd clap for you, if I could," Greer smiled to Vero.

"Heck, I'd give you a standing ovation," X said.

Vero walked to the pillar and knelt to untie Greer.

"How'd you do that?" Ada asked.

"I remember when Kane stuck his hand in the fire at C.A.N.D.L.E., the flames around his hand became real calm and still. But the second he removed it, they started dancing again. That imp was so darn greedy, I knew if he saw his reflection, he'd be convinced it was another imp. I stilled the water long enough for him to be able to see his reflection, and then pulled it out once he was knee deep. Although, I didn't expect him to stab himself."

"That was a bonus," Greer said, standing up and stretching her arms. "That little creep was going to eat us."

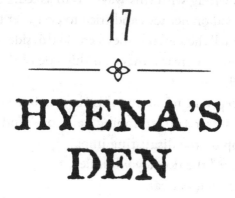

# 17

# HYENA'S
# DEN

"G reer, can you still feel the soul?" Kane asked as the
fledglings walked across the imp's bridge.

"Faintly."

"Anyone else getting anything?" Kane looked around at
the rest.

"No," Vero said.

X shook his head. "Me either."

"At least I've got something ..." Greer said.

Just as she was about to step off the bridge, Greer
screamed. The donkey had appeared out of nowhere again,
blocking their exit from the bridge.

"I wouldn't go that way," the donkey spoke.

Greer put her hand over her chest, trying to catch her
breath. "You gotta stop doing that, you freak!" she shouted.

"So unappreciative," the donkey said.

"What's wrong with this way?" Vero asked.

Greer stood on her toes and tried to peer over the donkey. "Yeah, I can tell the soul is somewhere on this side of the river."

"There is also great danger on this side of the river," the donkey said.

"You keep talking about this danger but won't tell us what it is!" Greer said, stomping her foot. "And thanks for the heads up on the disgusting imp!"

"Hee-haw!" the donkey whinnied.

Greer covered her ears.

"The imp is nothing compared to her," the donkey said. "Heed my words! Turn around!" The donkey vanished, and the fledglings looked at one another.

"This is truly a weird dream," X said.

Ada frowned. "Maybe we should listen to him and go back." She pulled Vero by the back of his shirt, stopping him from stepping off the bridge.

"We'll never win if we do because the soul is this way." Greer pointed to the land across the bridge.

"You sure you feel him?" Ada asked.

"One hundred percent. But I'm not convinced it's a him."

Ada thought for a moment then released Vero's shirt. They stepped off the bridge, but the moment their feet touched the ground, the landscape changed into a hallway lined with lockers on both walls and even on the ceiling.

"Whoa, how did this happen?" Kane asked.

"The soul is in here somewhere," Greer said. "But I can feel it's real confused."

"I've had this dream a bunch of times," X said, his eyes scanning the ceiling of lockers. "I can't remember which locker is mine."

"Me too." Ada grimaced. "And I have a test and need to get my pen out for it, but I can't remember the combination. It's a horrible nightmare." She shivered.

Greer gave her an annoyed look. Suddenly, the soul flashed around the corner.

"There it is!" Vero shouted, pointing to where the soul had just disappeared.

The angels ran down the hallway and turned the corner. The soul was frantically going from locker to locker, stopping momentarily in front of each one. Wherever the silvery being hovered, the locker handles rattled, as if an unseen hand were desperately pulling on each one, but none opened. Kane pulled the fort-i-fire from his pocket, but the soul took off down the long hallway once again.

"Don't let it get away!" X shouted.

The angels sprouted their wings and flew after it. The soul stopped and pulled on more locker doors, and Kane was able to get within a few yards of it. He paused his flight and took aim, but then a locker door opened, and just as he was about to throw the fort-i-fire, the soul slipped inside. The door slammed shut behind it. Kane lowered his arm.

"Quick! After him!" Vero shouted.

Kane hesitated, his eyes scanning the lockers. "Which one was it?" he asked in frustration.

"Definitely this one," Greer said as she flew past Kane. She tugged on the locker handle. "See? It's unlocked."

Then Greer screamed as the door swung open and the donkey poked his head out into the hallway.

"Nope, nope, not this way," the donkey said.

Greer slammed the door shut. "That stinkin' donkey is gonna kill me," she said, trying to catch her breath. From inside the locker, the donkey's voice was heard echoing, "So unappreciated!"

"Is it the wrong door?" Vero asked.

Greer stared at it and scratched her head. "I don't think so. It feels like the right one."

"Yeah, I'm pretty sure that's the door the soul went through." X nodded.

Pax tried to open the locker doors around it. None would open. He shrugged. "It's our only option."

Vero looked around at the others. "Okay," he said at last and opened the locker door.

The donkey was no longer inside. Greer stuck in her head. It was pitch dark. "Guess I'm going first," she said to the others, her voice echoing in the narrow metal space.

Greer stepped inside the locker and squeezed her body through. One by one, the others followed her. The back wall of the locker was nonexistent. The fledglings walked straight through, and Vero felt sandy ground beneath his feet. A hot, arid wind blew in his face. After a moment, a soft light began to grow, and he could see the land before him. It was barren, cast in shadows. He saw rolling brown hills dotted with sparse shrubs, the desolate horizon broken only by a few stone structures. Then Vero glimpsed a silvery light. It dove behind the cluster of stones.

"The soul just went behind those rocks!" Vero said, pointing.

Greer looked confused. "No, I'm not feeling it there," she said, shaking her head.

"I saw it too!" Kane said as his wings sprouted. "Let's go!"

"No, I'm telling you, that wasn't our soul!" Greer shouted.

Kane didn't listen to her. He took off in the air and headed for the rocks.

"Stop him!" Greer shouted as her wings shot out.

The others hesitated as they watched Greer fly after Kane. The silvery light had certainly looked like the soul, but why was Greer so certain that it wasn't? Vero threw his hands in the air. "Let's go."

Vero, X, Ada, and Pax chased after them. Kane hovered over the stone structure. He pulled the fort-i-fire from his pocket when Greer grabbed his wrist.

"Get off!" Kane yelled. The light moved from around the rocks into the open as Kane struggled against Greer. "It's a perfect shot!" he yelled. "Let go!"

But Greer wouldn't release his wrist. She twisted his arm behind his back. "It's too easy!" she yelled. "Don't you see that? He *wants* you to throw it at him!"

Kane stopped struggling. "What do you mean?"

"My best guess is that it's Melchor," Greer panted. "He can appear as light, the same as the soul."

"I think she's right," Ada told Kane.

Greer released Kane's arm. "Of course I'm right because I feel absolutely no connection to whatever that light is."

"It does resemble Melchor," Vero said.

The light figure extinguished itself and vanished.

Kane narrowed his eyes and jerked away from Greer. "That guy is getting on my nerves!"

Vero had to agree. "Yeah, he does have a hugely unfair advantage."

"He was trying to trick us into losing," Kane said. He paused and turned around to look at Greer. "Thanks, Greer, for stopping me."

"Anytime," she smirked.

Kane examined the horizon. "Which way now?"

"Toward those shadow lands over there," Greer nodded.

Vero got a sick feeling in his stomach as he looked at the darkened wasteland.

The fledglings flew over the barren lands with Greer leading them. Vero saw a circular depression about the size of a big pond below. Greer began to descend. "Land next to the big crater," she told the others.

The fledglings landed on the rocky ground. Greer scanned the area. "It's here somewhere."

With each step on the sandy ground, the fledglings' feet kicked up more and more dust. Vero looked down at his white sneakers, which were now brown.

"Sure this is the right way?" Kane asked Greer.

"Yes," she said, forging ahead.

"I wish it weren't," Pax said, his eyes nervously darting around. "I'd like to get out of here."

"There," Greer said in a voice barely louder than a whisper.

The others followed her gaze to a small opening in a hill. There was an archway dug out of the earth, though not tall enough for the angels to walk through; they would have to stoop to get inside.

"Let's go," Kane said.

As the angels walked toward the hill, a low demonic growl stopped them dead in their tracks. Their heads whipped around, looking for the source. Ada stepped behind Vero.

"What was that?" X asked, his voice squeaky with fear.

"Best case scenario . . . a bullfrog with a sore throat?" Pax said.

Another growling sound echoed over the barren land, sending a shiver up Vero's spine. Many more snarling sounds soon joined in. The angels stepped closer to one another. Then the sounds turned into loud, high-pitched cackling noises—almost like hysterical laughter. Ada grabbed the back of Vero's shirt again as they saw the source of the crazed laughter walking toward them.

"Worst case scenario . . . a pack of hyenas," Pax said, his face white.

"Why can't this soul just dream about pink ponies and rainbows?" Vero asked.

Four hyenas began to circle the angels as they huddled together. Their heads were broad, with dark eyes and large rounded ears, and they had golden-yellow coats speckled with black spots. But it was their legs that fascinated Vero most. Their front legs were much longer than the back legs, and this made their gait most unusual—it looked as if the hyenas were constantly walking uphill as they circled them. Vero noticed how the hyenas' cackling unnerved Ada. Her hands began to shake and she pulled harder at his shirt.

"They're really, really, really, really, creepy," Ada said.

The hyenas' circle tightened around the angels. Beads of sweat dripped down Ada's face.

"Fly!" Greer shouted.

The angels shot into the air. But Vero's heart sank when he heard X screaming below him. He looked down and saw two hyenas were playing tug-of-war with X's left wing.

"X! Hold on!" Vero yelled.

Vero rocketed to the ground and landed right behind

the hyenas. He scoured the desert floor and pulled a decent-sized club-shaped root ball from a dead tree stump — the only weapon he could find. One of the other hyenas turned its attention to Vero and sprung at him. Vero somersaulted into the air over it and hovered over X. He swung wildly at the two hyenas as they continued to pull on X's wing. Kane and Greer flew down and dive-bombed the hyenas, getting close enough to kick at their faces and retreat. Vero hit a hyena in the head, stunning it. It released its grip on X's wing.

"Yeah, who's laughing now, you stupid hyena!" Kane shouted as he kicked the other hyena attacking X on top of its head. But the hyena refused to loosen its grip on X's wing.

Ada and Pax had flown down, grabbed some stones, and shot back into the air, pelting the other two hyenas to keep them away from X. "Guys, it's killing me!" X shouted, trying to push away the hyena that still gripped his wing, his face contorted in pain.

Greer made a daring dive at the beast. "You get off my friend!" she shouted as she landed a roundhouse punch right to the hyena's gut with everything she had in her fly-by. Her eyes went wide as the pain in her wrist registered, but below her, she heard the hyena's laughter turn to gut-punched agony. As Vero continued to swing at the other hyena, it caught the club in its mouth and clamped down on it, snapping it in half. The hyena then turned its attention back to X who still lay helplessly on the ground. The hyena bit X's arm. He screamed in pain as the two hyenas dragged him across the sand toward the opening in the hill.

"Get them!" Greer shouted.

"With what?" Vero yelled. "I need a sword!"

Ada threw her last stone and missed. Pax flew to the ground and quickly picked up a few more rocks. But as he flew back into the air, a hyena caught his foot in its mouth, slamming him to the sand. His glasses flew off his face upon impact. "Help!" Pax screamed.

The others watched in horror as Pax tried to kick the hyena's head from his foot. But the hyena was too powerful. It also began to drag Pax toward the den in the hill. As the hyena moved under him, and Vero saw the fear in Pax's face, a steely resolve came over him. He flew at the hyena, grabbed it by its neck, and yanked. Momentarily free, Pax quickly flew away. The hyena bucked from Vero's grasp, knocking him from the air, and leapt on Vero's chest. Its front paws pushed deep into Vero, ripping his T-shirt. Vero struggled underneath its weight, but he could not get up. As the hyena lunged for Vero's jugular, Vero felt the weight of the hyena lift off him. Out of the corner of his eye, Ariel's massive paw swiped the hyena, knocking it to the ground. It lay unmoving. Vero sat up and saw four bloody scratch marks across the hyena's body.

Without hesitation, Ariel turned and bounded after the other two hyenas where they were still pulling X toward the den. She pounced on them, and the startled hyenas released X and retreated. X got to his feet, holding his injured arm as Ariel continued to attack the snarling hyenas.

After a few moments' time, both of X's hyenas lay motionless on the ground. Ariel turned to the fledglings.

"Ariel, behind you!" Ada shouted.

The remaining hyena jumped on Ariel's back and sunk its teeth into her spine. She reared up and flicked it off her back, slamming it against a rock with such force, it slumped to the ground. Looking totally unfazed, Ariel walked over to X and placed her paws on his broken wing and bleeding arm. His wounds began to heal themselves.

"Thank you," X said breathlessly. "You're an amazing fighter."

"Everybody knows lions and hyenas are natural enemies," Ariel replied.

Vero looked down and saw Pax's glasses lying on the ground. "Here," he said to Pax as he handed him the glasses.

"Thanks," Pax said.

"The soul is in the hyenas' den," Greer said confidently.

Kane looked at the den and smiled at the others. "Let's win this thing," he said as he pulled out his fort-i-fire.

X stepped in front of him, blocking his way. "Ariel gets the first throw," X said. "She saved us. She deserves it."

"Saved you and Vero, not me," Kane said. He walked around X.

X grabbed Kane's shoulder and spun him around. "We would have never gotten past the hyenas without Ariel."

Kane looked to his fellow fledglings. No one spoke, but it was clear they all agreed with X. Kane held X's gaze for a moment then put the fort-i-fire back into his pocket. "Go," he said to Ariel. "You take the first shot."

Ariel bowed her head to him then headed to the den. The others all followed her, except for Kane. Ada walked back to him. "You did the right thing," she said to him.

"Maybe, but I can't bear to watch someone else win."

The others walked over to the entrance in the hill. But rather than excitement, with each step, they all felt a sense of dread.

"I have a bad feeling about this," Pax said.

"Me too," X said. "Like there's something really evil in that den."

"The soul's in there too," Greer said. "I feel it."

They stood before the opening. Vero, Greer, and Ariel stooped over to peer inside. They saw the soul right away. It looked dim and dormant, hugged by a black carpet.

Greer nodded. "That's it," she whispered.

As they observed the soul, they noticed that the black carpet seemed to be gently stroking and caressing its head, almost as if it were comforting the soul.

"That's really weird," Vero whispered, not wanting to disturb the soul.

"What hasn't been weird about this dream?" Greer murmured back.

Vero nodded to Ariel. "Now's your best chance."

Ariel turned her paw upward and a fort-i-fire materialized inside it. But as she drew her paw back, the end of the blanket shot toward the angels with lightning speed and wrapped itself around her paw. The fort-i-fire fell to the ground and exploded like a bomb.

Vero gasped. "It's that thing that tried to grab us with the unicorn!" he shouted.

Just as quickly as it coiled itself, the blanket unwound from around Ariel's paw and went back to stroking the soul's head. Vero ran from the den, and Greer, X, and Ariel followed.

"What happened?" Ada asked.

"That hair rope creature stopped Ariel from throwing it," Vero said, trying to catch his breath. "The fort-i-fire fell to the ground."

A smile formed at the corners of Kane's lips, "She missed?"

"Forget the Trials," Vero said angrily. "We need to get out of here!"

A ball of light appeared outside the opening. It was a fort-i-fire. Kane's mouth dropped.

"It's Melchor!" Kane yelled as he pulled the fort-i-fire from his pants' pocket. "He's gonna throw it!"

Melchor's fort-i-fire drew back for the throw.

"No!" Kane yelled, and he threw his fort-i-fire straight toward Melchor's. A loud bang rang out as the two fort-i-fires collided in midair and exploded like fireworks. The sleeping soul woke up with a start, and the angels were gone.

# 18

❖

# MICHAEL

The fledglings sat up and found themselves on the amphitheater's stage before an audience of angels. Ariel, Dumah, and the silhouette that was Melchor also sat on the stage. Gabriel towered over them. Her expression told Vero that she was not happy.

"All of you have failed your second trial," she said sternly. "But the biggest loser is the soul who so desperately needed the strength of the fort-i-fire and now will not receive it."

Vero lowered his head.

"You were so caught up in the competition you lost sight of what was most important." Gabriel's eyes rested on Kane. "Injuring humans is not what angels are about."

Kane opened his mouth to protest, but Greer kicked his leg and shook her head. Kane shut his mouth.

"There is to be one final trial, and I hope during it, you remember who you are," Gabriel said, her voice crystal clear, yet not loud. "The second trial is now completed."

Gabriel walked off the stage. Vero stood up and chased after her. "Gabriel!"

Gabriel stopped and turned around.

"This soul, the one we failed," Vero said. "What will happen to him now?"

"This soul, as we told you, is under great spiritual attack," Gabriel said. "The attacks will intensify, and the soul may not be able to withstand them."

"Will you send other angels to complete what we couldn't?"

"Only if God wills it."

✦

Vero lay on his bedroom floor clutching the phone receiver in his hand. He heard a recording coming through the line. "Does your house need repairs? If so, we'll be in your neighborhood ..." Vero hit the "off" button. He yawned as he stood and looked at his alarm clock. It was two minutes to midnight, and he still had school tomorrow. Vero looked down at his feet—his new sneakers were now all muddy. Somehow Uriel had gotten his sneakers back. He crawled into his bed and fell into a deep sleep.

The next thing Vero became aware of was a pair of hands was on his shoulder, shaking him awake. He rolled over and saw his mother sitting on the edge of his bed, smiling down at him.

"Get up, Vero," Nora said. "This is the second time I've been in here. Why are you so tired?"

*Sorry, Mom. Rough night battling an imp, a pack of hyenas ...* Vero thought.

Nora nudged Vero again. As she brushed his hair away from his forehead and looked lovingly at him, a real sadness came over Vero, remembering the events of the previous evening. He sat up. "Mom, I'm sorry about your party. We should have put more effort into it because you really do everything for us. I feel like such a jerk."

"Thank you," she said, smiling at him. "That really means a lot."

"And even though I don't always act like it, I thank God you were the one who found me in the hospital that night."

Tears came to Nora's eyes. She hugged Vero tightly. "Now that was the greatest present you could have ever given me."

The telephone rang. Vero nervously glanced at it, afraid to pick it up, afraid to get electrocuted once again. Nora let go of Vero and answered the phone. "Hello?"

Vero breathed a sigh of relief.

"Yes, he's right here," Nora said into the phone, then cupped the mouthpiece. "It's a girl ... Ada?"

Vero was surprised, not because Ada had his number — they had spoken on the phone in the past — but rather, what was so urgent? Didn't he just leave her?

Nora handed the phone to Vero then stood to leave. "I'll give you your privacy," she smiled, before shutting the door behind her.

"Ada, what's wrong?" Vero spoke quietly into the phone.

"I was hoping you knew something?" she said.

"No, I got back and went straight to bed."

"I lingered at little bit, and I overheard Uriel and the others talking about the hair monster. That's twice it's attacked us. They were really upset."

"What did they say about it?"

"I couldn't make out much, but they're worried. Uriel said it was time for Michael. That has to be Michael the archangel. It has to be serious when they're talking about bringing in the most powerful angel."

Vero was the only one of the fledglings who had ever met Michael. The mightiest of God's warriors had rescued him from Abaddon. Vero knew firsthand how formidable Michael could be.

"What was that creature? Did they say?" Vero asked.

"No."

"I guess we'll just have to wait until they call us back," Vero said.

"Ada, get your butt in the car!" a boy's voice yelled through the phone. "Dad's driving us to school early!"

"I'm on the phone!" Ada shouted so loudly that Vero had to hold the phone away from his ear.

Vero knew Ada had four brothers. He had met them at her Bat Mitzvah. It seemed like their favorite pastime was tormenting her.

"Now!" the boy shouted.

"All right, shut up!" Ada screamed then spoke into the phone. "Those hyenas were nothing compared to four brothers."

Vero chuckled.

"Bye, Vero. Call me if you find out anything." Ada hung up.

Dressed for school, Vero sat at the kitchen table eating a plate of scrambled eggs as Mom diced up a banana, making a fruit salad. Dad drank a cup of coffee while reading the newspaper. Vero sniffed—something was burning! He looked over and saw smoke coming out of the toaster. He quickly picked up a butter knife from the table and ran to the toaster.

"No! Don't —!" Nora screamed as Vero stuck the knife into the toaster, attempting to get the burning slice of toast.

For the second time in twelve hours, his hair shot straight up as electric current tore through him. Vero fell to the kitchen floor, still clutching the knife.

The gym at C.A.N.D.L.E. didn't look all that much different from Vero's school gym. It was a huge empty space with racks of swords lining the walls. The only difference was the floor. It was bouncy, like a trampoline. Vero saw the other fledglings bouncing over to him.

"Long time no talk," Ada smiled to Vero.

"I don't think we've ever been called back so fast," Vero said.

Pax nodded. "Something's up."

The double doors to the gym blew open, and a rush of wind accompanied by an intensely bright light nearly knocked over the fledglings. The wind calmed a moment later, and the light vanished. Vero smiled as an enormous angel stood over them. It was Michael the archangel. At ten feet tall and muscular with striking, rugged features, Michael looked completely invincible. The angels cowered in his presence, except for Vero. Despite the intimidating presence, he knew Michael to be kind and compassionate.

"Hello, Vero."

"Hello, Michael," Vero said, looking into his riveting violet eyes.

"Aren't you going to introduce me to your classmates?" Michael asked Vero.

"Oh, sorry," Vero said. "Everybody, this is Michael ... the archangel."

The fledglings looked at him in awe. Even the normally nonplussed Greer stared at Michael, her mouth half-agape. It turned out that Vero didn't need to bother with names. Michael nodded to each of the other fledglings as he went down the line.

"Greer, nice roundhouse on that hyena."

Greer blushed and bit her nail.

"Pax, it was good thinking under pressure with the stones, but we'll need to work on your aim. You should have hit a few hyenas."

Pax blushed and nodded his head.

"Ada, your bravery, intelligence, and knowledge of the Torah are equally impressive. X, you endured great pain from the hyenas. Don't let that go to waste. Offer it up, and pray that you learn from that experience to become a fierce warrior." Michael paused for a moment as he continued to eye X.

X nodded. Michael turned to Vero.

"Vero, your courage and defense of X was admirable ... but a root ball?" he teased. He turned up Vero's hand. "And now this? A butter knife?" Vero's face flushed. He quickly stashed the knife in his back pocket and shrugged.

Michael walked over to Kane and stood before him. He placed his hand on Kane's shoulder. "Your blessings and talents are great. But you need to concentrate on things that matter most, instead of your own personal gains."

Kane lowered his eyes in shame. "I'm sorry. I shouldn't have wasted the fort-i-fire. I wasn't thinking."

"Remember that for the final trial."

Kane nodded.

"I know you're wondering why you were called back so quickly," Michael said. "You are here for sword training."

Kane smiled ear to ear.

"It can no longer wait. Had Ariel not been there, none of you would have survived the hyenas."

"I almost wound up in the choir of angels," X said.

"That's not the worst thing that can happen to you," Michael said seriously as he picked up a sword from the rack and tossed it to X. "All of you, get a sword."

The others pulled swords from the rack.

"The enemy is very strong so you must be stronger," Michael said. "This is a crucial time, and you all must be ready." Michael flicked the tip of the sword to Ada's face. Caught off guard, she stepped back and fell on the trampoline floor.

"Ada, a warrior steps back for no one," Michael sternly said. "Once you show fear, your opponent has the advantage." Ada nodded. Michael held his hand to her, and pulled her to her feet.

Michael thrust his sword at X who quickly deflected the blow with his blade. Michael swiped at him a second time, and X managed to repel that one, too. But when Michael came at him a third time, a door blew shut, X turned his head to the sound, and Michael's sword tip rested on his neck. X gulped.

"Never let anything distract you, X! Be it a closing door, hyenas, or worse." Michael lowered his sword.

Michael then held up his sword to Kane, and Kane raised his own to meet it. Their swords crossed to form an X before they each stepped back to spar. Kane was impressive and quick on his feet, meeting every one of Michael's thrusts. Vero felt a pang of jealousy as he watched Kane's prowess. As Michael thrust forward, Kane's wings shot out, and he rolled into the air, landing on his feet behind Michael with his sword drawn. Michael spun around swiftly and smiled.

"Well done, Kane," Michael said as he lowered his sword.

"Thank you," Kane said. "But these are only training swords. When Vero fought the maltures, he grew one out of his hand ..."

"Yes, at the very moment his ward on earth had prayed, God granted his prayer."

"So we can only get our swords when someone prays for it?"

"No, each of you has the power to will it, just as you will your wings to sprout. With practice, the ability will come."

"But how did Vero do it?" Greer asked.

"When the maltures attacked Vero, he was so desperate for a weapon. His desire along with his ward's prayer made the sword a reality."

"So there's a beast in here," Greer said as she looked at her palm, "just waiting to get out?"

Michael nodded.

"Would have been nice to know when foster dad number five locked me in a closet for days!" Greer said.

"We are never to use our swords against humans,"

Michael said sternly. "God will handle the humans in His own way. Only He knows their hearts."

"Sorry," Greer said, lowering her head.

Michael tipped her chin up. "To grow your sword, you need to clear your mind of other thoughts, visualize it, and it will happen." Michael turned to the others. "Try it."

The fledglings closed their eyes. Each tried to concentrate as hard as he or she could. But nothing happened.

"Envision yourself as a strong warrior, feel God's strength inside of each and every one of you," Michael said in a coaxing voice. "Picture yourself strong against the enemy."

Suddenly, an image of the old hag came into Vero's mind and stared him straight in the eyes. Although her dark hair covered most of her face, Vero looked right back into the black, hollow eyes. She gave him a smile, keeping her lips tightly pursed together. There was something truly horrible about the vision, and it made Vero terribly uneasy. And then she let out a loud hiss, exposing a mouth full of rotten fangs and a six-inch forked tongue. At that very moment, a sword sprung forth from Vero's hand with a sound like the ring of a sword being pulled from its sheath. At the sound of the sword, the hag's image instantly vanished from Vero's mind, and he opened his eyes. Just as quickly as it had appeared, his sword disappeared back into Vero's palm. He stumbled backward several paces until his back hit the wall, and he slid to the trampoline floor. Michael walked over to Vero as the others gathered around.

"Guess you won't be winding up in the choir of angels during these Trials," X joked.

"You think that's the worst thing that can happen during

the Angel Trials?" Michael said again, noting the fear in Vero's eyes.

"Well, yeah … isn't it?" X said.

"No, dying means nothing to an angel. Dying does not separate us from God," Michael explained. "Evil separates us from God … forever." Michael caught the angels' confused looks. "The Angel Trials are not just a game. Do you know the history of the games? Of the very first one?"

Vero shook his head. The others looked to Michael to explain.

"The original Trial took place in heaven, and only angels from two spheres, not three, competed. One from the first, and one from the third. Myself and … Lucifer."

Vero's eyes went wide.

"He was far superior to me, for he was an arch cherub of exquisite beauty, and his wisdom had no comparison. Anointed above all angels. He defeated me in every challenge until the very final one, a test that God had allowed. He had shown us His newest creation — man."

Ada gasped, twisting her finger through her long curls.

"Man is a much more complex being than angels. He has dual natures, both physical body and spiritual soul."

"But I thought angels were higher on the totem pole, being pure spirit," Vero said. "At least that's what I learned in Sunday school."

"Me too," Greer said. "But then again, if angels are higher, why are we training to guard humans? Maybe we've been wrong all along."

There was a moment of silence in the gym as the angels considered this novel idea.

"And God asked that for our final challenge, we pledge

our love and protection of man always," Michael paused, letting the words sink in for the fledglings. "I did so willingly. Lucifer would not do it. He became jealous of God's new creation. He feared God loved man more than He loved him, that he was being replaced. His pride was wounded. He raised his sword and swung at man to slice him in two. At that moment, a newfound strength coursed through me, and I met his sword with my sword, sparing man. Lines were drawn that day in the heavens, as one-third of the angels fought on Lucifer's side. During the battle, as our blades crossed and pressed against one another, I stood eye to eye with Lucifer. I watched as his effervescent violet eyes turned red with hatred. His beautiful face turned gruesome as the rest of him transformed into a diabolical monster. The light that had once shown through him was replaced with darkness. Lucifer spat in my face, vowing one day he would exalt himself higher than God and destroy man through sin. I shoved him, and he fell from heaven like lightning, taking his followers with him. After the battle, God created the Ether. A barrier to heaven, so Lucifer could never have access. And our battleground to fight him and his demons."

The angels were silent, trying to comprehend the story.

"God no longer tests me. However, for you fledglings, He still allows you to be tested, until the day you chose your destiny. So be very careful. God allows evil in the Trials. It serves a purpose and going to the choir of angels is nothing compared to falling victim to the evil forces out there."

A tear ran down Ada's face.

"I've seen the evil," Vero said, his fear evident in his voice. "She's the long-haired creature."

Michael nodded. "Which is why you need to learn how to control your sword."

"Who is she?" Vero asked Michael.

Michael paused as he studied Vero for a moment.

"Lilith."

# 19

## PEP RALLY

"D on't ever do that!" Mom shouted as Vero held a butter knife over the toaster.

Vero jerked his hand away.

"Unplug it first," Mom said, pulling the plug out of the outlet and breathing a sigh of relief. "You'll get electrocuted."

Vero looked around. He was back in his kitchen — his sword training obviously over.

"Sit down and finish your eggs," Dad said, lowering his newspaper from his face.

But Vero had Lilith on the brain.

"I'm full," Vero said. "I just remembered, I need to check something on my computer!" He dashed from the kitchen to his bedroom and shut the door. Vero turned on his laptop. He had to know who Lilith was. He typed her name into the search bar and began to read. There was a lot more information than he had expected.

Lilith was the wilderness demon who was shunned by the prophet Isaiah, but in later translations was referred to as the 'screech owl.' It was believed she was the mystery woman of Proverbs 2:18–19: "Surely her house leads down to death and her paths to the spirits of the dead. None who go to her return or attain the paths of life." She was also mentioned in the Dead Sea Scrolls. Vero read that Lilith was the 'night hag' who snatched souls, and she especially loved to possess women through mirrors. Then Vero gasped when he read, "she has enchanted hair, resembling a serpent."

"Vero, come finish your eggs!" Dad yelled.

Vero closed his laptop and walked to the kitchen. He sat down to his plate of now cold, scrambled eggs. He poked at the eggs with his fork, distracted by his thoughts of Lilith.

"Aren't you going to have some breakfast?" Dennis asked Clover as she rushed into the kitchen wearing a purple bike helmet.

Vero looked up from his plate of scrambled eggs. Mom put a glass of orange juice down on the table.

"It's getting late, so hurry and sit down," Nora said.

"Nope, gotta go!" Clover said as she picked up her backpack and slung it over her shoulder. "Kira's out front."

"Kira? Who's Kira? Did you know about this?" Dennis asked Nora.

"Relax, you met Kira at the mall, remember?" Clover said. "We're riding our bikes to school today." She grabbed the glass of orange juice and downed it. "Had my breakfast." Clover ran out of the kitchen.

"Clover!" Dad yelled, but she was already out the front door.

Vero watched through the window as Clover got on her

bike and pedaled off with Kira. When Vero turned back to his parents, he noticed their worried looks.

"At least she's wearing a helmet," Vero said, hoping it would comfort them some.

"We need to come down harder on her," Dennis told Nora. "She's out of control."

"She's not out of control yet," Nora said hesitantly, "but I agree we need to do something."

"Nora, you're being naïve here," said Dennis. "She's rude and inconsiderate, and I'm sick of it. She behaved like a little brat at your birthday last night!"

"What do you want me to do about it?" Nora raised her voice.

Vero hated when his parents fought. It happened rarely, so that when they did, it was all the more upsetting.

"I want you to stop putting on a hurt face every time she's rude in the hopes that she'll feel bad and come around. I want you to punish her!"

The doorbell rang. Vero jumped up from the table, happy for the excuse to get away. He opened the front door and saw Vicki standing there.

"Hey, Vero. Is Clover ready?" Vicki asked.

Vero looked over her shoulder and saw Vicki's older sister Molly waiting in the car. Dennis and Nora walked over and stood behind Vero.

"Clover already left with Kira." Vero shrugged.

"Oh," Vicki said, crestfallen.

Dennis shook his head at Nora. "Looks like her rudeness isn't just directed toward us."

"I'm sorry, Vicki," Nora said. "She must have forgotten to call and let you know."

"If it's any consolation, she forgot to let us know too!" Dennis's voice rose and his nostrils flared angrily.

"That's okay. I'll just see her in class anyway," Vicki said, forcing a smile. "You want a ride, Vero?"

"Sure." Vero picked up his backpack and walked out with Vicki. He glanced over his shoulder and saw the worried looks on his father and his mother.

⚜

"Is Clover mad at me?" Vicki asked Vero as they walked up the school steps. "Did she tell you anything?"

"No," Vero answered. "She's just not herself lately."

Vero couldn't help but feel partly responsible for Clover's behavior. He thought she was most likely rebelling because of him. She was freaked out about him being an angel. He knew she was having a hard time accepting his inevitable fate.

"Ever since Kira came to this school, she only hangs out with her," Vicki said. "It's like I don't even exist anymore."

"Well, it's not only you. She's been that way with me and my parents too."

"And that's supposed to make me feel better?"

Vero shrugged. Vicki gave him a peck on the cheek and walked into the school.

"You animal," a boy's voice said, admiringly. Vero looked over his shoulder and saw Tack racing up the steps.

"Not what you think," Vero quickly replied.

"Yeah, I figured," Tack said. "But I thought I'd try anyway. Hey, you ready for today?"

"What's today?"

"The pep rally. How could you forget?" Tack asked.

It had completely slipped Vero's mind. With everything that had been going on in the Ether, it was easy to forget all that was going on down on earth. And maybe subconsciously, Vero *wanted* to forget because Coach Cindy was forcing them to dress up in the hot, humiliating mascot costumes. He was dreading it.

"Wishful thinking," Vero said. "I was hoping they'd cancel it."

"You're nuts. It'll be a blast. We're gonna whip up the crowd."

Vero saw Davina heading toward them. Tack elbowed Vero. "Here's your chance," he said. "I hear she's done with Danny."

Vero stopped walking and looked at Tack. "Over the whole Kira thing in the library?"

"Yeah, but there was also something he posted online."

"What?"

"I dunno," Tack said.

"Hi, Vero," Davina said as she walked up beside him. "Can't wait to see what you guys have planned for today."

Tack elbowed Vero, "See?"

"Oh, thanks," Vero said.

"You too, Tack," Davina said as she walked ahead. "I just hope they don't cancel the rally."

Vero's eyes went wide with hope. "Cancel it?"

"There's still no water in the gym." Davina gestured behind her.

Vero looked over her shoulder and saw two plumbing trucks parked on the school property. A manhole cover sat on the blacktop as several plumbers worked on the main waterline.

"It's been a couple of days now," Davina said.

"And everyone reeks after gym class," Tack said.

"I wonder why they can't fix it," Vero pondered.

"Probably because they're looking in the wrong place down there," Tack said.

"How would you know?"

"Don't know. Just a feeling," Tack answered. A troubled look came over him as he continued to stare at the plumbers.

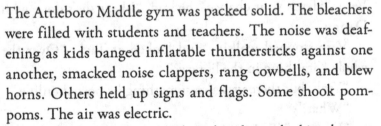

The Attleboro Middle gym was packed solid. The bleachers were filled with students and teachers. The noise was deafening as kids banged inflatable thundersticks against one another, smacked noise clappers, rang cowbells, and blew horns. Others held up signs and flags. Some shook pompoms. The air was electric.

A small but mighty marching band marched in place on the gym floor playing snare drums, bass drums, tubas, and trumpets. Coach Randy, wearing his ball cap, stood on the gym floor. He waved his hands, trying to quiet the crowd.

"Hold up! Everyone quiet down!" he shouted into a mic. It didn't work, so he put his index fingers in his mouth and loudly whistled. The marching band stopped playing. Gradually, the crowd grew silent.

"I love the enthusiasm," Coach Randy said. "We are ..."

"Attleboro Middle!" the crowd shouted back.

"We are ..." Coach Randy shouted.

"Attleboro Middle!"

Coach Randy gestured to the marching band. They began playing the "Chicken Dance" song as two ridiculous costumed chickens ran across the gym floor. The crowd got to its feet.

Vero had a hard time looking out through the costume's beak, but he glimpsed Tack in front of him dressed in a matching costume. They were covered with bright yellow feathers with a red wattle and red corn on their heads. Each had huge blue eyes and a large beak. It was a most unfortunate mascot—the fighting chickens. A big poultry farmer donated all the land for the school years ago, and, as a requirement, he wanted the school to name its team "The Fighting Chickens." Apparently, he had a cruel sense of humor.

As the music grew louder, Tack and Vero began to do the Chicken Dance to entertain the crowd. They flapped their wings and wiggled their tail feathers, and the crowd responded in kind. Even Coach Randy and Coach Cindy joined in the dance, especially the shaking of the tail feathers part. And when Vero and Tack stood up and clapped their hands four times, the noise in the gym was almost deafening as everyone joined them.

After repeating this part of the dance several times, Vero and Tack were supposed to link elbows and turn around in a circle for the grand finale. The crowd always went wild at this part. But when Vero turned to link elbows with Tack, he nearly stumbled. Tack was not there. Vero searched through the eyeholes in the beak for him. It was difficult with limited vision, but then he spotted him. Tack was standing in the middle of the marching band, staring up at the ceiling. Vero wondered if Tack had planned some gag that he wasn't in on. As the crowd continued to dance, Vero walked over to Tack.

He ruffled a few feathers as he squeezed his way through the band.

"What are you doing?" Vero shouted. "Don't leave me hanging out there."

Tack's eyes remained peeled to the ceiling. Vero grabbed his shoulder and spun him around, bumping into a tuba player who hit his teeth against the mouthpiece.

"Sorry," Vero said.

Tack jerked his head toward Vero. "We have to get everyone out of here!" Tack shouted.

"What?"

"They're gonna die!" Tack yelled through his beak.

"What are you talking about?"

Tack grabbed Vero and looked him in the eye, their beaks nearly colliding. "The ceiling is full of water, and it's going to collapse," Tack said with utmost seriousness.

"How do you know that?"

"Trust me." Tack let go of Vero and plowed through the marching band, causing the tuba player to hit his teeth on the mouthpiece once again. He raced over to the bleachers. "Everybody needs to get out!" Tack screamed.

But Tack couldn't be heard above the noisemakers and marching band. Vero looked up. He saw that a large portion of the ceiling was indeed sagging. Tack grabbed Coach Randy's mic from his hand. "Get out! Quick!" Tack shouted into the mic.

But no one paid him any attention. Throwing down the mic, Tack dashed over to the conductor and barked some orders to him, flapping his wings. The crowd thought it was all just mascot antics and laughed. After listening to Tack for a moment, the conductor gave the "cut" direction on the chicken dance song and held his hand up high with four fingers raised, indicating a song change to the band. Vero ran over to Tack to find out what he was doing as the band began to play the Conga Dance. Everyone was still laughing and dancing. "Grab my waist and follow me!" Tack screamed through the heavy costume.

Tack and Vero made a beeline to the stands doing the Conga. It was a new dance for the Fighting Chickens, but the crowd loved it! As they got to the stands, Tack started grabbing a few students and pulling them to their feet. He placed a girl's hands on his hips, bumping Vero off the line.

And that was all it took. The entire crowd flowed simultaneously into a conga line and latched onto Tack's lead. Vero continued to pull everyone off the bleachers and attach them to the line.

"Everybody, conga!" Vero yelled to the crowd, gesturing wildly.

Kids delirious with laughter rose from their seats and made their way down to the gym floor as the band played on. The entire student body conga'd across the gym toward the exit. Tack pushed open the gym's wide double doors and led the conga lines out into the football field. Still in the gym, Vero heard a loud noise. He looked up and saw a huge crack running down the ceiling directly above the band. Drops of water dripped onto the floor. Vero ran to the drum majorette and grabbed her baton.

"Hey!" she yelled. "Give that back!"

"The ceiling's gonna collapse!" Vero said turning her head upward. "Lead them out!"

Panic came into the drum majorette's eyes when she saw the bulging ceiling. She grabbed the baton from Vero, turned to the band, and marched them toward the door, following the conga line out to the field. The crowd was still dancing on the field as the band marched out, waiting to see what Tack had planned next. But the band stopped playing, and the crowd calmed down when Tack ran back inside to the now quieter gym. He yanked off his chicken head and raced over to the few remaining people in the bleachers.

"Get out!" he screamed at the top of his lungs.

Loud cracks pierced the air. The ceiling in a corner of the gym collapsed. Water gushed as if a dam had just broken. People sprinted for the doors. Mercifully, most were already outside. Then other parts of the ceiling collapsed. Vero's eyes scanned the gym, looking for Clover, but he didn't see her. It was total chaos as the final kids and teachers raced for the doors. Heavy sheets of plaster, beams, and lights fell as people scrambled out the exit. Vero and Tack barely got out the doors when they turned around to see the gym ceiling completely collapse.

Vero said a silent prayer that everyone had escaped safely.

# 20

## ✦

# UNLIKELY HERO

Fire trucks and police cars surrounded the gym. Scores of students lined up in the football field according to their classrooms as teachers took roll call. Vero and Tack also stood in line, peeling off their chicken costumes. Vero watched as firemen went in and out of the gym, combing through the rubble.

"How did you know that ceiling was gonna collapse?" Vero asked Tack.

"I had a gut feeling. For some reason, I was drawn to the ceiling right at that spot." Suddenly, Tack's eyes went wide. "Vero, I got it! I'm a dowser!"

Vero smiled. He knew how badly Tack had wanted to inherit the family dowsing abilities. "Your dad's gonna be so proud of you," Vero said putting his hand on Tack's shoulder. "You just saved everybody's life."

Vero noticed that Tack looked shocked by the enormity of it all. For the first time in his life, his friend was rendered speechless. Vero's happiness for Tack quickly dissipated when a glum Principal Meyers walked over to him accompanied by a police officer. Their serious expression told Vero something was very wrong.

"Vero, every class has taken roll call, and we matched it up with the front office's absentee list for the day ..." Principal Meyers said.

Vero began to sweat.

"And all but two students are accounted for ... Kira Mattox and Clover."

Vero's heart sank.

Classes were cancelled, and the students were sent home early. Vero sat in his living room across from a police officer. Nora nervously paced back and forth. The front door opened, and Dennis walked in. Nora ran to him, and he wrapped his arms around her. Tears fell down her cheeks. "Dennis, they still can't find her," Nora said, her heart in her throat.

"Anything new?" Dennis asked the officer.

"No. They're still going through the gym."

"Did they find her bike?" Dennis asked.

"Unfortunately the gym collapsed on the bike racks so we don't know yet," the officer said. "Is there any reason why Clover would not be at school?"

"No," Nora said pulling away from Dennis. "I told you. She left this morning for school with Kira."

"I'm sorry, Mrs. Leland. I know how hard this is," the

officer said. "Mr. Leland, did she contact you at any point in the day?"

Dennis shook his head. "No, we don't let her take her cell phone to school."

"I can't sit here anymore!" Nora said. "I'm going to that gym!"

Vero stood and went after his mom as she headed for the door. Dennis gently grabbed her arm. "Nora, they're doing all they can."

"No, they're not!" Nora yelled, pulling her arm away.

Nora opened the front door. The sight before her caused her to scream. A bewildered Clover stood on the front porch. Nora grabbed Clover and hugged her tightly.

"Thank God," Dennis said with a huge sigh of relief.

Nora released Clover. "Where were you?"

Clover looked surprised to see a police officer in her house. Vero could practically hear her heart pound as she stepped inside.

"Where have you been?" Nora repeated.

Clover looked at her mother's distressed face. She locked eyes with Vero, but Vero just shook his head, at a loss for words.

"The school gym collapsed during the pep rally, and you and Kira were the only ones unaccounted for," the officer said. "Were you with Kira today?"

Clover slowly nodded.

"So neither of you were near the gym this afternoon?" the officer asked.

"No, we left after morning announcements," Clover said.

"Do you have a history of skipping out on school?"

"No, she doesn't," Nora jumped in.

"This is the first time," Dennis said, narrowing his eyes at Clover. "At least I hope it is."

"Well, Clover, I'll have to report your truancy to the school, and we will find out if this is indeed the first time or not. If there are other infractions, you and your parents will have to attend a truancy hearing."

Vero saw his parents shoot nervous glances at one another.

"Now, do you know Kira's address?" the officer asked Clover. "We need to inform her parents."

Clover shook her head. "No, she just moved here."

"Officer 17 … Officer 17 …" A woman's voice came over the officer's walkie.

"Excuse me," the Officer said as he pulled his walkie from his holster and stepped out the front door.

"What is going on with you, Clover?" Nora said, her voice shaking with anger.

Clover didn't answer. She looked down.

"I don't recognize you anymore!" Dennis sat down on the couch and put his head in his hands.

The officer walked back into the room. "Kira's fine," he said. "She turned up at school looking for her bike."

Clover looked surprised upon hearing that.

"The gym collapsed on the bikes," Dennis informed Clover. "Don't think you'll be getting a new one anytime soon."

"The search has been called off," the officer said.

"Thank you so much," Dennis said as he walked him to the door. "We feel sick we had to put your department through this."

"It's a miracle no one was hurt," the officer said as he stepped outside. "That's the important thing."

A confused look came over Vero. A miracle? Had the

gym collapsing have anything to do with things going on in the Ether?

Dennis shut the door and turned to Clover. "How could you do this to us? We were worried to death!"

"I didn't know," Clover said.

"We thought you were dead!" Dennis yelled.

Clover locked eyes with Vero. He knew exactly what she was thinking — that someday in the near future, this scenario would be true. Except he would be the one his parents would mourn. Vero looked away.

Dennis was struggling to keep his voice under control. "Where were you?"

Clover looked down, silent.

"Clover!" Dennis yelled.

"We cut class, then walked to the metro to go downtown."

"Downtown?"

"They announced that there were an extra 600 seats available after they set up the stage for the Two Dimension concert. We wanted to be the first in line."

"You ditched school for a crummy concert while Mom and I were sick to death worrying about you?" Dennis was shaking.

"I'm sorry."

Dennis shook his head. "There were search teams combing that gym for you, firemen risking their lives for you, and you think sorry is enough?" He snorted. "What is going on with you?"

Clover looked at Dennis, flashing him a defiant glance, and didn't answer.

"Your friendship with Kira is over!"

Clover's eyes grew huge. "You can't do that!"

"Watch me," Dennis said. "You are grounded. You will take the bus to and from school each day. And when you come home, you will do your homework. There's no going out for two months."

"Two months!" Clover protested. "That's so unfair!"

"Want to make it three?" Dennis said, his voice menacing.

Clover bit her lip, trying to control her anger. Her look shot daggers at her father. Then she spun around and stormed upstairs. A few moments later, Vero heard Clover's bedroom door slam. Nora ran to the kitchen. Vero followed her, and found his mother sitting at the table, sniffling. He tentatively approached her. Nora looked up, her eyes wet. "I thought she had died." Nora burst into tears and grabbed Vero. She pulled him into a hug, crying into his shoulder.

"She's all right, Mom."

"You won't understand, Vero. Not until you have kids of your own," Nora said between sobs. She cupped his face. "I would die if anything ever happened to either Clover or you."

A tear escaped Vero's eye.

❖

Tack was suddenly the most popular kid at school. The jocks high-fived him as he walked down the hallway. Girls flirted with him. Teachers praised him. *The universe has turned upside down*, Vero thought. But as Vero watched Vicki hug Tack, he noticed Tack's face flushed red with unease at the embrace.

"Thanks, Tack," Vicki said as she released him and walked away.

Tack noticed the curious expression on Vero's face. "What? Why are you looking at me like that?"

"You finally got everything you've ever wanted," Vero said. "You're now an official dowser, suddenly the teachers think you're a genius, girls give you random hugs ... so why do you seem so bummed out?"

Tack shrugged. "I don't know. But you are right. I should be the top dog, but I feel kind of nervous."

"Well, yeah, when I think about how many people could have died ..."

"Yeah, that's all overwhelming, but it's more like I still have this feeling that ..."

"That what?"

Tack met Vero's eyes. "That there's something going on that's much bigger than me."

A ceremony honoring Tack was held in the school cafeteria since the gym was no longer an option. Marty and Mary Kozlowski, Tack's parents, sat front and center before the makeshift stage. Their three daughters sat directly behind them. All were older than Tack, yet all had the same strawberry-blonde hair. Vero sat next to Tack's sixteen-year-old sister, Mallory, while Tack stood on the stage with Principal Meyers.

Mallory elbowed Vero. "Who's that kid over there? He keeps staring at me." Mallory nodded over to Henry Matson who gazed at her, completely love-struck.

Vero sunk into his chair, shrugging his shoulders. Mallory squinted her eyes at Henry. Then she realized. "That's the little jerk who hacked into my Facebook account!" Mallory hissed. "I'm going to tell your principal about that kid!"

"Well, you might want to talk to Tack first before you do that ..." Vero said guiltily.

Mallory narrowed her eyes suspiciously at Vero. "Tack?"

Vero nodded as he sunk even further into his chair.

Mallory glared at Tack, as she put it all together.

"For his heroic bravery and keen sense of impending danger, we award Thaddeus Kozlowski—" a few kids snickered at Tack's real name "—the highest award given by Attleboro Middle ... the Service Award," Principal Meyers said as he placed a medal around Tack's neck.

The audience clapped. Kids hooted and hollered. Marty and Mary beamed with pride.

"I knew he was a dowser all along," Vero overheard Marty tell his wife.

Vero laughed to himself because Marty had been completely convinced Tack never had any dowsing abilities. No matter how hard he had tested him, Tack had never shown any aptitude for the talent.

"You know, he might turn out to be one of greatest dowsers in Kozlowski history," Marty added. Mary rolled her eyes.

Tack stepped off the stage, and a crowd of schoolmates mobbed him. He got friendly noogies, handshakes, slaps on the back, and hugs. Vero looked across the room and saw Danny standing off by himself near the exit. He was not part of Tack's love fest. Danny had become a leper once again at Attleboro Middle. A rumor had spread that he had posted some sort of threat against Attleboro Middle on the Internet the day before the ceiling incident. It was so serious that the police were investigating. Davina had told him she could no longer hang out with him. Vero feared that without Davina's support, Danny would become a thug once again. He knew it was his job to keep Danny on the straight and narrow, but the situation was pretty dire. He walked over to him.

"Hey," Vero said to Danny.

Danny gave him a suspicious look. "Hey."

"Guess we won't be having P.E. in the gym for a long while," Vero said.

Danny grunted. He had no interest in talking to Vero.

"I won't miss climbing the rope," Vero said with a laugh. "I could never do that. I can only get up a few feet. But you're pretty good at it."

Danny gave Vero a look. "Did they send you over here to get me to confess?"

"What? No," Vero answered. "Do they really think you caused the ceiling to fall?"

Danny nodded.

"That's crazy."

"Yeah, well, everyone seems to believe it," Danny said, crossing his arms. He looked out into the crowd.

Vero followed Danny's gaze. His eyes rested on Davina.

"I don't," Vero said. "Eventually, the truth will come out, and everyone else will come to believe you too."

Vero saw Danny's face soften. "Thanks," Danny muttered and walked away.

❖

Clover received a two-day suspension for cutting class, which made no sense to Vero. Punishment should be making a kid go to school, not letting them stay home. Clover spent the days mostly in her bedroom, doing schoolwork, or napping. She only surfaced for food. On the night of her second day of suspension, Vero knocked on her door, holding a dish of vanilla ice cream on top of a slice of apple pie.

"Who is it?" Clover shouted through the door.

"I have some dessert," Vero answered.

"Leave it by the door!"

"I don't think so. It's ice cream."

The door suddenly opened. Clover grabbed the dish then tried to shut the door. But Vero was too fast for her, and, taking a lesson from Balaam's donkey, he shoved his foot in between the door and the jam.

"What?"

"Do you know what the email said that Danny Konrad supposedly sent out?" Vero asked.

"Why do you care?"

"I just want to know."

"If I tell you, will you get lost?"

Vero nodded.

"I heard he wrote ... 'Fear me.'"

Vero's eyes went wide. Then the doorbell rang, startling him even more.

"We had a deal, now go!" Clover said.

"Hi, Mr. Leland."

Vero and Clover overheard Kira's voice. Clover shoved the dish back into Vero's hands and raced to the front door. Vero chased after her. Kira stood in the foyer with Nora and Dennis.

"Sorry, Kira, but Clover isn't allowed any visitors," Dad said.

"I didn't come to see Clover," Kira said. "I came to apologize to you and your family." Kira extended her gaze to the family. Dennis's expression softened a bit.

"Mr. and Mrs. Leland, Vero, I'm sorry for the trouble I caused everybody. I take full responsibility for everything. It wasn't Clover's fault ..."

Clover locked eyes with Kira.

"She didn't want to skip school, but my sister ..." Kira paused, her eyes filling with tears. "She died two years ago."

Vero watched Clover's expression. She looked surprised, as though she hadn't known about Kira's sister.

"And every year, it's really hard for me. Two Dimension was her favorite band, and I thought that somehow seeing them in concert would make me feel better, so Clover was just being a good friend coming along."

Dennis and Nora's faces softened.

"That's why we moved here. It was too hard for my mom to stay. She needed a change. But it was selfish of me, and I'm really sorry."

"We appreciate you coming over here to tell us," Dennis said.

"I wanted you to know the truth." Kira lowered her head and turned to walk away.

"Kira," Dennis said.

Kira stopped and looked back over her shoulder.

"We're very sorry for your loss."

Vero watched as Kira nodded and walked out to the street. He knew he should have felt terrible for her—but he didn't.

# 21

❖

# THE DREAMER

Vero threw on a pair of jeans and a navy blue sweatshirt over his T-shirt. It was Saturday morning, and he was going to meet Tack. Normally, he would have had swim practice, but because the pool's ceiling was also damaged in the collapse, practice was cancelled until the school could work out a schedule with the local recreation center for use of its pool. Tack's mother was going to pick up Vero and drop the boys off at the arcade while she had her hair done. Vero walked into the kitchen, opened the fridge, and pulled out a leftover slice of pizza.

"Not exactly a healthy breakfast," a voice said.

Vero spun around and saw Kira standing in the dining room.

"Oh, Kira ..." Vero said, surprised. "What are you doing here?"

"Don't sound so happy to see me," Kira said, a bit offended.

"Clover's not supposed to have any guests."

"Your parents said I could come over because Clover and I have a science project due Monday."

"Oh."

"So you and Tack are pretty popular, huh? I feel honored just being in your house."

Vero couldn't tell if Kira was being serious. "Really, it was all Tack."

"You're too modest. You know what? I think from now on, we should call you Vero the Hero."

Vero squirmed. He didn't feel flattered by Kira's compliments.

"It's like you're the great protector over at that school."

That hit a little too close to home. Vero gave her a curious look, but just then Clover walked into the room.

"I found it," she said, holding a glue gun.

Vero looked at the dining room table. It was covered with all kinds of arts and crafts supplies. "What are you making?" he asked.

"A desert ecosystem," Clover answered.

"Can you think of anything more boring?" Kira sighed. "We should be getting ready for the Two Dimension concert tonight not doing this."

"Clover's grounded," Vero said. "She can't go to the concert."

"Shut up, Vero," Clover snapped. "Get off my case."

Kira sat down at the table and picked up a pair of scissors. "I told your mom and dad it was my fault. They're being totally unfair to Clover."

Vero looked to see if Clover would defend their parents. She simply shrugged her shoulders.

"See?" Kira asked. "It's totally hypocritical 'cause I'm sure your parents must have ditched when they were in school."

Clover plugged in the glue gun and frowned. "She's right. Remember when dad told us about his senior ditch day? How he and his buddies went to the beach instead of school?"

"Everybody ditches on senior ditch day!" Vero said. "Teachers expect it."

Kira raised her eyebrows and lifted her chin. "Sorry, Vero. It's still ditching."

"We have to finish our project," Clover said. "Leave."

Vero stared hard at Clover. He was trying to read her mind the same way he had done in the Ether with Pax. But nothing. He couldn't hear any of Clover's thoughts. "Gladly," Vero said. He put his pizza on a plate and stomped out of the room.

Vero was sick of Clover. She was unbearable around Kira. As he walked past Clover's bedroom, his eye caught her journal lying on top of her pillow. He wasn't able to read her mind, but maybe her journal held some answers. Vero walked into the room and picked up the journal. It was Clover's dream diary. She had kept one ever since she was a little girl. If she had a particularly interesting dream the night before, Clover would record it in her journal. The last time Vero had snuck a peek at it, Clover had drawn an image of the Cherubim, the angels who guard God's throne. Strangely, that very same night, Vero had had the exact same dream in which he, too, had seen the Cherubim.

Vero's heart skipped a beat when he flipped it open and saw the pages — drawn with near perfect likeness were several hyenas facing off against seven angels: Ariel, Greer, Ada, X, Kane, Pax, and himself! Vero's breathing quickened as his mind put it all together. Clover saw this scene in her dream! She had been there. So she must have been the soul in desperate need of the fort-i-fire! Vero needed to talk to Uriel, and right now!

Suddenly, Vero's breathing became labored. He felt like his heart was going to burst. The pain was unbearable. He grabbed his chest and collapsed to the floor.

⊹

The first thing Vero heard was the distant sound of a crowd. He opened his eyes. Pax and Greer were standing over him. Greer nudged him with her foot.

"So nice of you to join us," Greer said. "Speeding bus?"

"No. Heart attack, I think," Vero answered.

"Clogged arteries at 13? You better lay off the junk food." Greer smiled at him.

As Vero stood up, his eyes took in C.A.N.D.L.E.'s great outer walls. He realized he was lying on the steps.

"I need to talk to Uriel," Vero said with urgency in his voice, thinking of Clover.

"He told us to go ahead without you," Pax said.

"What are you talking about?"

"The third trial," Pax said. "It's already begun."

Vero felt hurt. "Why wasn't I included?"

"He wouldn't give us an answer," Pax said. "But I got the feeling they don't want you to participate."

Vero's hurt gave way to anger. Why would they not want

him in the games? Why were they excluding him? He'd been chosen for the guardian team, fair and square.

Vero stormed up the stairs, determined to give Uriel a piece of his mind. As he walked through the massive doors, X, Ada, Kane, and Eitan were walking out with Uriel and Raphael. When Vero caught his eye, Uriel stopped, looking shocked. Raphael seemed equally startled, his jolly expression erased.

"Yeah, I'm here," Vero said defiantly. "Don't worry, I don't want to be in your stupid Angel Trials. I have more important things." Vero glared at Eitan, "And obviously, I've been replaced."

"Vero, how did you get here?" Uriel asked.

"I don't know, my chest hurt ... like an elephant was sitting on it ..."

"Self-induced heart attack," Uriel said, with wonder in his voice. "At this point in your training, no fledgling has ever been capable of self-transitioning to the Ether."

"Congratulations," Raphael smiled to Vero. "You willed yourself here."

Vero frowned. "Excuse me for not wanting to celebrate," he said, his eyes fixed on Eitan. "I'm glad you're replacing me because I need to help my sister. It was my sister, wasn't it? The soul we failed to hit with the fort-i-fire?"

Uriel and Raphael looked at each other with nervous glances. Greer gasped.

Uriel met Vero's glare. "You will go with your flight and participate in the Trials," he said firmly.

Vero snorted. "The Trials? You called everyone here except me. You were going to do it behind my back, and now you want me to compete?"

Uriel turned to Eitan, "You are to return to earth."

Eitan nodded, looking disappointed.

"No, let him stay," Vero told Uriel. He locked eyes with Uriel. "Clover's the soul under great attack? She was the soul in the cave with Lilith, wasn't she?"

Uriel looked to Raphael then slowly nodded.

Though Vero had been sure of it even before arriving in the Ether, hearing this confirmation caused him to panic. "I need to get a fort-i-fire to her!"

Uriel shook his head. "No, Vero, that time has passed."

"But she's in trouble! She's my sister—!"

"I know you love her, but Clover is not your ward."

"I don't care! I have to help her! What good is being an angel if I can't guard my own sister?!"

"You will do as you are told," Uriel said, the tone of his voice clearly meant that Vero was not to argue the point any further. "And, Eitan, you will return to earth."

Eitan nodded. "Yes, Uriel."

"But it isn't right!" Vero shouted.

Uriel turned to the other fledglings. "Good luck to you all." With that, he wrapped his wings around himself and disappeared.

Vero looked to Raphael, his eyes pleading. "Raphael, please..."

"Don't lose hope, Vero," Raphael said gently. "Not everything is as it seems. And you can always pray for Clover." Then he flew away.

"We're wasting time, Vero," Kane said, bouncing on the balls of his feet. "We're in a race here."

Ada gave Kane a look, then touched Vero's elbow. "I'm

sorry about your sister," she said. "How did you figure it out? Could you tell she's under attack?"

Vero sighed. "Sort of. She's suddenly become so self-absorbed and defiant to my parents, wearing inappropriate outfits and ditching school ..."

"Sounds like normal teenage stuff," Greer said.

"When you say it out loud, it doesn't sound that terrible," Vero agreed. "But you don't know Clover and how she really is. It's pretty out of character for her." Vero shot Kane a dirty look. "And if you hadn't thrown the fort-i-fire at Melchor's, Clover wouldn't be in the trouble she is."

"Not my fault! I didn't know she was your sister," Kane defended.

Vero could feel the rage building within him. "Even if you did, I bet you still would have done the same thing," he said. "Winning means more to you than anything else."

"Yeah, and this is why I never wanted you on my team!" Kane shouted back. "Trouble always follows you!"

Vero's face grew hot. He grabbed Kane by his shirt and shook him. Kane shoved him back. X swiftly inserted himself between the two and, with his impressive biceps, pushed them apart.

"Knock it off!" X yelled. "This isn't going to help anything!"

Vero and Kane stared at one another as they caught their breath.

"Look, I'm sorry about your sister," Kane said, wiping his face with his sleeve. "I really am. But chances are Clover will be right where you left her before you transitioned."

X nodded. "You need to trust that your sister's guardian will watch over her."

Vero stayed silent for a moment as all eyes awaited his response. Then he nodded slightly.

"Good," X said as he lowered his hands from both boys' chests. "Now we need to find Jacob's Ladder ... together." X looked pointedly at Vero.

Pax turned to Vero. "The third challenge is to reach the top of Jacob's Ladder first. And no one is allowed to fly."

"What did the archangels say about it?" Vero asked.

"Raphael told us the story," X said. "Jacob was Isaac's son and Abraham's grandson. One night he fell asleep and dreamed about a ladder that stretched all the way from earth to heaven. He saw angels going up and down it."

Vero remembered the story from Sunday school. "That's right. And he was the one who wrestled with an angel all night, wasn't he?"

"Yes," X chuckled. "Raphael admitted he was the angel Jacob wrestled with. It was during his own Angel Trials. He said Jacob whipped him good."

"So where is the ladder?" Vero asked the others.

"On earth," Ada said. "We were instructed to go back. Uriel said we should have an advantage over the other angels because they've never lived on earth."

"That, plus Ariel definitely won't blend," Kane said, smiling at the thought.

"Didn't think of that," Ada said.

"Uriel said we're to listen to our Vox Dei, pray to see the bottom rung, and we'll be taken back to earth," Kane said. "Just like how we normally do when it's time to leave the Ether."

"We're losing time, so let's do it," Greer said.

Vero closed his eyes. He blocked out everything as he

searched deep within himself for his Vox Dei. Gradually, he heard only the beating of his own heart. A peace overtook him. It was quickly shattered by the constant ding, ding, ding of what sounded like slot machines. Vero opened his eyes. He stood in the midst of an arcade. Bells and lights went off in every direction. He saw pinball machines, Skee-Ball bowling alleys, air hockey tables, photo booths, basketball machines, video games, a motorcycle racing simulator, a shooting gallery, even some kiddie rides. In short, it was a kid's paradise. Kids of all ages bounced from machine to machine. Vero was sure he had messed up his Vox Dei because he doubted the bottom rung to Jacob's Ladder could be in this place. But then he saw Greer, Kane, and Pax walking toward him. *If they also landed in the same arcade, then maybe it could be the place, after all*, he thought.

"Start looking," Greer told Vero.

"This is just crazy," Vero said. "I have a hard time imagining it's in here."

"This is where we all landed, so it's got to be the right place," Pax said.

"Not all of us," Kane said. "Has anyone seen X or Ada?"

Suddenly, Ada's shrill voice cut through the din of the arcade. Vero looked up and saw Ada sitting next to X on a kiddie Ferris wheel. She was clutching X's arm as the Ferris wheel spun around. The blood had drained from Ada's face, and she looked as white as a sheet.

"What the heck is she screaming for?" Greer asked. "It's a kiddie ride."

The attendant stopped the ride when Ada and X's carriage reached the platform. He unlocked the carriage door, and Ada dashed off the ride. Everyone looked at her as if she were crazy. Ada noticed the stares. She stopped screaming, and hugged her chest. "I hate Ferris wheels," she said.

"You can battle behemoths, imps, and hyenas, but you're terrified of a kiddie Ferris wheel?" Vero asked.

Ada hesitated then slowly nodded. "I almost fell off one when I was little."

"Oh my gosh, my heart breaks for you. Such a horrific childhood," Greer said mockingly. "Try and pull yourself together and find the bottom of that ladder please."

Ada flashed her a look.

"Maybe there's some secret door?" Pax said.

X looked to Pax, incredulous.

"It wasn't that brilliant of an idea," Greer said of X's expression.

"No." X smiled. "But we could understand him. Pax just spoke some of his first words ever on earth."

"Feels pretty good too," X said, stretching his legs. "Anybody want to race me? Vero?"

Vero wasn't paying attention to X. "Vero?" X tried again.

"Guy's I know where we are," Vero said, staring straight ahead.

"Where?" Ada asked

Vero's eyes shot wide with panic. "Maryland."

# 22

❖

# JACOB'S
# LADDER

A pit formed in Vero's stomach when he saw Tack wearing
a backpack and beelining toward him. How could this
happen? Didn't time on earth stop when in the Ether? Or
was it like before when he had battled the maltures, when he
had jumped in front of a fire truck and time had continued?

"Where were you? We sat outside your house, and then
my mom couldn't wait any longer," Tack said to Vero.

"Oh ... sorry," Vero said.

Tack pulled out his cell phone from his jacket pocket.
"I'll text my mom that you're here."

"Thanks," Vero said. "Did you knock on the door at my
house?"

"Yeah, nobody answered."

"You didn't see Kira or Clover?" Vero asked with concern.

"Nope."

"Oh ... yeah sorry, I guess there was a miscommunication somewhere."

"And what the heck? You told Mallory about Henry?"

"She was going to tell Principal Meyers!" Vero said.

"Thanks, because now I've got to do all her chores for the next two weeks."

"Sorry."

Tack squinted at Ada. "You're Ada, Vero's friend from the bat mitzvah."

"Nice to see you. I just happen to be in town with my friends ..." Ada covered, gesturing behind her.

Tack looked at Greer, X, Pax, and Kane.

" ... And I called Vero at the last minute."

"Oh. That's cool," Tack said. "My mom's next door getting her hair dyed. We can all play some games together."

"Um ... sure," Vero said despite Kane's panicked look. "I need some tokens. Can you get me some?" Vero fumbled in his pocket and pulled out a twenty. He handed it to Tack.

"Okay. I'll be right back." Tack took Vero's bill and walked over to the token machine.

Kane turned to Vero. "What are you doing? Get rid of him!"

"I can't!" Vero said. "What do you want me to do?"

"Ditch him!"

"Are we in your town?" Pax asked Vero.

"Yes."

"I wonder why?" Pax said.

Vero thought for a moment. "I don't know. But it's really complicating things. How about Ada and I go around with Tack, and you guys search for the rung? Then somehow I'll give him the slip."

Kane considered. "Do it fast."

Tack returned with a plastic cup full of shiny tokens. "Where are they going?" Tack asked as Kane, X, Greer, and Pax walked away.

"They just want to look around," Vero answered, nervously glancing at Ada.

"Hey, let's go to the shooting gallery," Tack said.

Vero, Ada, and Tack made their way through a throng of kids over to the shooting gallery. Vero's eyes were constantly scanning the arcade looking for anything that could be related to the bottom rung of Jacob's Ladder, but all he saw was a typical suburban arcade. The shooting gallery was Western themed. A mannequin wearing a cowboy hat sat at a piano. Frying pans and a dinner bell hung on the porch of a shack. Tin cans were arranged in a straight line on top of a bale of hay. A deer stood in between two trees next to a chipmunk sitting on a tree stump. A rattlesnake coiled up in a bush, and a bright red stick of dynamite lay on a wooden crate labeled "TNT." All the objects had red bull's-eyes in front of them. Tack put in enough tokens for three people, and Ada and Vero picked up their guns.

"We don't have time for this," she muttered to Vero.

Vero shrugged nervously then held the butt of the rifle to his shoulder and aimed at the bull's-eye in front of the piano player. He pulled the trigger. The piano player jerked forward, and his fingers moved across the keyboard playing a song.

"You got him!" Tack yelled.

Tack shot at the dinner bell. It began to clang.

Ada aimed at the tin cans, but nothing happened. Her aim was off. Other kids began to pick up rifles and shoot. Soon it seemed like every bull's-eye was going off. Vero shut one eye as he looked down the barrel of his rifle. A cat leapt across the gallery. The poor creature was completely frazzled. It jumped from object to object looking for a way out.

"What's a cat doing there?" Tack asked, putting down his gun. "Is it part of the gallery?"

The cinnamon-colored cat had long legs and a wiry body. Vero looked over and saw an employee pushing through the crowd. The chubby, balding man shouted, "Hold your fire" at the top of his lungs as he jumped over the counter after the cat. Trapped, the cat stood still. Its large almond-shaped eyes were frozen on Vero.

"Help me!" rang through Vero's head. It was a voice he recognized. The cat was Ariel.

"Ada," Vero whispered. "It's Ariel!"

The man slowly approached Ariel, backing her into a corner. She hissed at him. "Help!" she communicated to Vero.

As the man reached out to grab her, Vero shot the bull's-eye beneath Ariel. The rattlesnake jumped forward, startling the man. He stumbled back, giving Ariel the chance to escape. Ada ran after Ariel. Vero turned to Tack. "Quick, give me your backpack!"

"Why?"

"Just do it!"

"My lunch is in there," Tack said as he held out his backpack. "And my clothes. I'm spending the night at my aunt's house."

Vero grabbed Tack's backpack, zipped it open and dug out Tack's lunch. He handed it to Tack. "Here, eat it now! And I'll give it back to you later!"

Vero turned and chased after Ariel. But he wasn't the only one chasing her—the arcade employee was also in close pursuit. He pushed his way through crowds of kids, keeping an eye at all times on Ariel. Vero turned a corner around a photo booth and stopped in his tracks; she was gone. The man also stopped running. He looked around, scratching his head. Ariel was nowhere in sight. After a few moments, the employee walked away.

"Over here," Ada said in a low voice.

Vero saw Ada crouched behind the photo booth. She was wearing a heavy, bulky coat, and her right arm pulled the coat over her chest.

"I lost her," Vero said to Ada.

Ada smiled and opened her coat, revealing Ariel hidden underneath. "I grabbed some kid's coat off the floor and hid her in here," Ada told Vero.

"Smart thinking. But that kid will be looking for his jacket soon enough. Put her in here." Vero opened Tack's backpack. As Ada lifted Ariel from under the coat, Vero turned his back to shield her from view. "You should be safe in here," Vero said to the cat as he zipped her inside. He was careful to leave some room for air. "Just don't meow."

"Thank you," Ariel communicated to Vero.

"I was wondering how you'd look on earth," Vero mentally spoke to Ariel.

"An Abyssinian, of course," she answered.

Tack walked over holding a sandwich in a Ziploc bag along with an apple, a bag of chips, and a water bottle.

"Can I have my backpack please?" he asked as the apple fell from his hand and rolled under a video game. "Dang it."

"I'll give it back to you later. Okay?" Vero said. "I'm hiding the cat in there."

"Serious?"

"Yeah. Just 'till I find a safe place to release it."

Tack considered. "Okay. But it better not go to the bathroom in there."

Ariel loudly hissed. "Me? I'm the one stuck in here with his smelly socks … at least I hope they're socks," she spoke mind-to-mind with Vero.

Without warning, Tack was pushed from behind. His water bottle flew out of his hand and also rolled under the video machine. "What the …?"

Tack turned around and saw a gangly-looking teenage boy standing behind him. He wore white tube socks with pastel blue corduroy beach shorts and a striped red and yellow shirt. And if that wasn't bad enough, he had a mullet haircut.

"You need to look where you're going!" Tack said. "What? First day with the new feet?"

"Yes, as a matter of fact, it is," the teenage boy said.

"Weirdo," Tack muttered as the boy walked away. Tack turned to Vero, eyeing the boy's outfit, "Now that's a look that will make you stand out in a class photo. Why didn't I think of that?"

Vero and Ada watched as the teenage boy tried to make his way through the arcade. He bumped into the butt of a girl's cue stick as she lined up a shot on the pool table. She scratched. "Clumsy jerk!"

"Does that guy just have a death wish?" Tack asked.

"Looks like it," Vero answered. "C'mon, let's shoot some hoops."

As they walked to the basketball machines, Vero saw Kane out of the corner of his eye. He mouthed to him, "Anything?"

Kane shook his head.

"I'll meet you guys there," Vero said to Ada and Tack. He walked over to Kane.

"We checked every door, everything we could think of," Kane said. "They don't lead to anything. Can't find a portal anywhere. It's really frustrating."

"A portal?" Vero asked.

"Uriel's exact words were 'You must be the first to climb Jacob's Ladder, and the first step is just through the portal,'" Kane said as he eyed Vero's backpack. "Where'd you get that backpack?"

"It's my friend's."

"Come on! You're hanging out with that kid instead of looking," Kane said with frustration in his voice.

"What do you want me to say? Sorry, Tack, my fellow guardian angels and I have to find Jacob's Ladder?"

Vero's eyes darted over to an extremely handsome teenage boy standing before a three-way mirror in front of the funhouse. He appeared to be mesmerized by his reflection. Vero elbowed Kane. "It's Dumah."

"What's he doing?" Kane asked.

"Either he's looking for a portal through the mirror, or he's just staring at himself."

"The guy's off," Kane said.

Greer, X, and Pax walked over.

"I can't take it anymore," Greer said. "This is starting to feel like one big joke."

"It has to be here," X said. "We're just not thinking right."

"Uriel had to have given some other clue when they introduced the challenge," Vero said.

"Not really," Pax shook his head. "We were told that step one on the ladder was to find the portal."

"Anything else?"

"No," Greer answered. "Then Raphael told the story of his Angel Trial where he had to wrestle Jacob."

The clumsy boy tripped into a kid carrying a plastic cup full of tokens. They spilled all over the floor.

"Hey!" the kid yelled.

"Sorry," the clumsy boy answered.

"I bet that's Melchor," Vero said.

"Why?" X asked.

"'Cause he doesn't know how to walk. He must have never been in human form before."

Greer knit her brow as she took in Melchor's outfit. "He also doesn't realize that the 80s are long over."

Pax chuckled. "I guess the archangels have a sense of humor."

Recalling his theft of the jawbone, Kane shot daggers at Melchor and walked over to him.

"Kane, where you going?" X asked. His voice had a hint of warning.

Kane glared at X. "Maybe he can help us."

As Kane raced over to Melchor, the others followed. "If Virtues can see the future," Kane said to Melchor, "tell us how you see us getting out of here."

Pax's face lit up. "Yeah, can you do that?" he asked.

Vero's eyebrow shot up as he looked at Melchor as he considered something.

"No," Melchor answered. "I can only see what they allow me to see."

"You sure you're not lying to us?" Kane stared at him.

"You think I like being like this?" Melchor said. "If I could get out of here, don't you think I would?"

Kane considered for a moment.

"Vero," Tack called.

Kane turned and saw Tack and Ada walking over to them. "Oh great." Kane threw his hands up. "Here comes the friend again."

"Are we going to shoot hoops or not?" Tack asked as he leaned against an arm wrestling machine. It had a strong man's shoulder sticking out of the top connected to a hand bent at the elbow ready to arm wrestle. Lights blinked on a meter that measured people's strength.

Greer gasped as she gazed at the machine. But just then Tack's cell phone beeped. He pulled it from his pocket and read a text.

"My mom said your mom's been looking for Clover. She wants to know if you know where she is?" Tack shook his head. "Your family is all over the place today. If you had your own cell phone, you could keep track of each other."

"Clover's not at home?" Vero asked, the panic rising in his voice.

Tack shrugged. "I told you, no one opened the door for me when I knocked."

"I know," Vero said, palming his face, "but I thought maybe they didn't hear you or they were in the backyard."

"I'm sure it's not a big deal. She's probably out with Kira." Tack typed a text message on his phone. But when he hit "send" the message stalled. "Suddenly, I'm not getting great reception. I'm gonna go stand out front." Tack walked away. Vero was trying to control his racing heartbeat when Greer elbowed him.

"Guys, I may know where the portal is," she said. "Raphael was giving us a huge hint when he told us the story of wrestling Jacob." Her eyes landed on the arm wrestling machine.

Vero followed her gaze, though he was distracted with thoughts of Clover.

"Give me a token," Greer said to Ada.

Ada handed Greer a token. She slipped it into the machine, then bent her elbow and placed her hand in the machine's hand. "See you guys on the ladder," Greer said, as she pushed down with all her strength. The meter blinked like crazy. She struggled against the machine's hand, but then slammed it down, winning the match. And then, nothing happened.

"Darn it!" Greer said with huge disappointment.

"Good one, Greer," Kane said. "What the heck did you think was going to happen?"

"I thought for sure if I beat the arm-wrestler dude, I'd blast out of here and onto the ladder."

She stepped back and bumped into Melchor who stumbled and fell through the black curtain into a photo booth. A guy with tattoos on every inch of his arms and his girlfriend on his lap threw him out of the booth and onto the hard floor.

"You ruined the photo, you little jerk!" the guy shouted. He picked Melchor up by his striped shirt to hit him when his pierced girlfriend ducked out of the booth and stepped in between them.

"Don't do it, Ronny! He's not worth breaking probation for!" she yelled.

Ronny stared at Melchor then dropped him back onto the floor. The finished photo shot out of the side of the booth. Without looking at it, Ronny grabbed the photo and threw it onto Melchor's chest. "Here, something to remember me by," Ronny said as he wrapped his arm around his girlfriend's waist and walked away.

X stretched out his hand to Melchor and pulled him to his feet. With his free hand, X snatched the photo.

"Thanks," Melchor said then stumbled away.

X looked at the photo with suspicion. "That's it! I know where the portal is!" X shouted. "Look at the photo!"

The others crowded around X. In the photo, Ronny and his girlfriend had surprised looks on their faces.

"So?" Pax said.

"Do you see Melchor in the photo?" X asked. "He's not there. The camera should have captured his image. I say there's something going on with that photo booth."

"Yeah, but then why didn't Melchor get taken to the Ether?" Ada asked.

"Maybe because his whole body wasn't inside it when the camera went off," X reasoned.

"Whatever. I'm game!" Kane said, sweeping aside the black curtain. "Everybody in. Quick."

Pax and X stepped into the booth.

"Ada give me your tokens," Vero said.

Ada handed them to Vero, who took the curtain from Kane. "Go ahead," Vero said. Kane stepped in the booth, and Vero turned to Ada and Greer. "Pile in before Tack gets back."

"I'm not sitting on anyone's lap," Greer said, looking into the tiny booth.

"Fine, then you guys go. I'll be right behind you," Vero said.

"Get in, Greer!" Kane snapped.

Ada and Greer crammed into the booth, and Vero drew the curtain closed.

"When you get there, start climbing. I'll catch up. Just keep climbing," Vero said as he fumbled for a token. He put his hand over his heart, said a silent prayer, and dropped the token into the machine. There was a blinding flash, and then silence inside the booth. Vero drew back the black curtain, and saw it was empty.

With the other angels safely gone, Vero pulled Ariel from the backpack and let the bag fall to the ground. He looked around nervously. "Better go quickly."

"I owe you one," Ariel mentally said as she jumped into the booth.

"No, it was I who owed you one," Vero answered. He drew the curtain behind her.

"Hey!" a man's voice shouted. "Get that cat out of there! Grab it!"

Vero saw the employee racing toward them, his big belly bouncing with each step. He fumbled with the token, dropping it. He fell to his hands and knees and reached under the machine for the fallen token. He snatched it just as the man approached, and scrambled to insert it into the machine.

"Quick! Get in!" Ariel spoke mentally to Vero.

"I'm not going with you right now," Vero said.

"Why not?"

Vero didn't answer her. "Come on, come on!" he muttered as the token finally dropped into the machine.

Just as the man ripped open the black curtain, the flash went off, blinding him. When he was able to see again, the small cat was gone.

# POOL OF
# TRUTH

A bewildered look came over the man. "What the ..." he said. The man turned to Vero. "Where did it go?"

"Where did what go?" Vero dodged the question.

"The cat! I saw you let it into the booth!"

Vero shook his head. "Sorry." He leaned into the booth as if to check it. "No cat in here."

Vero turned and pushed his way through a crowd of kids. He wasn't ready to go through the portal. Not just yet. Vero spotted Dumah, still staring into the mirror, fascinated by his image.

"Dumah, did you see Melchor?" Vero asked.

Dumah did not respond. He was too mesmerized by his reflection. Vero flashed his hand in front of Dumah's face. No response.

"Hey!" Vero yelled.

Still no response from Dumah. Vero shook his head and turned to scan the arcade. He spotted Melchor walking with his hands in front of him as if he were blind. Vero raced over to him and grabbed his shoulder, spinning him around. "I know where the bottom rung is," Vero said. "I'll show you—"

"Why?" Melchor looked suspicious. "There's no reason you'd want to help me."

"I will, but I need something from you first," Vero said. "Can you show me a vision of where my sister is? I think she's in trouble."

"I can't do it here on earth. I need to be in the Ether."

Vero studied his face, trying to determine whether Melchor was telling the truth or not.

"I'm completely useless on earth if you hadn't noticed," Melchor added.

Vero had to admit this seemed to be true.

"But I can't guarantee I'll see anything even in the Ether," Melchor said. "I can listen to my Vox Dei, but it doesn't always mean I'll be granted a vision. But I promise I'll try if you show me how to get there."

Vero nodded. "Follow me."

He led Melchor to the photo booth and pulled the curtain aside. "Get in." Vero dropped another token into the machine and jumped behind the curtain with Melchor. He grabbed onto Melchor's shirt so they wouldn't be separated.

The light flashed bright, and Vero suddenly felt as if he were in a wind tunnel. All his senses dulled as an unknown force pulled him at an incredibly fast speed. When the wind stilled, and his eyes could make sense of things again, he found himself standing on a huge sparkling crystal stair.

Each step was nearly two feet tall, and as he looked up the staircase, he saw no end in sight. It wound round and round. Ariel and his fellow fledglings were nowhere to be seen ... and neither was Melchor.

Vero stood on the step and looked down. There were steps below him, and it wasn't an actual ladder as he had imagined, but his Vox Dei told him he was in the right place. White, billowy clouds surrounded him on all sides. He wondered if the others had also landed in the same spot. But more importantly, where was Melchor? He sincerely hoped that Melchor hadn't somehow deceived him. "I need to catch up to him," Vero said to himself, his wings sprouting from his back. Vero flapped his wings, but he could not get airborne. He tried again, but his feet remained firmly planted on the stairs. He had no choice but to climb up the staircase.

As Vero started up the crystal stairs, he remembered a quote from Martin Luther King Jr. "Faith is taking the first step even when you don't see the whole staircase." And Vero had no idea where the glass stairs would lead him because the staircase wound around and around, blocking his view of the flights above. There was no railing. He glanced at his watch as he climbed and climbed. Almost an hour had passed. He was becoming bored. Vero looked down at his feet. Faces came into view under the clear glasslike stairs. He was so startled that he stumbled toward the edge of the step and nearly fell off the staircase. Ugly, one-eyed monstrous faces hissed at him. Maltures! The same hideous creatures that had tried to push him off a nine-story building before he had even known he was a guardian angel! A single eye went clear through their heads, and their mouths were filled with yellow fanged teeth. What looked like deep burns ran across their faces. They thrashed underneath the staircase, salivating, as they tried to break through the steps' risers to grab Vero. Vero stepped up his pace, determined to reach the top. All his thoughts were of Clover. He had to find Melchor and see his sister's future.

More and more maltures appeared beneath the staircase with each step Vero took, but they seemed to be contained. Nonetheless, Vero was anxious as he watched their black jagged wings flap, holding them in the air. "Maltures with wings?" Vero said with trepidation in his voice. Then as he lifted his foot, he felt something sharp cut through his right ankle. He looked down and saw a claw pulling on his leg. The step's riser was open, and a malture was trying to drag him under. Vero screamed and fell on the staircase, banging his hip on the glass. With his other foot, he kicked the malture in the eye, momentarily stunning him. The malture released his grip, but before Vero could scramble away, another malture grabbed and dragged him farther under the stairs.

"Help!" Vero yelled. "Get off!"

Vero kicked this second demonic creature with all his strength, but the malture was strong. Its claws dug deep into Vero's leg. It had pulled Vero's legs completely under the stairs. Vero thought of his sword and tried to concentrate, willing it to appear. He tried to do what Michael had taught him. But he was too panicked to concentrate. He gripped the edge of a glass step when suddenly a pair of arms grabbed him around his chest. He turned his head and saw X pulling him out of the open stair. But even X's incredible upper body strength was not enough to save him from the malture. Greer, Kane, Pax, and Ada ran down the winding staircase and grabbed Vero's arms, and Vero felt as if he was being stretched in every direction. It was a game of tug-of-war, and he was the rope!

"Harder!" Kane yelled to the others.

But the malture would not release its grip on Vero's leg.

The glint of steel caught Vero's eye. He looked at Kane who stood over him, brandishing his sword. A pang of jealousy shot through Vero when he realized Kane had conjured up his sword, but Vero had not been able to. In a powerful tug, X yanked Vero back another foot. Kane wielded his sword over his head and struck the malture's arm with a punishing blow, severing it. The malture shrieked and a look of surprise came over its evil face. Its claw, still wrapped around Vero's ankle, began to wither. The fledglings watched as the claw disintegrated into a pile of ash along with the rest of its body. Through the glass staircase, Vero watched as the ashes blew into the clouds and disappeared.

"Hurry up," Greer said as she hoisted Vero to his feet. "We need to get away from this step."

The fledglings raced higher up the stairs. Vero limped a bit, but he managed to keep pace with everyone. After a few minutes, Greer stopped and sat down. "Take a breather," she said to the others.

Vero plopped down next to her and caught his breath. He pulled up his torn pant leg and saw bloody claw marks embedded into his skin.

Greer winced. "They hurt?"

Vero shook his head. "Not too much." He looked at the others. "Thanks, but how did you know where to find me?"

"We heard you screaming like a little girl," Greer said.

"For that matter, I think everyone in the whole Ether heard you."

"Actually, we were only a few steps ahead of you," X said. "But you wouldn't know because this staircase winds around so much."

Vero turned to Kane. "Nice swordplay."

"Yeah, not bad . . . my first malture kill," Kane said, looking into his now empty hand. "Too bad there's nothing left of it. I would have liked to have that malture stuffed and hung over my fireplace." He chuckled.

"Why are there maltures along the staircase in the first place?" Vero asked the group. "I would have thought this was sacred ground."

"Maybe there's still a chance they can pull souls off it," Ada said. "It's sort of a last-ditch effort."

"Have you guys seen any of the other angels?" Vero asked.

"Not yet," Pax answered, his glasses fogged up from the mist.

"Did I miss something?" Vero asked. "Because for some reason I can't get airborne."

"Uriel told us that flying up and down the ladder isn't possible," Pax said.

"Yeah, well, my legs are gonna be in great shape after this," Greer said standing up.

The angels trudged up the stairs. Their lungs and thighs burned.

"I once climbed the Great Wall of China," Kane said. "But that's nothing compared to this."

The staircase wound around and around, bringing them higher and higher into the unending clouds. As they climbed, Vero thought of Clover. From the moment he had realized her soul was under attack and that she was missing, worry had spread through his mind like wildfire. He needed to deliver a fort-i-fire to her while she was dreaming. But how could he? Uriel had blocked him from doing so. He needed Melchor to show him a vision of Clover's future. Even a glimpse might help him figure things out.

"Is anyone else getting dizzy?" Ada asked.

"Me," X answered.

"Me too," Pax said. "I'm getting vertigo."

Greer felt wetness in her shoes. She looked down and noticed water pooling around her boots. She bent down and ran her index finger through it. It was water, all right. She glanced farther up the stairway. A small stream of water dribbled down the stairs.

"It looks like there's a leak somewhere," Greer turned and told the others.

"Let's go see," Kane said pushing past her.

They climbed a few more rotations when Vero heard a low rumble. It grew louder. His eyes darted around for its source when a deluge suddenly came crashing toward them from above. The currents picked up the angels and knocked them off the stairwell, but they didn't fall into empty air. Vero felt as if a huge ocean wave had pushed him under.

He looked up at the turbulent surface above and kicked and swam towards it. He poked his head up out of the water. Vero saw that he was in the middle of a deep blue lake that had three waterfalls thundering down into it from up above. It was the lake Uriel had once shown him where the souls had bathed on their way to meet God. The water was cooler and more refreshing than Vero could have ever imagined. As the other angels began to surface around him, they all recognized where they were...they had been here not too long ago when they had begun their search for the unicorns.

"How did we get here and where have the stairs gone?" Kane asked.

"Gone for now," a voice said.

Vero cocked his head and saw Ariel sitting on the shore of the pool. She was no longer a cat. She had gone back to her Ether form with her human head and lion's body. Kane and the others swam towards her and walked up out of the water onto the shore.

"Great, now the competition has caught up with us," Kane said.

"Or the competition has caught up with me," Ariel shot back.

Vero smiled at Ariel. He was happy to see her. Kane would be furious if he knew he had helped Ariel escape the arcade. Ariel must have known it, too, because she discretely winked at Vero.

"I wonder why we're here." Pax said.

"It's the reflection pool," Ariel said. "The pool of truth."

"But I thought this is where human souls bathe before they see God?" Vero asked.

"It is," Ariel answered. "But that's not all that happens here."

"So what is it?" Pax asked.

"The waters show you the truth, no matter what," Ariel said. "It's impossible to lie to it. Try it."

Greer bent over the pool and saw her reflection staring back at her. "I'm a very charming, patient person with impeccable manners," Greer told the pool.

Instantly a stream of water shot Greer in the face.

"Ahh!" she yelled, pulling back.

"See?" Ariel said.

"That's one serious lie detector!"

Ada looked cautiously at the pool. "What's it here for?"

"It's mainly for human souls. After they shed their earthly bodies, their guardian angel—you guys—escort them up the ladder. Every soul must stop at the pool where they are stripped of all their lies before they meet God."

"So how do we get out of here?" Kane asked impatiently.

Ariel flicked her tail. Pax moved back, as her venomous tassel of stingers got a little too close to his face. Ariel noticed. "Sorry," she said. "I would never use my stingers on you."

"Nice to know." Pax eyed her tail, still a bit nervous.

Kane cleared his throat. "So how do we get out of here?" he asked again.

"You must reveal something deeply personal," Ariel said. "Something honest about yourself. Kind of like a confession . . ." she nodded to X. "If you do, you'll be returned to the next level of Jacob's Ladder."

"Out loud in front of everybody?" Greer asked, outraged.

"No, it can be silent."

Pax kneeled by the water. He looked hard into his reflection. His lips moved as he silently spoke. Taking the shape of Pax's body, the water rose out of the pool, wrapped its arms around Pax and pulled him under. Pax disappeared.

Vero turned to the others wide-eyed. "Was that a good thing or a bad thing that just happened?"

"That's how you get to the next step," Ariel said.

Kane narrowed his eyes at Ariel. "Why should we believe you? Why would you help us?"

"The pool of truth is common knowledge. I'm surprised Uriel hasn't covered this material with you yet. As for whether you believe me or not, that's up to you."

"I believe her," Vero said with great conviction. "She wouldn't lie to us." X then kneeled before the pool. He closed his eyes and concentrated. Nothing happened. After a few moments, he opened his eyes.

"What the heck? I just revealed something honest, so why didn't it take me?"

"Your eyes were closed," Ariel said. "They have to be open when you speak, so you can see yourself."

Vero thought about the expression, "You can't lie to yourself." Vero understood he had to see himself for who he was.

"Try it again, with open eyes," Ariel told X.

X stared at his reflection. With his eyes wide open, he spoke to his reflection mentally. A moment later, the water formed into his shape, reached out, and pulled him into the pool, and X was gone. Ada also knelt before her reflection. The "water Ada" grabbed her and pulled her under the water.

"You're next," Greer nodded to Kane.

Kane got down on both knees and focused on his reflection. After a few moments, his lips stopped moving. As he waited for a response, a stream of water shot into his face.

"Hey!" Kane yelled as he wiped the water from his eyes.

"Guess someone is holding back," Greer teased.

Kane knelt closer to the pool, closed his eyes, but once again, water sprayed into his face.

"Dude, you're doing something wrong," Vero said.

A look of resolve came over Kane. He stared into the water. As he silently spoke, Vero was surprised to see a tear escape his eye and roll down his cheek. The water took Kane's shape and pulled him into the pool. Kane vanished. Greer, Vero, and Ariel were left standing on the pool's edge.

"Vero, you next?" Greer asked.

Vero ignored her as he looked intensely into the water. He watched as a light bounced off the surface.

"Vero?" Greer said. "Hello?"

Vero spun around and grabbed the air next to him. He rolled around and wrestled with ... nothing.

"You lied to me!" Vero yelled.

"I think you're totally losing it, dude," Greer said.

But then Greer noticed that the air Vero was wrestling was reflected in the pool. It was the illuminated image of Melchor. She could see his wings, head, and entire body. Vero finally pinned Melchor.

"You promised to show me Clover's future! You're nothing but a little weasel!"

"I am not," Melchor said. "I've been looking for you ever since the arcade."

"Liar!"

"No, I must have landed on a rung lower than where you did. Let me up and I'll show you what you want to know."

"No tricks?" Vero asked.

"No tricks."

"Swear to God?" Vero asked.

"Swear to God," Melchor said solemnly.

Vero considered for a moment then slowly got off Melchor. Though he was invisible, Vero could still feel

Melchor's body. It didn't feel like skin and muscle, but rather like air that had weight and shape.

"You better not try to pull anything," Vero said.

Vero and the others could see Melchor's reflection in the pool—a silhouette image of his body.

"Keep looking at the water," Melchor said. "I will show you what I can of your sister's future."

Vero, Ariel, and Greer watched the pool of water. An image of Clover appeared on the surface. Vero thought it resembled a movie playing on a rolling screen. He saw Clover standing in a dark alley. She looked terrified as two dangerous-looking men approached her. Then the image disappeared.

"Wait! Where was she?" Vero asked as panic rose in his throat like bile.

"I don't know," Melchor answered.

"Can you show me more?"

"I see nothing past that point, but I might be able to show you events leading up to the moment."

Another image of Clover appeared in the water. She was sitting on a bus gazing out the window. She looked apprehensive as she watched the setting sun. Another person came into view. Kira was sitting next to her. The bus stopped in a rundown section of a city. Kira and Clover got up. As they walked toward the front of the bus, Clover suddenly stopped and turned back to her seat. She seemed to be looking for something. Kira picked up Clover's purse. Vero could read her lips—"I've got it," Kira told Clover with a sickly sweet smile.

Vero wondered where they were going. As Clover continued to walk up the aisle, she passed a man reading a newspaper. The image was so clear that Vero could read the print on the paper. He read the date, and it was today! *I thought Melchor was showing me the future? The concert! They're sneaking out to the Two Dimension concert!*

Clover stepped off the bus, and the doors shut behind her. Vero's heart jumped into his throat. Kira remained on the bottom step holding Clover's purse and cell phone, smiling as the bus pulled away from the curb. A frightened look came over Clover when she realized she was stranded and alone.

"She ditched her!" Vero yelled. "She left Clover without any money or her cell phone!"

"What kind of friend is that?" Ariel asked.

Vero thought for a moment. "Melchor, show me her friend, Kira. I need to see the truth of who she is!"

An image of Kira's face appeared on the water's surface. Vero stared intently at it. He needed the truth from her. The desire to know what was really going on with Clover consumed him. Suddenly, Kira's face began to break apart as the water swept away. Vero and the others looked on with great fascination as the water rushed back together and reformed into another image. To their horror, an old hag's face appeared in the water — the same one who appeared during Vero's sword training. She had razor-sharp fangs and hollow eyes. Ripples formed around her head, and soon the water was spinning in circles, creating a whirlpool. Vero saw the whirlpool resembled a chain of hair. Lilith! The whirlpool then swallowed her up.

"Kira is Lilith!" Vero shouted.

It all made sense to him now. Her influence over Clover

was what had caused Clover's personality change. Lilith had Clover under her power!

"Melchor, has this happened already?" Vero desperately needed to know.

"No, but it will tonight."

"But time is supposed to stop when we're in the Ether!" Greer said, now panicked for Clover as well.

"I willed myself here," Vero said. "With the heart attack. They didn't call me back. That's why time didn't stop in the arcade."

Then Greer remembered. When Danny had been under attack from maltures, Vero had jumped in front of a fire truck to get to the Ether. He wasn't called back that time either and, like now, time on earth had not stopped.

"I have to move fast!" Vero told the others. "I have to save my sister."

"How?" Greer asked.

Vero swallowed hard. "Slay Lilith."

All grew silent. After a moment, Greer locked eyes with Vero. "I'm going with you."

"Me too," Ariel said, stepping forward.

Everyone looked at Melchor's reflection on the water. He appeared confused. "It's okay," Vero said. "You helped enough."

"Sorry," Melchor said.

"Then at least tell the others what we've gone to do. And tell them to go on without us."

"I will."

Vero turned to Greer and Ariel. "You can go with him. You don't have to do this. I'll understand."

"No," Greer said, shaking her head. "My Vox Dei is telling me very clearly that I need to go with you."

Vero nodded then turned to Ariel. "It's the right thing to do," she said.

"Thank you."

"Where do we find old Lilith?" Greer asked.

"My best guess is the forest where we found the unicorns," Vero said. "That's where she first attacked us."

Vero thought he saw fear in Ariel's normally stalwart face. He put his hand on Ariel's shoulder. "Are you sure you want to do this? You're leaving the Powers without any competitor."

"I'd have a hard time hanging a medal around my neck know it came at the cost of your sister," Ariel answered.

Greer smiled. "I like this chick."

Melchor watched as the three sprouted their wings and flew towards the rivers above the waterfalls.

"God be with you," he whispered.

# 24

---

❖

---

# MARSH CREATURES

Vero, Ariel, and Greer flew at breakneck speed above the unicorn forest. The land below was thick with trees and shrubs. Vero spotted a small clearing.

"Down there!" Vero yelled to Greer and Ariel. "That's where the unicorns were grazing!"

Vero motioned with his head for them to land in the open area below. Greer and Ariel followed him to the ground. Vero scanned the area. Dense woods surrounded them on all sides.

"Okay, now how do we find her?" Greer asked.

"I'm not sure," Vero said. "All I know is that this is the spot where she attacked us."

"Then we have to ask those that live here," Ariel said. "They'll know her habits."

"Who lives here?" Greer asked.

"The animals of the forest."

"And how are we going to talk to them ...?" Greer asked.

"In case you haven't noticed, I'm half animal."

"Good point." Greer nodded, smiling.

Ariel turned her head toward the ground in front of her. Vero saw her human nose twitch as she picked up a scent. She then pounced on a patch of earth and began to dig furiously with her front claws. Dirt flew between her hind legs and splattered all over Vero. He watched as Ariel pulled something out of the ground. Ariel's claws were retracted, and she held a mole around its midsection.

"Please don't hurt me!" Vero heard the mole plead. He was surprised he could understand it.

"Answer my question, and I won't eat you," Ariel said forcefully.

Greer gave Vero a look. *Gross!*

"What do you want to know?" the mole asked.

Vero noticed how velvety its dark fur was. He looked for the creature's eyes, but all he saw were tiny slits nearly hidden by fur. Vero thought the mole was strange-looking with its large snout and sharp claws.

"We need to find Lilith," Ariel said.

Hearing Lilith's name, the mole panicked. It violently squirmed in Ariel's palm and freed itself. It hit the ground and frantically burrowed into the dirt. Ariel chased after it. Once again, she caught it in her paw.

"No, I won't speak of her," the mole squealed.

Ariel opened her mouth wide and dangled the mole over it. Vero shot Greer a disgusted look. Suddenly, she didn't look so beautiful to him.

"Please, don't make me!" the mole pleaded as it squirmed.

"Where is she?"

Ariel lowered the mole closer to her mouth.

"Okay, okay!" it screamed.

Ariel lifted him to her eyes.

"The marsh. You'll find her by the marsh."

"You swear?" Ariel asked, lowering the mole back toward her mouth.

"Yes! Yes, I swear! Straight ahead, the marsh under the towering cliffs."

"Go!" Ariel dropped the mole to the ground, and, within seconds, it burrowed deep into the earth.

"Were you really going to eat him?" Greer tentatively asked Ariel.

"You've never tried mole?"

Greer and Vero flashed one another disgusted looks.

"I've never tried it either," Ariel laughed. "We Powers are pure spirits and don't need food to sustain us."

Ariel, Vero, and Greer walked through the dense woods. Overgrown trees, shrubs, and thick-hanging moss made it impossible for them to use their wings. Vero could feel the ground underneath his feet squish with each step.

"We must be getting closer to the swamp," he said. "The ground is feeling soft."

"My boots are getting all wet," Greer complained.

"At least you have shoes," Ariel said.

Vero brushed the tree branches and underbrush away from his face and pushed through the foliage. Ariel and Greer followed. Minutes later, they found themselves standing in a low-lying marshy wetland. A ring of trees surrounded the marsh. Large rock cliffs stood behind the trees. On the edge of the swamp there stood the burnt-out remains of a huge bonfire and just beyond that an old abandoned well on the edge of the woods.

"This must be it," Vero said in a voice barely above a whisper.

"Be careful," Ariel said.

Vero scanned the marsh nervously. Dense clusters of reeds grew out of the swampy land, and stagnant pools gave off a foul stench. Something darted in the grass under his foot. Vero jumped back and screamed when he realized it was a snake. The slithering creature disappeared into the black mud.

"Thanks, Vero. Now Lilith will definitely know we're here," Greer said.

"There's a snake in there." Vero pointed.

"Man up!" Greer said.

Another snake slithered toward Vero. His face turned red as he tried to suppress a shriek. His wings shot open, and he rose into the air.

"Seriously?" Greer said, shaking her head.

"I hate snakes," Vero answered. "I'll just fly for now. They can't get me up here."

Without warning, a thick black snake jumped out of the muck and flew straight at Vero. Vero eyes shot wide, hardly able to believe what he was seeing. He screamed and quickly ducked. The serpent narrowly missed him.

"What the ...?" he said, his voice shaking.

"A flying snake?" Greer said.

"Yeah, but it doesn't have any wings!" Vero said. "That's even creepier!"

The snake slithered around in midair and flew back straight for Vero's face when—swoosh!—a sword sliced the flying reptile right across the middle of its long body. It fell to the ground in two pieces. Vero saw the sword belonged to Ariel. She had flown up to save him. He wondered how she could hold the sword in her paw. After all, lions did not have opposable thumbs. But when he looked closer—he saw that her paw had morphed into a sword—her paw and sword were one.

"I've heard of flying fish, and even flying squirrels, but who knew snakes could fly?" Greer said.

"I hope that was the only one," Vero said, trying to catch his breath.

As if on cue, more serpents launched out of the swamp and headed toward Vero. He ducked, swooped down to pick a long stick off the ground, and held it like a batter waiting for the pitch as the snakes altered their course and headed back for him.

"Ah—redemption! Time to show Michael you do know how to wield a stick as a weapon!" Greer shouted as she hovered in the air.

As Vero aimed it at an attacking snake's head, its mouth opened, and a burst of fire shot out. The direct hit burned the wooden stick almost immediately. Vero dropped what was left of it to the ground before the burning remnants scorched his hand.

"Or maybe not," Greer shook her head.

"And they shoot fire?" Vero moaned. "That's not a fair fight! This is my worst nightmare!"

"Enough with the sticks, Vero! I need to see real metal here!" Ariel shouted as her sword swiped at a flying serpent, killing it. As a serpent flew toward Greer, she closed her eyes, and . . . a sword sprung forth from her left palm. She wielded the sword at the creature, slicing off its head.

"What the heck are these things?" Greer shouted.

"Fiery, flying serpents ... Isaiah wrote of them!" Ariel yelled. "They're nasty!"

More serpents rose up out of the marsh. They coiled and slithered through the air as if they were skimming along the surface of a pond. Greer and Ariel wielded their swords every which way at the flying beasts while at the same time ducking shooting fire from their mouths. A flame caught Greer's shoe. She dropped to the wet marsh, putting it out.

"A little help here, Vero!" Ariel shouted swinging wildly at serpents.

Vero looked down at his hand, willing his sword to appear. He closed his eyes and concentrated so deeply that sweat began to trickle down his face. When he opened his eyes, he was face-to-face with a snake! The snake opened its mouth to spew fire when, suddenly, Vero's sword sprung from the palm of his hand. In a split second, Vero swung the sword's blade in front of him, beheading the serpent mere inches from his face.

"About time!" Greer called to Vero as more snakes attacked her while she shot back into the air.

Ariel and Greer swung at the flying serpents, killing one after another. When a serpent just barely missed Ariel, Vero could see that she was growing tired and her reflexes were slowing. Vero flew to her side to help her when he saw scores and scores of snakes flying out of a massive fallen, hollowed-out tree trunk lying in the marsh. Too many snakes to count slithered from the den. A sense of despair came over Vero, Greer, and Ariel when they realized they were about to be ambushed.

"Get behind that tree!" Ariel screamed to Greer and Vero as she nodded to a tree with a thick trunk growing out of the marsh.

They looked to one another; unsure of what she was asking them to do.

"Now!" Ariel yelled.

Vero grabbed Greer's arm and they flew behind the tree. Ariel roared. Vero peeked around the tree and saw Ariel turn her backside to the swarm of angry snakes flying toward her. Her scorpion tail fanned at the tip. Suddenly, barbs the size and shape of sewing needles shot out like bullets firing from a machine gun. The poisonous needles hit their targets, and snake after snake fell from the sky. *It's raining snakes*, Vero thought.

Soon the flying serpents were all lying lifeless on the ground. Feeling it was safe, Vero and Greer stepped out from behind the tree, but both carried their swords defensively out in front, just in case.

"That was amazing," Vero said, looking at the ground littered with hundreds of dead snakes.

Greer stared at Ariel in awe. "I guess that tail comes in handy."

"Don't let your guard down," Ariel panted. "She's here somewhere. Those flying snakes were nothing but her little welcoming committee, and she won't be happy we've killed her pets."

Ariel took a few steps, then screamed out in pain. She fell into the mud. Vero and Greer raced over to her, carefully stepping around dead snakes. Ariel's paw had swollen, and the pad had turned a bright red. Some sort of infection was rapidly spreading up her leg.

"They're still alive . . ." Ariel managed to speak.

Vero and Greer looked at the ground. Their hearts jumped up in their throats when they saw the severed head of a serpent spewing fire from its mouth — its eyes still darting around, seeking its next victim. Vero stabbed the tip of his sword straight through the center of the snake's head. It finally went limp.

"Get off the ground!" Ariel urged them. "You could step on another one!"

Greer and Vero flew into the air, hovering about a foot above Ariel. Greer felt Ariel's paw. It was hot to the touch.

"What can we do?" Greer asked, desperately. "Can you heal yourself?"

Before Ariel could answer, the angels heard a rustle behind them. Greer and Vero whipped their heads around in the direction of the ancient water well. It sounded as if the disturbance was coming from deep within it.

"Let's get her up!" Vero said to Greer, sensing danger.

Greer and Vero's swords retracted back into their palms as they landed on the ground. They were grabbing Ariel under her front legs when they saw a snake-like rope of thick hair crawl out of the well and head toward them.

"Hurry!" Vero yelled. "Ariel, your wings! Can you fly?" But Ariel had gone unconscious.

"Lift her!" Greer shouted as the hair rope slithered closer. "We have to fly her out of here!"

Vero and Greer lifted Ariel a few feet off the ground, but then, with an unnaturally fast speed, the tip of the hair rope spun itself around Ariel's body and pulled her from Greer and Vero's hands. Ariel was consumed and disappeared into the hair. The hair serpent retreated back into the well.

Vero turned to Greer, wide-eyed with terror. "Lilith."

# 25

---

# THE BLACK CASTLE

She has Ariel," Greer whispered in the now eerily quiet marsh.

Vero nodded slowly.

"We have to go after her," Greer said quietly, never taking her eyes off the well. Greer fought back tears. "She can't kill her, can she? We can still rescue her, right?"

Vero looked hard at Greer. He had the same fear, but he put on a brave face and gripped her shoulder. "We'll get her back."

Greer sniffled. Vero looked over at the well. "I have to go in there," he said resolutely. "But I don't want you coming with me. This is as far as you go. Go back to C.A.N.D.L.E."

"Nice try, Vero," Greer said, blinking rapidly.

Vero put both hands on Greer's shoulders and looked her square in the face. "Greer, Lilith is a monster. She just took

Ariel like she was nothing more than a stuffed animal. If anything happened to you ..."

Greer's tough-girl persona reappeared, and she met Vero's eyes with resolve. "I appreciate your concern, but we're in this together. I know I belong here, fighting for Clover and now Ariel."

Vero's eyes filled with gratitude. He grabbed her arm and shoved her in front of him like a shield. "Okay, you first."

"Jerk." Greer chuckled.

Vero released her arm.

"So do we go in there after her?" Greer asked, eyeing the well. "Or do we lure her out somehow?"

Vero thought for a moment. "Maybe lure? I could let one of those snakeheads bite me like they did Ariel. That might bring her back out," Vero said.

"One of those bites could also kill you. You saw Ariel's leg. And lower your voice," Greer whispered. "The well's only a few feet away. She could overhear us."

"Then we go after her." Vero sprouted wings and flew over to the well with Greer following. He hovered over the circular top and looked down into it. Darkness. Complete and utter blackness. He turned to Greer. "Your last chance to bail."

"No way," she said.

Vero and Greer flew down and stood on the edge of the well's decrepit stone wall. Vero gave Greer one last look before he jumped into the center of the well, feet first. The circular walls of the well were wide enough that Vero could flap his wings to slow down his descent. After a few minutes, his feet hit solid ground. Greer landed safely beside him. Vero looked around. The flicker of flames from torches hanging on the stone walls lit up the small chamber. But upon closer look, he realized those weren't torches lining the walls. They were the severed heads of flying serpents! And they were still alive! Fire shot from their mouths in steady bursts.

"Lilith's definitely into Goth," Greer said.

"Stay away from their heads," Vero warned. They're still venomous."

"Do you think she knows we're here?" Greer asked, looking around. "Wherever this is . . ."

"Yes," Vero said. "Stay on your guard." He nodded to a single tunnel that led away from the cavern. "That's the only way forward."

Greer nodded. Vero took the lead through the tunnel. It was a tight squeeze, so they retracted their wings and were careful not to brush up against a wall or else they'd feel the wrath of the snakes' flames. Foul smells began to attack their noses and burn their throats. Greer buried her nose and mouth in the bend of her elbow as she walked. Eventually, the tunnel opened up to a massive cavern. Vero put his hand up, halting Greer.

Before them, spanning some kind of foul, black river of sludge, swung a narrow bridge. On the other side of the bridge, a fortress wall of black stone rose into the darkness. Atop the wall, black bars stretched all the way to the ceiling of the cavern. There was a door in the center of the wall, but it was inside the mouth of a huge carved serpent head. Beyond the bars, Vero could see that the cavern opened up further and housed an ominous dark castle with tall turrets and a massive round tower in the center.

"Not much curb appeal," Greer commented, taking in the fortress wall.

"I know." Vero nodded. "Nothing says 'welcome' like bars and a giant snake head. This isn't going to be easy." A hot wind blew across the sludgy water, delivering its putrid smell to Vero's and Greer's noses. Vero gagged from the stench.

"If evil has a smell, this is it." Greer choked. "It's worse than the Leviathan."

"Let's go," Vero said, stepping out onto the footbridge. The hairs on Vero's arms bristled as they made their way across the rickety bridge toward the stone serpent's mouth. Once on the other side, they walked carefully through the mouth, anxiously glancing up at the massive stone fangs above them. Seconds later, a loud creaking sound rattled them. Greer and Vero spun around to see the serpent's mouth close tightly behind them.

"There's no turning back now," Vero said.

Greer shivered.

The serpent's mouth led to a tunnel that was fairly wide initially, but as Vero walked ahead, the passageway grew narrower and narrower. It, too, was illuminated only by the serpent heads.

Eventually, the passageway was so tight that Greer was forced to walk directly behind Vero. After a short distance, an opening on the other side could be seen. Vero stopped walking, and Greer bumped into him.

"Hold up. I think I can see a gate on the other side," Vero said.

"How far?" Greer asked, as she tried to peer over his shoulder.

"Maybe twenty or thirty feet."

"Good. Turns out, I'm getting claustrophobic. So hurry!" Greer said, pushing Vero forward.

Vero stumbled, and when his foot hit the ground before him, a geyser of flames leapt up from beneath it. The explosion pushed Vero back the way he had come, right into Greer. Vero's pants were on fire as the two tumbled to the ground. Vero rolled on the floor, trying to extinguish the flames, and Greer took off her jacket and began smothering the flames on his legs. Moments later, the fire on Vero's pants went out, but the flame that had knocked him backward was still burning on the floor of the passageway.

"Is your leg burnt?" Greer asked.

"No, only my pants."

They looked at the hallway before them.

"What the heck just happened?" Greer asked.

"After you pushed me, I stepped forward, and fire shot out from the ground under my foot," Vero said as he bent down and picked up a stone. "Grab some more. I want to see something."

Greer grabbed a few small rocks from the floor and handed them to Vero. He threw them down the hall. Wherever they landed, fire erupted.

"It's a mine field!" Greer yelped. "We can't walk across that, and we can't go back!"

Vero surveyed the narrow hallway before him. Greer was right about walking ahead.

"We're doomed already," Greer said. "If the hallway wasn't so tight, we could just fly over the fire floor."

Vero thought about that for a moment. As he looked down the tunnel, the flames from the rocks on the floor still flickered in the narrow passage, but he could see that they stopped directly in front of the gate.

"We'll see about that," Vero said.

Vero took a few steps back. He focused on the small tongues of flame on the floor before him. He put his hand over his heart and concentrated, then started running full speed like a gymnast about to begin a tumbling routine.

"Vero, what are you doing?" Greer screamed.

Just before he reached the flames on the floor, Vero leapt forward headfirst. As he flew, he grew his wings and positioned them straight back over his torso, since the narrow passage prevented him from spreading them. His wings scraped along the passage ceiling but gave him just enough lift to carry him forward, almost like a paper airplane. The gate was quickly approaching, but his glide altitude was beginning to decrease. As he got nearer and nearer to the floor, Vero realized it was going to be close. He stretched forward with his arms and pointed his toes, trying to make himself as thin as possible. Just before his torso scraped the ground, he slammed headfirst into the gate and collapsed onto the floor. He moaned in pain, but had cleared the fire floor.

Vero grabbed the gate and pulled himself to his feet.

"Vero, are you okay?" Greer called. There was panic in her voice.

Vero gingerly touched the top of his head. "Yep."

"You're a crazy jerk, you know that?!"

Vero turned around and peered at Greer in the flickering light. "The flight was tight, but it was only the sudden stop at the end that really hurt. You can do it, Greer. If you keep your wings pinned back behind you and get a good running start—Oooof!"

Vero was still talking when Greer head-butted into his gut. They both fell to the floor in a heap.

"Don't you EVER leave me behind again, Vero Leland, you stupid lunatic!" Greer punched his arm.

Vero had the wind knocked out of him by the force of Greer's impact. As his breath came back to him, he struggled to get the words out, "Okay, fine. Never again."

They pulled themselves to their feet before the gate and dusted themselves off. Vero tried the handle on the gate, and it swung wide. As they took a step forward, they saw they were standing in front of a courtyard, beyond which stood a formidable black, medieval-looking castle.

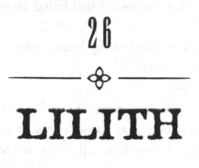

# 26

## LILITH

Vero and Greer flew slowly across the courtyard, but they didn't run into any trouble. No flying snakes, no fiery minefields, no Lilith. It was so easy that it made Vero nervous.

Vero and Greer landed in front of the huge castle door, and together the two of them pulled it open. After peering inside, they stepped into a massive room. Fiery serpent heads hung on the cold stone walls, spewing jets of fire from their mouths. Arched windows with solid black glass let in no outside light, not that there was any daylight in this great dark pit anyway. Massive cobwebs decorated the place, and a high, peaked ceiling enclosed the room like a tomb. But besides the cobwebs and the serpent heads, the room appeared empty. Greer moved in closer to Vero.

"And I thought Abaddon's cave was scary," Vero said.

*Thump! Thump!*

Terrified, Greer hugged Vero from behind and crouched down. Vero broke out in a cold sweat as his eyes scanned the room. Now that the sound had faded away, it was eerily quiet.

"Maybe the noise was just my heart pounding against my chest?" Greer said hopefully.

*Thump! Thump!*

Greer jumped. Vero tensed. Then his eyes focused on something moving in the far corner of the room. It was a tan wicker basket about three feet tall. Vero nodded toward it.

"Please, save me from her," a young girl's voice cried from inside the basket.

Vero tentatively walked toward the sound, but Greer grabbed his shoulders from behind.

"Probably a trick. Be careful," she warned Vero in a low voice.

Vero nodded. He and Greer cautiously approached the basket, nervously eyeing their surroundings with every step.

"Please, help me," the girl's voice said. "Lilith put me in here and won't let me out."

As Vero and Greer neared the wicker basket, they could see that while the cylindrical sides were woven from tan wicker, its lid was cast from heavy lead.

"How long have you been in there?" Vero asked the voice in the basket.

"I don't really know. There are no days in this place, only endless nights."

Vero crouched down and saw the girl's desperate gray eyes through the basket's slats. He was moved to pity.

"Please, take the lid off," she begged. "Have mercy on me."

Vero and Greer exchanged hesitant looks.

"I can take you to your sister."

"My sister? What do you know about my sister?"

"Lilith has her. Clover is her name. She's been talking about Clover for a long time now."

Vero looked to Greer, unsure. Greer bit her lip.

"It's not too late. There's still a chance you can get her back, but you need to hurry," the girl said.

Feeling a surge of hope, Vero stood and reached for the lead cover. Greer grabbed his hand, stopping him from removing it. She shook her head and held up her index finger, indicating for Vero to wait.

"What is your name?" Greer asked.

"My name? I don't know. I've been in here so long, I can no longer remember." The little girl sniffled.

"Greer, we don't have time for this!" Vero said, annoyed. Now that he was inside Lilith's horrible fortress, he felt a renewed urgency to rescue Clover from her grip.

"No!" Greer said. "You don't get it!" She tightened her grip on his hand.

"This is my sister's life we're talking about!" Vero shouted. He pulled away from Greer and shoved the cover to the ground.

The lid hit the floor with a loud clang and spun in circles like a fallen coin, echoing throughout the dark chamber. Vero and Greer stood back as the basket shook. They saw two little hands reach out and grab the rim. The back of a small child's head of golden hair popped up.

"Stop!" Greer commanded. "Tell me your name!"

The girl spun around, and Vero and Greer saw her eyes were no longer the pitiful ones they had seen inside the basket. Her eyes now appeared to be made of stone, the same black obsidian stone that made up the castle. Vero then realized that he had merely seen a reflection of his own desperate eyes mirrored in hers. The girl smiled at them, showing jagged fangs of black stone. Vero jumped back.

Greer's expression hardened. "I know your name!" she shouted.

"Liar," the girl hissed.

As Greer held the girl's gaze, she motioned behind her back for Vero to pick up the lid. Vero slowly bent down to retrieve it.

"I know exactly who you are," Greer said, trying to buy Vero more time.

"You know nothing, stupid fledgling," the girl growled as she put one foot out of the basket.

Greer saw that Vero had picked up the heavy lead cover. "Now!" she yelled.

Vero lifted the cover over the girl's head, but it was heavy, and he trembled from the weight. Greer pushed down on the girl's head, trying to shove her back into the basket. The girl fought back, snapping at Greer's hands with her sharp black fangs. She knocked the lid from Vero's hands. He scrambled after it. The girl was nearly out of the basket and smiling evilly. "You think you can overpower me so easily? I wonder what they teach you at that school these days?"

Greer looked into her soulless black eyes and said, "I'll tell you what they taught me, they taught me your name! You are Wickedness."

A look of shock came over the girl. She let out a shriek that echoed throughout the chamber.

"You are wickedness, and I command you into the basket!" Greer yelled forcefully.

The girl retreated into the basket and grew eerily calm.

Vero slammed the cover over the top and let out a sigh of relief.

"How did you do that?" Vero asked, panting.

"Demons hate to give up their names. Once you know their names, you have power over them."

"But how did you know her name?"

"Zechariah 5. The woman in the basket. Her name is Wickedness."

"Why do you think she's here?" Vero asked.

"I bet she's Lilith's attempt to corrupt us. If she gets out of the basket, her wickedness will seep into you."

Out of the corner of his eye, Vero saw something black scurry from the floor into the hallway. He did a double take, but it was gone. "Did you see that?"

"What?"

"Come on, it went that way," Vero motioned.

Vero stealthily rounded the corner with Greer. Crouching low, they proceeded down the hall, staying in the shadows. Vero saw what looked like the tapered end of a lock of hair slithering down the hall ahead of them.

"Lilith's hair," Vero whispered.

Vero and Greer followed it, keeping a safe distance behind. The truss of hair turned the corner, then disappeared.

"Forget it! She wants us to follow it," Greer whispered to Vero.

"Yeah, but she is who we came for," Vero whispered back.

Vero cautiously turned the corner and saw an enormous, windowless throne room framed by rows of stone pillars and arches. An ugly, black velvet chandelier hung from the ceiling but failed to illuminate. Flaming serpent heads attached to the pillars provided the only light. A long red runner ran the entire length of the chamber, up several steps, and ended at the foot of a throne whose back was forged from hundreds of scythes. Kira sat on the throne, looking very much like the 14-year-old girl Vero knew from school.

"Not bad for a teenager. Huh?" she said, her arms gesturing to her chamber.

"Is that her?" Greer asked in a hushed voice to Vero.

Vero nodded. He squared his shoulders. "Release my sister!"

"And Ariel," Greer added, stepping forward.

"But your sister is my new BFF," Kira said in a mocking tone.

Vero's voice shook with fury. "You tricked her."

Kira appeared not to have heard him. "And don't forget Danny. All I had to do was send out one little email, and I've got your entire school believing he rigged that gym ceiling," she laughed. "Humans really make it so easy for me. They love to believe the worst of a person. Just ask Davina about the kiss."

"Let Clover go!"

"Do you really think I'll take orders from two little fledglings?"

"You will from these two," Vero said with conviction.

Kira laughed then looked up at the ceiling. "Oh, Pavouci!"

Vero followed her gaze. Suddenly, the chandelier started to move. Vero and Greer watched in horror as the arms of the chandelier began to untie the main body from the chain from which it hung. It wasn't a chandelier at all but rather a massive spider suspended on its back! With lightning speed, the gargantuan spider jumped down and scurried on all eight legs toward Vero and Greer. Greer's eyes bulged in terror as a strand of web shot forth from its abdomen and lassoed her. Another sticky strand wrapped itself around Vero. Vero saw the spider had a mouth, but no eyes! Pavouci gave an evil gurgle as he pulled both angels toward him. He quickly wrapped his spindly legs around them and began spinning them together in layer after layer of thick sticky silk.

Greer screamed as she thrashed wildly, trying to claw her way out. But her struggle only caused the massive spider to gurgle louder. He was enjoying himself. Vero, by contrast, had put his hand on his heart and gone limp as soon as the spider had begun to blanket them, putting up no fight at all.

When Pavouci finished his work, he dropped the bundle of wrapped fledglings on the floor and sat on it like a mother hen on her eggs. Kira, still on her thrown, brought her hands together for a few claps.

Then Kira rose, a malicious victorious smile plastered on her face. She walked down the steps toward the spider and his bundle, which was now completely still. But her smile quickly vanished when she heard what sounded like a sword being unsheathed. Pavouci, still nesting atop the cocoon, stopped gurgling. To Kira's great anger and dismay, thick black blood gushed from underneath the spider's abdomen, staining the white bundle below him. A moment later, Vero rolled out from under the dead spider, brandishing a sword covered in its black blood. Kira's eyes grew big and rimmed red with rage as she let loose an unearthly scream.

Vero saw that Greer was still completely limp inside the spider's silk web. With his sword, he quickly cut the webbing, further opening the hole from which he had emerged.

Dazed, Greer rolled out of the pod, pushed back onto her butt, and shrank up against a pillar. Vero turned to Kira, brandishing his sword. "Give them up now!"

Kira let out another low growl and began to transform. Her teeth grew into rotted yellow fangs. Deep wrinkles cut into her face. Her bright hazel eyes changed to black stone. She had turned into the hideous, ugly hag. Kira was no more — the true Lilith had emerged. And then, from her scalp, the long hair train grew and grew. It seemed endless. Vero stepped back. Greer stumbled to her feet and stood beside him. Her sword shot forth from her hand.

"I will never let her go!" Lilith snarled, holding up her hands.

Vero and Greer's eyes went wide with fear as they watched a gleaming scythe grow from each of her palms.

"Oh no ..." Greer stammered as she studied the two curved blades.

"You have got to cut those nails," Vero taunted Lilith.

Swoosh! Vero felt the wind of the blades as Lilith sprang toward them and swung her arm, narrowly missing his head. Apparently, she didn't care much for his sense of humor. Vero spun and braced himself, his sword ready to block more swipes.

"Where is it? Tell me where it is," Lilith said, circling the angels.

"Where is what?" Vero asked, never taking his eyes off her.

"The book. The book poor pathetic Raziel lost. Tell me where it is, and I'll release your sister."

Then Vero understood what Lilith was really after — the Book of Raziel. It was the book Michael had told him would play an important part in his life.

"Release Clover first!" Vero yelled. "Deal?"

Lilith smiled, and her forked tongue licked her lips. She shook her head. "Nice try, boy. But you have no leverage here."

Vero held her gaze. "I know where the book is, and you don't. I would call that leverage."

Lilith shrieked and swung wildly at him with both scythes. Vero blocked her attacks, swiftly meeting each with the blade of his sword. With Lilith focused on Vero, Greer saw a window of opportunity. With incredible speed, she charged and brought down her sword nearly on top of Lilith's head. At the last moment, Lilith dodged the brunt of the shot, but Greer's blade found some hold and cut off Lilith's left ear. Black blood seeped down the side of Lilith's head. She let out a piercing screech that sent shivers down Vero's spine and lunged at Greer, both scythes swinging.

"Greer, watch out!"

Lilith backed Greer into a corner. The tip of her hair rose up, split in two, and struck at Greer like twin snakes, grabbing her from both sides. The hair enveloped her, lifting her off the ground, and brought Greer face-to-face with Lilith. Greer looked into Lilith's obsidian eyes and froze in terror. Lilith smiled wickedly. Her hair hurled Greer against the wall where she impacted with a bone-crushing thud and slid to the ground, knocked out.

"Greer, no!" Vero screamed.

Filled with rage, Vero blindly charged Lilith, swinging his sword wildly. Lilith easily deflected his reckless attacks. The clang of metal striking metal reverberated throughout the hall. Lilith laughed out loud as she effortlessly backed Vero up against a pillar. His wings shot out, and Vero rocketed into the air.

He didn't get far before the tip of Lilith's hair reared up and ensnared his right leg, pulling him back down to the ground. Vero swiped at the hair with his sword and sliced off the offending truss. Lilith's craggy face grimaced as she recoiled with pain. But a moment later, she swung her scythes with a deadly strength at Vero's head. Vero somersaulted over her as her blades sliced clear through a pillar like a circular saw, severing it.

"Lilith! I know your name, and I command you to give them back! Give them all back!" Vero shouted, his blade out in front.

Enraged at the sound of her real name, Lilith turned and struck his sword with such supernatural strength that it flew out of his hand and clanged to the ground. She flashed Vero a malicious smile as he backed away, bumping against a pillar. With her right hand, Lilith held the curved blade around Vero's neck. He could feel Lilith's foul breath on his face.

"Tell me where the book is. We could be so powerful together."

Vero looked into her hollow black eyes. He closed his eyes and silently prayed.

"Tell me!" Lilith screeched.

Vero opened his eyes. A confident smile came to his lips as he looked Lilith directly in her eyes.

"You think your faith is going to get you out of this one?" she scoffed, tickling his neck with the edge of the blade.

"Yes, plus a little help from my friends," Vero said.

And with that, Greer stepped from the shadows behind Lilith. Vero briefly saw her sword glinting silver before she thrust it into Lilith's lower back. Lilith hissed in agony and surprise. She spun around to Greer, releasing Vero from her deadly scythe. Black blood gushed from Lilith's side, but she did not appear weakened by the loss. Greer jumped back from Lilith's swinging blades, but the tip of one of the scythes caught her, slicing across her midsection. Greer instinctively covered the wound with a trembling hand.

Vero watched as Lilith advanced on Greer, going in for the kill. Greer raised her eyes to meet Lilith's hungry gaze and knew she didn't stand a chance. "Vero," she whispered. "Catch!" Greer threw her sword to Vero who caught it by the hilt.

Lilith raised her right hand, winding up for the blow that would end Greer's life, when Vero leapt toward her and grabbed a handful of hair, jerking Lilith's head back. With all his might, he swung Greer's sword, severing Lilith's mane of hair at her neck. "You will release them all, Lilith!" he shouted.

Lilith let out a bloodcurdling shriek as she lost her balance and stumbled back. Her scythes disappeared into her palms.

"No!" she screamed as she fell to her knees and desperately scrambled to collect her fallen mane. But suddenly Lilith dropped the hair and clutched her stomach as if just then feeling the deep wound that Greer had inflicted. Lilith looked up at Vero and snarled, "This is not over! It is never over!" She stretched out her arms and grabbed for Vero, who stepped back. "Fear me!" Lilith hissed.

Vero ignored her and raced over to Greer. He whipped off his sweatshirt and pressed it against her wound to stop the blood loss. He put his other arm around her, and together they watched as puffs of black smoke wafted from Lilith's nostrils. Then her entire body spontaneously combusted into flames, though her howl of pain never ceased. The flames grew so intense that Vero pulled Greer into his shoulder to shield her eyes. After a few moments, the fire disappeared, and where Lilith had stood only a black scorched mark on the red carpet remained.

"She's a goner," Vero said.

Greer looked up a Vero, sadness in her eyes. "I think I am too."

"No, don't say that," Vero said, near tears. "I'm gonna get you out of here."

Greer shook her head. "Maybe the choir isn't so bad ..."

Suddenly, a warm glow filled the room. Vero looked for the source of the light. It was the pile of Lilith's fallen hair — the black strands had turned golden. The hair coiled around itself and formed into the shape of a volcano as Vero and Greer looked on, wondering whether this was some new evil they would have to fight. Then Ariel shot out of the cone's top. Being a cat, she landed gracefully on her feet, albeit dazed and confused. Vero and Greer smiled at her.

"Welcome back," Greer said weakly to Ariel.

"Can you help her?" Vero pleaded.

Ariel's smile quickly dropped when she saw that Greer was clutching her stomach, blood oozing between her fingers. She bounded over to Greer, gently removed Greer's hands, and placed her paw over the seeping wound. Vero and Greer looked down in amazement as the wound resealed itself. It was perfect — not even a blemish.

"You could have left a little scar," Greer joked. "I have an image to uphold after all."

"Thank you," Vero said to Ariel, hoisting Greer to her feet. Vero handed Greer her sword and then picked up his own.

"I guess the choir will just have to wait," Greer chuckled. "Right, Vero?"

Vero didn't answer. He was staring desperately at the fallen hair. Ariel and Greer walked over and stood on either side of him.

"Were there others in there?" Vero asked.

Ariel shook her head. "It was only darkness. I saw and heard no one else."

Disappointment swept over Vero. A tear came to Greer's eye. "Clover ..." she whispered.

Suddenly, a loud cracking sound shook the chamber like an earthquake. The ceiling above the angels began to crumble. Sheets of black stones fell at an alarming rate. Greer grabbed Ariel with one hand and Vero with the other, pulling them under the safety of an archway. They watched as not only the ceiling's stones collapsed but also the earth directly above it. Cool fresh air rushed down, caressing Vero's face. A large opening clear to the outside had formed high above them.

But before Vero, Ariel, and Greer had time to fly back into the beautiful night sky, the hair cone began to shake once more. Hundreds then thousands of different colored, ethereal beings with heads and flowing bodies drifted out of it. Each soul would rise several feet then slowly fade away like smoke. It was as if floodgates had been opened. Vero, Greer, and Ariel stood back and watched anxiously, hoping to catch sight of Clover's soul.

"Do you see her?" Greer asked.

"Not yet."

"How could Lilith have had all these souls within her grasp?" Greer asked.

"These are only the souls of those still living on earth," Ariel said. "Sadly those who have passed away while serving her interests have gone on to another place. But these souls are lucky. You have freed them from her influence. On earth, they will feel a true weight has been lifted, and they can begin anew."

Vero continued to watch the flood of souls, desperately searching for Clover. But then his face turned pale as a thought occurred to him. "You said these souls are the ones still alive on earth ..." Vero said, trying not to hyperventilate. "What if she's not ..."

"Don't say it!" Greer cut him off. "It's not true. I can feel she's still alive, and she's in there!"

Vero studied each soul as it emerged. He was growing more despondent by the minute. But then a soul rose up and seemed to turn to him. It was the same silver cloud being from the dream challenge ... it was Clover!

"That's her? Isn't it?!" Vero asked.

"Yes," Greer said as relief swept over her. "She's free."

"And so are we," Ariel said.

And with that, Greer, Ariel, and Vero flew out of the chamber through the ceiling's opening.

# 27

❖

# WREATHS OF GLORY

Vero, Ariel, and Greer walked through C.A.N.D.L.E. The main hall was filled with angels, and it felt as if every eye was on them. Angels everywhere were whispering and staring. Vero saw an angel tip his head to him as he passed.

"You guys getting the feeling that we're being watched?" Greer asked. "And I mean not just by the Thrones."

As they stepped through the doors to the packed auditorium, every angel bowed to them. Vero, Greer, and Ariel exchanged confused looks. Had everyone heard about their fight with Lilith? Ada and Pax ran over to them.

"Is it true?" Ada asked Vero excitedly.

"About Lilith?" Pax looked at them with amazement.

Ada pushed back her copper curls. "They say you left the competition to hunt her down in her castle!"

Vero looked at Ariel and Greer and nodded. "She had my sister, so we had to go. I'm sorry about ditching you guys."

"Yeah, sorry, guys," Greer said.

Pax's eyes were big and round. "They're saying you whipped her, and freed thousands of souls?"

"All true," Greer said. "I guess we lost the ladder challenge?"

Ada shook her head. "No, we actually made it to the top of Jacob's Ladder first."

"You ..." Pax looked at Ariel. "You were gone, and Dumah never left the arcade. Uriel had to rescue him and bring him back or else he'd still be staring at his reflection."

Ada laughed. "Turns out the Dominions' one flaw is their vanity. They need to learn to resist their beauty. Dumah had never seen a mirror before, and he became totally fascinated with his reflection."

"What about Melchor?" Vero asked.

"He finished after us," Pax said. "I guess being invisible doesn't make you run stairs extra fast."

Uriel walked over to them. He caught Vero's eye, and for a moment, the two of them just looked at each other. "Welcome back," Uriel said at last, looking around at the others.

Vero wondered if the archangel was upset with them. "I'm sorry, Uriel. I know I shouldn't have taken off like that, but—"

Uriel smiled warmly. "God's work always comes before a competition."

Vero sighed a breath of relief. He wasn't going to get into trouble.

Uriel turned to Greer and Ariel, "You all fought bravely and performed wonderfully."

Ariel nodded and looked at the ground shyly.

"No biggie." Greer smiled.

"How did you kill Lilith?" Pax asked.

Greer chuckled and nodded. "Vero gave her a long overdue haircut and—"

Uriel held up a hand and cut her off. "She isn't dead."

Greer spun to face Uriel, her forehead wrinkled in confusion. "But we watched her burn. The only thing left of her was a scorch mark on the carpet ..."

"She is very much alive," Uriel said. "Only greatly weakened ... for now."

Greer's heart sank.

Recalling the similarly burnt floor in Dr. Walker's office, Vero asked, "The nurse that attacked me on earth, before Kira ever showed up? Was that Lilith too?"

"It was," Uriel said.

"She kept asking me about the ..."

The herald angels' trumpets blew, cutting Vero off. Vero was familiar with Uriel's habit of causing an interruption whenever Vero was about to say something he shouldn't. When he heard the trumpets, he looked at Uriel. Uriel shook his head almost imperceptibly, confirming Vero suspicion— they would have to wait to talk about the book later, and in private.

"Time for the final ceremony," Uriel said with a smile, and he turned to walk toward the stage.

Ariel, Vero, Greer, Pax, and Ada followed. As they got closer, Vero saw that Kane and X were already standing on the stage. Dumah and the faint light that was Melchor were also there. They joined everyone on stage. X shook Vero's hand. Kane nodded to Vero, "Glad your sister's all right."

"Thanks," Vero said.

Once again, Vero had the feeling that his every move was being observed. He looked up and saw the Thrones breaking through the sky, appearing from thin air. The eyes on the wheels spun round and round. Gabriel, Uriel, Raziel, Raphael, Charoum the Dominion, Camael the Power, and Vangelis the Virtue took their positions on the stage. Vero's eyes lit up when he saw Michael walk out. Michael looked to the Thrones, and Vero could tell they were conversing mentally with one another. The archangel nodded, and the Thrones disappeared from sight. Michael turned to the audience.

"Before we crown the overall winner of the Angel Trials, we will announce the winner of the third trial—the ascent of Jacob's Ladder."

Kane grinned ear to ear. Michael walked over and stood before Kane, placing a palm branch in his hand. "To Kane and his fellow guardians," Michael announced. The crowd erupted in cheers. Kane held the palm branch high for all to see as he stood proudly at attention, soaking in the adoration. When the applause and cheers died down, Michael faced the spectators. "And now for the winner of the Angel Trials ..."

"Here we go," Kane said in a low voice as he elbowed Vero. "We got this ... I mean I won the third challenge, plus we found the jawbone and should have won the first challenge too."

Vero didn't say anything. He didn't share Kane's confidence.

"As you know, we hold the Angel Trials to test our young

angels in the areas of ability, endurance, and belief," Uriel said. "Our angels did their best, and, for the most part, honored God with their talents and strengths. We are proud of all of them. The Thrones have made their decision, and due to unforeseen events, their verdict is unusual. For the first time ever in the history of the Trials, the Thrones have decided to award the honors to three individual angels from two different groups."

Kane nodded with confidence to Vero.

"For her bravery in battle and generosity in helping fellow competitors, Ariel for the Powers, has won top honors!"

The crowd exploded in applause, and the Powers rattled their tails loudly. Ariel looked shocked but pleased.

"And for the first time ever," Michael continued, "top honors go to two Guardians! For their exceptional skill in battle and their courage to give up everything in order to follow God's will, to Greer and . . . Vero!"

Vero exchanged surprised looks with Greer as the spectators clapped and cheered. Kane looked shocked. Then his expression hardened as he watched Vero and Greer wave shyly at the audience.

Michael put his hands up to calm the crowd. "Angels, we salute you. Together, these three angels sacrificed personal glory to follow their inner voices. And in so doing, freed numerous souls trapped under Lilith's malicious influence."

Michael motioned to Gabriel. She walked over holding three round laurel wreaths. Michael placed the first wreath on Ariel's head.

"God bless you."

Ariel looked down, humbled.

Michael placed a wreath on Greer's head. "May God bless you."

Greer blushed.

Michael placed the final laurel wreath on Vero's head. "Well done, Vero. May God bless you always."

As Vero looked into Michael's piercing violet eyes, he fought back tears. Michael placed his hand on Vero's shoulder and smiled.

Dumah turned to Greer. He nodded to her. "Congratulations," he said.

Greer's eyes went wide. "He speaks! Dumah speaks!"

Dumah smiled.

X, Pax, and Ada walked over to Vero. Ada hugged him. Pax high fived him, and X knuckle bumped him. Vero looked for Kane but only caught a glimpse of him storming off the stage.

X leaned into Vero. "He looks pretty upset. I know you two haven't been getting along lately, but Kane's not a bad guy. When Uriel put Eitan on our team, Kane fought him, told Uriel it wasn't right."

"Really?" Vero said, moved.

"Yeah."

Vero scanned the crowd and spotted Kane. He chased after him, but Kane had already disappeared into the audience. Struggling to avoid the congratulatory hugs and embraces of angels on all sides, Vero spread his wings and shot up a few yards for a better vantage point. He glimpsed Kane walking back into C.A.N.D.L.E. Vero flew after him, but he bumped into several angels who had flown up to give Vero their accolades. Shaking them off, Vero finally caught up to Kane as he entered the main hall.

"Kane!" Vero alighted just outside the giant door and raced after him.

Kane turned around in front of the torch. "What do you want, Vero? Come to gloat?"

"No," Vero said, shaking his head. "I wanted to explain ... I went for my sister. You would have done the same for yours. I wasn't trying to outdo anyone."

"But you do every single time," Kane said. "That's why I didn't want you on my team in the first place."

Vero looked down. He hadn't expected Kane to say that.

"I wanted to shine." Kane glanced at the giant torch. "I wanted to stand out ... " He sighed. "Right after my baby sister was born, my parents went through a divorce. My dad came to pick up my brother and me for a weekend visit, but my dad only took my brother. He gave some excuse about how he thought I looked like I was coming down with a cold so I should stay home. But I felt fine. When the weekend was up, he didn't return with my brother. He told my mom he was keeping him to live with him."

"Did he ever bring him back?" Vero asked.

"Yeah, after a few days. My mom had to agree not to call the police on him, and no one ever spoke about it again."

"You're lucky you had a cold or else you would have been kidnapped too."

When Kane looked at Vero his eyes were full of pain. "I told you. I wasn't sick, and my dad knew it. And ever since, I had to live with knowing that he didn't want me. Why take my brother and not me? And since then, no matter what I've done, I can never get his attention ... and I guess it's the same with the archangels."

Kane turned and walked away.

"But you do stand out," Vero said, striding after him. "You were selected the leader of the group by Aurora. I wasn't. And I'll admit it, I was jealous when the unicorn gave you the blessing and not me. And you pulled the fort-i-fire from the flames."

"But that 'special blessing' was just one big fat lie. What good did it do?" Kane's voice was shaking. "I did what they asked of me. I gave this competition my all, and what do they decide to do? They change the rules!"

"It's only a contest. It has nothing to do with who we are. It doesn't mean anything."

"It meant something to me!" Kane yelled.

Kane turned and walked toward the main doors. Vero's heart felt heavy. He saw Kane was in a bad place, and he wished there was something he could do to help. And then an idea occurred to him. Without any fear or hesitation, Vero reached into the swirling torch and pulled out a fort-i-fire. He drew his arm back and threw it at Kane. "Kane!"

Kane turned around. With an amazing reflex, Kane grew his sword and batted the fort-i-fire all the way past Vero and way up to the ceiling of the vast dome, where it exploded into fireworks.

"Don't waste one on me," Kane said as he walked out the doors.

# 28

❖

# VERO'S TASK

The auditorium had emptied out. Only Vero, Greer, X, Pax, and Ada sat on the stage. Ariel lay beside them.

"He'll get over it," Greer said.

"I'm not so sure," Vero said. "You should have seen the look on his face."

"In some ways, I get where Kane's coming from," X said. "They never really explained the rules to us. It was really unfair when Melchor stole the jawbone after Ada was the one who solved the riddle ... and Kane did reach the top of the ladder first. When you—" X looked at Vero. "When you and Greer disappeared after the reflection pool, we had no idea where you went. It's not like we could have helped you or come after you even if we had wanted. Melchor didn't say anything to us about Lilith or Clover until after we reached the top. So, yeah, I totally get Kane's frustration. We did our best to play by the rules, and apparently the rules didn't matter. Not that I'm upset ... but I understand where Kane is coming from."

Uriel appeared at the side of the stage and walked over to the group. "It's time for everyone to go back," he told them.

The angels got to their feet. Vero turned to Ariel. "You saved our necks so many times during these Trials. Thank you."

"Ditto," Greer nodded to her.

Ariel smiled. "I hope to see you again." She closed her eyes and disappeared.

Ada hugged X and then the others. She hesitated for a moment.

"What?" Pax asked her.

"Going back feels different this time ... it's like our universes collided. It used to be our angel world was here, and our human life was there. But now, I'm not so sure," Ada said.

"Yeah," Greer said.

Ada looked serious. "She went after Vero's family. And I have a sinking feeling that Lilith was nothing by comparison to what's coming." She turned to Vero. "Be safe."

Vero nodded, then Ada closed her eyes and vanished. X looked at Vero and then he too disappeared.

Pax turned to Uriel. "I don't want to go back. Being in that institution is torture."

"But it's only half the torture your parents feel at having put you there," Uriel told Pax as he placed his thumbs over Pax's eyes and closed his eyelids. Seconds later, Pax vanished.

Greer eyed Vero, deliberating whether or not to hug him. Finally, she grabbed him and wrapped her arms around him. Embarrassed by her own gush of emotions, she quickly pushed Vero away. "Get off, weirdo."

Vero chuckled. "Thanks for helping me with Clover. You really didn't have to do it, but you helped anyway. I couldn't have done it without you."

"Who says she didn't have anything in it?" Uriel asked.

"What do you mean?" Greer asked.

"She had her ward to protect."

Understanding dawned in Greer's eyes. "I'm Clover's guardian angel?"

Uriel nodded.

"I knew it!" Greer said, pumping her fist in the air. "I knew I felt some kind of connection to her. That's why I was able to track her in the dream."

Vero smiled. "I couldn't have hoped for a better guardian for my sister. I guess this sort of makes us family."

"Don't push it," Greer said. She smiled at Vero then closed her eyes and vanished. Vero looked at Uriel. He wasn't ready to leave the Ether just yet. He needed some answers.

Uriel read his mind. "You're upset."

"Yes, I'm upset!" Vero snapped, holding back tears. "I'm upset about Kane! I'm upset about Pax living in an institution! And I'm upset that you didn't want me in the Trials!"

"There are a few things I think you should see," Uriel said, opening his wings.

Vero looked at Uriel. Though he was still full of emotion, he stepped toward Uriel, and in the blink of an eye, they were standing inside a nursing home back on earth. Elderly people sat at tables in a small dining room. Some were feeding themselves. Others had nurses feeding them. One elderly man banged his hand repeatedly on the tabletop. An elderly woman slumped over in her wheelchair, while another old woman sang a Broadway song to herself.

"This is the Alzheimer's wing at Mercy Medical," Uriel said to Vero.

Vero looked upon the seniors with great sadness in his eyes.

"I know when you look at them, you feel bad for them. You think their suffering is humiliating and dreadful. Don't you?" Uriel asked, as he observed Vero looking at the patients. "Well, the truth of the matter is, you shouldn't. They are the blessed ones, Vero."

Vero gave Uriel a disbelieving look. "Blessed?"

"For the patient, Alzheimer's is a blessing from God. You see, Vero, God wants these people to be with Him in heaven one day. So He makes them childlike again, removing all their worldly concerns, one by one, in preparation for their transition. So that when these people meet their maker, they will accept Him with the faith of a small child."

Vero's brow furrowed. Uriel was proposing a very unconventional way of thinking about a horrible disease. He'd never thought of Alzheimer's that way. The elderly woman stopped singing and looked directly at Vero.

"Are you two here to take me? Because I'm ready. But can I just finish my song?" she politely asked Vero.

Vero did a double take, startled that she could see him.

"The veil between earth and the Ether is very thin when humans are quite young, and again as people become elderly," Uriel said in a low voice to Vero. "It makes the transition to and from the spiritual world less jarring."

"Well?" the woman asked Vero.

"No, Estelle, we're not here to take you just yet," Uriel answered.

"Then I suppose I can finish my song," the woman said, and she continued singing.

Uriel wrapped Vero in his wings, and before he knew what was happening, Vero found himself standing with Uriel in a hospital room. A little girl, maybe seven or eight years old, lay in a bed sleeping. Bright balloons and colorful school drawings hung on the walls. Stuffed animals sat on a window bench.

"This is Leah. She has a congenital heart condition. She will endure many painful surgeries, but eventually the doctors will fix her heart. Her ailment is also a blessing. Through all of her suffering, Leah will emerge with great compassion and empathy for the suffering of other people. She'll take this experience and become a powerful woman dedicated to the comfort and well-being of others during her lifetime."

Vero didn't say a word as he looked upon Leah, his mind trying to make sense of Uriel's words. Uriel's wings blanketed Vero again, and in an instant they were standing in the aisle of a small bus. The seats were filled with middle school-aged kids, all of whom had Down syndrome. One boy blew his breath onto a bus window, creating a fog on the glass. Vero watched as he drew in the fog with his index finger. Another boy clapped his hands together, laughing, but Vero couldn't figure out what was so funny. A girl braided another girl's hair sitting in front of her.

"These people, Vero, are not who you think they are. They are not unfortunate people to be pitied. Rather, they are the greatest of God's teachers. Those lives fortunate enough to be touched by these youngsters will see in them the true face of God."

Vero considered what Uriel was showing him. "But how?"

"Vero, these children love unconditionally, and see only

beauty in everything around them. They trust easily and forgive just as easily. There's no malice in these precious beings. Their souls are the most spiritually evolved of all humans. They are born with Down's because God does not want their souls corrupted, and they are here to guide humans back to God."

Vero was silent as he took in Uriel's words. The steamed bus window caught his attention. The boy had written the name "Vero" on the glass. Uriel's wings hugged Vero once more, and they stood in a small fenced playground. A boy kicked himself high up in the air on a swing. A girl crawled through a tunnel as another little girl slid down a slide. A boy sat on the bottom step of a jungle gym. He wore a protective brown foam helmet as he leaned his head against a woman's chest. She held him close.

"It's Pax and his mom . . ." Vero said, tears flooding his eyes.

Uriel nodded. "Now tell me, does that look like someone who doesn't love her son?"

Pax's Mom gently rubbed his arm.

"Then why did she put him here?"

"What Pax does not see is that he needed to go to an institution *because* his parents *do* love him so much. When it is his time to die on earth, it would be too painful for them, especially his mother. But this way, God is starting the separation to spare his mother some of the agony she will endure."

Vero watched Pax with his mother, thinking of the agony his own mother will also one day suffer. Uriel's wings wrapped around Vero, and they returned to the auditorium in the Ether. Uriel sat down on the edge of the stage, and Vero joined him.

"Do you know why I showed you these people?" Uriel asked Vero.

"I think so. To demonstrate how not everything is as it appears," Vero said recalling Raphael's words to him.

"Vero, very often the judgments you make are based primarily on your very limited earthly knowledge and experience. You still view things through your human eyes, and it shows a lack of faith. All of you do it." Uriel looked Vero squarely in the face. "I did not want you in the Trials, but not for the reason you think. Rather the opposite."

Vero gave him a curious look.

"I did not want you to win."

"But why?"

"I wanted to hide your identity for as long as possible. Now Lucifer knows for sure you're the one. I guess he may have suspected for a while, but now he knows. And that means you will not be safe. I was trying to protect you, as were the others."

"Then why crown me a winner?"

"The Thrones disagreed with our strategy, and they are in commune with God's will. And as much as we sought to protect you, it's obvious He feels that it's time for you to do what you must."

Vero looked at Uriel, unflinching. "Find the Book of Raziel."

"Yes. God has entrusted you with the task."

Vero put his head in hands, totally overwhelmed. Ada had first told him about the book, then Michael had. It was the book that God gave Adam to comfort him after he was expelled from the Garden of Eden. It listed all the secrets to the laws of the universe, the names of all the angels, and how to interpret dreams, but, most importantly, it listed all the souls yet to be born into the world.

"Lilith wants it," Vero said.

"Yes, Lucifer sent her after you. And as you've seen, she tried to get to you through Clover. But Vero," Uriel tilted Vero's chin to him. "Now, he will come after you himself. He will declare war on you and everyone you love."

Fear washed over Vero's face. "But I have no idea where the book is."

"Nor did you know where the unicorn, jawbone, or portal were when you began those challenges. But He has given you the gifts you need to overcome obstacles and find it. There was a reason you were the only one who could read the parchments in the golems' mouths."

Vero remembered that no matter how hard Ada or Pax studied the parchments, they appeared blank to them. Yet, he saw the words clearly.

"And you possess a strength ... no one has severed Lilith's hair in more than a millennium. It is confirmed for all to see. Even before Gabriel placed that laurel on your head, Lucifer knew you were the one."

Vero looked up at Uriel. "Will Lilith come after me again? You said she's not dead."

"Lucifer will use whatever and whomever to stop you. Lilith is no exception," Uriel said in a warning tone.

"Why do they want the book so badly?"

Uriel appeared surprised by the question. "What would the lord of darkness possibly want with all the secrets of the universe? You could just imagine how he'd use a book like that to lead even more people farther from God."

Vero's brow furrowed as he thought about that.

"But the gifts you possess aren't the only weapons you will have to find the book. Your fellow fledglings at C.A.N.D.L.E., even Clover and Tack ..."

"Tack?" Vero interrupted.

"Yes, Tack. They have also been given gifts to help you succeed."

"Tack? You sure?"

Uriel chuckled. "Especially Tack." Uriel's eyes filled with emotion as he looked upon Vero. "I'm proud of you, Vero. I'm sorry I had to let you think otherwise."

Vero looked out across the empty amphitheater. "I know. Everything in its own time."

"And always remember ... you don't find out who you are when the going is good. It's under adversity that we find our strength."

Uriel wrapped his wings around himself and disappeared. In his wake, something round and shiny caught Vero's attention. As he looked closer, he recognized it as his crown, the crown waiting for him in heaven. The last time he had seen it, it had been adorned with a single jewel. But to his surprise, several simple gemstones were inlaid into the circular base, nearly completing it. He should have been thrilled at the sight of it, but he wasn't ... because he knew once the crown was completed, so would his time on earth.

# 29

---

# THE BURNING HATRED

Vero walked through the front door of his home. He saw his mom and dad hugging a sobbing Clover. Vero walked over to the sofa. "Is she okay . . . ?"

"It's all right now," Dad told Vero.

"What happened?"

"That horrible Kira talked Clover into sneaking away with her to that stupid concert tonight, the one we forbade her to go to. But your sister only got as far as the Attleboro metro stop before she had the good sense to call Mom to come get her."

"I don't ever want to see Kira again," Clover said sniffling. "I'm sorry I've been such a brat."

"We've got our old Clover back now, and that's all that matters," Mom said.

Vero looked at Clover. She held his gaze.

Mom patted Clover's hair and stood up. "Come on, I've got to get dinner on the table."

"I'll help you," Dad said, and together they walked into the kitchen.

Vero sat next to Clover.

"Please don't say you told me so," Clover said.

"I won't. It's my fault," Vero said. "Unfortunately, I brought Kira into your life."

Clover looked to Vero in confusion.

"Kira isn't just a bad kid, she's a very powerful demoness."

Clover gasped as a terrified look came over her.

"She was trying to get at me through you," Vero explained. "She had you under her influence."

"But why?"

"Because I have to do something very important, and she wants to stop me. I can't tell you anything about it yet, but I can tell you that you and Tack are meant to help me."

"Tack?"

Vero chuckled. "I know. I had the same reaction. Both of you have gifts to help me succeed."

"You mean my visions? The dreams?"

"Probably."

"I think they've returned because I had another dream the other night. I saw you with the other guardian angels in my dream. You were there, weren't you?"

"Yeah, we were there," Vero answered.

"That's freaky." Clover looked down. "I'm scared, Vero. What if this happens again?" When she looked up again, her eyes were full of fear.

"I won't lie to you. They're going to keep coming after

us. But you've got a great guardian angel looking out for you." Vero put a hand on Clover's. "She's a close friend of mine."

Clover smiled.

$$\maltese$$

Vero noticed that things at Attleboro Middle seemed to have settled down. A sense of normalcy returned to the school. Tack could once again walk down the hallway without the girls giving him spontaneous hugs. Teachers went back to chiding Tack for his lousy grades, and the jocks ignored him. But Davina and Danny were still on the outs, so when Vero saw Davina sitting on a bench in front of the school, he realized it was time to make things right.

"What are you reading?" Vero asked Davina.

Davina looked up from her book. "Hey, Vero. Studying for today's science test."

"I'm glad I caught you because I wanted to tell you something," Vero said as he sat down next to her. "That day in the library when you saw Danny kiss Kira, well, I was also there. It didn't happen the way you think."

"What do you mean?"

"Danny was on his computer, minding his own business, when Kira, just out of the blue, leaned over and kissed him. She did it right when you were coming, for you to see. She wanted you to think she and Danny were romantic. Danny was freaked out by it."

Davina's eyes softened. "Really?"

"I swear. Kira kissed him before he knew what was going on. He's crazy about you. He'd never do that to you. And when he chased after you, I saw Kira sit down at his computer. She sent out the threatening email, not Danny."

"Why would she do that?"

"Kira is not a nice person. She's just full of hate. Unfortunately, that's what motivates her. The inspectors said the whole ceiling collapse was caused by years of faulty plumbing from back when the sprinkler system was installed. Danny could never have masterminded that. Everybody now knows that."

"I know."

"But it would be nice if he heard it from you ..." Vero nodded to Danny who was walking up the stairs to the main doors.

Davina followed his gaze and saw Danny.

"Thanks," she said to Vero.

Davina walked over to Danny. As Vero watched Davina talk warmly to Danny, he realized he must have been becoming more angel than human because, here he was, encouraging his crush to be with someone else. It was a bittersweet feeling.

A hand slapped the back of Vero's head. He spun around to see Tack standing there.

"Hey!" Vero yelled.

"That's for ditching me at the arcade," Tack said. "You could have let me know you left. Luckily, I found my backpack on the floor in front of that photo booth."

"Oh, sorry," Vero said. "I was pretty upset about Clover, so I left in a hurry. I'm really sorry."

"Your mom called mine and said Clover was okay. She tried to sneak out with Kira."

"That won't happen again—"

"Yeah, I heard Kira left school," Tack interrupted.

Vero nodded.

"She was hot, but there was definitely something weird about her."

"Trust me, she would never be your type," Vero said, as he stared at Tack, recalling Uriel's prediction, *"Tack has been given gifts to help you succeed."*

Tack squirmed under Vero's gaze. "What? Do I have a booger hanging or something?" he said, quickly wiping his nose with his sleeve.

"No," Vero laughed. "I was just thinking that God works in mysterious ways."

Tack gave Vero a look then put him in a headlock, and the two walked up the stairs and into the school.

&#10070;

A fire burned brightly deep in the forest. Lilith kneeled before the flames, her face old and hideous and her head now bald. Only a few sparse hairs grew from it.

"You are pathetic, my bride," the blaze spoke. "You have disappointed me."

Lilith spat on the fire. It roared. The flames intensified then formed into the shape of an arm. The burning arm shot out of the fire and grabbed Lilith around her neck, lifting her off the ground. She choked as the hand tightened.

"I should feed you to Abaddon," the fire said.

"Except even you, Lucifer, are afraid of him," Lilith gurgled.

The hand squeezed hard. Then it let go. Lilith fell to the ground, gasping for air.

"You will get what I need to know or else!"

"Or else what?" Lilith interrupted. "We chose hate a long time ago, you and I. We care for no one or no thing. We even despise ourselves. So your threats mean nothing to me. Yet, I will do what you ask, but only because that same hate that destroyed us, is all we have."

Lilith turned and walked into the blackness of the woods as the fire extinguished itself, smoldered, and turned to ash. She stepped over a fallen branch then came to an abrupt stop. Two eyes willingly met hers. They belonged to a boy, a dark-haired angel with angry eyes ... they belonged to Kane. Lilith smiled eagerly.

# The Dragon's Descent

## An Ether Novel

*Laurice E. Molinari*

As part of his training, Vero participates in the Angel Trials, a set of three challenges similar to the ancient Greek Olympic games. He and his group of fellow angels compete with angels from other realms. On earth, his sister, Clover, has a new friend who is leading her down the wrong path. Clover no longer has time for her family or her schoolwork. During the third trial, it becomes obvious to Vero that Clover's new friend is actually Lilith, the demoness of the Bible and Dead Sea Scrolls. Vero must defeat Lilith in order to release her hold on Clover. During the struggle, to Vero's great distress, one of his fellow angels joins Lilith. Vero frees Clover and it is revealed to him that he is the one fated to find the Book of Raziel, the book that contains the names of all the souls yet to be born and specifically, the baby soon to be born who will usher in an era of peace.

To start reading *The Dragon's Decent* turn the page!

# 1

# TRAIL OF LIGHTS

A panther's piercing gold eyes gazed through shimmering leaves as it relaxed on the well-worn curve of an ancient tree branch. As the large, black cat looked upon the green, conical mountain in the distance, it yawned, losing the fight to an afternoon nap. Above, a chattering family of langurs carelessly stuffed their gray-black faces to their heart's content, allowing shreds of leaves to fall onto their white beards. Below, in the marshy lowland, a small herd of shaggy-coated Sambar deer stood shoulder deep in the water, eating water lilies and refreshing themselves in the cool water. A petite white egret hitched a ride on the back of one of the deer, pecking insects from its fur while green and brown frogs made their presence known with boisterous croaks.

Silently, heavy clouds rolled into the jungle, burying

the tranquil afternoon in mist. The vibrant ecosystem was transformed into a blur of fog in a moment's time. And then, just as quickly, the mist dissipated, revealing the now quiet darkness of night. On the face of the distant mountain, an illuminated trail wound its way up the mountainside. The zigzagging path seemed endless, lit up by thousands of flickering lights that stretched into the stars.

Clover woke with a start. After sweeping her long blonde hair from her face, she grabbed a small journal and a pencil off her nightstand and began to cover the blank pages with detailed images from her dream. Moments later, she glanced at her old princess alarm clock: 5:22 in the morning. She would need to be up for school in an hour, but something screamed to her that she had to record what she had seen before the images faded from memory.

Clover had kept a dream journal ever since she was a little girl. She felt her dreams were special, and as she grew older she found it harder and harder to shake them—in fact, her dreams had always been so vivid, so real to her, that she often needed to stay in bed for a few moments to reorient herself after waking. Clover knew the images she dreamt were trying to tell her something and had discovered that many did hold messages. These visual messages used to terrify her, but finally, at the ripe old age of fifteen, she had learned to embrace them—and not only her dreams, but also her visions. She had once thought she was seeing hallucinations, that she was crazy. But in time, she had come to realize she saw real things other people could not see. And she saw them because of Vero, her guardian angel brother. Her prophetic gifts were meant to somehow support Vero in his mission. Of this, she was one hundred percent sure. And that's the reason she took such painstaking efforts to sketch the mountain, the animals, and the jungle as accurately as possible.

❖

Clover walked past Vero and playfully boxed his ear while he sat in the kitchen eating an egg-in-the-hole. It was his favorite breakfast—an egg fried inside a hole cut in the middle of a slice of bread.

"What was that for?" Vero scowled, tugging on his left ear.

Clover opened the refrigerator door and pulled out a peach-flavored Greek yogurt. "Making sure you were awake." Clover smirked then picked up a spoon from inside a drawer before slamming it shut with her hip. "Where are Mom and Dad?"

"Dad went in to work early," Vero said, shaking the saltshaker over his egg. "And Mom's out jogging."

"Good. Hold on . . ." Clover said, dashing out of the kitchen.

"For what?" Vero asked, but Clover was already gone.

When she rushed back with her dream journal, he had stuck his fork into his egg, and yolk spilled out onto the fried bread. Before he could take a bite, however, Clover slammed the book down on the table with a thud. It was open to a sketch of the landscape from her dream.

"Does this mean anything to you?" she questioned urgently and curiously.

Vero's gray eyes narrowed as he studied the drawing. He

looked thoughtfully at it, as if trying to trigger some sort of recognition. He focused on the winding trail of lights up the side of a steep mountain that rose high above hills and the exotic animals below.

"Anything?"

Vero shook his head.

"Are you sure?" Clover tapped her index finger on the drawing. "Because I have a really strong feeling about this."

"Nothing," Vero mumbled in between bites of egg. "Maybe in time, it'll make sense."

The front door opened and quickly shut. Clover snatched the journal from Vero and snapped it shut just as their mother, Nora, walked into the kitchen. Nora's face was bright red. Sweat had formed on her forehead.

"The bus is almost here! What are you doing still eating? Go! Get ready!" Nora yelled, out of breath.

"Shoot! I gotta brush my teeth," Vero exclaimed, jumping up from the table and sprinting out of the room.

"I'm ready," Clover said to Nora. "But I totally miss when Molly would pick me up."

"Well, you better make friends with the bus, because Molly graduated, and I'm sure not driving you." Nora studied Clover's face. "Why do you look so tired? Were you on your phone last night? Because you know, no electronics in your room."

"No, Mom." Clover rolled her eyes. "I just woke up super early."

"You probably heard Dad. He went to work while it was still dark," Nora said as she pulled a bottle of flavored water from the fridge. "He's worried about his project."

"He worries about every project," Clover said.

"Why don't you want me to see that?" Nora asked, motioning to the journal tucked under Clover's arm.

Clover froze.

"You don't have to show me. I'll just sneak a peek like I normally do once you're on the bus." Nora smiled.

"You do?!" Clover asked with a look of outrage.

Nora laughed. "Oh yeah! And I also throw out all your old toys too!"

Clover eyed her, not sure if she was joking.

"But you have no problem showing Vero," Nora said, a bit hurt.

Clover considered for a moment. "Fine," she said as she handed her mother the well-worn journal. "It's on the next to last page."

Nora flipped to the sketch of the mountain. Clover watched her mother's eyes soften as she studied the drawing. At forty-two, Clover thought her mother looked great. Sure, she had to highlight her hair to remain a blonde, but she could still fit into most of her college clothing, and last week when Nora bought a bottle of champagne for a housewarming gift, she was carded! Clover hoped she had inherited her mom's genes.

"You're really good."

"Thanks, Mom." Clover blushed.

"Was this in one of your dreams?"

Clover nodded. Down the block, the school bus horn blared.

"Gotta go!" Clover snatched her journal from Nora's hands and zipped it inside the front pocket of her purple backpack. "I'll take it with me. That way you won't be tempted to snoop around for it." Clover smiled.

As Clover left, Vero ran down the stairs with frothy toothpaste around his mouth. Nora chuckled to herself.

❖

Clover got off the bus before Vero. The high school was the first stop, followed by the middle school then elementary. Vero always felt a tinge of sadness when he watched Clover step off the bus without him. Even though he would join her at the high school next year, it was of little consolation because he knew that someday the separation would become permanent. He hoped and prayed they'd both be given the strength to survive once that time came.

"Hey, move over," a boy's voice cracked.

Vero looked up and saw Tack standing over him. Sometimes he thought his eyes were playing tricks on him when he looked at his best friend of twelve years, because Tack no longer resembled the pudgy little kid Vero had grown up with. Tack was now nearly six feet tall, and all the places that once had been prone to baby fat had transformed into well-defined muscles. As Tack sat down next to him, his hairy, long legs bumped up against Vero who had also grown considerably. And Vero had even started wearing deodorant a few months ago, after Clover complained that he stunk up the whole room with BO, as well as mentioning the pungent aroma whenever he took off his socks.

But it wasn't only Tack's physical appearance that had changed—he had become more serious. He no longer held the title of class clown and had even made honor roll for the first time in his life. Most people attributed the change in Tack to the natural transition to maturity. But as Vero glanced at the stack of books on Tack's lap, he wondered—was Tack being prepared for whatever part he was to play in helping Vero find the Book of Raziel? The archangels had told Vero that it was his mission to retrieve the all-knowing book. It blew Vero's mind when he thought about all the knowledge contained within its pages: the laws of the universe and of creation, the names of every human ever born and those yet to be born, and the names and duties of each angel. It was mind-boggling. The book had originally been given to Adam to console him after he was expelled from the garden, then passed down for generations until it eventually became lost. And though it was up to Vero to find it, the archangel Uriel had told Vero that Tack would play some part. Maybe Tack could somehow sense he had a higher purpose . . . he was a proven dowser, after all, and could sense things ordinary people could not. Perhaps that was why childish things were falling so quickly by the wayside?

"Did you figure out what you're going to do for service hours?" Tack asked Vero as the bus drove away from the curb.

"I'm not sure yet," Vero said. "How many do we need to do?"

"Fifteen hours or else they won't pass you to ninth grade."

"My mom wants me to volunteer at the hospital. She says lots of kids do. Plus, I can drive in with her to work," Vero said.

"I'll do it with you," Tack said. "My sister volunteered there and said she was delivering flowers and reading books to little kids, stuff like that."

"I can handle that," Vero said.

"Then ask your mom to sign us up."

"Okay."

"Oh, but I can't do Saturday mornings," Tack said. "That's when my dad takes me out on dowser jobs with him."

Vero nodded. He knew how important being a dowser was to Tack. Up until last year, his friend had shown no aptitude in the ancestral talent; then Tack's abilities sprung forth with a vengeance when he sensed that a busted pipe had caused water to pool in the gym's ceiling. He'd led everyone outside moments before disaster hit.

"Hi guys."

Vero and Tack looked up and saw Davina Acker quickly move to the seat next to them as the bus rounded a corner. Davina always made Vero smile. She was stunning, with sparkling blue eyes and soft brownish hair, but it was her warm smile that Vero found most endearing.

"Hey, Davina." Tack nodded.

"I thought I heard someone say service hours," she said. "I worked this weekend at the nursing home."

"How was it?" Vero asked.

"Sort of sad at first, but then you start to notice how grateful all the residents are that you're there, and then you're glad you went," Davina said.

"I hear you. My grandma lives in one in Virginia," Tack said. "When you first get there, the place kind of smells like mothballs . . . sort of like Vero's feet."

"Hey!" Vero looked offended.

"But then my grandma and her friends are so happy to see me, it kind of becomes fun."

"Then you guys should volunteer with me," Davina said.

"We're gonna do the hospital," Tack said as the bus came to a stop in front of Attleboro Middle School.

"My mom works there," Vero added.

"Oh, there's Danny." Davina smiled dreamily, glancing out the cracked, finger-smudged window.

Vero followed her gaze. Danny Konrad stepped off his black skateboard and kicked the tail with his right foot, flipping it into his hands. Danny looked like the all-American boy—blond, dimpled, and confident.

Tack nudged Vero. "And this is where we become invisible."

"That's not true!" Davina exclaimed indignantly.

"Really?" Tack smirked.

"Well, maybe a little, but only because I need to talk to Danny," Davina said as she walked up the aisle.

Tack rolled his eyes as he and Vero followed her off the bus. Danny walked toward the school's metal front doors as Davina chased after him.

"Danny! Danny!"

Danny stopped and turned around. Vero and Tack stood behind Davina.

"Hey . . . How come you didn't text me last night?" Davina asked.

"I was busy." Danny shrugged.

"Really?"

"My dad was home . . ."

"And?"

Vero watched as a flicker of anger crossed Danny's face.

"And what? I don't have to tell you stuff that's between my dad and me," Danny snapped.

Hurt instantly clouded Davina's eyes as Danny turned and walked away. Tack elbowed Vero, who was concerned.

"The universe must be off," he whispered to Vero, watching Danny make his way into the school.

❖

Deep beneath the ground wriggled the bodies of creatures—so many that they crawled over and under one another like clumps of earthworms. These beasts lived underground because light was the enemy. Darkness sustained them.

Each monster was equally hideous. Sparse, matted bunches of fur clung to their nearly emaciated bodies—bodies that resembled decomposing corpses. They hissed with grotesque, dirt-covered fangs. Their clawed hands swiped at one another, cutting into scaly, sallow skin. The lone eye that penetrated their heads could not see beneath the dark earth, yet somehow they knew the master had come into their presence. Their anger intensified, their attacks becoming more furious. The violent frenzy pleased the master. The creatures were tired of waiting for the master to release them so they could do the thing for which they were created—spread hatred. But it was not the right time. So their master kept them hidden beneath the surface, seething with chaos and hunger. When the time came, their festering hatred would erupt with a vengeance.